UNQUIET LAND

UNQUIET LAND

Sharon Shinn

ACE
New York

ACE

Published by Berkley

An imprint of Penguin Random House LLC

375 Hudson Street, New York, New York 10014

Copyright © 2016 by Sharon Shinn

Penguin Random House supports copyright. Copyright fuels creativity, encourages diverse voices, promotes free speech, and creates a vibrant culture. Thank you for buying an authorized edition of this book and for complying with copyright laws by not reproducing, scanning, or distributing any part of it in any form without permission. You are supporting writers and allowing Penguin Random House to continue to publish books for every reader.

ACE is a registered trademark and the A colophon is a trademark of
Penguin Random House LLC.

Library of Congress Cataloging-in-Publication Data

Names: Shinn, Sharon, author.
Title: Unquiet land / by Sharon Shinn.
Description: New York, NY : Ace Books, [2016]
Identifiers: LCCN 2015049930 | ISBN 9780425277034 (hardcover)
Subjects: | GSAFD: Fantasy fiction.
Classification: LCC PS3569.H499 U57 2016 | DDC 813/.54—dc23
LC record available at http://lccn.loc.gov/2015049930

First Edition: November 2016

Printed in the United States of America
1 3 5 7 9 10 8 6 4 2

Cover illustration © Jonathan Barkat
Cover photography: mountains © naturemania/Shutterstock;
ivy © photo5963_shutter/Shutterstock
Cover design by Judith Lagerman

For Mom

I figure you deserve a dedication once every twenty years or so.
Expect the next one when you turn one hundred.

Who's Who in Welce

PRIMES & POLITICIANS

DARIEN SERLAST, Corene's father and the regent
ZOE LALINDAR, the coru prime and Darien's wife
CELIA, Darien and Zoe's daughter

TARO FROTHEN, the torz prime
VIRRIE FROTHEN, Taro's wife
LEAH FROTHEN, Taro's niece
MALLY, Leah and Rhan's daughter, formerly the decoy princess

NELSON ARDELAY, the sweela prime
BECCAN ARDELAY, Nelson's wife
RHAN AND KURTIS ARDELAY, Nelson and Beccan's sons
NAVARR ARDELAY (NOW DECEASED), Nelson's brother and
    father to Zoe and Josetta

KAYLE DOCHENZA, the elay prime
MIRTI SERLAST, the hunti prime and Darien's aunt

ROYALTY

KING VERNON (NOW DECEASED)
QUEEN ELIDON, Vernon's first wife
QUEEN SETERRE, Vernon's second wife
QUEEN ALYS, Vernon's third wife
QUEEN ROMELLE, Vernon's fourth wife

PRINCESS JOSETTA, Seterre's daughter

RAFE ADOVA, Josetta's betrothed

PRINCESS CORENE, Alys and Darien's daughter

NATALIE, Romelle's oldest daughter

ODELIA, Romelle's youngest daughter and previously heir to the throne

FRIENDS & VISITORS

ANNOVA, Zoe's closest friend

YORI, a driver for Darien Serlast

JAKER AND BARLOW, itinerant merchants

CHANDRAN, a merchant from Cozique

THE CROWN PRINCE OF THE KARKADES

SEKA MARDIS, an attendant to the prince of the Karkades

WELCHIN AFFILIATIONS AND RANDOM BLESSINGS

ELAY (AIR/SOUL)	HUNTI (WOOD/BONE)	SWEELA (FIRE/MIND)
joy	courage	innovation
hope	strength	love
kindness	steadfastness	imagination
beauty	loyalty	clarity
vision	certainty	intelligence
grace	resolve	charm
honor	determination	talent
spirituality	power	creativity

CORU (WATER/BLOOD)	TORZ (EARTH/FLESH)	EXTRAORDINARY BLESSINGS
change	serenity	synthesis
travel	honesty	triumph
flexibility	health	time
swiftness	fertility	
resilience	contentment	
luck	patience	
persistence	endurance	
surprise	wealth	

Quintiles & Changedays

The calendar of Welce is divided into five quintiles. A quintile consists of eight "weeks," each nine days long. Most shops and other businesses are closed on the firstdays of each nineday.

The first quintile of the year, Quinnelay, stretches from early to deep winter. It is followed by Quinncoru, which encompasses late winter to mid-spring; Quinnahunti, late spring to mid-summer; Quinnatorz, late summer to fall; and Quinnasweela, fall to early winter.

The quintiles are separated by changedays, generally celebrated as holidays. Quinnelay changeday is the first day of every new year. Since there are five changedays and five seventy-two-day quintiles, the Welchin year is 365 days long.

Money

5 quint-coppers make one copper (5 cents → 25 cents)
8 coppers make one quint-silver ($2)

5 quint-silvers make one silver ($10)
8 silvers make one quint-gold ($80)

5 quint-golds make one gold ($400)

ONE

It was Quinnasweela changeday, and the whole world was on fire. Leah strolled through the Plaza of Women just as night came on and watched in silent appreciation as candles and oil lamps were set in every window of every building in Chialto. The city had been largely converted to gaslight during the past five years, but on this autumn holiday, those pale imitations of fire had been turned off in favor of the real thing.

Leah hadn't realized she'd be back in Chialto in time for the holiday. Well, really, she hadn't given much thought to changedays in the past five years, since she'd been living in the country of Malinqua, where the turn of the seasons had never been cause for celebration. If you'd asked her a quintile ago—say, on Quinnatorz changeday—she'd have said she was never returning to the country of Welce. Yet here she was, wandering through the Plaza, mingling with the crowds, buying a cup of spiced apple wine from a streetside vendor, and feeling a rare moment of contentment.

She had to admit she loved being back at the Plaza of Women. Situated on the edge of the formal shop district, it was a big, paved space that would have been flat and open except that it was crowded with booths and stalls. Even on ordinary days, those booths held an endless variety of merchandise, from fresh flowers to used clothing to alcohol of dubious origin. Tonight, there were ten times as many stalls, each crammed to bursting with cheap trinkets, bundles of cloth, samples of flavorful food, and candles in every shape, scent, and color.

And other oddments.

Leah had decided to head back to her apartment for the night when she came across a large, rickety booth tucked off the main path. It was shaded by a wide sheet of blue fabric, which hung perilously close to the torches illuminating the unexpected merchandise for sale: dozens of exotic fish, each swimming in its own clear glass bowl.

She'd never seen anything like them before—triangle-shaped creatures with narrow, pointed faces and frills of diaphanous fins completely encircling the widest portion of their bodies. They came in vivid colors, glittering green, rippling gold, dusky blue, rich purple, but all of them had eyes so dark they appeared to be an unblinking black. They were like living jewels suspended in crystal water.

The booth was crowded with other customers moving with amazement from one glass bowl to another. Three slim, dark young men—looking enough like each other to be brothers—ran between tables, answering questions and begging the onlookers not to dangle their fingers in the water.

"They'll bite," one of the brothers warned a young girl whose hand was suspended over a bowl. "Hard enough to draw blood."

The girl hastily dropped her arm. The woman with her, most likely her mother, asked, "What do you feed them?"

"Anything, really, but they prefer meat. They'll eat each other if you put two together."

Leah moved from bowl to bowl, bending down to marvel at each occupant. "I've never seen anything like them," she said when one of the brothers was close enough to hear. "Where do they come from?"

"Cozique, these days," he answered. "That's where the breeders live, anyway. But the first pairs were caught in Yorramol and shipped back to the southern seas."

"*Yorramol!*" a few of the other customers murmured. Yorramol was practically a mythical place, so distant that almost no one in this part of the world had ever sailed there. Leah figured the chances were about even that these fish had actually originated in that faraway spot. More likely they could be found in the seas off Berringey or Dhonsho, where they were so thick in the water that you could scoop them out by hand. Unless you were afraid of being bitten.

"I don't understand. Are they good for eating? They're so small," complained a man who was looking around the booth with some bewilderment.

"Of course you don't *eat* them!" exclaimed one of the other onlookers, a middle-aged woman in fashionable clothing. "They're for looking at! They're just for having a pretty thing in your life. Like a painting, but alive. Like a flower."

The man's expression suggested he didn't bother much with art or botany, either. Practical and unimaginative; hunti, at a guess, or torz. "I just don't get the point," he said in a grumpy voice.

"Then the reifarjin is not for you," the vendor said.

The man made a disgruntled noise and stalked off, no doubt to seek out something more sensible, like a handsaw or a milking bucket. A small girl danced around the fashionable woman, tugging at her wrist.

"I want one," the girl begged. "Please, can I have one? Can I?"

"I don't think your mother would like it," the woman answered.

"We can leave it at your house and I'll just come visit."

"Oh, so *I'm* the one who has to feed it and give it fresh water every day?"

"Maybe it wouldn't be very hungry," the girl said hopefully.

Leah smiled, listening to them, and stepped to the last table. There were only three bowls here; soon she would have seen everything on offer in the booth and she could go home. It was ridiculous that she had spent so much time here anyway. She didn't want a fish, whether or not it had a lovely name like *reifarjin*. Like the petulant man, she was not in the market for a purely decorative acquisition. She had spent too many years caring only for herself; she wasn't sure she should be trusted with the responsibility of keeping something else alive.

The fish in the first two bowls were both small, copper-colored, and lethargic. Leah wondered if they were sick, or maybe only half grown. That was something else she should ask one of the brothers: How long did reifarjin live? Were they so delicate that one would barely survive the trip back to her lodgings, or so hardy that she'd be stuck with it for the next decade? If she was silly enough to buy one. Which, of course, she wouldn't be. There could hardly be a more coru purchase than a fish, and Leah had never had much affinity for the element of water. She was a torz woman, tied to earth and flesh. Reliable and practical and dull.

Well—except for the past five years. Past six.

She shook her head and bent down to get a closer look at the reifarjin in the final bowl. It was slightly larger than the others and gorgeously colored, with streaks of brilliant raspberry fading into cobalt blue. It sported a double row of the feathery fins, one in each color, fluttering so rapidly in the still water that they seemed to form one vibrant shade of heliotrope. Most of the other reifarjin had seemed unaware of their human audience, but this one knew she was there, Leah thought. As soon as she ducked down to examine it, it sidled closer to the glass, watching her mistrustfully from one large eye while its circlet of fins quivered in agitation or resentment. When she lifted a hand and traced her finger from the top to the bottom of the bowl, the fish lifted its gaze to track her movement.

I want you, she thought, so powerfully and so unexpectedly that it was almost as if someone else had whispered the words in her ear.

One of the brothers materialized at her side. "What do you think?" he asked.

"Why does this one look different from the others?" Leah said.

He shrugged. "Don't really know. Maybe one in fifty is a blended color like that. They behave the same as the others. Eat the same food. They just look different."

"Do they cost more?" she wanted to know.

He eyed her, sensing a sale. "Sometimes."

Leah straightened up, took a step away. "Well—"

"But not this one," the vendor said hastily. "Regular price."

"Which is?"

He eyed her again, trying to gauge her monetary status from her appearance. She didn't think her clothing gave much away. She was wearing a plain green tunic and matching pants, both out of season; she'd pulled her dark brown hair back into a messy knot and hadn't bothered with cosmetics. She'd lost weight while she was in Malinqua, so she looked a little underfed for her stocky body, and the wariness she'd developed in the past five years could sometimes be read as worry. It was extremely unlikely he would peg her for what she really was: a prodigal daughter of the Five Families who had finally made her way home.

"Two quint-golds," he said.

"*Two quint-golds!*" she repeated, her voice as shocked as if he'd named a price twenty times that high.

"Usually," he added. "But we're offering a special price for Quinnasweela. One quint-gold. That includes the bowl and everything."

She spared a moment to wonder how they could possibly sell the fish *without* the bowls and another moment to think she was a complete idiot. And then she firmly shut down her brain so she wouldn't think at all. "I'll take it," she said. "This one."

It would have made sense to go directly from the vendor's booth back to her lodgings, carrying the reifarjin by the handles of the sturdy woven bag that was also part of her purchase price. But as Leah tried to avoid the worst of the changeday crowds, she ended up passing the center of the Plaza and the raised dais where the blind sisters sat. By the light of their own ring of torches, she could see that one of the three seers was not, at the moment, entertaining a visitor. So she climbed right up the wooden steps, sank to her knees before the other woman, and carefully set her new acquisition down on the planks beside her.

"Blessed changeday to you," Leah said. "I have some questions to ask."

The blind seer tilted her head to one side, as if planning to listen closely to all the things Leah would and would not say. This woman and her sisters had operated in this very same spot for as long as Leah could remember—for decades, probably. There was some speculation that they were not the same women who had first commandeered the dais here in the heart of the Plaza, that they were the nieces or daughters or granddaughters of the first sisters who had unrolled their mats and began trading in information. But they knew everything about everyone in the city—perhaps in all of Welce. You could buy their knowledge with coins or pay for it with information of your own. Never, as far as Leah knew, had their information been false. And never had anyone been able to tell them apart. They were three big-boned, soft-skinned, blank-eyed women who harvested secrets and shared the rich bounty.

"Ask, then," the woman replied.

"How much do I owe you?" Unlike the fish vendor, the seer wouldn't haggle. She would name a price and Leah would pay it or go somewhere else to try to discover what she wanted to know.

"I can't answer that until I know the questions."

"I want to learn about . . . about . . . the decoy princess."

The seer didn't seem surprised or skeptical. She didn't ask why that would be a topic of interest to anyone. She merely nodded. "The little girl. Mally."

"That's her name. What do I need to pay you?"

"Two silvers," said the other woman.

A low price. Clearly none of the information about Mally was particularly sensitive. Leah handed over the coins and then said, "Tell me about her. Everything."

The woman fingered the coins. "Your accent makes you a native Welchin. And yet you know nothing about the child?"

"I've been living abroad. There is much about the current political situation that I don't know."

The sister nodded. "Well, then," she said. "This is her story. Odelia is the daughter of King Vernon and his fourth wife, Romelle, and she had been named as heir to the throne. Darien Serlast—you do know who Darien Serlast is?"

Leah was tempted to answer, *I know him very well, in fact. I was in Malinqua at his request, spying on a foreign nation.* But, of course, she never told anyone that. "He's the regent."

"When Odelia was born, he was still just an advisor to the old king. But Darien Serlast is the one who thought it would be a good idea to find another child who could stand in for Odelia to keep the true princess safe in case danger ever threatened. Taro Frothen—the torz prime—is the one who discovered Mally. The resemblance between the two girls is said to be remarkable, although it is not clear if they are actually related."

They were, Leah knew, in the way that all the members of the Five Families were related after years of intermarriage, but the connection was distant. Romelle was Taro's fifth or sixth cousin; Leah could never remember exactly. Torz, anyway, with a faint thread of Frothen blood in her veins. And Mally was Taro's great-niece, though only a handful of people were aware of that fact.

"No one knows who Mally's parents are?" Leah asked.

The seer shook her head. "I imagine Taro Frothen knows, but they say that even Romelle is in the dark."

"So once Taro produced this girl, how was she used over the past five years?"

"Odelia had been certified as King Vernon's heir, but he died not long after she was born. Romelle and her baby and her older daughter went to live on Taro's estates because she said she wanted to raise her children away from the scheming at court. But, of course, they had to come into Chialto on many formal occasions. On those visits, sometimes Romelle brought Odelia and sometimes she brought Mally. No one ever knew if it was the real princess or the fake one, and this is one of the reasons, or so everyone believes, that there was never any attempt on Odelia's life."

"And no one could ever tell them apart?"

The seer smiled slightly. "Well, the primes could," she replied, "but they had every reason to keep up the fiction."

The primes. Of course. Each prime had a deep connection with one of the five elements, and this translated into an almost mystical ability to decipher truths about the people around them. Taro Frothen was a man of earth and flesh—he could touch a stranger's hand and instantly identify him, recite his genealogy and probably describe the state of his health as well. Nelson Ardelay, the sweela prime, could sift through anyone's thoughts and pick the truth from the lie. Leah had heard that the coru prime could read a person's blood; she didn't know how the hunti and elay primes decoded people and arranged them into family groupings, but she was sure they could do it.

"The primes," Leah echoed. "But no one else?"

"No. And so the arrangement continued for the first few years of Odelia's life. But then, back in Quinnahunti, there began to be questions. It turned out that Mally was the only one who had been seen at court for several quintiles. Odelia never left the Frothen estates. Darien Serlast demanded to know why, and the truth came out about the princess."

"What truth?" Leah had heard some of the story, but incomplete pieces of it, filtered through travelers who had made the long journey between Welce and Malinqua and who weren't as fascinated by this tale as she was.

"She has a condition. Her body is healthy, but she seems trapped in her own mind, seeing things and experiencing things in a way that is different from the rest of us. She understands words but rarely speaks them—knows who her family is, but rarely touches them. As soon as the primes understood her situation, they realized she would never be fit to rule."

"And so they chose Darien Serlast to be the next king," Leah said impatiently, because she already knew this part of the story and she didn't care about it much.

The seer offered another one of her faint smiles. "After much debate and disagreement and political maneuvering, they chose Darien Serlast," the woman amplified. "Deciding against the other three princesses, who might also have been considered candidates for the throne."

"Yes, but— Didn't it turn out that those other princesses were not actually Vernon's daughters? That his various wives had—ah—relied on the services of other men when it looked like Vernon would not be able to sire children of his own?"

The seer looked amused now, though Leah imagined it had been quite a shock the first time she and her sisters had absorbed *that* particular bit of information. "You are correct. And it was in large part due to the fact that Josetta, Corene, and Natalie were not Vernon's blood that the primes decided to look elsewhere to bestow the crown."

Yes, fine, but Leah didn't really care how Darien's story had unfolded. "So. Once Odelia was no longer the heir, what happened to Mally?"

The seer shrugged. "Her life has not changed much, though it is much quieter now. She still lives with the torz prime and his wife on their country estate. Romelle and Odelia and Natalie live there also, as they always have. They just do not come to Chialto nearly as often."

"And Mally—she is happy there? With Taro and his wife?"

"It is hard to judge the happiness of a five-year-old girl," the blind sister replied. "But the prime and his wife are kind and loving people, and she has been given every material comfort. Compared to most other orphans, her situation is very good."

"Orphans?" Leah repeated. "I thought you said you didn't know anything about her parents."

The seer shrugged. "It has been more than a quintile since the truth came out about Odelia," she said. "In all those ninedays, no parents have come forward to claim Mally as their own. If they had turned her over to Taro merely to serve the crown, they have no reason to keep their silence now. But they have not. Which means they are either dead or . . ." Her voice trailed off.

"Or?"

The seer shrugged again. "Or they are careless and irresponsible people who have no business raising a child. If they have not come forward by now, it seems unlikely that they will—and better for Mally if they never do."

TWO

Leah stayed up too late watching the changeday revelry from the second-story window of her small apartment, so she slept in on firstday. Once she'd dressed and eaten breakfast, she wasted the rest of the morning trying to figure out the best place to set the fishbowl. Too much sunlight was bad for the reifarjin, the vendor had told her, but it couldn't survive in constant shade. It liked to observe movement. It enjoyed being near colorful things. It needed to be fed every day.

Leah was finding it more and more absurd that she had burdened herself with such a fanciful acquisition. *What was I thinking?* And yet she still felt a little possessive thrill of happiness every time she glanced at its wide, gorgeous shape.

She ultimately placed it on a small table just inside her door, within the open rectangle that served as the kierten. A kierten never included furniture or any useful items; its very emptiness signaled that the tenants had so much space they could allow some of it to go unused. But a kierten often sported some purely ornamental touches, such as plants or vases or paintings. Leah figured a decorative fish qualified. And, since her lodgings consisted of a single chamber with the tiniest of bathing rooms tucked into one corner, the reifarjin could observe her every movement, even if she thrashed in her sleep.

"So I suppose you'll be quite happy here," Leah observed as she bent down to study it through the glass. It fluttered its variegated fins and positioned itself so it could stare back at her from one of its oversize eyes. She wasn't sure that expression indicated happiness. "Are you hungry?"

She dribbled meat scraps into the water and was amused to see the reifarjin abandon its wary reserve to go chasing after each piece before it settled to the bottom of the bowl. Once it had gobbled up the last morsel, it turned its dark gaze on her again, so she sifted a few more bits into the bowl, and those were quickly devoured as well.

"I wonder if you would eat yourself to death if I just kept feeding you," she said. "I didn't think to ask. Maybe Chandran will know. I'm going to write and tell him all about you. Maybe he's heard of reifarjin before."

She brushed the last crumbs off her palms and went hunting for writing materials. She'd only been in Welce three days, and she'd already written Chandran twice. But, of course, the journey itself had taken almost two ninedays, and a great deal had happened since she'd seen him last.

She really hadn't expected to miss him so much. She'd known him barely a quintile as she worked beside him in his booth in the Great Market, selling expensive goods to Malinqua's wealthiest citizens. It had been clear early on that both of them were refugees from other countries, other lives, and that they were not interested in sharing their secrets with anybody. At first this had led them to distrust each other, but gradually it had helped build a sort of bond between them. She didn't know when she had started to think of Chandran as the one person she would want to confide in. She didn't know when she'd started to hope *he* would confide in *her*. But now that he was more than a nineday's journey away, she found herself wanting to talk to him all the time, tell him what she was thinking, describe what she was witnessing, get his measured insights on the events of the day.

Now that he was so far away, she wished they had had the chance to get closer.

But that was foolish. He was very well-established in Malinqua, and she was determined to find her place in Welce; neither of them was likely to uproot again. It was pointless to keep writing letters, keep calculating how many days it would take for his first reply to cross the ocean once he knew where to send a letter in return. It was ridiculous to find herself mourning a friendship that had been so brief and had no future.

But she was still going to tell him about the reifarjin.

She had just located a blank piece of paper when there was a knock on the door, brisk and peremptory. Not the landlord's usual timid rap, but she couldn't think who else would be calling on her. No one else even knew she was in the city. Except—

She wasn't surprised, upon opening the door, to see two soldiers standing in the hall. They wore royal livery—severe black uniforms ornamented only with the five-colored Welchin rosette—and polite expressions.

"We've come from the regent," said one in a pleasant voice. "Would now be a good time for you to visit him?"

She was tempted to answer *No*, just to see what the guard would say next, but there was really no point to it. She had to talk to Darien Serlast sometime; might as well get it over with now.

"Of course," she said, equally as pleasant. "Let's go."

The trip to the palace was accomplished in a small elaymotive. The two men sat up front, one of them driving, while Leah lounged in the well-padded passenger compartment behind them. She'd only been in a smoker car a few times before she left for Malinqua, but since she'd been gone, the gas-powered vehicles had clearly become more luxurious. They'd also become more common—it seemed like half of the conveyances they passed were also elaymotives, some small like this one, others twice its size. She even saw a couple that she thought might be public transports capable of holding twenty or thirty people.

It wasn't long before they were on the winding road leading to the palace, which was situated halfway up a low mountain. It was an extensive and pretty building of golden stone—not nearly as big or dramatic as the royal residence in Malinqua, but still impressive. Its most dramatic feature was the great waterfall that gushed beside it, tumbling all the way down from the top of the mountain, pausing to fill a lake beside the courtyard, and then rushing along the eastern edge of the city before making its way out to sea. *Malinqua doesn't have anything to compare to the Marisi River, now does it?* Leah thought with a certain satisfaction. *Chandran would love the Marisi.*

She shook her head to shake the thought away.

Soon enough, she had disembarked in the courtyard and was turned over to a servant who escorted her through the cavernous kierten of the palace. He shepherded her to the stairwell that led to the right section of the palace, the wing that had always been Vernon's. The stairwell on the left led to the queens' wing, where Vernon's four wives had lived in a far from harmonious state. Leah wondered if Darien and his wife similarly kept separate quarters. He was married to Zoe Lalindar, the coru prime, who, by all accounts, was an unpredictable and strong-willed woman. Leah thought that if *she* were married to Darien Serlast, she'd probably want the width of the palace between them. She liked Darien, but . . .

The servant led her to a second-floor room with high ceilings, huge windows, and comfortable furnishings. Her immediate impression was that this was a place where someone wouldn't mind staying for hours at a time. Probably Darien's office, the place where he did most of the work of governing.

"Leah Frothen," the servant announced as she stepped through the door.

Sure enough, there was Darien, sitting behind a tidy desk but rising instantly to his feet. "Leah. I'm so pleased you could come right away," he said, and she could hear the edge of sarcasm in his voice. Clearly he had expected her to visit him the moment she set foot back on Welchin soil, and was not pleased that he had been forced to summon her. "Come sit by the window and we'll talk for a while."

The servant closed the door behind him as Leah strolled over to a table already set with tall glasses and a pitcher of fruited water. The windows overlooked the placid lake, which reflected back bright sun and cloudless skies and the honey color of the palace walls.

As they settled into their chairs, she took a moment to study him. The past five years seemed to have left him remarkably unchanged, considering how much he'd been through in that period: He'd seen his king die, had taken on the burdens of regency, gotten married, and sired a second daughter. But whatever turmoil he'd experienced barely showed. His face was still handsome, narrow, and impossible to read; his gray eyes were coolly assessing and gave nothing away. Maybe there were a few strands of silver in his dark hair, a couple of new lines on his face. Otherwise, the intervening years sat lightly upon him.

Not as true for her, apparently. "You look different," he observed.

"Different how?"

"Thinner. And your hair—"

"Yes, I cut it and colored it while I was in Malinqua," she said. "Not that I really needed to disguise myself, since no one there knew me, but—" She shrugged.

"A wise precaution," he said. "But now that you're back in Welce, perhaps you will revert to your true appearance."

"And perhaps I'll keep changing it," she retorted.

He smiled at that and poured water for both of them. "A very coru sentiment," he said. "Have you changed your affiliation as well as your outward aspect?"

She thought of the reifarjin even now fanning its gaudy frills in her apartment. "I'm not sure I could manage to sustain coru for longer than a defiant moment or two," she said.

"It does seem to be the most exhausting of the elements," he agreed, sipping his water. "Though frequently rewarding."

She smiled. Like most people who met him, she'd always found Darien intimidating. He was so smooth, so assured, and so well-informed; she always felt like he knew everything about her and she knew nothing about him—and the imbalance would never work to her advantage. But years of living on her own in a strange country had given Leah a large measure of confidence in her own skills and intuition. She was a lot harder to impress these days.

"You didn't call me here to discuss the elemental traits," she said. "So what would you like to know?"

He didn't even blink at the abrupt question. "I'd like your final report about the empress of Malinqua and her current situation," he said. "But first, I'd like to hear your version about what exactly is going on with my daughter."

For the first time, Leah felt a twinge of guilt that she hadn't made it to the palace as soon as she arrived in Chialto. She'd been focused on her own emotions at being back in the country of her birth. She hadn't thought about Darien or how worried he must be about Corene.

Eighteen years ago, Darien had been one of the trusted court favorites who had helped King Vernon produce a series of heirs. Corene had been born to Vernon's third wife, Alys, but it was years before anyone realized Darien was really her father. Upon Vernon's death, Darien began to take an active role in Corene's life—even more active once it turned out Alys was the least nurturing mother any child could have—but he had never developed an easy relationship with that redheaded wild child. A quintile ago, Corene had run away to Malinqua against Darien's expressed wishes. He had sent Nelson Ardelay to bring her home, but once the sweela prime arrived on the scene, Corene ran even farther away. From what Leah had seen, Corene didn't intend to come home anytime soon.

"I thought Nelson must have explained all that," Leah said.

Darien looked briefly and deeply annoyed. "Nelson explained that Corene went to visit Cozique with a friend she had made at the Malinquese court," he said. "He didn't explain why he or Corene or *anybody* would consider that a good idea."

Leah held back a smile and spoke in a serious voice. "While she was in Malinqua, Corene seemed to come into her own," she said. "She grew more certain of herself. She developed close friendships and seemed to give a great deal of thought to the kind of person she wanted to be. I think she's still on that journey, and she thought by coming home she would cut that journey short. But I believe you would like the person she is becoming."

Darien narrowed his gray eyes but didn't answer, just nodded at her to continue.

"Anyway, you have to admit that Corene could hardly have picked a more strategic place to run away to than Cozique," Leah added. It was the largest, wealthiest, and most powerful nation in the southern seas. "That friend she made at court? The daughter of the Coziquela queen. A *very* good friend to have."

"Nelson says she is envisioning herself as some sort of international ambassador for Welce."

"I think she is. And I think she'll be a good one."

Darien drummed his fingers on the table. "Well, it does us no harm to achieve closer relations with Cozique," he said at last. "Whether

Corene is capable of cementing those relations—and whether she is actually *safe* while she sojourns there—I am not so certain."

"Surely you have spies at the Coziquela court," Leah said softly.

He smiled reluctantly. "Yes, of course," he said. "But none of them with quite the same level of—sophistication—as you. Would you be interested in taking an assignment in Cozique?"

She sat up straighter, because she hadn't expected that. "What? No. Thank you for your faith in me, but I've been away from Welce too long. I don't know that I'm happy to be back, but—but I need to stay awhile and find out."

He watched her a moment, as if trying to determine what she hadn't said, since it was likely to be more interesting than what she *had*, then he nodded. "Very well. We'll revisit that in a moment. First, tell me your impressions of the current situation in Malinqua. Coziquela forces came in and took over the harbor—did the empress make terms? Has she been left powerless, or will she recover from this disaster?"

"I think she is already scheming how to recover, and I don't think it will take her that long," Leah said, launching into a recital of the last exciting days at the Malinquese court.

When she was finished, Darien remarked, "I rarely say this, but I'm glad Nelson was on hand to play a part."

Leah laughed out loud. "He was magnificent," she said. "I'd forgotten how impressive the power of the primes could be."

"Yes, well, we strive to live in times where they are not called upon to show off their fearsome abilities," Darien replied dryly.

She decided not to ask him how often his own wife worked her elemental magic on water. Zoe Lalindar had flooded the Marisi a few years back; Leah supposed you didn't need to do that too often to remind people what you were capable of. "Calm and serenity," she agreed. "That's what we want."

Darien surveyed her a moment. "Is that what you're hoping to find now that you've returned to Welce? What are your plans?"

She lifted her chin. "I want to see Mally."

He nodded. "Of course. But in what capacity? Do you plan to walk into Taro's house and pull her aside and introduce yourself as her mother? Speaking as one who had no claim on his oldest daughter until she was nearly twelve, it is not so easy to become a parent overnight. For you *or* the child."

Darien Serlast, offering a personal example from his own life to make a point. She couldn't remember that ever happening before. "I haven't thought it through," she admitted. "I thought maybe Taro would let me stay with them for a while. Get to know her slowly. I don't know."

He was still watching her with those intent gray eyes. "And that's another consideration," he said. "Have you given any thought to what you might do to fill your time? Do you want to take up court life again? Or are you looking for more meaningful occupation?"

She had been prepared to respond with another helpless *I don't know*, but that last question stopped her. *I'm an idiot,* she thought. *Darien didn't ask me here to learn about Corene or to inquire about my feelings. He wants to offer me another job.* She lifted her head and gave him back a stare as cool and assessing as his own. "Just come out with it," she said. "What is it you want me to do?"

That made him smile, which warmed his face to an amazing degree. "I was thinking about your situation," he said. "I had some thoughts about a course you could take that might ease your way *and* serve the crown."

"'Serve the crown.' I like that," she said. "It sounds much more noble than 'Do some secret business for me.'"

He shrugged. "If you're interested, say so. If not, I won't trouble you with my ideas."

That was something else about Darien. He could make you feel like you were in the wrong even when you weren't. "Please, majesty, I'd like to hear how I might be of service to my liege."

He paused a moment, as if marshaling his thoughts. Before he could speak, there was a quiet knock and a man entered. He was tall, bald, ageless, and expressionless; he looked like he could disappear into the walls of the palace if he were so inclined. Leah had never seen him before—then again, she guessed that he probably went to a great deal of trouble *not* to be noticed. She had the sense that he was high on the list of Darien's trusted army of spies. He had that look.

He glanced briefly at Leah, and when Darien nodded, he said, "There's been another one."

She could feel Darien's attention narrow into a sudden cold fury, though his voice remained carefully neutral. "Where?"

"On the banks of the Marisi. Where the vagrants camp."

"Now that surprises me," Darien said. "The camps are patrolled."

The man nodded. "It seems she—"

"'She'?" Darien interrupted.

"Yes. It seems she made her way there afterward. So it happened somewhere else."

"There was nothing she could tell you?"

"No."

Leah was looking idly out the window, trying to pretend she wasn't interested in the conversation and thinking that whatever had happened to this unfortunate woman must be pretty awful if Darien allowed his spymaster to interrupt him while he was conducting other business. She waited until she heard the *click* of the door closing, then she turned her head to give the regent a look of wide-eyed curiosity. "That sounded mysterious. And unpleasant."

"It is both those things," Darien agreed. "But it's not what I want to talk about with you today."

Leah didn't even bother asking more questions. There was never any point in badgering Darien. "You were going to tell me how I could be of assistance to you."

"Indeed I was," Darien responded. His voice was perfectly calm, perfectly level. Maybe whatever had just happened wasn't so bad after all. "As I think you know, during the past eight or nine years, Welce has increased its international trade partnerships and strengthened alliances across the southern seas. We have made even more progress in the past two or three years—though obviously we have experienced a slight setback with Malinqua. We have been hoping to develop tighter bonds with Cozique, simply because Cozique is so powerful. And yet we must always be mindful of the fact that our near neighbors can be our truest allies or our most bitter foes, just because of their geographic placement."

Our near neighbors . . . "Do you mean Soeche-Tas?" she demanded. "What have they done now?"

Soeche-Tas shared a continent with Welce, though dense mountains on Welce's northern border had generally served to enforce peace between nations. Over the centuries, the two countries had sometimes skirmished over fishing territories and mining rights, but they had managed to avoid outright war. About six years ago, Vernon had thought to improve relations with Soeche-Tas by marrying Corene off to its aging viceroy, but Zoe had strongly objected, and the wedding had been called off in the most dramatic way possible. Leah had left the country shortly afterward, so she didn't know how that broken covenant had affected relations.

"The Soechins haven't done anything—that I'm aware of," Darien said. "But they're making alliances, too. And one interesting trading partner they have begun to woo is the Karkades."

Leah frowned. "But—isn't that a possession of Cozique? Though not a very big one."

"Right on both counts. Except certain factions in the Karkades have been suing for independence during the past few years. And these factions have begun treating with other nations of the southern seas. They already have a partnership with Dhonsho. They are close to signing a deal with Soeche-Tas. And some of their representatives want to call on me to discuss strengthening relations with Welce."

"That might not make Cozique's queen too happy," Leah observed.

"No. In fact, it might make her quite irritable."

Which put Corene's flight to Cozique in an entirely different light. "So you really *are* worried about your daughter's safety."

"Cozique is too civilized to murder foreign diplomats in a fit of pique," Darien said softly. "But I admit this is an unexpected complication."

Leah was still thinking. "And, of course, you don't want to reject a treaty with the Karkades out of hand, since you would like to keep the peace with Soeche-Tas."

"Precisely," Darien said. "But I am not sure how easily the Karkades will be put off by vague promises, since the ruling factions are eager to make a point to Cozique. They want allies, they want them now, and they want them to swear unwavering support. It is a delicate situation, to be sure."

"Maybe send someone to Cozique to bring Corene home," Leah suggested. "She's become politically savvy. Once she understands how the situation stands, I think she'll fall in line."

"Yes, but even if I subtract Corene from the equation, I don't know that I will rush to sign treaties with the Karkades," Darien said. "I don't like being manipulated, that's one thing. And—I don't know enough about the place, that's another."

"What? No Welchin operatives in its primary cities? I'm shocked."

Darien shrugged. "The Karkades never seemed important enough to investigate," he said. "I have people on the way now, of course, but they might not arrive in time."

"So what do you want *me* to do?" Leah asked.

He studied her again as if trying to gauge how much duress she could handle before collapsing in exhaustion. "As I said, we are expecting an influx of visitors from the Karkades and Soeche-Tas. I suspect a few advance spies are already here, in fact, but the first official delegation doesn't arrive for a couple more ninedays. I thought—it's such a small thing—but these foreign arrivals might feel more at home if they had access to some of their favorite native traditions. Food, clothing, spices—"

"You want me to open a shop," Leah said. For a moment she was so surprised she couldn't tell if the idea delighted or horrified her.

"I do," Darien replied. "While you were in Malinqua, you reported that you worked at the city's Great Market, and you seemed to find it an agreeable experience. If you were a purveyor of exotic goods, you would be in an excellent position to make international contacts, since you would frequently interact with both suppliers and customers. And if you actually enjoyed running a business—" Darien shrugged. "All the better."

"I did like it, but I wasn't doing most of the work," she told him. "I was employed by someone who ran the business. Invested the money, dealt with suppliers, set the prices, paid the taxes—all of it."

"The Welchin crown would be your principal investor, and I would not expect an accounting of your profits," Darien said gravely. "If it turned out this was an enterprise you eventually wanted to run on your own, we could discuss terms for how you could buy me out. Otherwise, it would exist only until this particular crisis is past, and you would not need to display any business acumen to operate it."

"But I'd still need to—locate a property and set it up and find suppliers and order goods—" She was protesting, but Leah had to admit she was intrigued. She *had* enjoyed being Chandran's assistant in

Malinqua's Great Market. She'd had a knack for picking merchandise that would sell, and she'd found it easy to develop a rapport with even the pickiest of customers. Of course, one reason she'd liked the work so much was she'd liked being around Chandran. The retail life wouldn't be nearly so enjoyable if she were running the business on her own.

"As to getting the enterprise started, Zoe has some thoughts she could share," Darien said. "I believe you would be able to open your doors much sooner than you might anticipate."

Leah wondered how exactly the coru prime would be able to assist her in setting up a shop. It would be worth it to say yes just to learn the answer. But there was one very large objection to the whole scheme. "I can't stay in Chialto and run a business for you, Darien," she said, and the regret in her voice was real. "I came back to Welce to see Mally. That means I have to go where Mally is."

"Yes, but Mally will be in Chialto for the next quintile," he said. "I have made arrangements."

Her breath caught in her throat. Of course he had. Darien must really want her to take on this little venture; he had gone to some trouble to remove all possible obstacles. "What arrangements?"

"Taro's wife has agreed to bring Mally to the city for an extended visit," Darien said. "Taro, as I'm sure you know, generally refuses to leave his estates except on explicit order from the crown, but Virrie is much more sociable. I hope to convince her to stay at a property I own in Chialto so she is not even responsible for running a household while she is here. Once you determine how you would like to introduce yourself to your daughter, you can visit with her as often as you like."

Leah's heart was beating strangely fast; the thought of seeing Mally made her feel faint with excitement and dread. "You're trying to make it impossible for me to say no to this scheme of yours, aren't you?" she managed to say.

"I wouldn't put it that way," Darien said. "But I am certainly trying to make it easy for you to say yes."

She wondered if she could shock him. "And if I said I'd do it, but only if you made sure I never accidentally ran into Rhan Ardelay? Would you kidnap him and hustle him out of the city?"

It felt strange to say Rhan's name out loud. She had spent so much energy in the past five years trying to forget that Nelson Ardelay's youngest son even existed, and now here she was using him as a way to taunt Darien Serlast. But Darien was one of the few people who knew that Rhan was Mally's father. Darien had known even before Nelson.

The regent lifted his eyebrows. "Is that one of your requirements? If so, let us discuss it."

She had to laugh. He was bluffing, she thought, but she was tempted to see how far Darien would go to get what he wanted. "It's not a requirement *at the moment*," she said. "I'll let you know if it becomes a condition in the future."

"So you'll do it?" he said. "Run the shop?"

She wanted to say she needed to think it over, but she could tell her mind was already made up and it seemed pointless to make Darien wait for her answer. Well, except to teach him that he couldn't just move people here and there like pieces on a game board. But since he obviously could, she didn't think he'd learn the lesson anyway. "I will," she said. "I think it sounds like fun."

THREE

L eah was hungry, and she was curious, so she accepted when Darien asked her to stay for lunch. He led her up two flights of stairs to the level where he obviously kept his private quarters. She was trying to remember if she'd ever been in this particular corridor when he gestured her into a charming room full of afternoon sunshine and a round table set for three. A lone woman stood by the window, contemplating the waterfall. She turned to face them as they stepped in.

"Oh, you *do* look like Mally," was her greeting before any introductions had been made. "A little bit like Romelle, too, but I suppose you'd have to for your daughters to appear so similar."

Leah thought that she heard Darien sigh behind her. "Leah, this is Zoe Lalindar. Coru prime, my wife, and a woman sadly lacking in manners. Zoe—well, you've obviously figured out that this is Leah Frothen."

Zoe was laughing as she came over to give Leah a friendly bow. The coru prime was tall, lanky, and relaxed; by her plainly styled brown hair and loose-fitting tunic, it was clear that she didn't have much patience with formality. But her smile was warm and her black eyes were bright with interest. Leah thought that this was someone who liked people far more than she liked things.

"I don't think we've met before, but I saw you from a distance a few times before I left Chialto," Leah said.

"Let me guess. I was calling up floods or threatening to make a man's blood boil in his veins," Zoe said.

That actually made Leah laugh out loud. "No, but—*could* you? I mean, I know you actually did flood the Marisi, but—blood boiling? Really?"

"She threatens it all the time, but she never delivers," Darien said, as they took their places at the table. It was already laden with a diverse selection of breads and meats and sauces. "I've begun to think it's a hollow boast."

Zoe reached for a pitcher of fruited water and regarded him with a lurking smile. Leah was seized with the sudden conviction that not only did Darien believe her, but he'd seen her demonstrate a skill that was at least similar and awfully damn impressive. "I *could* do it," she said, "but it's so very extreme. You have to be prepared for the direst of consequences once you've done something like that."

Darien accepted a glass from her hands. "Not that Zoe shies away from extreme behavior, you understand," he said. "Or minds dire consequences."

"That comes from being coru, I suppose," Leah said, taking her own glass. "I've often wished I had a little more coru in me. I would like to be more spontaneous."

They began passing the serving plates around, for all the world like an ordinary family having a casual midday meal. Though the food on the plates was far superior to the fare the average merchant or carriage maker would serve at the most elaborate dinner. "Are you torz?" Zoe inquired. And when Leah nodded, she asked, "And what are your blessings?"

Leah made a face. "Endurance, honor, and time."

Zoe considered those while she finished her first mouthful of food. "Not exactly carefree," she decided.

"My mother said once that they meant I'd become some kind of scientific researcher, discovering the mysteries of the stars. I always figured they meant I'd grit my teeth and make it through some horrible situation without complaining."

"And instead you've become one of Darien's secret operatives! Which actually sounds more interesting than those other options."

"She's agreed to run the business," Darien put in. "I told her you'd help."

"Oh, can I sign on as a sales clerk? I don't mind working long hours."

Leah was laughing again. "What? No. Of course not. You're the coru prime."

"But I have experience," Zoe argued. "I worked in a cobbler's shop a few years ago. I liked it, too."

Leah glanced between Zoe and Darien, because she wasn't sure Zoe was joking. Darien sighed again. "She did," he said. "It was during her more vagabond days."

"Which I still miss."

Really? thought Leah. *Myself, I've been a vagabond too long. I'd like to come home.* Aloud she said, "So when Darien said you could help me—"

Zoe took a spoonful of fruit compote. "My cobbler friends advised us on property we could buy for the shop."

Leah looked at Darien. "So you were pretty sure I'd say yes."

He shrugged. "You or someone. I was hoping you."

"If you had said no, you would have had many even more enticing opportunities to say yes," Zoe told her. "That's how Darien works."

"Maybe I should have held out awhile to see what else he offered."

"Exactly! That's what you should do *next* time he wants a favor."

"I don't see how it can be considered a favor if it's an arrangement that benefits us both," Darien replied.

"Which is why so many people say yes to Darien," Zoe noted.

"We stray from the point," Darien said. "As Zoe mentioned, we have procured a shop in a prime location. The place still must be furnished—"

"And *stocked*," Leah said. "What you carry is at least as important as where you're located."

"I can help you out there, too," Zoe said. "I have friends who are itinerant traders, and they deal in fairly unusual merchandise. They'll work with you to get the place opened quickly."

Itinerant traders? Leah was beginning to think the coru prime's "vagabond days" had lasted a lot longer and been a lot more interesting than anyone would expect. "That would be great at the beginning," she said. "But I made some contacts in Malinqua and I think I can start importing very quickly. The problem will be the lag time between sending out letters and getting responses."

"Yes, and unfortunately even Darien can't speed up sea travel just by commanding it," Zoe said.

"I *have* tried," he said. He spoke so solemnly it took Leah a second to realize he was joking.

Zoe patted his wrist. "Don't give up. Someday you might master the trick."

It was astonishing how human Darien Serlast became when he was in the presence of his casual wife. Leah wouldn't have believed it if she hadn't seen it for herself. She hid a smile and said, "How quickly do you want the shop opened?"

"How soon *can* it be opened?"

"Not until it's stocked with enough merchandise to last for at least three ninedays," she said firmly. "And I have to have more supplies on the way. And I'll need someone I can trust to work there on the days I have to be gone."

"Me, of course," Zoe said, but she was grinning.

"Have you asked Annova?" Darien inquired.

Zoe nodded. "She liked the idea." She glanced at Leah. "Another friend of mine from the vagabond days."

"Can she speak Coziquela?" Leah asked. "Because if you're expecting international customers, that's probably the language they'll use."

"She can," Zoe said. "She taught herself a few years ago when she got bored during one very cold Quinnelay." Zoe shrugged as if to say: *A little odd, I know, but that's Annova.*

Leah took a deep breath. "Then I guess all that's left is to go look at the property."

"And to finish lunch," Zoe said, passing another plate. "We'll be spending the afternoon looking over the shop. We don't want to go hungry."

As soon as they finished their meal, Zoe left to find Annova. Darien reached into a pocket of his tunic and said, "This letter arrived for you a day ago."

Leah had stood up when the other two did, and now she stared blankly at the regent. "A letter? For me? Came to you? At the palace?"

"I was surprised as well," Darien said, handing it over. "You can wait for Zoe here. She'll be back in a minute with Annova."

Leah was a little concerned about being saddled with a stranger as she took up a new double role on behalf of her liege. What if she didn't like or trust Zoe's friend? "Who is Annova, exactly?"

Darien's face was expressionless. "Someone Zoe encountered when she was camping down on the river. Before she was recognized as coru prime."

"Camping—with the vagrants—on the Marisi?" Leah was almost too astonished to get the words out.

"Just so," Darien said. "Annova and her husband, Calvin, are both devoted to Zoe, however, and entirely to be trusted. Also—I think you will like them. It is difficult not to."

"I suppose you tried."

A smile flickered across his face so quickly she might have imagined it. "Of course not. I like everybody."

Which made her laugh out loud. Darien's smile widened and he said, "Read your letter. Go visit the property. Then come let me know what you need from me, and we will do what it takes to get you in business."

He left and Leah glanced down at the envelope in her hand. And then almost fell over from surprise.

Chandran's handwriting. Chandran who had sent a letter to the palace, assuming it would somehow make its way to her. She had never told him her place in Welchin society, but he knew she was a spy for the crown. Even so, it took a certain reckless nerve to imagine a regent would be willing to serve as your courier.

She sank back into her chair and broke the seal. It looked as though Darien had not bothered to read the letter before handing it over, though Chandran would have assumed that *someone* might. He would be circumspect.

The letter was brief.

Leah,

You have been gone only three days and already it seems like a quintile. I expected to miss you, but not this much.

But whenever I am sad that you are gone, I picture you back where you were meant to be, and I persuade myself that I am happy.

As you might imagine, things have been tumultuous in the city of Palminera ever since Cozique sailed into the harbor. No one has any time for shopping, of course, so the merchants all voted to close the Great Market for a nineday so that the building could undergo some necessary repairs. I find myself with more free time on my hands than I am accustomed to and no idea how to use it. I did spend an afternoon in the Little Islands district, visiting some of the places you used to tell me about. I liked the food in the Welchin café, but possibly only because it reminded me of you. I also went to the Welchin temple and tried my hand at pulling blessings. Three strangers were there, so, as you directed me, I asked them to pick my coins. They gifted me with travel, honor, and resolve. Am I right in remembering that one of those is also a blessing you possess? That is what I told myself, anyway.

You said that you would write, and I hope you do.

Chandran

Leah read the letter through three times, not sure whether she should lay it against her cheek and smile, or hug it to her heart and weep. She was happy to know Chandran missed her, too, but it scarcely mattered; what reason would she ever have to return to Palminera? Why would he ever come to Welce? She probably would never see him again, and mooning over him did her absolutely no good.

There were voices down the hall, so she tucked the letter inside her tunic and rose to her feet. Zoe swept in, accompanied by a small, thin woman who might be anywhere from sixty to eighty years old. Her wrinkled brown face was smiling and kind; her black hair was so short it was barely more than a shadow across her skull. She was wearing what looked to be a very fine tunic and shoes, but there was something raffish about her. It wasn't hard to picture her living a footloose lifestyle and enjoying it very much.

Zoe made introductions and Annova's smile widened. "So we're going to start running a shop for Darien Serlast," she said in a pleasant voice that had the faintest burr of an accent. "Every time I think life doesn't hold anything new for me, I find out I was wrong."

Leah tilted her head. She'd heard that particular cadence before, and recognized the deep color of Annova's skin. "Are you originally from Dhonsho?" she asked.

"My mother was," Annova replied. "My father was Welchin."

"What? Dhonsho? You never told me that," Zoe said.

"Do I have to tell you everything?"

"I don't see why not. Anyway, I always thought you were from one of the southern provinces."

"I was. But my ancestors came from farther away." Annova nodded at Leah. "Not many people in Welce recognize Dhonshon faces."

"I met a few expatriates in Malinqua," Leah said. "They didn't make it seem like Dhonsho was a place I'd want to visit."

"My mother told some of the same stories. I've never been tempted to go there, either."

"But some of the fabrics they make there are gorgeous," Leah added. "I was hoping to import a few items from that country."

Annova gave Zoe a sideways glance. "You were right. I'll like this job."

On that harmonious note, the three women set out for the shop district.

Darien had supplied an elaymotive and a couple of guards, though both Zoe and Annova looked disgruntled when the soldiers appeared. Traffic was heavy on the Cinque, the road that encircled the city, and so dense when they got close to their destination that the three women elected to get out and walk. The soldiers followed suit.

The shop district was a collection of high-end boutiques filled with the most luxurious wares to be found in Chialto. Anyone could stroll under the fluttering awnings and linger outside the big display windows, pointing and gawking, but only people with a lot of gold at their disposal would actually walk through the doors and hope to buy. The Plazas were for fun; the shop district was for serious acquisitions.

The space Darien had acquired was a narrow spot sandwiched between two much larger boutiques. Zoe produced a key and they all stepped inside, looking around with interest. The place was wholly empty, but warm and appealing even so, Leah thought. Afternoon sun streamed through the windows and picked out the patterns on the wood floor, the stubbled finish of the plaster walls. Elevated floors in both display windows provided space for setting out the best merchandise; hooks in the ceiling could be used to hold baskets or banners. There was a short counter near the front door where a worker could complete transactions and hide a money box. The shop held nothing else except floating dust motes in the air and crunchy grit underfoot.

Still, it was bigger than Chandran's booth in the Great Market and rife with possibilities.

Leah did a slow pivot, waving her hands at walls and corners. "Tall shelving units there—a cabinet there—a table or two in the middle of the room to hold all the cheaper stuff that you don't mind somebody stealing. The real problem will be storage, because I don't see a back room and you have to be able to restock quickly."

"There's an upstairs unit," Zoe said, gesturing toward a door set in the far wall. "A lot of the merchants live in apartments above their shops."

"Let's go see," Leah said, and they all filed through the back door. It opened onto a poorly lit space that featured another door—which probably led to an alley—and a cramped stone stairway going up. Once they climbed it, they discovered that, like the bottom story, the top level was almost twice as long as it was wide. It also was completely empty, except for a small closet-size space that offered running water and a little privacy.

"Perfect," Leah said.

They clattered back downstairs and spent twenty minutes deciding what furnishings to buy, how to lay out the shop, and how quickly the place could be stocked. "I have contacts in Malinqua, but it takes about two ninedays to sail between countries on a commercial boat," Leah said. "I know there are cutters and mail ships that can go faster— would Darien want to employ one of those on my behalf?"

Zoe was grinning. "I'm sure he would."

"Then I'll write letters tonight and get them to Darien in the morning."

"Don't forget there are traders who are already in town," Zoe said. "My friends Jaker and Barlow will be around a few more days if you'd like to meet with them."

"I'd love to, thank you. After that, I'll go to the harbor and see what's for sale there."

"Then I think we're finished here," said Zoe, handing Leah the key. "Unless you can think of something else we need to do?"

"We ought to pull blessings," Annova said. "You should always ask for blessings when you set out on any new enterprise."

"Oh, good idea. There's a temple nearby," Zoe answered. "We can walk there."

The temple wasn't quite as close as Zoe's cheerful assertion had implied, and Leah thought she could hear the soldiers grumbling as they made their way through progressively narrower and less prosperous streets. But they eventually found themselves before a small, quaint building whose exterior incorporated all five of the elements: walls of gray stone decorated with climbing ivy and painted butterflies, lit by hanging oil lamps and serenaded by fluttering water fountains. For a wonder, the place was empty when they stepped inside.

Annova plopped down on the bench painted blue for water, reinforcing Leah's hunch that the older woman was coru. "Three of us, so we'll each pull a blessing for the shop," Annova decided. Threes, fives, and eights were propitious in Welce, and most everybody was superstitious about keeping some combination of those numbers in all their transactions. "Then maybe we each pull a blessing for ourselves as well."

Zoe tossed a few quint-silvers into the tithing box before stepping up to the barrel and vigorously mixing the coins. She grinned at Leah. "You've been gone how long now? Five years? When's the last time you had a blessing bestowed on you?"

"More recently than you'd think. There was a Welchin temple in Palminera's international district, and I went there now and then. Even had strangers pull blessings for me from time to time, to be sure I was doing it properly."

Annova looked interested. "So what was the last set of blessings you received from strangers?"

It took Leah a moment to remember, and then she let out a strangled laugh. "Hope, serenity, and change. At the time I thought the only one that really applied was change."

"That's the thing about blessings," Zoe agreed. "The ones that seem most unlikely are the ones that come true." She dipped her hand back in the barrel and came up with her fingers closed around a coin. "And so the first blessing I pick for the shop is—" She opened her fist. "Beauty."

She flipped the coin once in the air, caught it, and dropped it back in the barrel. "That seems fitting, if you're going to sell lovely things."

Annova pushed herself to her feet and approached the barrel. Closing her eyes, she skimmed her fingers through the top few layers of metal before plucking one at random. "Wealth," she said, after squinting at it in the temple's low light. "Another good omen."

Leah plunged her arm elbow-deep into the cool pile of coins and grabbed the first disk that didn't slip through her fingertips. "Surprise," she said when she identified the glyph. "Hmm. I'm not sure that's the best sign when you're starting a business."

"Surprise is always good," Annova said.

"Not for torz people," Leah retorted.

Zoe was smiling. "I've liked most of the surprises that came my way," she said. "But some of them have definitely required an adjustment."

Annova was sorting through the coins again. "Now, let us each choose blessings for ourselves," she said. "Since we're here." The coin she came up with showed the glyph for fertility. She laughed and slipped it into her pocket. "Calvin will like that," she said.

Zoe's blessing turned out to be change. "I don't know why I even bother," she said, tossing the coin back.

Leah's was honor. A blessing she already possessed, a blessing that had been bestowed on Chandran the first time he visited a Welchin temple. She felt a little shiver go down her back. "I guess this means you can trust me to keep any bargain I make with Darien," she said.

Zoe waved a hand. "We already trusted you. This means something else." She grinned. "Or nothing. Sometimes the blessings are obscure."

Leah shrugged and dropped the coin back into the barrel, where it landed with a musical splash. "At any rate, I think we're all set," she said. "I'll write notes tonight and bring them to Darien tomorrow—and then we'll get started."

The reifarjin watched Leah for the entire hour it took her to compose a letter to Chandran. So she told him about the fish, which, when the day began, had seemed like the most interesting thing she would have to report. She told him about Darien's plan to bring Mally to Chialto for a quintile, and how afraid she was to see the girl for the very first time—how afraid and how excited. Chandran had learned about Mally on the day he met Leah; he was one of the few people in the world who knew she had a daughter.

But, of course, she devoted the bulk of the letter to outlining Darien's extraordinary request. She was careful in how she described their arrangement because she did not want to baldly proclaim, "The regent is employing me to spy on foreign visitors." So she said that she'd proposed the idea of opening a shop and Darien had offered to fund it as a way to make expatriates feel more at home. Chandran would be able to interpret that statement correctly.

She wrote:

> *I'm so glad he agreed. I need some structure or I think I'll go mad. I can't go back to my old life, but I haven't figured out my new life. I know I want it to include Mally, but I haven't even had the courage to go to her yet. Maybe this shop will be my anchor. Maybe it will be my tall tower, the place from which I can look out on the world.*

Chandran would understand that reference, too. They'd spent an evening standing together on one of Palminera's high towers, gazing at the city below. That's where they were when she told him she was leaving. That's where they were when they promised to write.

> *But I need your help to launch my new enterprise! I'm hoping you'll be willing to make some purchases for me with the money I've enclosed. I'd like a selection of items from Dhonsho, Berringey, and Cozique. You know the pieces I like best—the scarves, the jewelry, the glass boxes—but I trust you to pick out anything else that you think would appeal to me. In return, I'll be happy to send you Welchin merchandise for your booth, if you tell me what you're looking for.*

She paused then, trying to think of what else to say. She wanted to keep writing; she wanted to ball the paper up and throw it in a corner and start over, writing something much less scattered and chatty. She didn't know how it had happened, this change in their relationship. While she was in Malinqua, she had never felt moved to pour her heart out to Chandran, and now she wanted to tell him everything she was thinking and feeling. She supposed it was because he was so far away, so unreachable; it was safe to confide in him now. She couldn't think of anyone in Chialto she would want to confide in.

Well, she'd never really been the confiding type.

It was nighttime before she finished the letter. She stood, stretched, and wandered over to the window to watch the gaslights of Chialto spring up all along the boulevard. Some were streetlamps, some were house lights, and all of them threw small circles of illumination over other people's lives. Her own lights were on. Had passersby glanced up to see her bent over the table, scratching out her letter with great concentration? Had they wondered who she was writing to, whether she was sharing good news or bad? Or had they kept their heads down and continued walking, indifferent to her entire existence?

"You're thinking silly things," she said, half aloud. "You must be hungry. Eat, then go to bed. If tomorrow is anything like today, it will definitely live up to the blessing you pulled for the shop."

It had always been the blessing she found most unwelcome. Surprise.

FOUR

In the morning, Leah took a public elaymotive to the palace—a much less comfortable experience, though the large vehicle was well-maintained and not too crowded. Darien's admirable servants recognized her name immediately, so she didn't have long to wait before he joined her in his study. He agreed to have one of his personal couriers deliver her letter and asked how much money she wanted to send to Chandran. When she named a sum, Darien lifted his eyebrows.

"You must be convinced of his honesty," he said.

"He tried to poison me the first day I met him," she said, partly because it was true and partly to see Darien's reaction.

But it was hard to astonish the regent. He merely raised his eyebrows again and said politely, "It is usually the behavior I look for among my closest friends."

"But I do think he's an honorable man," she said. "I guess we'll find out."

"Yes, if he never sends any goods in response to your plea, we can assume he's a scoundrel."

She laughed. "Well, I plan to go to the harbor soon to see what I can find among the ships in port. So I should have something to sell even if Chandran betrays me."

"I hope you're not planning to travel to the harbor today," Darien said. "I'd like you to join me for lunch. I have guests."

Something about the way he said it made her stomach tense. "Guests?"

"Taro and Virrie Frothen. And Mally. They arrived last night and are currently staying at the palace."

For a moment, she couldn't breathe. *Mally. Mally. Mally.* Leah had returned to Chialto for just this moment, just this reunion, and yet she wasn't sure she could endure it. Her heart would hammer open her rib cage; her bones would shatter from longing and dread. "I—" she said, though it came out barely a whimper. "Darien, I—"

"If you would prefer to meet her alone in a room, that could be arranged. But Virrie and Zoe both thought it might be easier if there were other people around and the conversation was casual," Darien went on.

"What other people?" she managed.

"Just us. You and Zoe and me, Taro and Virrie and Mally. Oh, and Celia."

That surprised a smile from her. "Your baby daughter?"

"She's just over a year old now," he said. "We don't bring her to the dinner table if we've got company—which we usually do—but Zoe likes to include her at informal lunches to get her used to social situations. Josetta says that she and Corene had had a meal with every prime and political player in the city before they were five years old and that it's simply part of a princess's training. More to the point, Mally likes her. Her presence might"—he waved a hand—"make things easier."

Leah nodded and gulped some air. "Yes," she said. "I'd love to stay for lunch."

They headed back to the small dining room they'd used the day before, to find only one person awaiting them. It was Taro, a big mountain of a man with brown hair and brown eyes and loose brown clothing. Even on state occasions, he looked like he'd spent half the day in the fields, coaxing the crops to grow by digging through the dirt by hand.

As soon as he saw her, he said her name in his deep rumbling voice and enveloped her in a hug. She gulped for air again and tried not to burrow into his shoulder, to bury herself in his warm embrace. He was the torz prime; he was the most human and compassionate of the five, with a gift for affection, but he had always been more to Leah. He was her mother's brother, her surrogate father, the man who had held her up when every other support in her life had failed. Once her mother died, he had been the only person Leah believed loved her without reservation.

Naturally, she had trusted him to raise her daughter.

"How good it is to see you again," Taro said, pulling back just enough to get a look at her face. "Though you're thinner than I like. And you've done something to your hair."

She laughed a little and pulled back even more, though she was pleased when Taro kept hold of her hands. "People keep talking about my hair! Does it look that bad?"

"It's just different," Taro said. He surveyed her critically a moment. She wondered what he was searching for—shadows of the old emotional scars or signs that she had outgrown them. Maybe he was looking for new scars, damage done by her recent life. Maybe he was just taking in the sight of her face. "You look good," he said finally.

"*You* look just the same."

"No need to insult me," he said, then let loose a booming laugh. She couldn't help but join in, and so that was how it happened that she was laughing the first time she saw her daughter.

There was a swirl at the door and then suddenly there were four more people in the room. Zoe, holding a small blond toddler on her hip. Virrie Frothen, a serene, big-boned woman who looked perfectly sized and constructed for the torz prime. And a little girl who trailed behind them, glancing around with interest at the people and the objects in the room.

For the third time in ten minutes, Leah found it impossible to breathe. She felt light-headed, as if she might faint. Lights flickered at the edges of her vision. She wanted to run from the room, but she was paralyzed. She wanted to stay and never take her eyes off her daughter.

Mally looked like she might be a little tall for her age and hadn't grown into her height yet. Her hair was darker than Leah's had ever been until she started coloring it, and long enough to take on a spiraling curl as it fell down her back. Her eyes were huge, a gold-flecked brown. Just like Leah's mother's eyes.

She wasn't smiling. The serious expression on her face seemed natural to her, as if she didn't smile very often, but she didn't seem somber or worried. Observant, maybe. Watchful. Not quite sure what the world would throw at her next and wanting to be ready for it.

No, that's how you *look,* Leah reminded herself. She couldn't stop staring.

Zoe crossed over to her, jiggling the child on her hip. "Leah! I'm so glad Darien talked you into staying for lunch. I wanted you to meet Celia, who I am hoping will be on her best behavior. Celia, this is Leah. Can you say hello?"

Leah dragged her gaze from Mally and managed to give a moment's attention to Celia. She had her father's smoky eyes but her mother's lively face, and an expression that said she could be as stubborn as one and as wayward as the other. She watched Leah for a moment, then stuck her fingers in her mouth and looked away.

"I think she's hungry," Zoe said. "We all are."

Not Leah. She thought she might throw up.

"Leah. There you are. When Darien told me you might join us—" Virrie didn't bother to finish the sentence, she just folded Leah against her soft body and hugged her close. When she pulled away, she was smiling. "*Now* the world is right again."

"It is so good to see both of you," Leah said, but she was back to staring at Mally. Virrie motioned to the little girl, who promptly joined them.

"Mally, dear, this is Taro's niece, Leah, who's been traveling in exotic lands," Virrie said. "How would you like to greet her?"

Leah watched as Mally considered for a moment, clearly remembering hours of etiquette training. Then she offered a perfectly judged bow—not as low as she'd give to a prime, deeper than she'd dip for most other members of the Five Families. "She gets extra respect because of Taro," Mally said, her voice ending on a slightly interrogative note.

"Very good," Virrie approved. "Now how should she acknowledge you?"

Mally considered again, lifting her flecked brown eyes to Leah's face. "She doesn't know," she said after a moment. "You didn't tell her who I am."

Who do you think you are? Leah wanted to ask. But she didn't wait for the introduction. She bowed in return, to almost exactly the same depth. She wanted to sink to the floor in an obeisance lower than she would offer to a queen, but she forced herself to maintain some decorum. She was proud of how normal her voice sounded when she explained, "You're here with my uncle, so you deserve to be treated with honor."

Mally replied to that only with a grave smile, but she seemed pleased.

"Everybody, sit!" Zoe exclaimed, gesturing them all to the table. The coru prime didn't seem to have orchestrated anything, but somehow it turned out that Mally was sitting between Leah and Zoe, while Zoe kept Celia on her lap. Virrie sat across from Mally, and the men pulled their chairs close together at the head of the table. Well, it was a small table; they were all close together.

"So, Leah. Tell us about your travels," Virrie requested as they began passing around serving dishes. "Darien dribbled out bits of information, but we have been famished for news."

Once again, Leah forced herself to look away from Mally, and she glanced guiltily between Virrie and Taro. "I know I should have written," she said. "But everything was just too—difficult."

"Sometimes it is," agreed Zoe, who was amazingly adept at holding a child on her lap with one hand while serving herself food with the other. "Celia, use a spoon if you're going to eat from my plate. Thank you. I once disappeared for ten years and didn't tell anyone where I was. Mally, can you handle that platter? Do you want Leah to help you?"

"I can do it," Mally said, and very carefully dished out a portion of fruit compote before handing the platter to Leah. Their fingers didn't touch.

"No one knew where you were that whole time?" Virrie asked.

"Well, they knew I was with my father," Zoe said in a dry voice.

"Your mother's family must have been worried to death," Virrie said.

Zoe gave Celia a bite of vegetables before eating from the same spoon. "It turned out they were," she said. "Though I didn't know it at the time. That's what happens when your parents come from families that despise each other."

Taro snorted an appreciation of that and looked straight at Leah. "That's exactly what happens," he said.

Zoe glanced at Leah, too. "I don't really know your story," she said.

"I was thirteen when my father and I left Chialto, you know, so I missed all the scandals for the next few years."

Leah was quickly doing the math. Zoe must be only twenty-nine or thirty, a year or two younger than Leah, though the prime had such presence she seemed older. "I'm not sure it qualified as a scandal," Leah said.

"Celia, do not eat off of Mally's plate!"

"I don't mind," Mally said. She tore a piece of bread into small chunks and offered one to Celia.

"You don't have to discuss it if you don't want to," Zoe added.

Leah shrugged. She could barely choke down food, so she might as well talk. "My mother was Taro's youngest sister, and very wild, everyone said," she explained. "Born elay, if you can believe it."

"You couldn't help but love Rinda, but she was *so* difficult," Virrie said. "Stubborn and selfish and dramatic. And beautiful."

"She joined an acting troupe when she was seventeen and married the lead actor three ninedays later," Leah went on.

"*Said* she married him," Taro muttered into his goblet of water.

"*Taro,*" Virrie reprimanded him, gesturing subtly at Leah.

As if Leah hadn't always known that she was probably illegitimate. As if knowing that had kept her from having an illegitimate daughter of her own.

Though the torz prime, who understood the ways of the flesh more than most people did, tended not to be judgmental about such things.

"By all accounts, they were very happy for their first few years together," Leah said. "They traveled all over, putting on theatrical productions."

"They even traveled to Soeche-Tas and there was some talk of sailing to Cozique, though they never did," Virrie said. "I saw them perform several times. They were quite good."

"Then I was born—"

"Let me guess. Suddenly your father was not so keen on his young wife once there was a baby in the picture," Zoe said, wiping a smear of milk off of Celia's face. Mally continued to feed Celia bits of bread, first dipping them in honey.

"You would have expected that," Virrie agreed, "but, in fact, he was quite delighted with Leah. Fussed over her and played with her and bought her expensive and wildly inappropriate gifts. When he remembered she was alive."

"Ah," said Zoe. "The kind of person who feels like a baby is a little doll to be played with when one feels like it, and put away when one doesn't."

Darien said humorously, "Though you have to admit, it would be much easier to raise a baby if that were true."

"Babies need a *lot* of attention," Mally said. "Or else they cry."

The adults all laughed. "That they do," Virrie said.

"But I like them anyway," Mally said.

Zoe leaned over and kissed her dark hair. Leah was so jealous her stomach hurt. "I like them, too," Zoe whispered.

"At any rate, he was very fond of Leah and devoted to Rinda and everything might have been just fine, except that Rinda died when Leah was eight," Virrie said.

"Oh, that's so hard," Zoe said. "My mother died when I was young, too." She shook her head. "You get past it, but you never get over it. It's always there."

And what is the grief like when your mother abandons you the day you're born? Leah thought. *When you never have a mother to lose?* She watched Mally give Celia another piece of honey-soaked bread and smile when the little girl stuck it in her hair instead of her mouth.

"Celia!" Zoe exclaimed, snatching it out of the blond curls. "You're supposed to *eat* that! Not decorate yourself with it."

"My father tried to raise me on his own but he— Sometimes he didn't always remember that I— There were always other people from the troupe around, but it was a somewhat precarious existence," Leah said.

"So Taro and I took her in," Virrie said. "And raised her like any good daughter of the Five Families, just like one of our own children. Brought her to court, when Taro could be convinced to leave the estate, and introduced her to all the eligible men in the city." Clearly remembering how *that* ultimately went wrong, Virrie sighed.

"What about your father?" Zoe asked.

"I saw him from time to time. He was still very . . ." She searched for a word. "Improvident. I felt guilty because I thought I should miss him more than I did, but every time I was with him, all I could think was how grateful I was that I was living with Taro and Virrie instead of him." She shrugged slightly. "He died before I turned twenty."

"Well, I must say, your own father makes mine seem a little better," Zoe remarked. "Someday we'll have to sit down and swap stories." She sipped from her water as she appeared to think something over. Finally she said, "I'm trying to figure out the time line. You must have left the city shortly after I arrived. Or shortly before."

Taro was frowning. "I can't remember the exact timing, either."

"I was in Chialto when Zoe arrived, but I was already—" *Pregnant*. "In difficulties. I left right after the regatta, in fact."

"Oh, the regatta!" everyone exclaimed almost in unison.

"That *was* an exciting day," Virrie said.

Princess Josetta had been crewing one of the boats, and it had almost gone rushing down the waterfall, carrying her to certain death. But Zoe had stopped the Marisi in its banks. It had been her first public act as coru prime.

"How *is* Princess Josetta?" Leah asked. They had discussed her own sad life long enough. Time to turn the topic to other people. "I sailed back from Malinqua with Nelson Ardelay, and he told me a good bit of her story. She seems to have turned into a remarkable young woman."

"She has," Zoe said. She and the princess were half sisters, since *her* father had slept with Queen Seterre in the hopes of providing Vernon with his first heir. It was all so complicated; Leah could hardly keep straight who was related to whom. "She's running a homeless shelter in the southside slums, in love with an aeromotive pilot. So very elay."

The rest of them shook their heads. All the elements were important, of course, and respectable, but anyone who wasn't elay had a hard time understanding anyone who was. "I do wonder sometimes how elay people make it through the day," Virrie said.

Leah managed to look casually in Mally's direction. "I hope *you're* not elay."

"I'm torz," Mally said.

"Well, that's a relief," Darien said.

Zoe shook out a bracelet hanging with charms. "These are my blessings. Beauty, love, and power. What are yours?"

"Intelligence, loyalty, and patience," Mally said, enunciating them clearly as if she had practiced them many times.

I didn't even know that, Leah thought, feeling a swift stab of self-loathing. *I didn't even know my daughter's blessings.* One sweela for her father, one torz for her mother, and one hunti for herself. All of them, from what little Leah had observed, true.

"Those are all most excellent," Zoe approved.

"What are Celia's blessings?" Mally wanted to know.

"Charm, determination, and grace," Zoe said. "So far we've seen plenty of evidence of the first two, but none of the last one!"

Virrie tilted her head to one side. "What's her affiliation? Have you been able to tell?"

"Not yet," Zoe said. "I think she'll turn out to be coru, like me, or sweela, like my father." She glanced at her husband. "Naturally, Darien says she'll be hunti, but he says it with less conviction all the time."

"Of course, the whole city is hoping she won't be coru," Taro said. "They'd rather she was next in line to take the throne than to become coru prime."

"I don't see why she couldn't do both," Zoe said, but it was clear she was just trying to be provocative. Everyone scoffed at the notion with a wave of the hand or a shake of the head. The primes were instrumental in choosing and certifying the next ruler—and shielding the king or queen from their own remarkable magic. For instance, the hunti prime could snap a man's bones in his body, but once a monarch was chosen, the prime gave up all power over that individual. Or something. Leah found it all a little murky.

"We just need to produce many more children so that we have multitudes to choose from for either position," Darien said.

"Well, I don't know about *multitudes*," Zoe demurred. "But I would like to have several more." She wiped Celia's mouth and added, "Although I don't feel like I need to be in any great hurry to identify my heir. As far as I can tell, Nelson is the only one who's done so."

In fact, he had named his elder son as the next prime long before Leah left Chialto. She had always wondered if that was one of the reasons Rhan was so wild.

"I do think Kurtis is a most excellent choice," said Virrie. "He's so much more sober and thoughtful than most of the Ardelays. It will be odd to have a sweela prime who's not always getting into trouble."

Darien was frowning at Zoe. "Until you said it, I didn't realize it was true," he said. "None of the other primes have identified their heirs." He gestured at Zoe. "Obviously, you haven't made much progress on producing candidates yet, but the rest of them should have been thinking about this for years now."

"I've been thinking about it," Taro said mildly. "I just haven't come to any conclusions yet."

"It's more complicated than that," Virrie said. "It's a very spiritual thing, or so Taro has always led me to believe. The elements themselves have to speak up to claim their next representative. You can't just look over your sons and daughters and say, 'I choose you.' Fire and water and earth have to choose you, too."

Zoe was laughing. "Well, apparently the elements had picked me, but nobody told me before my father and I left Chialto. So I didn't find out until the day I didn't drown in the Marisi when I should have. I was underwater for, I don't know, fifteen minutes, and never had to draw breath. That's when I knew something strange was happening in my life." She sipped her water and added, "And my life had already been pretty strange."

"So is the new prime always a direct descendant of the old one?" Leah asked.

"No," Zoe and Taro said at the same time.

"No," Zoe repeated. "Darien's father was the hunti prime, and when he died, the power didn't go to any of his children, but to his sister, Mirti."

"And Mirti doesn't have children of her own," Darien added. "So if that was a requirement, we would be in desperate straits right now."

"But the power usually follows lineage," Taro amplified. "Zoe's heir might be her cousin's daughter. Mirti's heir might be—well, might be one of Darien's children. But neither one is likely to be some random stranger currently living in obscurity somewhere in Welce."

"So if Nelson hadn't already chosen Kurtis, the sweela prime could be anyone with Ardelay blood," Leah said. Thinking, *It could even be Mally. She's Nelson's granddaughter. She's abandoned by her parents and she spends the first five years of her life pretending she's somebody else, but maybe all those hurts would fade away if she got to be sweela prime.* But that wasn't how the world worked, she supposed.

"That's right," Darien said. "Even Zoe, who is Nelson's niece."

"Even better, *Josetta*!" Zoe exclaimed, laughing. "She's just as much an Ardelay as I am. Oh, she would *hate* that!"

Leah's eyes widened. "I would think it would be an honor to be prime."

"Also a responsibility," Darien said. "And Josetta much prefers to lead her own life without having to fulfill the expectations other people have of her."

Yes, the princess sounded elay to the core. "I hope I'll get to meet her soon," Leah said politely.

"I hope so, too," Darien said. "Though she can be very elusive. I have convinced her to take up residence in the house where Zoe and I lived before we moved to the palace. However, she probably doesn't spend even half of her time there. I hate to have the place stand empty."

"It's a lovely house," Zoe said with a sigh. "I miss it." As if she had suddenly been struck with a good idea, she straightened in her chair, jostling Celia, who protested. "Hush. Virrie—it just occurred to me— you're planning to stay in the city for a while, aren't you? Maybe you and Mally could move into Darien's house, too."

Mally had been playing a game with Celia, covering her own eyes with her hands, then flipping back her fingers to peer at the little girl, who screamed with laughter. But she looked up at that. "We're staying in the city? Aunt Virrie and me?"

"I thought we might do that for a few ninedays," Virrie said, elaborately casual. "You could see Celia all the time. Wouldn't that be fun?"

"Probably," Mally said cautiously.

"And you'd love my house, I know you would," Zoe said to Mally. "There's a room—Darien had it built just for me, because I'm coru. It has a river that runs around the inside, with bridges and fish and everything."

Mally looked fascinated. "Inside a *house?*"

"Yes! That's why it's the best house ever!" Zoe said.

"It is a beautiful place," Virrie said. "We'd love to stay if you're sure there's room for us."

"There would be room for everyone at this table," Darien said. He nodded at Leah. "You, too, if you're looking for lodgings."

Virrie turned her serene face in Leah's direction. "Now, that's an interesting idea," she said.

Leah felt enveloped in panic. It was too much, it was too soon, she didn't want to frighten Mally away with eager, obsessive affection. She didn't want to break her own heart every minute of every day. "Well—maybe—I'd have to think about it," she said, stumbling over the words.

"Where are you staying now?" Taro asked.

"In a room near the Plaza of Women. Small but comfortable."

Taro snorted, clearly indicating that he didn't think any small rented room was good enough for his niece. Leah couldn't help teasing him by adding, "Much nicer than some of the places I stayed in Malinqua."

"Well, you're not in Malinqua now," he growled.

"Think it over," Darien said, and something in his voice made her believe he would find a way to get her transferred to his residence even if it meant burning down the building where she currently lived. "I feel you'd be more at ease in my house."

"We'll see," Leah said.

"Yes," Darien said, "I suppose we will."

FIVE

By the end of the meal, Leah was exhausted from reining in her constantly changing emotions. Elation, remorse, fear, hope, worry, and too many others to identify. She did manage to say a creditably cool goodbye to Mally as Virrie and Taro shepherded the little girl to the door. But the minute they left, she collapsed back into her chair and waited for her heart to stop pounding. She was sure she would never breathe normally again.

Darien had left right behind the others and Zoe had disappeared with Celia, but Zoe was back in the room before Leah was fully recovered. "I thought that went well, didn't you?" Zoe asked, reclaiming her own chair.

"I don't know," Leah said honestly. "I'm too shattered to be able to think clearly."

Zoe surveyed her a moment, seeming to search for the right question to ask. "You don't have to tell me," she said at last, "but I've been wondering. Why exactly you—" She hesitated.

"Why I abandoned my daughter?" Leah said bitterly. "Why I looked at her exactly once, then handed her off to Virrie, and ran away as fast as I possibly could?"

"I wasn't going to phrase it like that."

Leah spread her hands, not sure she could explain. "I didn't think I could do it—didn't think I could raise a child. I had had such an odd upbringing myself that I didn't know how you were *supposed* to take care of a baby. And I was so unhappy and miserable and angry and hurt and—well. I could hardly take care of myself, let alone someone else. I just wanted to get away from Welce. Away from everybody."

"Away from Rhan."

Leah felt her mouth twist. "So you know that, too. I suppose Darien told you."

Zoe shrugged. "I'm the coru prime. The first time I took the girl in my arms, I knew who her father was."

"Yes. I wanted to get away from Rhan. I had been so in love with him. I had thought I had finally found my place in the world. And then he—then he—when he found out I was pregnant—" She shook her head. "He told me he wasn't prepared to marry me. He wasn't prepared to be a father to my baby. He wouldn't be part of our lives. He *said* that."

"I adore Rhan," Zoe said. "He's my cousin, you know. But he might be the most irresponsible person I've ever met."

"I used to think that," Leah said. "And then I realized I was no better."

"Maybe you weren't, five years ago," Zoe said. "But I bet you are now."

"I hope so," Leah said. "I plan to be."

"So will you move into the city house so you can be near Mally? It's a very comfortable place."

"Not just yet. I need to think about it."

"Darien can be very persuasive."

"I've gotten a little better at resisting the blandishments of men."

That made Zoe laugh. "Well, I think it would be a good arrangement for you, but since I always like to see people defy Darien, I won't bring any pressure to bear! Now, are you free for the rest of the afternoon? I could take you to meet Jaker and Barlow."

On the one hand, Leah wasn't sure she had enough energy left over to manage another event. On the other hand, she needed a distraction. She came to her feet. "Excellent," she said. "Let's go."

. . .

Of course Leah liked Jaker and Barlow. She was beginning to suspect that she would like anyone the coru prime counted as a
friend, because Zoe had a taste for unconventional people.

Barlow was expansive and talkative, a little self-important but quick
to laugh at himself. Leah had the thought that it might be easy to get
mad at him but hard to stay mad. Jaker was quieter, more thoughtful,
more serious, though he had a constant twinkle in his blue eyes that
made it clear he appreciated life's incessant ironies. Zoe and Leah met
them in a small, cramped apartment overflowing with oddments—small
sculptures made of unidentifiable stone, plants with twisted stems and
purple leaves, wall art showing no landscape to be found in Welce. They
served a hot beverage that tasted like cinnamon and pepper, pouring it
into tiny cups the color of translucent jade.

"This is like living inside a storybook of fantastic tales," Leah said,
glancing around.

Jaker laughed. "Yes. That's our life. Full of wild fantasy."

Barlow grinned. "When the wheel doesn't come off the elaymotive
ten miles from the nearest town, and the man who promised to sell you
his entire cargo actually shows up when and where he promised, and
when you're not fighting flood or snow or sleet—yes, it's the fantasy life."

"Oh, stop complaining," Zoe said. "You know you wouldn't do
anything else."

The men first demanded to know the details of Corene's adventures
in Malinqua, since it turned out they had a fondness for Corene and
Josetta as well as Zoe. Then they pulled out boxes and satchels and
wrapped bundles and began showing Leah their wares.

They weren't specialists in any particular kind of products, Jaker
explained; they separately invested in items that appealed to them and
sold their goods to customers across Welce. It was easy to see why they'd
been operating successfully for years, Leah thought. Their choices were
idiosyncratic but exquisite. Gloves made of gray-and-black striped fur,
spices that smelled like citrus and cocoa, lengths of wool dyed in royal
colors, goblets of blown glass fused to etched silver.

"What I'm thinking," Leah said, "is that I want to set the shop up around the five elements. Each section will be full of items from all over the southern seas—but tied to that section's element. So these"—she picked up two of the goblets—"would be in the coru section. The spices would be torz. I could divide the bolts of wool by color. Put the red and orange ones in the sweela section, maybe, and the yellow and white ones in elay."

"Well, then, here's something for the torz aisle," Jaker said, and pulled the lid off a box about the size of a pillow. Inside was a tumble of rocks, all different sizes but all with the same curious composition: layers of black and white interspersed with bands of muted blue, coppery green, and thin crystallized streaks of scarlet. The colors of the elemental affiliations. Some had sharp, jagged edges as if they'd been hacked out of a mountainside; others were smooth and polished as if they'd been rescued from a river. "We found an old miner up near the Soeche-Tas border. He'd been collecting these for years while he was prospecting for precious gems. We were only going to take a few, but they were all so pretty."

"I like these," Leah said, dipping her hand into the pile. The polished stones were silky against her hand; the raw ones felt grainy and primal as dirt.

"And still in the torz section—" Barlow said as he opened a small leather satchel to reveal a tray of cut jewels. "These you might keep locked up, though, because they *are* worth something."

"Did these come from the miner, too?" Zoe asked.

"They did. Cost way more than the rocks."

Leah looked up with a smile. "I can see this will be a profitable association."

The next few days passed in an enjoyable but exhausting blur of travel, negotiation, and physical labor. Leah spent a day and a half at the harbor, canvassing the ship captains and buying whatever caught her eye. She had made the trip in an elaymotive supplied by Darien and driven by a stocky young woman named Yori, who had a pleasant face and an attitude of careless confidence. Yori was strong enough to carry large boxes, patient enough to wait for hours without getting bored, and quick-witted enough to navigate the crowded harbor streets without incident. More than once during the extended buying spree Leah had been tempted to say, *I wish I was you.*

By noon of the second day at the harbor, they couldn't stuff another item in the elaymotive, so Leah figured that it must be time to go home. On the trip down, she'd sat in the back of the coach like any high-born lady, but for the return journey, she joined Yori in the driver's compartment. There was no room anywhere else—and it was more fun to talk to Yori than to stare out the window and watch the flat countryside roll past.

"So are you glad to be back in Chialto?" Yori asked as they crossed the canal into the city limits.

"I'm not sure yet," Leah admitted. "Sometimes I think it would be easier if I was still in Malinqua."

"If easier is what you want."

"Isn't it what everyone wants?"

Yori shook her head, never taking her attention from the road. They were on the Cinque now, the five-sided boulevard that made a complete loop around Chialto, and traffic was almost as bad as it had been at the harbor. "What I want is to *feel*. I know that means sometimes I'll feel bad. I can't stand the idea that I might just drift through my own life. At the end of it, I want to look back and be a little impressed."

"You're sweela," Leah said almost accusingly. "The past two days I've thought you must be torz or hunti, because you're so patient. You tricked me!"

"I am. Sweela with three elay blessings. I try not to tell anybody."

"I would think not!" Leah exclaimed, and they both laughed

It took nearly an hour to unload the elaymotive at the shop, and by then it was almost dark. Yori offered to drive Leah back to her lodgings, but Leah wanted to walk. "Too many days cooped up in dining halls and smoker cars," Leah said. "I need to clear my head."

This early in Quinnasweela, the night air was cool enough to make a brisk walk welcome. Leah detoured through the Plaza of Women to pick up dinner from a food vendor since she couldn't remember if she'd left anything edible in her rooms. The instant she stepped inside the kierten and turned up the gaslight, the reifarjin fixed her with its unblinking stare, managing to convey its sense of deep betrayal.

"I know, I know. I wasn't here to feed you this morning, and I'm so sorry!" Leah said. She unwrapped her sandwich and pulled out shreds of meat to drop into the bowl. The fish devoured them almost before they hit the water. She stopped feeding it when almost a third of the food was gone. "Do you *ever* get full? You're the oddest creature."

She moved slowly through the room, kicking off her shoes, pouring a glass of water, settling into an old chair with a sigh of contentment. She was almost as hungry as the reifarjin, and she ate the rest of the meal in about ten minutes.

"Maybe I should go back out and get us some more food," she said to the fish. It frilled its fins as if in reply; she took that as an affirmative. "Well—"

A sharp rap on the door made her sit up straighter and wish she hadn't discarded her overtunic and shoes. "I imagine that will be a messenger from Darien, wanting me to come up to the palace and report," she said on a sigh, pushing herself to her feet. "Maybe I can put him off until tomorrow."

But it wasn't Darien or Yori or one of the regent's guards or the landlord or any of the few other people who knew she was in the city.

It was Rhan Ardelay.

Leah stared at Rhan for what seemed like a full minute. He stared back just as intently. She had not forgotten a single detail of his face—handsome, roguish, always on the verge of laughter. He'd managed to tame his dark red hair, but it still retained an irrepressible curl. He was dressed in a fashionably dark tunic and trousers, well-cut and expensive. He looked like he was on his way to attend a fancy dinner or to break some young girl's heart.

"Rhan," she said, her tone absolutely blank.

"So you do remember me." When that caused her face to go just as blank, he added, "I thought you might not. Since you have pretended for the past five and a half years that I did not exist."

"Maybe it wasn't pretending so much as wishful thinking," she shot back.

"I have a lot of ex-lovers—"

"I'm sure you do."

"But you're the only one who has wished me dead."

"Are you sure? Have you asked them all?"

He laughed. He actually *laughed.* Then he slipped past her to stroll into the room, looking around critically. "Well, all right, maybe one or two of the other ones wouldn't mind if I suffered a little," he said. "This is where you're living now? It's awfully stark."

"I don't want you here. Get out. Who told you where I was living? Who told you I was even in Welce?"

"My father. Since apparently you sailed back from Malinqua with him."

Leah felt a strong surge of irritation with the sweela prime. "I *knew* I should have made him promise not to tell you anything."

Rhan shrugged. "I would have found out sooner or later."

"So why are you here right now?" she asked.

He was still surveying the apartment, doing one slow pivot to take in the entire space. "I couldn't stand living here," he said. "It's depressing."

"And I was going to ask you to move in," she marveled. "Now I can save myself the trouble."

He laughed again. "It doesn't suit you," he said.

"I rather think you no longer know what suits me and what doesn't. If you ever did."

"I know what you *like,*" he countered. "And this isn't it."

Leah shrugged. It had been a long time since what she *liked* had had much bearing on what she did, where she lived, or how she moved through the days. "Why are you here, Rhan?" she asked again, a little more wearily. "What do you want from me?"

"A friendly conversation?" he said. "Would that even be possible?"

No, she wanted to say. *I don't feel friendly toward you. I don't love you anymore, I don't hate you, but you'll always be the man who broke my heart. If I've pretended you don't exist it's because that's easier than remembering that you do.* She recalled Yori saying she didn't want life to be easy; she wanted it to be full of experiences that made her feel. *Well, I'm not Yori. And Rhan makes me feel too much.*

"Conversation about what?"

"Come on, Leah," he said in a wheedling voice. "Put on your shoes. Put on your tunic. Let's go somewhere and talk. You can't avoid me forever. Let's get all the nasty things said now and then move on."

"Just saying the nasty things out loud won't make them go away."

"Maybe not," he said. "But it's a start."

I n the end, she went with him because she didn't know what else to do. If she refused to talk to him, shoved him out the door, she would still be thrumming with the shock of his presence; talking to him could hardly make things worse. But she wouldn't let him take her to some quiet, romantic restaurant with soft lighting and expensive wines. She insisted on loud, brightly lit, and public, "so no one will look twice if I throw my water in your face." They ended up at an outdoor café near the Plaza of Women where the food was greasy and cheap. Braziers ringed the metal tables set out under a canopied patio, supplying almost enough heat. Tubes of gaslight hissed under the awning, sending down a garish illumination. Three other couples sat at nearby tables. All of them appeared to be arguing.

Perfect.

Rhan asked for a liqueur that made the waitress stare at him uncomprehendingly, so Leah ordered wine for both of them. "You won't like it, it's too sweet, but it's the best they've got," she told him. "So don't complain."

"Your sojourn in— Where was it? Malinqua?—has blunted your sensibilities, I see," Rhan said. "What exactly did Darien have you doing? Running ghetto taverns and smuggling illegal goods?"

"Consorting with the people who did," she said.

His eyes widened. "I was joking."

"I wasn't."

"But weren't you—afraid? Disgusted? Offended? *Depressed?* You're a daughter of the Five Families and you were living in *squalor*—"

"First, I wasn't actually living in the slums and I mostly kept to the respectable establishments, though I learned my way around the riskier districts quickly enough. And second—" She considered him a moment. *How* she remembered those first giddy ninedays when Rhan was courting her. This laughing, handsome, charming scoundrel who luxuriated in hedonism. He was a connoisseur of the exquisite, a devotee of the extravagant. Of course she had wanted him to believe she shared his tastes.

"And second," she went on, "I never cared about material things as much as you did. Until I moved in with Taro and Virrie, I didn't have any idea what the lives of the Five Families were like. You always forget that."

"I barely knew it," he retorted. "Since you didn't *tell* me about your life before I met you."

"I wanted you to think I was good enough for you."

"But as Taro's niece—"

"My father was an *actor*. We stayed in grubby hotels and left sometimes without paying the bill. The best clothes I owned were the costumes we saved for the historical dramas. I was happy when someone remembered to give me dinner at *all*—I didn't care that it wasn't from the finest restaurant in town. Maybe Taro's niece deserved to dine at the palace and live like royalty, but I was sixteen before I knew what it was like to be a daughter of the Five Families. Of course I didn't want you to know any of that back then! But that's why none of this bothers me now."

Whatever reply he might have made was cut off by the serving girl returning with a carafe of wine and two glasses that were none too clean. Leah poured for both of them and watched in appreciation as Rhan took his first sip. He didn't quite gag and spit it out, but he swallowed hurriedly and then gazed at the glass as if it might be filled with poison. *In Malinqua, it would be,* Leah thought a little wistfully.

"Any life that led you to consider this wine worth drinking is a sadder existence than I ever want to contemplate," Rhan said.

"Good. I'll have it all."

"And I figured it out eventually, you know," he went on. "I knew you hadn't been brought up with finery and wealth. But my own life was something of a charade just then, too. My father—even though he was the sweela prime—had been ostracized because his brother Navarr had offended King Vernon, and the whole Ardelay family suffered for it. I seemed to be in desperate pursuit of luxury, but I was just trying to compensate for my unfortunate situation. I, too, was trying to prove to everyone in Chialto that I was good enough to sit at the table."

"It's not even comparable."

"Maybe not," he said. "But I was never quite as shallow as you seem to want to think."

She shrugged. It didn't matter. An overindulged dilettante, an anxious pretender trying to fit in—he could be either of these things or something else entirely, but it didn't matter. He held a place in her memory that was charred and deep in ashes, and how he made her *feel* was more important than who he actually *was.*

The serving girl was back, asking if they wanted to get food. Rhan looked horrified at the thought, but Leah ordered another sandwich. This time she wasn't sharing it with any stupid fish.

"Do you really think anything they serve here is safe to eat?" he asked once the girl had departed.

Leah sipped from her glass and wondered how much wine she'd have to put away to blunt the sharp edges of this evening. More than she was willing to drink, she decided. "I've been here twice in the past few days and survived both times," she said. "I think I'm safe enough."

"So what's your plan?" he asked. "Now that you're back in Welce? Do you *have* a plan?"

Apparently he was moving past recriminations and straight to informational exchanges. Just as well. Otherwise the recriminations could go on forever. "I want to bring Mally into my life," she said.

Rhan raised his red eyebrows. "Tell her who she is? Who *you* are?"

"Eventually. I hope. Once she's gotten to know me. Darien has arranged for Virrie and Mally to live in town for the quintile, and I'll hope to see her often. I don't know how long it will take to gain her trust and affection, but I'll try. And then—then we'll see."

"Do you plan to tell her about me?"

She eyed him a moment. "I don't know. Do you want me to?"

For a moment, Rhan looked vulnerable and uncertain. It was an expression that sat oddly on his laughing face. "I don't know. But—like you—my mother is determined to find a place in Mally's life, and you can hardly tell a child who her grandmother is without mentioning her father as well."

Leah shrugged. "In Welce, it seems to be easy enough to conceal the parentage of high-born children. King Vernon managed it for years. I think we could get your mother involved in Mally's life without giving away any secrets. So you may step forward or stay in the shadows, whichever you choose."

He was silent a moment while the waitress brought a plate holding a hearty sandwich that smelled absolutely delicious. Leah took her first bite and swallowed it while Rhan was still thinking.

"I do want to apologize," he said at last, "for behaving so badly when you told me—when you first found out—it just had not occurred to me that you would get pregnant."

Leah swigged some more wine. The more she drank, the less she minded how bad it was. "It hadn't occurred to me, either," she said. "Which was obviously stupid."

"I didn't know what to *do*," he said. "And I didn't want to tell my father, since I was sure he'd be furious."

"As if Ardelays haven't been siring bastards across the Welchin countryside since the dawn of time."

He gave her a reproachful look, but could hardly deny it. The Ardelays were famous for their indiscretions. "I talked to Kurtis, to see if he had any advice. He already had his own children by then, of course, and he was full of the glories of parenthood." Glancing into the past had clearly unsettled Rhan enough that he needed the calming effects of alcohol. He took another sip of the sweet wine, grimaced, and polished off the glass.

"So I thought, all right, I can find some way to make this work, I don't know how, but Leah and I can discuss it. But you were gone." He poured himself another glass. "Vanished." He gulped that down, too. "No one knew where you were."

"I'd gone to Taro's to wait out the last ninedays of my pregnancy."

"It was half a quintile before I was able to worm that information out of anybody."

Leah didn't bother to hide her incredulity, and Rhan correctly read her expression.

"Very well, maybe I didn't try very hard. I didn't hire spies and try to track you down. But I did look for you. I was worried. Eventually I had to ask for my father's help—and you do *not* want to hear the things he said to me when he learned I had failed to provide for a woman who was carrying my child. *Or* for the child itself."

"Oh, I think I do want to hear."

"Well, I'm not going to repeat them. But within a single day he had uncovered the rest of the story, down to the fact that you had delivered a baby girl on Taro Frothen's estate—and left the baby behind. But beyond that no one, not even my father, could discover what had happened to you next."

"Say what you will about Darien Serlast," Leah said with a tight smile. "He knows how to keep a secret."

"Taro does, too, though apparently he didn't know as much as I believed at the time," said Rhan. "Merely that you had left and that Darien had funded your way. If he knew you were in Malinqua, he never said." Rhan sipped at his wine more slowly, watching her over the glass. "I was certain I would hear from you eventually. I was sure you wouldn't have a child—*my* child—and never tell me where the baby could be found. If nothing else, I was sure you would have so much anger left inside you that you'd have to spill it out in a letter. And then I would find you, and we would talk, and we might not have fixed things between us, but we would have made things *better*. But you never wrote. You were well and truly gone."

"It seemed easier." Yori's voice in her head: *I don't want easier. I want to feel.*

"Easier for you maybe," Rhan snapped.

She spread her hands. "So now I'm the one who says I'm sorry. But you had made it clear that you were not interested in the upheaval a child would bring to your life. It didn't occur to me you would change your mind. Therefore, it seemed pointless to tell you she had arrived."

"And what about you?" he demanded. "You despise me for shirking my responsibility, but *you* didn't want a baby, either, from what I can tell. At any rate, you didn't keep her."

Leah nodded calmly, but her stomach was churning with self-hatred. "Oh, I never said I was any better than you. I was terrified at the idea of having a child—having another human being given over to my care. I was heartbroken and wild with grief, afraid I would harm the baby or myself. I left her because I was a coward, yes, but also because I wanted her to have someone better than *me* to look after her." She hunched her shoulders. "I wasn't thinking clearly. Or maybe I was. I thought she would be better off with Taro and Virrie than with me. But I'll never forgive myself for leaving her."

"My father wanted her, too, once he found out the truth," Rhan said. "And my mother—you can imagine. Kurtis offered to take her in and raise her along with his own children. But before we had a chance to make this offer, the course of her life had already been set."

Leah nodded. "She'd been discovered to be Odelia's lookalike."

"She was suddenly the decoy princess. So not only could we not claim her, we had to pretend we did not know who she was. It was very hard." He looked away. "I admit, I didn't make a special effort to get to know her even so. I could have found a way. I could have visited Taro's estates when both girls were in residence. I could have fashioned myself some kind of uncle. But I didn't do it."

"I think Taro would have discouraged you from developing a relationship with her while she was masquerading as Odelia."

Rhan snorted. "I'm not afraid of Taro. Have you ever seen my father in a rage? Hardly to compare."

That made Leah laugh. "Taro's the torz prime. He could cause boulders to shake loose from the earth and smash you to the ground. You don't want to make him angry."

"Well. So I didn't. And now Odelia is no longer the heir and Mally can be herself, and I can be her father if I want to, if I can figure out how."

"And I can be her mother if I can figure out how."

"I know you hate me," he began.

"I don't *hate* you. I just find it painful to be around you."

"But perhaps we can find some way to be friends, at least where Mally is concerned. Unless you think it would be better—unless you think I don't deserve . . ." His words trailed off and he watched her, his face a study in dejection.

Leah took a hard breath. "I don't envision the three of us going on pleasant excursions or setting up a household together and pretending to be a family," she said bluntly. "But I had such a troubled relationship with my own father that I would never keep Mally away from hers. I would be *glad* if you made her a part of your life. Just a part of your life that doesn't include me."

Rhan gazed at her, his eyes narrowed in speculation, and for a moment she thought she could tell what he was thinking: *Are you sure? Couldn't we try to make our lives intersect, overlap, combine?* But he didn't say the words. Maybe he wasn't even thinking them.

"Then that's all I want," he said simply. "I will let you get to know her first. As long as you swear you will let her get to know me next. I won't interfere, I won't cause trouble, I'll hold off. But I think it's time I stepped forward."

"Time we both did."

"You can choose," he said, "when to tell people. What to tell people. Everyone in our circle."

Your circle, she wanted to say, but didn't. "Who already knows the truth? Do you have any idea? Besides your parents and Taro and Darien, I mean. And Zoe, of course."

"Zoe knows?" he said with a groan. "I suppose she does. I suppose Kayle Dochenza and Mirti Serlast know, too, then—all the primes can tell when someone is related to someone else." He straightened his shoulders. "Well, it hardly matters, since everyone will soon learn the truth. I suppose it will be quite a topic for conversation at the next formal dinner."

Now she laughed. "It might be, but I won't be there to hear the gossip. I don't plan on reentering court life any time soon."

"You don't? Then what do you plan to do with your time?"

She took another big gulp of her wine and smiled a bit maliciously. Finally, she was starting to enjoy herself. "I'm going to become a shopgirl."

SIX

Annova looked around the shop and said, "You're ordering more goods? How do you think you'll sell all of *this*?"

Leah and Yori had left yesterday's acquisitions on the ground floor of the building, and Leah had to admit that the disorganized bundles and boxes looked like one big mess. But she saw potential. "If I manage a steady rate of sales, I'll have constant turnover and need to be replenishing on a regular basis," she said. "And if the first things I put out don't sell, I'll need to try new things and—trust me. This isn't too much."

"I know we're supposed to be helping," Virrie confessed. "But I keep getting distracted. I love these little wooden bowls."

Mally looked up from the window embrasure, where she was carefully arranging the multicolored stones Leah had bought from Barlow and Jaker. "I like these rocks," she said.

"I thought you would," Leah said. "You can sit there in the window and play with them as long as you like."

"And when you're done playing with them, we can store them on one of the shelves to get them out of the way," Annova said practically.

While Leah had been bargaining with ship's captains, Annova and Zoe had been furnishing the shop, setting up open shelving units on the two long sides of the store and interspersing them with closed cabinets, wooden chests, and tall tables. Now the trick was deciding which pieces of merchandise should initially be on display, which should be within easy reach downstairs, and which should be stored upstairs until replacements were needed. For the rest of the morning, Leah and Annova and Virrie spent their time determining what went where and then hauling boxes up the steps. Afterward, Annova and Virrie stayed upstairs, organizing the replacement goods by elemental affiliations, while Leah returned downstairs to begin arranging merchandise in the showroom.

Mally spent all of that time sitting quietly in the window alcove, sorting through fifty or sixty rocks of varying sizes. As the morning wore on, Leah couldn't resist perching on the edge of the elevated floor and spending a few moments watching her.

She didn't think it was accidental that Virrie had found a way to leave her alone with Mally. Leah had to swallow against her tight throat and put some effort into speaking in a casual voice.

"Show me what you've been doing," she invited.

Mally looked up and gave her a grave smile. The window embrasure was perhaps five feet deep and raised about two feet off the floor. Three tall windows made a half-hexagonal shape around it and admitted satisfying amounts of unfiltered light. The sunshine through the glass also warmed up the space to a degree that was right on the edge of uncomfortable. Leah could see a few strands of dark hair sticking to Mally's damp forehead. Otherwise, the girl didn't seem to be aware of the temperature.

"First I put them in piles," she explained. "The flat ones here and the tall ones here and the round ones over there. And then I started making a pattern."

Leah looked more closely. What she had first taken as a random assortment of stones on the wooden floor was really an elaborate mosaic. Mally had carefully chosen slabs of stone and fitted them together—a jagged edge against a broken corner, a concave curve against a convex bow—so that they formed one more or less continuous surface. She hadn't completed the pattern yet, but it looked like she was making a giant rectangle, flat edges to the outside to define the border.

"That's—really stunning," Leah said faintly. "Who taught you to do that?"

"I never did it before. I just thought it would be fun."

"You're almost done with your shape. It would have taken me a year to fit all the pieces together like this."

Mally lifted her flecked eyes to Leah's face. "Don't you like rocks?"

"I do! I just never—I guess I just never sat down and played with them much."

"Natalie says rocks are silly."

"Natalie?" Leah repeated reflexively. In a moment, she remembered the name. Queen Romelle's daughter, a year or two older than Odelia and Mally. Naturally, she had been living on Taro's estates while Mally was growing up there.

"My sister," Mally said. She picked up a flat stone, nearly square except for one missing corner, and considered where to place it. "Or—maybe not my sister." She flicked Leah a look as if wondering how to explain.

"I don't know much about your life," Leah said softly. "Would you like to tell me about it? I know you live with Taro and Virrie."

Mally nodded and found a place for the stone she'd been holding. She picked up another one and ran her fingers over its smooth edges.

"Taro and Virrie and Natalie and Mama, except I'm not supposed to call her *Mama* anymore," Mally said. "And Odelia lives there, too, but sometimes I'm Odelia. But sometimes I'm not. Mama says— *Romelle* says—I'm not ever going to be Odelia anymore."

"Did you like being Odelia?"

Mally shrugged and discarded her current stone in favor of another one. "Odelia had to be good and sit quietly and let people stare at her and never say it was rude," Mally said.

"Did you ever get mixed up? Think you were Mally when you were supposed to be Odelia?"

Mally shook her head. "Not even when people tried to trick me."

"Tried to— How would they do that?"

"They would ask me. 'What's your name? What's your mama's name?'"

"And you knew when to tell the truth and when to lie?"

Again, Mally gave her a brief look from those wary eyes. "I just always said I was Odelia. Even if Taro asked me. Even though he *knew*."

Well, Leah supposed that was one way to make sure a young child didn't give away a desperate secret. Tell her exactly what to say, no matter what the circumstances. "So if I walked up to you and said, 'Hello, young lady, what's your name?' what would you tell me?"

"I'm—" Mally hesitated. "I'm not supposed to be Odelia anymore."

"So maybe you can be Mally if anybody asks."

"Maybe nobody will ask me."

Leah's heart squeezed down. What a sad predicament for a small girl! So well-versed in deception that she didn't even know how to claim her own name. "It's hard to pretend to be somebody else," Leah said. "I know."

Mally glanced at her. "Did you ever?"

Leah nodded. "I did! For five years! I lived in another country and I pretended to be a different person."

"What was your name?"

"Nobody knew who I was, so most of the time I just used my own name. Not always. But I told people that I had run away from Welce and I didn't have any money, when really I was there because Darien Serlast sent me to Malinqua to work for him."

"Was it fun?"

"Sometimes."

"Was it dangerous?"

"Sometimes."

"Did you ever forget who you were supposed to be?"

Leah thought about that. "Sometimes," she said at last. "Or—more truthfully—sometimes I forgot who I really was. I forgot all the people back in Welce who loved me. And it was a while before I realized I needed to remember them."

Mally moved one rock that was already in place and replaced it with another that was more suited to the spot. "Are you glad to be back?"

"I think so."

"And did anybody forget you while you were gone?"

Leah was so surprised by the question that she let out a little huff of air that was halfway between a laugh and a sob. "Oddly, it doesn't seem like it," she said. "I thought that they would have."

"Are you going to go away again?"

"Oh no. I'm never leaving Welce."

"I don't think I am, either," Mally said.

Leah smiled. "You're just a little girl. You could grow up and want to have all sorts of adventures! Look at Princess Corene. She seems determined to explore the whole world. Maybe you will, too."

"Maybe," Mally said. "But I don't think so."

There was a clatter at the back of the shop and Annova and Virrie reappeared. "We're hungry," Virrie announced. "Shouldn't we take a break and get something to eat?"

The next nineday passed in a virtually identical manner. Leah and Yori returned to the harbor to shop for new merchandise; Jaker and Barlow swung by to introduce one of their trader friends. Rhan insisted on another dinner, and Leah went, but at the end of it she told him flatly she didn't want to see him again. "Not like this, anyway. I can stand it if we see each other at big dinners when other people are around. But it's too unsettling to sit here and talk to you like we're old friends."

"We *are* old friends."

"We're old lovers, and I'm not good at those transitions."

She wasn't sure, even so, that he would stay away. Rhan had never been very good about observing other people's rules.

She wrote Chandran every night, but she didn't mail any of the letters. She wanted to wait and see how he responded to the one she'd sent through Darien, the one that had included the list of items she'd like to buy and the heavy bags of money. It might turn out they only had a business relationship, which would certainly be sensible. But in that case she wouldn't want to share all the thoughts she'd put down on paper over the last nine days.

I've met my daughter. I've talked with her father. I am facing my ghosts and demons, my abandoned dreams and my bitter hopes. So far I have survived each encounter, but each one has made me dizzy in its own way. I can't tell if I'm starting to recover my balance or if I'm getting used to the constant spinning. At any rate, I'm not unhappy. Lonely sometimes, despite being surrounded by people on most days. But not unhappy.

They were not the sorts of letters you sent to a man who cared only about how many quint-golds you would pay him for his Coziquela gemstones. Leah folded each piece of paper and stuck it in a drawer. She would see how he responded to that earlier letter, and then she would decide how much to show him of her heart.

During the hours when she wasn't compiling her inventory or communicating with the men in her life, she concentrated on putting her shop in order. And getting to know Mally.

Virrie brought the little girl to the store every day for a couple of hours and usually found some way to leave Leah alone with her at least briefly. Leah had invited Mally to help her set up the torz section of the shop, a task Mally took as seriously as she seemed to take everything else. Torz was the earth sign, often symbolized by blossoms and vines and crops, and Mally spent a solid hour arranging a tray of cut-glass roses.

"The first time somebody buys one of those, all your work will be wasted," Leah told her with a smile. "And we *want* people to buy things."

"I know. I'll arrange them again."

Leah had bought a small flowering fruit tree at the Plaza of Men and potted it in a dark green planter, but Mally wouldn't let her put it near the torz items. "That's hunti," she said.

"But it's so little!"

"It's still a tree," Mally said firmly. "Put it over there."

"Relegated to the inferior corner of wood and bone!" exclaimed Zoe, who had dropped by to check on Leah's progress. "Darien will be downhearted when he learns how low his status is."

"Hunti isn't *bad*," Mally told her. "It's just not torz."

"Well, that will be a relief to Darien," Virrie said.

"Does he like trees?" Mally asked.

"He does," Zoe said. "And anything made of wood."

Leah glanced around. "I have something upstairs. A wooden skeleton. I thought it would be perfect for some hunti collector with a macabre turn of mind."

"Now that I'd like to see," Zoe said.

"Annova's upstairs," Virrie said, tugging Zoe toward the back door. "Let's ask her to show it to us."

Leah turned to Mally as soon as the women were out of sight.

"Well, let's move the tree to the hunti section and then see what else we can do there. I like the tall basket with all the canes in different kinds of wood."

"The striped one is my favorite."

"Isn't that one nice? Or the one of very dark wood. It's harder than metal, I think. Oh, and did you see the necklace that arrived yesterday? It's made of silver, but it looks like little branches woven together. Definitely hunti."

Mally and Leah had just started rearranging items on the hunti table when the front door opened and a gust of cool air swirled in. Leah looked up, expecting to see Yori or one of Darien's guards, but the man who stepped inside was a stranger.

"I'm sorry," she said with a smile, "the shop isn't open yet."

He didn't answer, merely looked around. He was wiry, thin, of medium build; he seemed to lean forward a little, balancing on his toes, as if preparing to make a sudden leap or to dash out the door. His clothes were dark and nondescript, a little too big on him. Chandran had taught Leah early on that a visitor wearing loose clothing was often a thief who tried to casually slip merchandise into his oversize pockets.

Her hand closed over the smooth, round head of one of the hunti canes. "I'm sorry," she repeated, this time without the smile. "We're not open. You'll need to leave."

He gave her one long hard stare, as if trying to gauge her strength and swiftness, and clearly decided she wasn't much of a threat. He pivoted toward the nearest shelving unit and starting scooping up merchandise. A bag of semiprecious stones, a bowl of hammered gold, an inexpensive stone figurine.

Leah slid the cane free from the basket. "Run upstairs," she ordered Mally in a low voice. Then she charged across the shop, yelling, "Get out of here! Get out!"

Lifting the cane over her head, she swung it down on his shoulder. He *oofed* with pain and spun back to confront her, his hands raised to fend her off. She swung again, changing her angle, hitting him hard directly under his left rib cage. He grabbed at the cane before she could raise it again, yanking so hard he almost pulled her off her feet. So she went with the momentum, stabbing her weapon forward like a sword, driving the tip deep into the middle of his chest. He grunted and let go. She batted at his head and shoulders, but his hands were raised and she could tell she didn't do any real damage.

"Get out of here!" she shouted again.

Suddenly he jumped forward, knocking her hand aside, sending the cane skipping across the floor. He grabbed her by the shoulders and shook her so brutally she thought her head might snap off. She kicked him between the legs, not connecting as hard as she wanted to, but enough to make him hiss a curse. He tightened his grip on her shoulders, then shoved her violently away from him.

She stumbled into the shelving unit and felt the whole thing tremble as if it might topple over. She clutched at one of the racks, trying to catch her balance, and sensed a shift in the weight of some of the storage boxes. She flung up her hand to protect her face just as rocks started raining down from the topmost shelf. Big and small, rough and polished, dozens of them, pelting the intruder as if aimed by a marksman. He cried out and put his own hands up, but Leah could already see red marks forming on his cheeks and wrist. He hunched his shoulders and bent double, trying to scrabble for safety. But his foot slipped on one of the smooth, marble-size rocks, and he crashed to the floor in a great clatter of flesh and stone.

Leah snatched up the cane again, but she didn't need it. Two royal guards tore in through the front door, and the three women came bounding down from upstairs. Everyone was crying, *What happened? Are you all right?* though the guards were also efficiently tying up the intruder while they inquired after everyone's well-being.

"Mally!" Leah gasped and spun around, but Virrie had the little girl close in her arms. Everybody else looked fine, just agog with curiosity.

"What happened?" Zoe demanded.

Leah put her hand to her chest, suddenly aware that her heart was pounding. "He—that man—came in off the street and started putting things in his pockets," she said breathlessly. "I told Mally to run, and I started hitting him with a cane. He threw me against the display unit and a whole box of rocks came down on top of him." She nodded down at the soldiers. "I was certainly glad to see *you* arrive."

One of them looked up. His face was friendly but rueful. "Escorting the prime," he said. "We were outside and saw this man come in, but we didn't realize he would cause trouble. Until we saw you fighting."

Annova bustled over to take Leah's face between her hands. "Did he hit you? Are you hurt?"

Leah rubbed her shoulder. "He grabbed me—here—I might have bruises. Otherwise, I'm fine."

"The regent will want to talk to him," one of the soldiers said, hauling the intruder to his feet. The man scowled down at his shoes and wouldn't look at any of them.

Virrie raised her eyebrows. "Why would Darien want to talk to a common thief?"

The soldier looked apologetic. "Because he might have harmed the prime," he said.

Zoe glanced at Leah, then back at Virrie. "Or the princess."

"But she's not—" Virrie hugged Mally closer and didn't finish the sentence.

"I think he was just stealing," Leah said.

The soldier nodded. "Probably. But the regent will want to talk to him even so." A few minutes later, the guards had hustled the thief out the door.

"You must hate that," Leah said, turning back to look at Zoe. Annova was already on her knees, cleaning up. A glass vase was broken and a wooden figurine looked like it had been damaged beyond salability, but the worst of the mess was just the spatter of stones. Mally squirmed out of Virrie's hold so she could crouch beside Annova and start gathering them up. "Knowing that you're always being watched so closely by royal soldiers."

"It is an affront to my carefree coru heart," Zoe agreed. "And yet people I love have been saved more than once by the vigilance of Darien's guards. And after I had Celia—well—I stopped caring so much about my own independence and more about her absolute safety. So I have learned to live with the shadow of constant supervision."

"Well, I'm glad they were following you today!" Leah exclaimed. "I thought I could fight him off, but he was stronger than he looked."

"You should have screamed for help. We would have been down here in seconds," Virrie scolded.

Leah could not help her look of disbelief. "Two old women—and the coru prime? To join a brawl? I don't think so."

"I'm not *that* old," Virrie said.

"I am," Annova said, looking up from the floor, "but I fight dirty."

"And the coru prime is very handy in a fight," Zoe said cheerfully. "I could have made all the blood rush to his head and rendered him unconscious in a moment."

"So we didn't really *need* the guards," Leah said.

"Exactly. But I do like Darien to think he's being useful."

"Well, let's get this all cleaned up," Leah said. "And then—how about lunch?"

The next nineday unfolded in a similar manner, though the temperature was decidedly colder and the wet weather much more unpleasant. Rhan didn't drop by. No one tried to rob the shop. But Leah was starting to find a rhythm to her days and she liked that. It would be completely disrupted when she opened her doors and began dealing with customers, but then she would find a new rhythm. She was looking forward to it.

She and Annova were alone in the shop late on eighthday when a delivery cart drew up out front and the driver began carrying in crates. Maybe a dozen, most of them quite large.

"What's all this?" Annova demanded.

But Leah had seen the firm, well-formed handwriting on the shipping manifest, and she felt a pulse of excitement. "It's from my merchant friend in Malinqua," she said. "*This* is the stuff that will set our shop apart."

"Then I can't wait to see it."

Leah tipped the driver extravagantly and locked the door behind him, not wanting anyone else to stroll in while they were distracted by opulence. Annova was already prying the lid off the first crate. "It smells good, at any rate," she said.

Leah had expected Chandran to provide her with a diverse and high-quality selection of goods, but he had outdone himself. One crate contained mostly foodstuffs—dried lassenberries from Cozique, seed-wax cakes from Dhonsho, keerza leaves and lovely pots for brewing them in from Malinqua. Another held primarily artwork—Berringese sculptures, Dhonshon masks, paintings from the Karkades. Several were filled with clothing, everything from simple, subtle Coziquela dresses to formal Malinquese jackets to embroidered ladies' gloves from an island Leah had never heard of. There was even an assortment of turbans from Berringey.

But what Leah was most interested in unwrapping, what she was certain Chandran would have included, were the bright, gorgeous fabrics of Dhonsho. Sure enough, the fifth crate they opened practically burst with color. "*Oh!*" Annova exclaimed, reverently lifting out layer after layer of cloth. Some were bolts of loose fabrics dyed in complex patterns; others were finished pieces such as skirts, shawls, and tunics. Each one was more beautiful than the last.

Annova could hardly bring herself to put any of them down; she kept laying pieces across her lap, as if to look at them more closely later, and then crooning over the next one she gently slipped out of the box.

"You know you can have anything you want," Leah told her. "All of these things were bought with Darien's money. He'd figure it's just part of your paycheck."

Annova had found a long, filmy scarf woven from strands of blue and green and gold, and hung with jangling charms shaped like shells and starfish. "Look at this," Annova said, wrapping it twice around her head, throwing the long ends over her shoulders. The colors were vibrant and cheerful against her dark skin. "Even the ugliest woman would be pretty in something like this."

"Well, you're not an ugly woman, but consider it yours," Leah replied.

Annova's fingers came up and played with the edges that lay against her cheeks. "My mother had a scarf like this—almost the same colors— she said it had belonged to *her* mother," she said. "It was one of the few things I kept when Calvin and I were living on the river. But it wore away to thread. I still have the pieces in a box in my room."

"There was a family of Dhonshon shopkeepers living in Palminera," Leah said. "I became friends with them and they did me a huge favor one day. I loved their store. Everything in it was just like this—beautiful and brightly colored."

"Dhonshon craftspeople make beautiful things," Annova agreed. "My mother said they have to, to make up for all the wretchedness in their country."

"I know the king is a terrible man," Leah answered.

"Dhonsho has had a long succession of terrible kings, but the current one is among the worst," Annova said. "But how would *you* know anything about him?"

"When Corene was living at the palace in Malinqua, she made friends with a princess from Dhonsho," Leah answered. "Alette. The king's daughter. It turned out he was planning to have her killed."

Annova looked briefly sorrowful for a woman she'd never even met. "Then she must be dead by now."

"I hope not," Leah said quietly. "We helped her flee the country. It was all Corene's idea, though I played a part as well. But I don't know that Alette made it to safety even so."

Now Annova looked intrigued. "Corene helped a Dhonshon princess escape? I don't think I've heard this story. Does Zoe know it?"

"Maybe not. As you can imagine, we were eager to keep it a secret."

"Where did she go?"

Leah laughed softly. "To Yorramol, or so we hope. I know she boarded a ship bound for there, because I put her on it. But there was a war going on, and I can't be sure she slipped through the blockade." She lifted her hands. "She promised to write Corene if she could. I hope one day a letter will arrive."

"I don't know anyone who's been to Yorramol," Annova said. "You hear people talk about it, and you think they must be lying."

"That's why we thought she might be safe there from her father's vengeance," Leah answered.

Annova smiled. "We will assume she arrived there unharmed. And that she will write. And then you can write her back and ask her to send you spices and fabrics and masks and music boxes and anything else they might sell in that strange place. And *then* you will have the most distinctive merchandise in all of Chialto!"

Leah laughed and indicated the piles of exotic goods arrayed all around them. "I think I already do."

At the very bottom of the last box they unpacked, they found a thick sealed envelope bearing Leah's name. Leah had been looking for something of the sort—a letter, a note of some kind, a personal acknowledgment amid all this welter of commerce—but Annova was the one who found it. She handed it over without comment. By its bulk, it contained multiple sheets of paper, and maybe something else besides.

Leah could hardly wait to open it, but she wanted to be alone when she did.

Just in case. Just in case Chandran said something that made her smile, or made her blush, or made her sigh.

"Well! Let's decide what stays down here and what goes upstairs," Annova said when they had cleared out every last item from every last box. "And then—you're ready, aren't you? You could open your doors whenever you wanted."

Leah nodded. "On secondday, I'm thinking," she said. "A lot of the local shopkeepers stay closed on firstday, so I should, too."

"Zoe wants to have a party for you—here in the shop," said Annova. "She'll invite her cousin Keeli and her aunt Saronne, and they can bring all their fashionable friends."

"Although it's the foreign visitors we want to attract, not the local buyers."

Annova put her hands on her hips and looked around. "I think you'll attract them all."

Finally they had hauled all the boxes upstairs, swept up the detritus of unpacking, and declared themselves done for the day. Annova set off for the palace; Leah made her way home. She detoured through the Plaza of Women to pick up two meals at the inexpensive cantina where she'd taken Rhan—one for herself, one for the insatiable reifarjin. While she was there, she bought one of the more costly bottles of wine, though it was still ludicrously cheap. She would light candles and sip wine and read Chandran's letter, and pretend she was having dinner with a friend.

She followed this excellent plan as soon as she made it home. It was full dark when she let herself into her room, so the candles were welcome. The fish practically leapt out of its bowl in its eagerness to feed, so she spent a long few minutes crumbling up a meat pie and dribbling the bits into the water. All the while, she felt the drag of the letter in her pocket. It seemed to carry heat as well as weight. Emotion as well as substance. She supposed that was her imagination.

Finally she sat at the little table by the window with her meal spread out before her, and she broke the seal on the envelope. Yes—several sheets of closely written paper and a slim packet holding—something. She lay the packet aside and began reading.

Leah,

I was so pleased to receive your first letters, telling me of your safe arrival in Welce and your early days there. Yes, I am sure it feels strange to be back in the city you once knew so well, and to find it has changed only a little while you have changed a lot. I have been gone from my own homeland much longer than five years and, while I find it difficult to imagine ever returning, I do sometimes wish I could walk down the streets of the capital city one more time and breathe in the scents I have never encountered anywhere else. If I ever learn that I am dying and have only a few ninedays to live, I will go back. I would like those spires and rooftops to be the last images my eyes ever see.

I am also pleased to hear that you will be opening a shop in what I remember you describing as the most elegant district of Chialto. You said once that if you ever returned to the city, you would like to run a business there; the fact that you can pursue this dream in partnership with your regent makes the plan even more agreeable. I know you like the notion that you are independent and require the help of no one, including Darien Serlast, but I think I know you better than that. You are independent, no question, but you do not like being unbounded. You do not like being without purpose. I do not know if you ever managed to be frivolous when you were younger, but it is something I think you lost the knack for long ago.

Finally, what pleases me the most is that you have turned to me to aid you in this enterprise. I miss you very much; being of some use to you now makes me feel that you are not so far away. And I flatter myself that I have just the right skills to enable you to succeed at your new venture. Thus, even though you are gone from my life, I am still in some small way a part of yours.

By now you will have unpacked the boxes and found all the items I have chosen for you, based upon your requirements and my own intuition. If there is anything you decide you do not like well enough to attempt to sell, return it to me and I will replace it with something of approximately the same value.

You mention that your regent is expecting visitors from the Karkades and you would like to lure some of these travelers to your shop, so I have included a number of items from that country. You were in luck, for the very day your letter arrived, I was visited by a trader carrying Karkan goods. The people of Malinqua tend to prefer items from Cozique, so I have never carried much Karkan merchandise, but I know enough about it to judge what is good quality and what is inferior. So I have made some purchases on your behalf.

What might be even more helpful for you to know, as you deal with the natives of that country, is the attitude with which they approach the world. Their history is long and dramatic, with periods of brutal violence followed by equal periods of peace and enlightenment. They are governed generally by a sense of balance, but not in the way you Welchins find harmony among your five elements or the Malinquese strive to find a middle ground between their two towers of light and darkness. Rather, they operate in the extremes and expect their cumulative actions to somehow even out.

Their primary philosophy is one of atonement. An act of great evil can be erased by an act of parallel generosity. Their most famous king slaughtered nearly one hundred children to punish a rebellious noble. To expiate this monstrous sin, he became the greatest benefactor of schools and orphanages throughout the country. His entire personal fortune went to founding a university that only the very poor can attend, at no cost to themselves. It is the best university in the realm.

The corollary to this philosophy is the belief that even the very virtuous have some darkness at their core. No one is surprised to discover anyone is capable of deep wickedness. It is hard to shock Karkans. Hard, also, to impress them.

Of course, the country was annexed more than one hundred years ago by Cozique. To the Karkans, this is a great and terrible wrong that has yet to be righted. The whole country is out of balance, and this has led to a certain debauchery among the ruling family. (They are no longer the ruling family, of course, merely figureheads who do as the Coziquela bid them; but they are descended from the last true rulers of the country and they live at the royal palace, and their people still look to them for guidance.) I know stories of their excesses that I do not want to repeat here for fear of sullying my pen.

You say that representatives from the Karkades are coming to Welce to negotiate with your regent. If you have his ear, I would encourage you to whisper this information into it: The Karkans are determined to win back their independence. They believe it is the only way to atone for the humiliation of the past, that it is their right to achieve it, and that nothing they do to attain their goal can be considered too outrageous. On the surface, they will not appear to be fanatics—they might even possess some charm. But the regent should remain on his guard even so.

I half wish I was upon friendly terms with the empress Filomara of Malinqua, for I would give her the same warning. You remember, of course, that Coziquela warships invaded Palminera shortly before you departed. While hostilities were short, Cozique continues to maintain a military presence here, and this has caused stress and strain among the Malinquese citizens. It is said that Filomara and her oldest nephew are constantly scheming for ways to eject Coziquela forces completely from their soil. Naturally, the Karkans are aware of their discontent, and they have sent envoys here to investigate a partnership between their nations. In normal times, Malinqua would have so little to gain by such an alliance that the idea would be laughable—but these are not normal times. Malinqua may be so eager to rid itself of Cozique's influence that it will sign a treaty with the Karkades, and then I do not know what terrible consequences may follow.

There! Have I filled you with uneasiness and disgust? The more I know about the royal houses of the southern seas, the more I think they are all full of murderers and madmen. Dhonsho with its rampaging king, Berringey with its barbaric habit of slaughtering royal heirs, Malinqua with its long history of poisoning rivals, the Karkades with its self-righteous brutality. For many years, I believed the only civilized court could be found in Cozique; but, from what you tell me, Welce is a place of relative sanity. A place anyone might be happy to live.

I hope, as you settle in there, that you are indeed finding yourself happy. I am eager to receive your next letters, hoping to hear news of a glad reunion with your daughter. Hoping to hear any news at all.

I think of you often, never more so than when I am sorting through goods brought to me by some trader. I wonder which pieces you would like, which ones you would believe in so wholeheartedly that you could convince almost any customer to take them home. The other day, a Berringese merchant came by selling jewelry, and there was a piece that reminded me so strongly of you that I had to purchase it. It is not for you to sell in your shop, you understand; it is for you to keep. I hope you will wear it from time to time and think of me.

Chandran

Well. This was a letter that would require a few readings. Leah momentarily laid it aside to pick up the slim packet that held Chandran's gift. Her mouth formed an *O* of pleasure as she unwrapped it to reveal a pair of earrings. Each one was made of simple gold wires wrapped around three small emeralds, holding them in place like buds on a filigree branch. They were a perfect match to a necklace Leah had bought during one of the first ninedays she had worked at Chandran's booth.

He had remembered.

They were not just business partners after all.

Not that such a realization could do her much good when he was a long ocean journey away and she was pretty sure she was never leaving Welce again. But it was a comfort nonetheless. Leah finished her meat pie, took another sip of wine, and read the letter again from the beginning.

SEVEN

The very next day, Leah had her first encounter with a Karkan. She had gone to the palace to share Chandran's assessment with Darien. The regent had listened closely, nodding a few times, but kept his conclusions to himself. Well, of course he did. Darien never told anyone what he was thinking. His only comment was, "And this information comes from the man who tried to poison you?" She couldn't tell if that made Darien more or less likely to trust Chandran's word.

"Well, yes. But in his defense, he knew I was lying to him."

"If everyone I ever lied to had tried to poison me, I'd be dead a thousand times over."

"Perhaps you should start practicing honesty."

"I practice vigilance. So far it seems just as effective."

She rose to go and he stopped her. "If you have a little time," he said, and she sank back into the chair.

"Of course I do."

"There are a handful of visitors in a room down the hall, awaiting an audience with me. Two are from the Karkades, two from Soeche-Tas. They know that I am busy for an hour or two and seem content to sit there until I am free. I can have a servant escort you there so that you, too, appear to be waiting upon my convenience. You might over-hear something useful."

"I might," she said, "if they're not speaking in one of their own languages. I don't know either Soechin or Karkan."

"If that's the case, you can loiter a few moments, then storm out impa-tiently. But my guess is that they communicate in Coziquela since they have not been allies long enough to study each other's habits of speech."

"I'll see what I can learn."

He was silent a moment, thinking something over, then he said, "Officially, so far only a couple of Karkans have arrived in Welce. Envoys who will gauge my level of interest in speaking to someone with more power and influence. Unofficially, I believe a member of the royal family is already staying in a rented house near the Plaza of Men and using an assumed name—which is ironic, since one of his affectations is that he tells no one outside of the royal family what his true name is."

He sounded so disgruntled that Leah couldn't help smiling. "What? And your spies in the Karkades haven't discovered what it is yet?"

Darien did not look remotely amused. "They have not been in place long enough to do so."

"Is that what you want me to find out?"

"I don't really care what he calls himself," Darien replied. "I would rather have you bend your attention to gathering information of more value."

She nodded and came to her feet. "I'll do my best."

A few minutes later, one of Darien's impassive servants showed her to a pleasant but very dull room with a few formal couches, a couple of spindly desks, and a view down the mountain road toward Chialto. A long table in the back of the room held basic refreshments—clusters of fruit, platters of bread, pitchers of water. Four strangers sat together on two of the sofas, leaning forward, elbows on knees, deep in conversa-tion. Leah acted as if she was totally uninterested in them, catching only glimpses from the corner of her eye.

"And how long might it be before the regent has time to see me?" she asked the servant, allowing an edge of irritation to come to her voice.

"I am very sorry. I do not know." The man bowed and showed him-self out.

Leah smothered a sigh, glanced around, spotted the table, and helped herself to refreshments. Then she sat at the desk closest to a window, glared out at the sunshine, and gnawed discontentedly on a roll.

The other people in the room had stopped talking when she entered, but after a moment or two they resumed their conversation. Darien appeared to be right that they were speaking Coziquela, but not loudly enough for her to hear more than a few phrases at a time. And none of their words sounded particularly incendiary.

". . . one of the better hotels . . ."

". . . not like Cozique . . ."

"Oh, but dinner was good! Not what I expected . . ."

". . . though not exactly entertaining . . ."

If they didn't start outlining the details of their villainous plots pretty soon, she'd throw down her half-eaten roll and stalk out.

Five minutes after Leah entered, the sole woman of the group stood up, refreshed her water glass—and came over to where Leah was sitting. Leah looked up in surprise that wasn't entirely feigned.

"I noticed you, too, were waiting for the regent," the woman said in flawless Coziquela. She had an accent, though, drawing out each vowel just a little too long. Leah had heard enough Soechin speakers to know this woman wasn't from that country. Karkan, then. Good. "Could you tell me, is he generally prompt?"

Before answering, Leah tried to take in as many details as she could without being obvious about it. The other woman looked to be in her late thirties, but her face was so expertly made up that she might have been ten years older, Leah thought. She was strongly built, somewhat below average height, with frosty blond hair randomly strung with glittering beads. Instead of the tunic and trousers favored by the Welchins, she wore a dress in the Coziquela style, though somewhat more ornate and fitted. Her hands were heavy with rings and her throat hung with necklaces—what Leah might consider an excessive amount. She couldn't tell if this was normal attire for the Karkans or if the woman had gone to extra effort because she was seeking an audience with the regent.

She decided to tone down her malcontented attitude; the last thing she wanted to do was paint Darien as uncooperative. He could manage that all on his own. "Prompt enough, I suppose, if you've got an appointment," she said. "I don't. And I know he's busy." She shrugged.

"Is he generally responsive? Reasonable? What kind of man is he?"

Leah straightened in her chair, allowing her interest to show this time. *Anybody* would be intrigued to be asked such questions about the local ruler. "He *listens* to everybody, whether they're from the Five Families or the southside slums," Leah said. "He doesn't always take the action you might want, but he does hear you out."

"That's good, I suppose."

Leah warmed to her role. "And you'll never know what he's thinking. He'll be very polite, and he'll nod in all the right places, but he keeps his thoughts to himself."

"Also a good thing, for a man planning to be king."

"But he's honest. If he does make you a promise, he'll keep it."

The woman nodded. "And what kinds of things does he respond to? Some kings like gifts, for instance. Some like to be introduced to new friends."

What does that *mean?* Leah wondered. She remembered that Chandran had called the Karkan royal court debauched. Was this woman asking about Darien's sexual preferences? If Darien had any that could be satisfied by foreign visitors, Leah didn't want to know about them.

"He likes information," she said. When the woman cocked her head to one side, Leah expanded. "He likes to know things other people don't. He likes to put pieces together. If you have knowledge about—" She waved a hand. "Something that's happening in Soeche-Tas. A secret alliance between Cozique and Berringey. A plan that's about to be launched by the Karkades. He likes to know. Give him information and he's more likely to give you what you want."

"Now, that's a very useful tidbit," the woman said. She bestowed a warm smile on Leah. "I am Seka Mardis, by the way," she added. Leah had no idea if *Seka* was her title, her first name, or some other identifier. "I am visiting from the Karkades."

"I'm Leah," she answered. "I'm just about to open a boutique in the shop district." She faked a start of realization. "I specialize in foreign goods. You might drop by and see if there's anything that would interest you."

"I would be happy to do that. I have only been in Welce a short while, but already I miss some of the scents and colors of home."

"I spent five years in Malinqua," Leah said. "It was a couple of quintiles before I got used to the food."

"It is both the biggest advantage and biggest disadvantage of foreign travel," Seka Mardis agreed. "I have not traveled often beyond our borders, but I am hoping that one day soon—"

She didn't get a chance to complete her thought, because there was a sudden quiet presence at the door. Darien's servant was back, bowing deeply. "The regent will see you now," he announced to the room.

"Excellent," Seka Mardis murmured.

Leah worked hard not to let her irritation show as she tried to figure out a casual way to remind Seka to visit her shop. But she didn't have to; Seka seemed just as interested in initiating a friendship as Leah was. "I would so much like to see the goods you have in your boutique," she said. "Where exactly is it?"

"I'll write down the address for you," Leah replied, scrawling the information on a piece of paper that someone had left behind. "I won't be open for a few more days, but I'd love to have you as one of my first customers!" She gestured at the men, who were waiting impatiently at the door. "And all your friends."

"We'll be by soon," Seka Mardis promised. "Leah." And she nodded and hurried out.

Leah sank back in her chair, watching the visitors walk out. Many of her conversations back in Malinqua had started the same way when she was trying to cultivate new sources. She had exchanged a few words with a café owner, a bartender, an ostler, a maid. Asked no questions, made no promises, just appeared amiable and mildly curious. Some of the friendships had yielded nothing but a few desultory conversations; others had provided a valuable stream of useful information. It was hard to know for sure, but she thought a relationship with Seka Mardis would fall in the second category.

And so it begins again, she thought. She could feel herself smiling.

Virrie and Mally didn't drop by the shop during the afternoon, but they were waiting outside Leah's apartment when she got home that night. The evening air was cool, but they weren't shivering in the street. They were sitting inside an idling elaymotive, with the heating system activated in the back and a grinning Yori sitting in the front.

"What are all of you doing here?" Leah demanded, leaning in through a window.

"We've come to take you to Nelson's," Virrie said. "He's having an impromptu party. Mostly family."

Leah took in such a quick breath that she almost started coughing. "So then why are *we* invited?" she said a little sharply

"Oh, Nelson knows Taro's gone home and Mally and I are here without him, and he wants to make sure we aren't lonely," was Virrie's affable response. "And I think he's worried about you. Living in this little place all by yourself. He thinks you just sit here all night and brood."

Nelson indeed might have said that. Virrie could have come up with it on her own, too. Leah eyed the older woman with a certain hostility, but they both knew she wouldn't be able to resist going. Especially not when Mally stretched forward to smile at her.

"I think it will be fun," Mally said. "Virrie says there will be lots of kids! You should come, too."

"Well—" Leah glanced down at her clothes. She'd dressed up to visit Darien, but after working in the shop for five hours she'd managed to get dirt on her trousers and dust on her tunic. "Maybe I should change."

Virrie pushed the door open. "Oh, don't bother. You know no one at Nelson's house cares what you look like."

Leah sighed and settled onto the bench seat, Mally's warm little body between her and Virrie. "No one at *your* house ever cares what anyone looks like," Leah corrected. "When Nelson feels like it, he can put the rest of us to shame."

Yori put the car in motion and soon they were winding down the Cinque to the most prosperous part of town, where the majority of the Five Family members had their city houses. "It's a little funny, isn't it?" Virrie said. "*None* of the primes really care about fashion. Taro always looks like an old farmer. Zoe would rather wear rags and camp on the river than dress in formal attire to attend a banquet. Kayle Dochenza—if he even *remembers* to change clothes once a nineday, I'd be surprised. And Mirti Serlast—well. It's pointless to even speculate what might be in her closet. Of course Nelson can outdo any of them! It's not difficult."

Leah laughed. "I assumed the primes were always like that. Interested in things that were so much more important than how they looked."

"Oh, it depends on the individual. Christara Lalindar—Zoe's grandmother, you know—she had a fine sense of opulence. She could sweep into a room with so much style that you'd have thought she was one of the queens. And Darien's father was an elegant man, much like Darien himself. Very aware of what was due to him and what he owed to the office he held. But Kayle's mother—" She shook her head. "You think *Kayle* looks like a lunatic. You'd have sworn that woman wandered homeless through the slums for the whole of her existence."

The placid Virrie was not usually so talkative; she was probably trying to distract Leah from thinking about their destination. But Leah felt her tension rise throughout the duration of the drive, and it ratcheted up a notch as they arrived. The three of them climbed out and Yori drove off. Then Leah stood there a moment gazing at the achingly familiar house. It was the most sweela building in the entire city. It was built of red brick and orange roof tiles, and light shone from every one of its wide windows on all three stories. Small lighted candles lined the walkway from the street to the door. Even from where they stood, it was clear the place was bursting with life and energy and conversation and laughter.

"Ardelays," Virrie said with satisfaction. "There's no one quite like them."

They entered into a chaotic swirl of people and activity; it was so loud that the servant at the door didn't even bother to announce them. But Nelson bellowed, "Leah!" from half a room away, and a few moments later she was enveloped in his enthusiastic embrace. She could only laugh and submit.

He drew back to examine her a moment, smiling down at her. They hadn't seen each other since they had arrived in Welce after the long journey home from Malinqua. "You look good," he said. "Not quite so scrawny. It suits you to be home. I can tell."

"Maybe," she said. "Nelson, of course you know Virrie, but have you ever met Mally? She's one of Taro's wards, and she and Virrie are living in the city for a few ninedays."

Nelson dropped to an easy crouch so he could be eye to eye with the little girl. Mally didn't look at all discomposed by his wild red hair and exuberant manner, though she kept hold of Virrie's hand while exchanging a long stare with the sweela prime.

"Well, hello, Mally," he said, gentling his voice. "I don't know that we *have* ever been properly introduced, though I'm sure I've seen you from time to time. I'm very glad to have you in my house at last. My wife will want to meet you, no doubt."

"Virrie said there would be boys and girls here," Mally said. "I could play with them?"

"There are! My grandson and granddaughter are in the other room—are they sixteen now? I lose track—and any number of nieces and nephews. I warn you, they're all a little rambunctious, but friendly as can be."

Virrie was looking beyond Nelson. "And Celia's here, too, apparently. *With* Zoe." She motioned them over.

Mally looked around in excitement. "Celia? I love Celia."

Nelson rose to his feet, grinning. "Well, of course Zoe is here," he said. "She's my brother's daughter."

"So's Josetta," Virrie reminded him.

He laughed. "And the princess is also on the premises! She didn't tell you she was coming? I understand you're sharing a house."

"She's gone more often than she's there," Virrie explained. "She has some kind of lodgings down in the slums. I think Darien hoped that playing hostess to me would oblige her to stay in his house most nights, but it didn't turn out that way."

"I'm always pleased anytime Darien's plans don't quite work out," Nelson said with satisfaction. Virrie and Leah both laughed.

Zoe was upon them at that moment, a squirming Celia in her arms. "She would *not* be still until I promised her Mally was coming," she said. "Nelson, is there some quiet place I can take them so they can play together? I'll supervise."

Nelson had a soft smile on his face, an almost wistful look Leah hadn't seen him wear before. "Actually, my wife would love the opportunity to spend time with Mally—with *both* girls," he corrected himself quickly. "She loves children, and none of the ones that belong to us are really little anymore."

Not hard to interpret that, Leah thought. *Mally is her granddaughter, but until now she's always had to hold back and love her only from a distance.* A difficult thing to do for a woman as warmhearted as Nelson's wife, Leah supposed. Beccan Ardelay was as hearty and impulsive as Nelson, as shrewd and generous, too. Mally was about to be smothered in love.

"Then let's go find Beccan," Zoe said. "*Happy* to turn Celia over to someone for even a half hour."

Nelson lifted Celia from Zoe's arms and settled her on his hip as easily as Taro might have. "Come on, Mally," he said, reaching down to take her hand. "Let's go find my wife. You'll like her."

Mally trotted off, happily chatting with the sweela prime. "Look at that," Leah said. "I never think of Nelson as being the paternal type, but he's managing quite well."

Zoe snorted. "Since bastard Ardelay children turn up on a regular basis, I imagine Nelson is quite comfortable holding babies."

Leah choked on a laugh. "Do you think Mally has half siblings lying around somewhere? For some reason, I never thought of that. It would be just like Rhan."

"It would be," Zoe agreed. "Kurtis married fairly young and seems *much* more stable than most Ardelay men, so I like to hope that he's remained faithful. But I probably delude myself. I've often wondered if Josetta and I have half siblings of our own, since our father was famous for his affairs. But if we do, I haven't encountered them yet."

"I wouldn't mind coming across a few more of Navarr Ardelay's daughters someday," Virrie said. "I like them all." Someone caught her attention from across the room and she waved. "Oh, I have to go talk to Lilias and the twins. Leah, don't sneak out of here without letting me know you're leaving."

"How did you know that's what I was planning to do?"

Virrie smiled, patted her cheek, and ambled off.

Zoe said, "I can never decide if I like Virrie or Beccan better. I sometimes think if either one of them had had the raising of me, I'd have turned out much better than I did."

Leah's smile was a little crooked. "Well, Virrie *did* raise me, at least for a few years, but I'm not sure I'm much credit to her."

"I think she finds you completely satisfactory. And she adores Mally."

"Yes. I was lucky I had someone like Virrie to leave Mally with."

"If I ever ran away, I'd give Celia to Annova," Zoe said. "But these days I don't run away as often as I'd like." She sounded regretful.

"I often wondered," Leah said. "Is there a decoy princess for Celia like there used to be for Odelia?"

"No. Darien and I discussed it when she was born, but I wouldn't agree to it." Leah raised her eyebrows in a question, and Zoe continued,

"It was his idea to have the decoy for Odelia, you know. Josetta, Corene, and Natalie never had anyone masquerading on their behalf. Well, it would have been difficult to pull off, since they all lived at the palace and it would have been hard to conceal their lookalikes. But there were three of them, and no one *said* so, but everyone believed that meant there were a couple of spare princesses if something happened to one of them."

"That *is* why you want your king or queen to produce a healthy number of heirs," Leah said.

"But Romelle lived out in the country with Taro, so it was easy to swap Mally for Odelia when we needed to. And because we were then down to one certified heir, Darien wanted to take extra measures to ensure her safety." She shook her head. "But I won't agree to the decoy for Celia."

"Why not?"

"First, I don't believe I'd be able to pull it off. I don't think I'd be able to convince anyone that I loved any other child as much as I love Celia. I don't think Romelle carried it off very well, either, to tell you the truth. I just think no one was paying close enough attention to realize that she didn't really like Mally." She must have seen Leah wince, because she added, "I'm sorry."

Leah just gestured at her to continue.

"Second, I don't think a decoy worked out so well in Odelia's case. If Mally *hadn't* been substituting for her, we would have learned the truth about her condition much sooner, and that would have been better for everyone."

"That's a good point."

"And third—" Zoe paused as if considering, and then she smiled. It was an angry and beautiful expression. "And third, I'm the coru prime. If someone touched my daughter, I'd boil the blood in his veins. And everyone who lives in Welce knows it. They'd have to kill me to be able to harm her."

In some countries, that's exactly what they'd do, Leah thought. She didn't bother saying so. She liked the idea of a mother so fierce she would destroy anyone who threatened her child. She wished she'd had that kind of mother. She wanted to be that kind.

"So Darien said, fine, no decoy princess," Zoe finished up. "But who knows? He might be grooming someone in secret to play that part just in case I ever change my mind."

That made Leah laugh out loud. "Oh, now that you say it, I'm sure he is!"

Zoe laughed, too. "I look forward to the day I finally meet her."

Someone approached Zoe from behind, calling her name. Zoe turned into a warm embrace and then introduced Leah to what turned out to be the first in a long line of cousins and second cousins and other Ardelay relatives who all wanted to say hello to the coru prime. Leah would have wandered off so Zoe could visit with her extended family, but Zoe kept a hand on her arm and introduced her to everyone in turn. The implication was clear. *These are Mally's relatives, too. Someday you'll have to get to know them all, so you might as well start now.*

After about a half hour of that, Zoe waved at someone across the room and tugged Leah in that direction. It took a little time to navigate the crowded space, since everyone they passed knew Zoe and looked curious about Leah, but they managed to avoid getting drawn into any more conversations. Eventually they made their way to a couple standing a little apart from the rest of the guests—a slim blond woman, who looked to be in her early twenties, and a dark-haired man, who might be a few years older. Leah was fairly certain she'd never seen the man before, but he looked oddly familiar. The woman she recognized on sight.

"Princess Josetta," she said, bowing deeply.

"Oh, not *here*. Not at Nelson's house," Josetta protested. "That's the best part of coming to Nelson's parties. Everyone acts like I'm nothing special."

"Nonsense," Zoe answered. "They act like *everyone* is special. Delightful and brilliant and full of potential. But it's true they treat you like everyone else, and that *is* refreshing."

The man with the princess gave Leah a friendly smile. He was handsome and slightly rakish, but almost preternaturally alert; she had the impression he was thoroughly and quickly sizing her up. It was an ability she herself had honed during her years in Malinqua as she tried to gauge who would be useful to her and who wouldn't. Her assessment of this stranger was that he would always be agreeable and would *appear* more cooperative than he really was. She figured he was good at collecting information but not so quick to reveal it. Her guess was that he'd come to the same conclusion about her. She smiled back.

"I'm Rafe," he said. "Since it doesn't look like either of them is going to introduce me."

"Leah," she replied.

"Sorry, sorry," Zoe said over Josetta's own hasty apology. "But you might as well be complete about it. Leah Frothen and Lerafi Adova. Or do you go by Lerafi Kolavar?"

"*Adova*, thank you very much," he said.

"Frothen?" Josetta repeated. "Then you're—"

Before she could complete the sentence, Leah put the pieces together. "You're the empress's other grandson," she said. "The one who *wouldn't* come to Malinqua."

"That's right," he said. His attention sharpened as he scanned her face. Maybe not everybody was privy to this information and he was wondering how she knew it.

"I'm just back from spending a few years in Malinqua," she explained. "I got to know Princess Corene a little, and your brother, Steff, was with her some of the time. He was a very likable young man."

Now Rafe's face showed eagerness. "So you've seen Steff lately! How was he? He's written me maybe two letters since he's been gone. I try not to worry, but—" He spread his hands.

"You must be Darien's spy! The one Corene told me about!" Josetta exclaimed. She glanced at Rafe. "Corene was better about writing than Steff, but I think it was only because she liked hinting at all the intrigue she then wouldn't tell us about." She laid a hand on Leah's arm. "Could we find someplace to talk for a while? I would love to hear all about Corene's adventures. And Steff's. Or are there other people here you need to see?"

There are people here I would prefer not *to see,* Leah thought. She hadn't spotted Rhan yet, but she was sure he was present. She wondered how much of her story Josetta knew, and she couldn't help a quick look at Zoe. The coru prime smiled very slightly and shook her head, so Leah took that as a blanket negative. No, Josetta didn't know that Mally was Leah's child, or that Rhan was the girl's father. She surely realized that Mally was Odelia's double, but she didn't have the rest of the details.

Though the princess would hardly be a harsh judge. She was a bastard Ardelay herself, and she didn't seem at all unhappy.

"I would *love* to go someplace quiet to talk," Leah said. "I find all these Ardelays overwhelming."

Zoe decided to mingle, but Josetta led Rafe and Leah through a back corridor to a small room clearly designed for private conferences. Leah and Rhan had spent a few leisurely afternoons in this very spot. Leah closed her mind to the memories.

"I can see you've been to this house many times before," Leah said as they disposed themselves in comfortable chairs. She noted that Rafe appeared entirely relaxed, but he chose a seat that faced the doors and conducted a quick, surreptitious survey of his surroundings. It amused her a little. This was someone who was used to living a precarious existence and hadn't quite gotten over his watchful habits. She remembered some of the gossip Nelson had shared with her on the long voyage back from Malinqua. Rafe had been a professional card player before he met the princess. Currently, he worked for Kayle Dochenza, piloting the infamous new flying machines that the elay prime called aeromotives. Oh, and he was related to the royal houses of both Berringey and Malinqua. Leah knew some of the details of that story, but she'd bet the most interesting parts were still shrouded in mystery.

While Leah was studying Rafe, Josetta was glancing fondly around the room. "Once I found out I was Navarr Ardelay's daughter, my life realigned," the princess said. "I had led a very circumscribed and careful existence, and I'd mostly hated it. But then to suddenly find out the truth—to have Zoe as my sister and Nelson as my uncle—and to no longer be a blood princess of the realm—my whole world got bigger. So yes, I've come here often. The sweela prime's house is the place to be when you want to open your mind."

"So you weren't too upset. When you discovered your true heritage."

"I was glad. Once I got over the shock."

Leah looked at Rafe and raised her eyebrows. "If Nelson told the stories correctly, you also received something of a shock when you found out who you really were. But were you glad, in the end?" *Will Mally be glad when she realizes I'm her mother?*

He laughed. "Well, I wasn't so pleased about it when people were trying to kill me, but once we managed to stop *that* activity—yes, I've been glad to know the truth." He kept his friendly smile, but she had been right in her first assessment: He was constantly weighing her words, constantly sifting for the meaning behind them. "Why? Do you think maybe there's a secret in your own background?"

"Rafe," Josetta murmured.

Leah managed a tight smile. "Not me. Someone I know. Just wondering how that conversation will go. If it ever happens."

Rafe pulled a pack of cards out of his pocket and idly shuffled them. A way to seem like he wasn't paying attention, Leah thought. A way to make you think he was half absorbed in something else. It was a good trick. She wondered how she could come up with something similar.

"It worked out for my brother, too," Rafe said. "Learning about his past. He was eager to go to Malinqua and take up his life as the empress's grandson." He gave her an inquiring look. "Unless things haven't gone so well for him since he's been there?"

Now she really admired his style. He'd realized that she was uncomfortable and smoothly changed the subject.

"Well, there were some rocky times, and Malinqua has some rough days ahead, but Steff seems to have found his place," Leah said, launching into the tale of her last quintile in Palminera. They both listened closely. Josetta frequently nodded as if Leah's stories matched the reports she'd heard from Corene, though clearly neither of them knew the details about Princess Alette or the series of murders at the palace.

"Much more exciting than I realized!" Josetta exclaimed at the end. "And now she's gone off to Cozique! I'm so sad that I won't get to see her again for a quintile or more—but at the same time, I'm so proud of her. She was—she was *flailing* in the past year or two. Simply at a loss for what to do with her life. If she's found her calling—well. *Nothing* will stop Corene."

"That was my impression as well."

"So what took you to Malinqua?" Josetta asked. "And what brought you back?"

The same thing: Mally. Leah managed a rueful smile. "I wasn't happy with the life I was living here so I thought I'd try someplace else. And eventually I realized that the things I'd left behind were still in my heart, so I might as well come back and deal with them. Not to be too mysterious about it."

"So Darien sent you to Malinqua to spy for him, because Darien never minds capitalizing on anyone's misfortunes," Josetta said dryly. "But how did he know you? If you're a Frothen, you must be related to Taro somehow? Which means I must have known you, too, but I don't really remember you. I'm sorry."

"My mother was Taro's youngest sister, but she died when I was a girl. When I wasn't with my father, I was with Virrie and Taro. But I wasn't at court much. And I have to be ten years or twelve years older than you. No reason for you to remember me."

"So now that you're back—what next?" Josetta asked.

Leah wasn't sure how many people should know the details of her arrangement with Darien, so she said carefully, "I'm opening a boutique in the shop district that specializes in foreign goods. The regent is one of my backers."

Josetta's face showed instant comprehension. "*Is* he?" she replied. "Then I'm sure it will be quite successful."

"I've imported some beautiful things from all around the southern seas," Leah added. "I'm opening on secondday. You should come."

"I'm not much of one for shopping," Josetta said. "But I'll come anyway."

They talked a few more minutes before Josetta observed that Nelson would be disappointed if she didn't speak to at least a few of her cousins. They headed back to the main room, to find it even more crowded with people, a good half of them redheads and all of them talking as fast and loud as they could.

Naturally, the first person to spot them was Rhan. He had a drink in each hand and a somewhat disheveled look, but he was smiling as he sauntered over. "How long have you shy little flowers been hiding away?" he asked, leaning over to kiss Josetta on the cheek. "Here, do you want some wine? It's very good."

"Surely you fetched it for yourself," Josetta said.

"I can find more."

"I'll get some," Rafe said, and lounged off.

Leah perforce accepted a glass from Rhan but only pretended to sip from it. Josetta said, "Rhan, do you know Leah Frothen?"

He gave Leah a lazy smile. "I do. I was so pleased to learn she was back in town after a long absence."

"She's opening some posh store," Josetta added. "You'll have to go buy things." She glanced at Leah. "Rhan is *much* more interested in shopping than I am."

"*And* I have better taste."

"That's because I keep my mind on loftier things."

"That's because no elay woman in the history of Welce ever had a sense of fashion."

Wasn't this unexpected? Rhan Ardelay bantering with some other woman while Leah stood casually by. Of course, Josetta was his cousin and in love with another man, so they weren't really flirting. But Leah wouldn't have thought she'd be able to endure even this much light conversation without wanting to scream her lungs out.

He turned to Leah with his easy smile. "And what brings you to this very noisy party at my father's house?"

Her own smile was strained. "Virrie brought me. And Mally."

"Mally," Rhan repeated, raising his eyebrows.

"You remember Mally, don't you, Rhan?" Josetta put in. "Taro and Virrie want to start introducing her to the world as *herself* now that she doesn't have to pretend to be Odelia anymore. I think it's so kind of them."

"It is kind," he said. "Now that you mention it, I don't think I've ever laid eyes on the girl when I was sure it was her."

"You know, I haven't, either," Josetta said. "We should go meet her formally. I wonder where she is?"

"Nelson took her and Celia off to play with Beccan," Leah said in a subdued voice.

"Then I know where they'll be," Josetta said, turning toward the hallway that led to the grand stairwell.

"What about Rafe?" Leah asked.

Josetta laughed. "He'll find us. Or not. He won't be worried." She motioned to her cousin. "Come on. You should meet her, too."

Rhan apparently couldn't resist the chance to give Leah one quick, sly smile. "I think I should," he said. "Seems like it's about time."

They found Beccan with Mally and Celia in a playroom on the second level of the house. The room was full of toys and half-size furniture and pillows scattered on the floor. Beccan was seated on a pillow, Celia on her lap. Mally knelt beside her on a tufted rug, arranging colorful marbles in some kind of design.

Beccan glanced up when they walked in the room and looked straight at her son. Her gaze was full of regret and delight in almost equal measure, sprinkled with remnants of anger and reproach. She was a slim brown-haired woman with elegant hands and a patrician face only just now showing the lines of age. She was the only person Leah had ever known who could silence Nelson with a single word.

"Rhan," Beccan said. "I was hoping you'd come look for me."

"Leah told me you were watching our younger guests, so I thought I'd say hello," he answered.

He dropped to a crouch next to Mally and spent a moment admiring her design. She paused, a blue marble in her hand, to give him a considering look. "Hello," she said.

"Hello yourself," he replied. "I'm Rhan. I hear you're Mally. That's a pretty name."

"Rhan's a nice name, too," she said politely.

He grinned. "So what are you making here?"

"A picture."

"Can I help?"

Mally frowned, clearly not interested in collaborating. "There's another box over there," she said, pointing. "You can make your own picture."

Rhan fetched it, then settled on the rug next to Mally. Josetta and Leah pulled some of the small chairs closer to Beccan and tried to make themselves comfortable on the insufficient seat bottoms.

"I'll take Celia if you're willing to give her up," Josetta offered.

"She's getting sleepy," Beccan said, handing her over. Celia had settled on Josetta's lap with her cheek against the princess's chest, but her eyes were still wide open. Leah thought she was doing her best to stay awake. Josetta kissed the top of the child's head and began swaying very slightly.

Rhan was unpacking the contents of the second box and spreading them on the floor in front of him. These weren't marbles; they were game pieces carved from a variety of different stones and woods, and they all seemed to have been thrown in this box because their companion pieces were lost or broken. "I used to play with these when I was a little boy," Rhan told Mally as he began arranging them in rows on the rug. "Everything in this room."

"Did you come here to visit?"

"I lived here." He nodded at Beccan. "That's my mother."

"Are you sweela?" Mally asked.

Rhan laughed. "What gave it away? My red hair?"

"It's a sweela house."

"It is that," Beccan said. "Though I did my best to add a little stability. To the house *and* the people who lived in it."

"You succeeded a little better at that with Kurtis than with me," Rhan said. He finished a row of wooden disks and started on a row of stylized white quartz horses. "I was a wild child."

That caught Mally's attention. "Were you bad?"

"Not *bad*," he equivocated. "I just didn't always do what I was told." He sorted through his pile to find more quartz pieces. "What about you?"

"I always do what I'm told," Mally said.

Rhan leaned down to whisper in her ear, loudly enough for all of them to hear. "Sometimes life is more fun if you don't."

Mally took up a handful of yellow marbles and began working them into her design. "Sometimes it's dangerous."

"Dangerous?" Rhan repeated.

Mally gave him a serious look. "People can get hurt if you're not careful."

There was a small silence while the four adults contemplated how often Mally must have heard that from Romelle, probably even from Taro and Virrie. *You must tell everyone your name is Odelia. You can't ever let anyone guess the truth. Do you understand? Something terrible could happen to Odelia. Do you understand?* Leah pressed her hands against her cheeks, hoping to push back the tears.

"I used to always do what I was told," Josetta announced. "Always.

I was *such* a good girl! And then one day I decided I wouldn't let anybody else tell me how to behave."

Now Mally looked at her. "Were you bad?"

Josetta laughed. "No! I didn't do anything *mean*. I just made my own decisions and didn't let anybody talk me out of them."

"To be fair, you were about sixteen before you became a rebel," Beccan said. "Mally is a little young to suddenly start deciding the course of her own life."

Leah slid from her chair and went to her knees beside Mally. The rest of the yellow marbles were in a pile just slightly out of the little girl's reach, so she scooped up a handful and held them out. Mally delicately picked two from her palm. "It's tricky," she said to her daughter, "to know when to do what you're told and when to think for yourself. Sometimes the adults in your life really do know better and all they want is to keep you safe. But sometimes they don't know better. Sometimes they're wrong. And *some* adults aren't very smart, or aren't very nice, and you *shouldn't* do what they say."

Mally considered that for a moment, her flecked eyes searching Leah's face. "How do you know the difference?" she asked at last.

"That's the hard part," Leah admitted. "What you need to do is find a few people you can always trust. Who will never hurt you. And who won't ever let you get hurt."

"Like Virrie," Mally said, going back to her work on the picture.

"Absolutely like Virrie," Leah confirmed. "And like any of the people in this room."

Mally looked up and glanced from face to face as if committing each one to memory. Her gaze lingered a little longer on Rhan's countenance, as if she wasn't positive he would be her best guide or champion, but then she nodded. "Not Romelle," she said.

Leah heard Beccan's swift intake of air, caught the sharp way Josetta turned her head to stare at Mally. But Leah just nodded. "Not Romelle," she agreed. "I'm sure what Romelle wants is to keep Odelia safe. That probably means she doesn't always think about what's good for anyone else."

"Well, I can't say I blame her," Beccan said on a sigh. "I probably would have sacrificed the whole world on behalf of Rhan or Kurtis."

"And I'm sure Zoe would do the same for Celia," Josetta added.

Beccan looked over at Josetta. "Is she asleep? Good. There's a crib over there if you'd like to put her down."

"I like holding her when she's not squirming to get away. It happens so rarely."

"She is quite an active little girl," Beccan agreed.

"Celia *never* does what she's told," Mally said.

They all laughed. "Well," Beccan said, "no. But I'm not sure I would let Celia be the model for my behavior."

Mally sat back on her heels. "I'm done," she said.

They all leaned forward to study her completed design in the short tufts of the rug. A swath of blue marbles arched over a field of green; a squarish block of brown ones anchored the left side, while a swirl of yellow ones collected in the upper right corner. Individual red marbles randomly dotted the border between green and brown.

"Look at that," Leah said. "It's a landscape. Grass and sky and sun and a big house."

"Taro's house," Mally said, pleased. She pointed at the bits of red. "Those are flowers."

"How clever of you!" Beccan exclaimed. "Much better than whatever Rhan's been making."

"I'm just organizing," he defended himself. "I wasn't trying to be creative."

"Organizing is better than nothing," Mally told him, clearly trying to make him feel better.

He laughed in delight. "It *is*! But next time I'll try harder."

"Leah keeps rocks for me at her store," Mally said. "You could come play with them, too."

He didn't even look in Leah's direction. "Thank you, Mally," he said. "I might do that."

There were loud footsteps at the door, and Nelson's burly form burst in. "*Here* you all are!" he exclaimed. "Just what I'd expect of Josetta and Leah, to be hiding away like this, but Rhan? You're a disappointment."

Beccan tilted her head back to look at him. "He's been getting to know Mally. It's been very nice."

"Good. I'm glad. Now everyone else wants to get to know her," Nelson said. "Come on, all of you! On your feet! There's a party here, or don't you remember?"

EIGHT

The next day was firstday, and Leah spent it preparing to open her shop the following morning. Made sure every display was just right. Laid in plenty of paper at the cash register so she could write out receipts. Swept the floor one last time.

Since she figured she'd spend far more time at the shop than the apartment, she'd brought the reifarjin with her in the morning and set it up in a big glass tank on a pedestal near the coru table. It seemed happy in its new surroundings, watching all the activity with its inscrutable eyes and fanning its frills as if in excitement.

"You think this is going to be fun, don't you?" Leah asked, feeding it the leftovers from her lunch. "So do I."

Late in the day, an elaymotive pulled up in front, and Zoe, Annova, and Yori climbed out. "We've brought you a present!" Zoe called as she and Yori wrestled a large, unwieldy, and well-wrapped item from the back of the smoker car.

"I'm supposed to be selling things, not collecting things," Leah said. But they carried their bundle inside anyway and set it up in the smaller of the two display windows. Zoe whipped off the cover to reveal a swirly tube of red glass that had clearly been bent into some kind of pattern, while Annova tinkered with a connector designed to hook into the gas feed.

"It's a sign for your shop," Zoe explained. "Go outside and look in."

Leah had barely stepped out onto the chilly street when the red tubing came to life, spelling out **LEAH'S** in glowing scarlet letters. She laughed and bounced back through the door.

"That's fantastic! Where did you get that?"

"There's a crazy sweela boy who's just started making these sculptures," Zoe said. "He's working with one of Kayle's nephews."

"We couldn't think of anything else you might need," said Annova. "I love it."

Yori looked around with her hands on her hips. "So you're ready? Everything's set for tomorrow?"

"Everything's set," Leah said.

"Well, then," Zoe said. "We'll see you in the morning."

Leah knew she should go home early, eat a light dinner, and get a full night's sleep so she was rested for the grand opening. But there was a buzzing in her blood, a humming in her head; she couldn't settle. So just as dark began falling, she put on a warm coat, took a public transport to the Plaza of Men, and walked around for about an hour, hoping to siphon off some of her nervous energy.

The Plaza of Men had an entirely different feel than the Plaza of Women. The outer perimeter was defined by stalls and booths that had been in place so long they had an air of permanence; they were almost as solidly built as some of the establishments in the shop district. The goods and services on offer were very different as well, provided by bankers, moneylenders, horse traders, carriage makers, and recorders of legal documents. Leah had no reason to seek out the betting booth, though she supposed it might be interesting to lay a wager on how successful her shop would be, but she found herself halting in front of the booth of promises. Here patrons could swear, before witnesses and for all eternity, that they would accomplish specific tasks, and their vows were recorded in books kept by the booth owner and his family.

According to legend, Darien Serlast had gone to the promise booth to put in writing that he intended to marry Zoe, and he had made this vow only one or two ninedays after meeting her. Leah doubted the story was true—it seemed so unlike Darien—but she wished that she might someday find the courage to ask.

Leah could think of many commitments in her own life she would like to be able to keep. *I will stop caring about Rhan Ardelay. I will willingly and unselfishly serve the crown. I will become the calm and courageous woman I want to be.* But really, there was only one vow that she was absolutely determined to uphold. She didn't need a piece of paper to serve as a reminder; it was written on her heart.

But she wanted the piece of paper anyway.

So she loitered outside the booth for a few minutes, keeping mostly to the shadows, watching the other patrons come and go. The booth had a sturdy wooden roof and three solid walls, but the front was open and several hanging lamps provided ample illumination for the activity under way. Men and women spoke their vows while two young men carefully recorded their words, first in the pages of a huge leather-bound book, then on separate sheets of thick, pressed paper. The patrons signed both copies, then the loose papers were rolled into scrolls, sealed with wax, and handed over. Leah noticed that everyone who left looked both excited and a little anxious, as if wondering: *What have I just done?*

When the place had emptied out except for the two workers, she stepped in and said, "I want to make a promise."

"Excellent," said one of the young men. He was sleek and deferential and looked about Leah's age. She had to wonder what he thought of his job—what kinds of declarations he had heard over the years, which ones had moved him, which had appalled him, which had made him silently snicker to himself. It was the sort of job that would lead you to great compassion, she thought, or complete cynicism. "Would you like to make a public recording that anyone may see for the asking, or a private one, that will not be released until you grant permission or are declared dead?"

Leah hadn't even known there were options. "Public," she said.

"And do you want a copy for yourself?"

"I do."

"Then come with me to the table where we keep the public records, and I will fetch materials."

In a few moments, she was standing beside him watching as, in extraordinarily beautiful handwriting, he inscribed a simple sentence in one of the oversize volumes: *I will be a mother to my daughter, Mally.* She watched with equal intentness as he wrote the words a second time on a sheet of heavy paper. He added the date to both documents, then had her sign them.

"Sealed or unsealed?" he asked when she was finished.

If the paper was unsealed, she could look at it anytime she wanted. If it was sealed, she could hand it to Mally at some point in the future and say, *Here is the proof of how long ago I swore to cherish you.* "Seal it," she said.

"And do you have a signet ring that you would like to use to mark the wax?" he asked. "If not, we have a variety of stamps you can choose from."

Who would ever have expected to make so many decisions for a simple promise? "What kind of stamps?" she asked helplessly.

"The most popular ones are the letters of the alphabet. Perhaps an L or an M," he suggested. "Other people choose blessing glyphs, particularly if one of their own seems appropriate. Otherwise we are happy to stamp the wax with our own seal—*certainty*—which our family has used as its motto for generations."

"Honor," Leah said, almost before he finished speaking. "That's one of my blessings. And that's what I'm going to do. Honor this promise."

"An excellent choice," he murmured.

A few moments later he had rolled the paper and closed it with a seal made of green wax, which he had chosen after ascertaining that she was torz. She handed over three silvers for the transaction, thanked him gravely, and tucked the scroll into an inner pocket of her tunic before leaving the shop.

Now she was *really* restless, on edge. Making the promise had left her even more unsettled, not less so, though she thought the emotion glittering through her blood was a form of determined elation. *I will keep my promise. I just have to figure out how.* It was as if she wanted the night to shrink back, the morning to leap forward, so she could more quickly get started on the rest of her life.

Pointless to head back to her lodgings while she still had this much chaos clamoring through her brain. She would just keep strolling through the Plaza until she wore herself out or until all of the shopkeepers covered their goods, locked their storage bins, turned down their gaslights, and went home.

She had just paused outside of a money-changer's booth to shake a rock out of her shoe when she spotted a face that looked vaguely familiar. By habit, she shrank back into the shadows so she wouldn't be seen until she decided whether or not she wanted to be recognized. At first she couldn't put a name to the woman who was stepping out of the booth with her fingers fisted tightly in her pocket. It could hardly be more obvious that the woman was carrying a large amount of money that she didn't want anyone to steal. *Don't be stupid,* Leah thought. *Move your hand.*

The woman turned to the man accompanying her and said something in a low voice. Leah couldn't hear what she said, but her face was full of excitement. She was short and somewhat stocky, wearing a tunic and trousers that looked expensive and well-cared for, but Leah didn't think the woman was a daughter of the Five Families. It was hard to say exactly why. Her companion looked wholly unfamiliar to Leah, though he wore similar clothing and a similar expression.

Like children setting out to do something naughty, Leah thought. *And they just traded a bunch of big coins for smaller ones so they could spread out their payments over a long evening.*

Just then the woman turned her head and the gaslight from the overhead lamps set something in her hair to sparkling.

Glass beads. Part of her coiffure. *The woman from the Karkades,* Leah realized. Seka Mardis, that was her name. She'd changed into Welchin clothing so she could blend into her surroundings more convincingly, but she hadn't bothered to comb the jewels out of her hair. *And she stopped by the money-changer's booth to swap Karkan coins for Welchin ones,* Leah thought. *So what is she planning to buy?*

Leah was sure Darien Serlast would like her to find out. And in her current state of mind, an adventure perfectly suited her mood. She hovered in the shadows a few moments, watching the Karkans confer. When they finally walked forward in a purposeful fashion, she followed them.

They circled halfway around the Plaza of Men before pausing in the shade of a horse-trading booth that had been shut up for the night. Moments later, they were joined by a third figure whose movements were even stealthier than theirs. The shape was tall enough for Leah to assume the newcomer was a man, though not a particularly robust one. Although he a wore a hooded cloak, which obscured his face and completely hid his body, he still gave the impression of being almost painfully thin. She couldn't tell anything else about his physical characteristics or style of dress. But Seka Mardis and her companion were definitely Karkan, so Leah was guessing he was, too.

A man taking extraordinary pains to make sure he was not seen—or, if seen, not recognized. Could this be the crown prince Darien believed had arrived secretly in Chialto?

Seka Mardis and the two men continued their circuit of the Plaza, staying out of the light as much as possible. Leah followed suit. Eventually they veered onto the walkway connecting the Plaza to the closest loop of the Cinque, where traffic was heavy even at this time of night. *If they've got a smoker car waiting, I'll never be able to keep up,* Leah thought.

But they didn't. They idled over to join a ragtag group waiting for the next public transport; when it wheezed into view, they hopped on. Leah had to scramble to cross the road and swing onto the omnibus before it took off at its typically sedate pace.

The transport was large enough to hold thirty or forty people—some seated, some standing—all of them swaying in unison with the vehicle's movements. A few, like Leah, clung to handles welded to the exterior and planted their feet on the low ledge that ran around the sides and the back of the vehicle. The interior was dimly lit, so she peered in through the window to see if she could get a better look at her quarry. Seka Mardis and her male companion still looked furtive and excited; she continued to hold her hand clenched firmly in her pocket. Their tall friend kept his hooded head turned away from the others, as if he was staring out the window, watching the city glide past. Leah looked away so they wouldn't catch her staring.

They had started out on the northwestern edge of the Cinque and were traveling steadily south, very soon passing the Plaza of Women. Leah remained poised to jump off the transport as soon as the Karkans disembarked. But they stayed on board through the neighborhoods populated mostly by young unmarried men, where the crown prince might have gone seeking companionship if his tastes ran that way. They kept to their seats as the vehicle lumbered past the poorer neighborhoods where a wealthy visitor could purchase almost any type of hallucinogen or narcotic. The Karkans didn't get to their feet and ask the omnibus to stop until it was halfway down the long, nervous section of the Cinque that overlooked the southside slums. Then they exited as one tight-knit group and began striding straight south, Seka Mardis giggling a little.

Leah jumped down from the transport, hastily fading into the closest shadows but hesitating a moment before cautiously following. Five years of living on the fringes of Malinquese society had taught her to never leave her lodgings without a weapon, and she hadn't managed to shake the habit since she'd returned to Chialto. But she wasn't really armed for self-defense in the southside ghettos. She had a pretty wicked blade strapped to her ankle, but no backup weapon and no real desire to be in a situation where she might need one. She almost couldn't believe the Karkans had really intended the slums to be their destination; she was tempted to run after them, a kindly stranger warning them that they must have taken a wrong turn somewhere.

But she remembered Chandran's letter, where he wrote of the debauchery and excesses of the royal family. Maybe the crown prince was looking for something he didn't think he could find anywhere else in the city, though it was hard to imagine what he could obtain here that he couldn't procure elsewhere under less perilous circumstances. Well, Leah would follow them as long as she felt safe.

She bent to retrieve her dagger from its sheath and melted behind them through the chilly darkness.

It was probably a couple of hours before midnight, and the southside was just waking up. About half the buildings she passed were dark and shuttered, apparently wholly abandoned, but the other half were pulsing with life and noise. Light spilled out through broken windows and half-hung doors. Everywhere were the sounds of men arguing, women laughing, glass shattering, bodies falling. Every shadow Leah passed seemed to have two or three darker shadows hiding within. When she looked quickly enough, she could catch the gleam of eyeballs before the lurkers hurriedly glanced away. There were no gaslit streetlamps, as there were throughout the rest of Chialto. The only illumination came from the windows of those taverns and flophouses. Leah stepped carefully, not wanting her feet to land in piles of refuse or puddles of unidentifiable fluid.

The three Karkans kept moving steadily ahead of her, sticking to the middle of the heavily potholed road. Leah was a little surprised that none of the locals had crept up behind them, attempting to lift a wallet. Then she caught the glint of metal in Seka Mardis's hand. Ah. So the clever little envoy had left off clutching her pocket full of coins and was now openly displaying a dagger. A much smarter posture in her current environment.

Leah was so focused on her quarry that for a moment she forgot to pay close attention to her surroundings, and she felt the brush of light fingertips along her left arm. She spun that way, showing her knife, and a child-size shape tumbled back from her and disappeared. She cursed under her breath and hurried to catch up with the Karkans. They were just rounding a corner and veering to the left when she spotted them again. She warily followed.

Nothing ahead of them but more broken houses, ruined pavement, and desperate souls. In fact, the farther they got from the Cinque, the worse the streets looked. Fewer and fewer buildings showed any evidence of life; if any commercial activity was going on, it was of the most unsavory kind and taking place behind triple-locked doors. It wasn't hard to imagine scenes of horror behind any of those dilapidated walls—drug-addled bodies writhing on filthy mats, rooms full of underfed orphans waiting to be sold into slavery. Leah felt her shoulders itch with revulsion. Her dagger suddenly seemed flimsy and unconvincing in her hand.

Seka Mardis and her companions slowed their pace. They peered into the narrow spaces between buildings, the alleys between streets. The young male Karkan even bent low to check behind empty barrels and under squat bushes. They weren't looking for a specific address then, Leah surmised. They were looking for . . . something they would know when they found it.

Leah was pretty sure she wouldn't like whatever it was they found.

The Karkans went another broken block before they came to an untidy halt and whispered among themselves. Leah slunk back to huddle under the eaves of what she devoutly hoped was an empty building. She was close enough to hear the sound of Seka Mardis's feet tapping across the pockmarked pavement, the low tones of her voice as she bent to address what looked like a bundle of rags on the edge of the street.

"Hello," she said in Coziquela. "How would you like to make a little money?"

There was silence for a moment. The bundle of rags might be dead, Leah thought, or so juiced on drugs that nothing else registered. But then the pitiful pile stirred and gathered itself into what might be the shape of a sitting creature.

"How much money?" it answered. The high, thin voice was that of a teen girl or a somewhat younger boy. Leah was betting girl.

"Two quint-golds," Seka Mardis replied.

The pile seemed to consider, then shook its head and sank back into an amorphous puddle.

Seka Mardis glanced back at the crown prince, who made a sharp gesture. *Try again* was Leah's interpretation.

Seka Mardis's as well. She leaned over again and said, "Five quint-golds."

The girl levered herself to a half-sitting position. "To do what?"

"Come with us and see."

"How far?"

"Very close."

The girl held her hand out and Seka Mardis carefully balanced five glinting coins in her palm. The girl tucked her hand into some hidden pocket, then pushed herself with some effort to her feet. Seka Mardis stepped close enough to take the girl's wrist in one hand, putting her other arm around the girl's waist. Even from where she was hiding, Leah could tell that the creature stank of vomit and feces and urine. But Seka Mardis did not hesitate or flinch as she guided the girl to where the others were standing.

"Where to?" Seka asked.

The male pointed behind them. "We passed a place about a block that way. Door was half open, but it looked empty. I'll go in and scout around." He glanced at their new employee. "Take you a while to walk that far, anyway."

"I'll walk with you," the crown prince said to Seka, speaking for the first time that Leah had heard. His voice was surprisingly deep and resonant. "For protection. For anticipation."

Leah felt serpents of horror slither up her spine. What did they intend to do to this poor child?

The young man stepped briskly away, swiveling his head from side to side to watch for danger. The rest of them followed. The prince had taken the girl's other arm, so now the two of them were helping her down the street with an almost unbearable solicitousness. Leah let them get a few paces ahead, then silently trailed after them.

Should she stop them? Whatever the Karkans were planning to do, it had to be carried out with the greatest stealth. That didn't mean it was something terrible, she supposed, just something they didn't particularly want their foreign hosts to witness. And as long as they had paid the young girl—as long as she was willing—

Almost as soon as Leah had the thought, the Welchin girl seemed to change her mind. She stumbled and appeared to try to pull back against the hands that held her. Leah heard her voice raised in a ragged question, heard Seka Mardis's comforting response: "Everything will be fine, you'll see."

"No," said the girl, growing more agitated. "No, I don't want to. No—"

Seka Mardis uttered an impatient oath and yanked the girl forward. The girl started wailing and moaning, thrashing her body about, trying to get free. Leah glanced around quickly, wondering if anyone might hear and come to her rescue. But there were no royal guards in the southside slums. No one to call on for help. She might scream her throat raw and no one would even glance her way.

The crown prince raised his voice above the girl's keening, asking Seka Mardis a question. "Right there," she answered, pointing at one of the nearby abandoned structures. Leah assumed that was where their third companion had slipped inside to prepare for the night's activity. The prince nodded, took a stronger grip on the girl's arm, and began dragging her in that direction with no more pretense of gentleness. The girl cried out and fell to her knees. The Karkans pulled her roughly off the street and through a sagging doorway into darkness.

Leah could still hear the girl's desperate cries. She had to do something.

A whiff of acrid smoke tickled her nose, and she jerked her head around to track the source. Three young men had gathered around a barrel and were passing a grimy bottle from hand to hand. Their faces were partially illuminated by a small fire they seemed to have started deep inside the barrel—possibly to stay warm, possibly to cook whatever drug they were sharing now.

I can work with that, Leah thought.

She glanced back at the one-story building where the Karkans had taken cover. It was so ancient and tumbledown that it looked as if it might collapse on top of them if they accidentally bumped into the walls. Leah thought she saw a brief flash of light within, as if one of the Karkans had struck a match or lit a candle. Illumination so they could see whatever they planned to do next.

She took a deep breath, balanced on her toes, then crashed through the darkness, straight at the young men around the barrel. She grabbed their contraband bottle before any of them realized what was happening.

"*Hey!*" one of them shouted, swiping at her arm. But she backed away, spun around, and ran for the building the Karkans had occupied. There were more yells behind her and the sounds of footfalls racing in pursuit. She burst through the door, the addicts right behind her, and then everything turned to mayhem.

Seka Mardis screamed, the prince let out a yelp of surprise, and suddenly there were bodies everywhere, punching, flying, staggering, rolling across the floor. There was barely enough light to see, and there was so much commotion that it was impossible to tell who was landing a blow and who was taking it. Someone crashed against the wall with such force that the whole place shivered. Someone else must have gotten sliced across the arm, because Leah could see a figure holding up a hand and crying, "I'm bleeding!" Leah hurled the bottle all the way across the open room and heard the satisfying sound of glass shattering against wood.

That caused more of an uproar as the addicts wailed and the Karkans shouted in alarm. The crown prince uttered a panicked cry in words Leah didn't understand, and suddenly the three foreigners were shoving each other to get out the door. Two of the young slum dwellers went after them, while the third one sank to his knees and began sobbing.

Leah turned her attention to the figure in the filthy strips of clothing. Yes—as she'd thought—a girl, whose ruined face looked like it belonged to someone barely sixteen years old. "Let's get you out of here," Leah said, slipping a hand under her arm.

The girl fended her off. "Go 'way—go 'way!" she shouted. Her eyes were wide with fear and maybe a narcotic.

"I won't hurt you—"

"That's what *they* said!" the girl snarled, snatching her arm free from Leah's grip. As if that act of defiance had sapped her of all energy, the girl sank to the floor and pillowed her head on her stick-thin arms. "Just leave me alone," she mumbled.

Leah stared at her helplessly, then turned to look at the boy, who was still crying, silently now. He, too, had dropped to the floor, but he had curled himself into a tight ball as if to keep the misery from bursting out in one long, uncontrollable howl. The liquid that had flowed out of the smashed bottle had started to scent the stale air with a harsh, oily odor that made Leah want to gag. The single candle the Karkans had lit was still burning in a holder on the floor, undisturbed despite all the commotion.

"I can't stay here," Leah said to the girl, who might be sleeping by now, might be dead. "I'm going to be sick. You need to leave."

But the girl didn't answer. The addict didn't answer. Leah put a hand to her mouth and hurried out the door, ducking around the corner of the building to try to get a read on the situation.

The Karkans were long gone. She didn't know if they'd run all the way back to the Cinque or if she had just thwarted them from preying on this particular prize and they were even now trolling the slums a few streets over, hunting new game. She doubted that the addicts had chased them very far; they hadn't looked like they had the physical or mental stamina to engage in a real fight. She guessed they'd be back eventually—soon, if they had any kind of semipermanent base here, later if they'd gotten distracted by other possibilities in the night. They might not recognize her if they saw her again, but even so, she couldn't linger.

She cast one doubtful glance over her shoulder, as if she could see through the wall to the girl inside. Leah might have saved her from the crown prince's depredations, whatever they might be, but she could hardly hope that the young woman would be safe even so. She might not even live through the night.

Still. She's no worse off than she was when the prince found her, Leah thought. *Better—she has five quint-golds now. I have to think I did the right thing.*

But who else had she failed to save tonight? And what had she failed to save them from?

NINE

The day that followed the night could not have been more different.

By the time Leah had gotten back to her lodgings, it was so late she was barely able to manage four hours of sleep before she had to get up again. She didn't look quite as haggard as she would have expected, maybe because excitement flushed her face and she took extra care with her appearance. She braided her hair back with bits of gold thread, and she donned a dark green tunic heavily embroidered with the same thread in patterns of leaves and flowers. She added the emerald earrings Chandran had sent her, the emerald necklace she had bought at his shop, and a green Dhonshon shawl that she had also bought from Chandran.

I wish you were here to see me through this occasion, she thought as she made final adjustments in front of the mirror. *I wish you were here to help me figure out the world. I wish you were here.*

She was at the door of the boutique a little past dawn to find Annova there before her. "And yet they'll tell you coru folk are completely unreliable," Leah greeted her.

Annova looked amused. "You can rely on coru folk to do whatever they're interested in doing," she said. "I'm interested in this." She surveyed Leah a moment. "I like the jewels, but your face is tired."

"I had an interesting evening."

Annova waited for a beat, but when Leah didn't add any more, she just said, "Let's get started."

They set up a table in the back and laid out delicacies for the customers they hoped would drop by: keerza from Malinqua, fruited water from Welce, berries from Cozique, and pastries and candies from a half dozen other sources. Then they fed the reifarjin, filled the coin box with money, and flipped on the switch to illuminate the swirly sculpture that spelled out Leah's name.

At the propitious hour of eight in the morning, they formally opened the shop. By noon, they had had a hundred customers.

It was all due to Darien's connections, of course. Zoe came with a whole cadre of friends and relatives, who strolled around the shop and exclaimed over the merchandise and purchased an eclectic selection of treasures.

"I think the reifarjin adds just the right touch," Zoe said as she paid for a silver starfish charm that had been crafted in Berringey and displayed in the coru section. "Exotic and unexpected. Like everything else in this shop."

"Thank you," Leah said, handing back a few quint-silvers in change. "I need to talk to Darien."

Zoe raised her eyebrows. She didn't say, *Tell me the news and I'll pass it on.* She merely asked, "How soon?"

"As soon as he has time."

"I'll let him know."

About an hour after Zoe left, Princess Josetta arrived, accompanied by a middle-aged blond woman who was a bit overdressed for a shopping expedition but gratifyingly pleased with many of the wares on display.

"Look at this feathered mask! I must have it—for the next opening, you know, everyone dresses in such an *opulent* style that it is impossible to appear too gaudy. Oh, and this! The butterfly hair clip! In my colors, too."

"Queen Seterre," Annova murmured to Leah. "Josetta's mother. She's a patron of the theatrical arts."

That explained the overdramatic style. "She seems nice enough."

Annova shrugged. "These days. Not always in the past."

"Well, we all change," Leah said.

She went over to see if they were looking for anything they hadn't been able to find, and Josetta offered more formal introductions. They were quite a contrast—quiet, earnest Josetta and her flamboyant mother—but Leah sensed a strong bond of affection between them.

"I love your shop! You have such fresh merchandise!" the queen exclaimed. "I will be back, I promise you, and will bring many of my friends with me."

"Majesty, I will be delighted."

Seterre wandered off to examine items on the hunti tables; Josetta smiled at Leah. "I hope you like actors."

Leah laughed. "I spent half my life around them."

"Ah. Then you already know."

Leah smiled but immediately grew serious. "I was in your part of town last night and wishing I'd known exactly how to find your shelter."

Josetta looked intrigued. "I can draw you a map, if you like. There are scarcely any street signs so it's hard to give directions. It's best to visit in the daylight, at least the first time you're trying to find it. Why were you there?"

"It's a long story. But I encountered a young woman who seemed on the verge of complete disintegration. If I'd had someplace to take her—"

Josetta nodded soberly. "There are people like that throughout the southside. I'll take in anyone who comes to my door but—some people don't want to stay. Even if you brought her to me, you couldn't be sure I'd do her any good."

"Maybe not. But at least I'd have tried."

"That's all any of us can do."

Josetta and her mother were still wandering through the store, along with five or six other customers, when Virrie arrived with Mally.

"I gave her three silvers and told her she could spend them all in the shop," Virrie confided to Leah as Mally gravely toured the tables.

"She can simply *have* anything she wants," Leah answered.

Virrie shook her head. "Mally likes to have boundaries. She likes to know that making a choice means she has to give up something else. She likes to think that actions have consequences. It makes her feel like the world makes sense."

"The world *doesn't* make sense," Leah grumbled.

Annova laughed at her silently. "Maybe it does," she said. "It's just that the pattern is too big for us to see."

"She'll buy rocks," Leah predicted.

"Probably," Virrie replied.

New customers swept up to the front counter just then, and Leah spent the next twenty minutes explaining the provenance of some of her more unusual items, then finalizing sales, making change, and wrapping purchases. That group was barely out the door before Virrie was leading Mally up to the sales counter.

Leah smiled down at the little girl, who was digging for money in the pockets of her tunic. "And what has caught your fancy today, young lady? Something from the torz section, I'm guessing?"

"Well, that's what I like," Mally said, setting her selection on the counter. It was a small object carved from a smooth, glassy chunk of rock so red it appeared to be tinged with blood. The shape was a broad spreading flower—a lotus or an overblown rose—with a flat base so it sat easily on the counter. There was a slim hollow in the center of the bloom, about the size of a woman's smallest finger.

Leah picked it up and examined it as if she hadn't seen it before, as if she hadn't selected it herself from a shipment of goods that had come directly from Berringey. "It's beautiful," she said solemnly. "The shape and the material make it torz, but the color is pure sweela. And you see this hole here? In the middle? You can fit a small candle right there. Sweela again. I couldn't decide where in the shop I should put it."

"I like sweela," Mally said.

"Wouldn't know it from the things you're interested in doing," Virrie said dryly. "Or eating or wearing."

"Nelson's sweela," Leah said.

Mally nodded. "And Rhan."

Leah's heart skipped a beat. "And Rhan," she agreed calmly.

"Rhan dropped by to visit us yesterday," Virrie said casually.

"Did he?" Leah said, her voice neutral. She hoped. "How friendly of him."

"They played games. She enjoyed herself. I was glad he came."

"Then so am I." *Surely he won't give her so much attention that he steals her from me. Surely I can't be jealous of her own father's affection.*

It's just that I have so little of her already. I hate to give up any more. "I don't think of Rhan as being particularly good with children."

"Well," Virrie said, still dry, "he's not very adult, now, is he?"

"I suppose not," Leah said, forcing herself to shake off her mood. She smiled down at her youngest customer. "That will be three silvers exactly! Let me wrap this up for you."

There wasn't time to visit with Mally, or brood over Rhan, because a new cluster of customers clattered into the shop just then. And once again Leah and Annova were showing, explaining, and selling merchandise. They continued to be just as busy till nightfall signaled closing time, and they could turn off the **LEAH'S** sign and lock the door.

"An *exceptional* opening day!" Leah exclaimed. "I would have been happy with *half* this many customers."

"Good thing you insisted on filling your storeroom upstairs with so much merchandise," Annova said. "Should we restock now or wait until the morning?"

Leah fought back a yawn. "We *should* do it now, but I'm too tired to think straight," she said. "I'll just make sure to get here early tomorrow."

"I'll come as early as I can," Annova said.

Leah strangled another yawn. "Go on. I'll lock up."

Leah found it rather pleasant to putter through the shop now that it was deserted, though it still seemed to hum with the remembrance of many voices, many bodies. She moved slowly through the aisles, straightening a pile here, folding a length of fabric there, moving a basket from one shelf to another. At the back wall, she flipped the switch that killed the interior lighting, so shadows leapt forward from all corners, though the gaslamps from the street outside threw faint illumination through the big display windows. She went through the door on the back wall to make sure the alley entrance was securely locked, pausing a moment to glance up the stairs. *I really am too tired to make the effort,* she thought, slipping back into the shop and locking the inner door as well.

She turned around and almost screamed. There was a large figure standing just inside the front door. Motionless. Focused on her. The light was behind him so she couldn't see his face or any details of his clothing. For a moment, she could neither move nor breathe.

Then he extended his hand and turned his face just enough so she could make out his profile: a prominent forehead, generous nose, thickly bearded cheeks and chin. "Leah," he said.

"Chandran," she whispered.

Now she really couldn't breathe.

"*Chandran*," Leah repeated. Her voice lightened and her heart lightened and all of her weariness melted away. "Chandran! I can't believe it! Why are you here?" She flew across the shop with her hands outstretched.

She didn't know if she would have hugged him—should have hugged him—but before she had to decide what, exactly, she would do with her arms, he stepped forward and took her hands in his. His grip was warm and powerful and exceedingly comforting, and he tucked her hands against his chest and smiled down at her.

"You got my earrings, I see," he said.

She laughed. She felt giddy. *Not enough sleep, not enough air, too much delight.* It took her a moment to realize he had spoken in Coziquela, the language they had always used when talking together in Malinqua. She couldn't even remember what language she had used to greet him. But, of course, happiness and excitement translated in any tongue. "I wrote and thanked you! Didn't you get my letter?"

"I have received many letters from you and cherished them all. I meant—you got my earrings and you chose to wear them. I am so pleased."

"But what are you *doing* here? I've missed you so much! But I never thought— Did something happen? Is something wrong?"

He considered. She had forgotten that, how he could take his time formulating an answer to even the simplest question. "Many things have happened," he said. "Nothing new is wrong. But old wrongs might have reappeared."

Her smile contracted into an expression of worry. "That sounds ominous. That sounds *bad*. Can you tell me about it?" *Will you tell me?* was what she really wanted to ask. During those ninedays when she had worked beside him in his booth in the Great Market, Chandran had learned a great deal about Leah, while she had learned very little about him. She knew he was an exile from his homeland. She knew he was convinced he could never return. He had never described the circumstances that led him to flee.

"I can tell you some of it," he replied.

Slowly she pulled her hands free, and slowly she gestured at the front door. "Can you tell me the story while we're somewhere that we can get food? I've just had scraps all day and I'm starving."

He thought about that, too. "I am not anxious for my tale to be overheard," he answered at last.

Ah. "Then . . . we can buy something and take it back to my apartment."

Chandran glanced around the storefront. "Or we could bring it back here," he countered.

He didn't want the suggestive intimacy of being in her private quarters, Leah realized. She couldn't tell if she was relieved or offended. But she thought she knew Chandran well enough to guess at the meaning behind his reluctance. He did not want to put *her* at a disadvantage. He did not want to encroach or presume. He knew that his arrival was sudden and disruptive and that she had had no time to think about how she might fit him into her life—whereas he had obviously had a long ocean journey to mull over that very question. He did not want to take advantage of taking her by surprise.

"We could bring it back here," she agreed. "There's a place up the street that offers a different menu every day. Let's see what they've got."

A half hour later, they were back at the shop, setting up a small feast. Leah cleared off the hunti display to serve as their dining table, and Chandran moved storage units over to take the place of stools. Leah added both water and fruit to one of the glass pitchers from the back table and heated up a pot of keerza.

They did all this by candlelight, sacrificing a few of the least expensive sweela items in the shop. "I'm afraid if I turn the gaslight back on, someone will think the place is still open," Leah said with a laugh. "We were *so busy* today!"

"I know. I walked by once or twice but I decided not to interrupt you."

"Interrupt?" she retorted. "I'd have *hired* you! Put you to work! We could have used the extra hands."

"Ah. Then I should have come right in."

Their banter was easy and light, the meal preparation companionable, but Leah was aware of a sharp current of tension. Clearly they had much to discuss; clearly he didn't want to discuss it until they were settled and focused on each other, unlikely to be distracted. It was hard not to feel uneasy.

Finally everything was ready and they took their unconventional seats. Chandran raised his glass of fruited water. "To Leah's," he said.

"To Leah's," she echoed. "May it always be successful, just not quite this successful."

"Surely some of today's customers came simply for the novelty."

"And because the regent's wife brought her friends and Corene's sister brought *her* friends and because I myself have contacts among the Five Families," Leah added. "But yes. Because people were curious and wanted to see what might be for sale in this new shop."

"Were you surprised by what people bought? What went differently than you expected?"

They talked commerce for a while, debated retail strategies, and estimated how quickly she'd have to replenish her backup supplies. All the while they ate their food, drank their water, and watched each other by candlelight. Not much to be learned from Chandran's face in such faint illumination. Truth to tell, there was never much to learn from Chandran's face.

"So tell me," she finally said, when they'd each finished their last piece of bread, their last spoonful of compote. "Why are you here? I'm happy to see you—but I'm worried that your arrival signals a calamity in your life."

"Maybe," he said. "A calamity that was a long time coming."

She sipped her water and waited, watching him collect his thoughts. The candlelight left his dark eyes enigmatic, his bearded face a mask. Or maybe that was just always how he looked.

"I have lived in Malinqua for nearly fifteen years," he said at last, speaking in slow, thoughtful tones. "You knew me as a merchant, but when I first arrived in Palminera, I had no thought of setting up a retail shop. I needed a job and I was good with horses, so I hired on at the large commercial stables down by the red tower."

"I know that place."

"Life is full of unexpected connections, so after I had worked in the stables for a year, a man who liked my way with his horses hired me for a post at the Great Market, in one of the horse trader's stalls. While I was there, I became friendly with a family who owned a booth on the fourth floor. They were importers and had received a shipment from Cozique that baffled them. I was able to explain. I began to help out when they needed assistance in the booth. Gradually I became a full-time employee and then part owner."

"Was there a woman involved?" Leah asked. "I used to think you must have married into the business."

Chandran regarded her for a moment. "There was a woman who *could* have been involved," he said. "But that interest waned when I explained that I had a wife."

"*Ohhhhhh.*" Leah didn't know what to say. He'd never mentioned a wife. He'd never mentioned anybody. *I'm an idiot,* she thought. *I've built him into some kind of romantic figure, and even though I knew half of it was my imagination, I never realized just how impossible that picture was.* She felt her cheeks redden in the dark. Had he realized how she'd thought of him? How she hoped he'd think of her? She thought of all those letters she'd written him in the past few ninedays, pouring out her thoughts and her dreams, hinting at her desires. She could only be unutterably grateful that she had never sent them.

"I did not mention that my wife was dead," Chandran added. "I let her assume—let all of them assume—that we were merely estranged. The woman's attentions were quickly engaged elsewhere, which was better for all of us."

Leah still felt flushed and embarrassed, though a little more cheerful upon learning that he was a widower. But that made her feel heartless, so she quickly said, "I'm sorry about your wife. That must have been very difficult."

"'Difficult' is hardly a big enough word to cover it," he said quietly. "It has been fifteen years now, and I still think about her death."

"I'm sorry," she said again.

"As I say, I continued to work for the family of merchants. When it became clear that the owner's son was not interested in running the business after him, and neither was his daughter, or her new husband, my employer allowed me to systematically buy him out. I have been part owner, and then the owner, of the business for more than ten years. It has been a very good life."

Leah found herself leaning forward slightly. "So what happened? Why are you here now?"

"A couple of ninedays ago, when I was working at the Great Market, I was recognized by someone I had not seen in fifteen years. He thought I did not see him, but I did. And I saw the look that crossed his face when he realized who I was. He did not approach me then, but I knew it was only a matter of time. And so I locked up my booth as I always do, and I went to my lodgings and gathered my things, and I went straight to the harbor and booked passage on the first boat I could find that was headed to Welce. I figured that as long as I was starting my life over, I might as well start it in a country where I knew at least one other human being."

"But—why—I don't understand. Just because he recognized you—"

"He is a member of my wife's family," Chandran said, as if that explained everything. "A cousin. And all of them hate me beyond reason."

"But why?" she said again, a little helplessly. He was telling his story, but in a very roundabout fashion, and she felt like she hadn't even come close to the heart of the tale.

"First, I must explain about my wife and her family," Chandran said. "You have always known, I think, that I come originally from Cozique."

"I guessed you did," she said. "You never actually said so."

"My father was a man of some wealth, who derived most of his money from trade. It has always been common among people of my station to marry for the good of the family. For connections."

Leah nodded. "It's common among the Five Families in Chialto, too."

"My father wished for me to marry into the family of one of his trading partners in the Karkades. The woman he had selected was beautiful, fascinating, and full of charm. And I was young—barely twenty-two. I was dazzled. I believed I was in love. I was happy to marry her."

Something in his voice made Leah sit up straighter. Just a few moments ago, he had said he was still not recovered from his wife's death, so she had pictured him heartbroken, inconsolable, bravely hiding grief behind a stoic mask. But she sensed that a different picture was about to emerge.

"Both of our families wished for us to live in the Karkades, and I was willing to do so," Chandran continued. "But I found their customs strange. They were—I believe I mentioned this in a letter to you—a people of extremes. Capable of great kindness and great cruelty. More than that. They relished cruelty—they embraced it. Because they believed they could erase the most heinous act by doing something equally magnificent to balance it out. Most people will not do truly awful things because they fear the consequences—the wrath of an angry mob or the castigation of a righteous god or the measured punishment of a respected legal system. These deterrents keep them somewhat in check.

"But the Karkans have no such fears. They do what they want, no matter how brutal or selfish it might be, because they have already accepted that they must atone. Sometimes they atone beforehand. A woman who wants to cheat on her husband, for instance, might buy him a very expensive gift before she ever strays, and they both understand this means that she has banked her forgiveness in advance. I had a difficult time understanding this particular form of moral barter."

"I can see why," Leah said. "But it seems like a system that would only work for the very rich."

"Certainly, it was among the wealthy that you would see the greatest excesses," Chandran admitted. "But the attitude prevailed at every level of society. There was a story about a woman who lived in the most impoverished section of town. She threw her infant son from a bridge one afternoon because she could not stand the sound of his crying. What redemption can there be for a woman who kills her own child? Later, she took in the children left fatherless when her brother died, and she raised them to be fine, strong men and women, sacrificing everything to keep them warm and fed. The children knew why she was so generous to them. Everyone knew. It was accepted that she had expiated her first unforgivable sin."

"I would find it a difficult system in which to operate," Leah admitted.

"As did I. And yet the Karkades are a beautiful place, and I had a beautiful wife, and I had quite a lot of money, and life seemed very good. My wife was—she had an incredible delicacy of complexion. Skin so white, with the faintest flush along the cheekbones, and the loveliest, most elegant hands. I used to be afraid to touch her sometimes, she looked so fragile, so perfect. I did not want my clumsy fingers to leave behind a bruise. When she slept at night, her face was so innocent it looked like it belonged to a child.

"There was a town nearby—a dreadful place—the wretched spot where they consigned anyone who had been touched by one particular disease. It was hereditary and incurable, and those who contracted it died a lingering and painful death. Most of the philanthropists of the day would throw money that way, funding research into possible cures and paying for nurses and physicians who would treat the ill. But my wife would go there, several times every quintile, and minister to the sick. She would bring food that she herself had cooked in our kitchens. She would take their fevered hands in hers, she would bathe them in cool water. She became attached to the members of one particular family, and she was there beside every single one of them when they died. She paid for every funeral. There were seven of them, I believe. Maybe eight. All dead now."

It was an act of staggering generosity, but Leah was starting to feel her lungs tighten up. If a woman would do something so benevolent, so selfless, for so many, what great sins might she commit without fear of condemnation? "I suppose," she said, speaking carefully, "this was only one side of her personality."

Chandran nodded. "You have perceived the drift of my tale. For the first two years that we were married, I saw only Dederra's sweet side. Her goodness. I thought she had escaped the Karkan taint—that she was perfect and pure. It turned out not to be so." He gazed for a moment at the dregs of keerza leaves in his cup. "I cannot imagine any circumstances for the rest of my life that will ever leave me so disillusioned," he said at last.

"Did she— What did she do?" Leah asked.

Chandran stared at his cup a while longer, then lifted his eyes to hers. "Terrible things," he said. "Unspeakable."

"You won't tell me if I ask?" she said, pressing a little.

He shook his head. "I do not want you to entertain those images in your head. I wish I did not have to live with them." He gave her a serious look. "I realize this means you might not believe her actions were as monstrous as I claim."

"I believe you," she said instantly.

"I am grateful for that."

"So these terrible things . . . Had she been doing them all along, or did she start after she had—had banked her forgiveness in advance?"

"I am not sure when she began indulging in this particular vice, but within a few years of our marriage, she was completely in its thrall. I would even say she was out of control."

"What did you do?"

"At first, I went to her family members, thinking that by speaking of her behavior publicly I might shame her out of repeating it. But they were indifferent—her siblings, her parents, her cousins. They said, 'Yes, but she has already atoned.' They said, 'Oh, that is not so shocking. Do you want to know what this *other* fellow did?' They were unmoved.

"I was distraught. I wrote my own family—not sharing the details, not explaining what I had learned, merely saying that Dederra and I had found we were ill-suited after all and I planned to petition to dissolve the marriage. Divorce is not impossible in Cozique, though there are many inconvenient legal details, and my parents were deeply unhappy that I planned to sever this connection. But I was adamant. I filed the necessary papers and waited in the Karkades until the decree came through."

Leah was slightly confused. "So you are divorced then. You said your wife was dead."

"Yes," Chandran said. His voice sounded muffled, as if he was projecting it through his folded hands, or as if the thought of the words he had to say made him almost too exhausted to speak. "She died before the divorce was finalized."

"So she knew you were leaving her."

"She did, and she thought it was amusing that I would abandon her for such a reason. We were still sharing a house—if I had simply walked out, I would have lost all claim to the fortune we had amassed between us as our families continued their trade arrangements. But my belongings were packed. I had purchased my tickets for the journey home to Cozique. I was merely waiting for a single final paper to be signed."

Leah's stomach was in knots. She wished she hadn't eaten quite so much of the delicious meal. She was filled with dread. "So then—what happened?"

"I found evidence of something she had done—inside our own house. I confronted her, and she laughed. She said, 'Just think what I will be capable of after you are gone.'"

Chandran looked at Leah, his eyes deep pools of darkness. "So I killed her. And then I sailed for Malinqua."

TEN

For the longest time, Leah couldn't move. Her body had ossified to startled stone; she was a statue of shock and horror. She did not feel the air enter or leave her lungs. Her fingers, spread on the table, could detect no texture of wood or cloth against their skin. The shop was filled with a roaring silence that pressed against her ears, blocking out any sounds of the surrounding night.

They were alone in this place. No one in the entire city knew that Chandran was in Chialto—no one even knew who Chandran *was*. He was taller than Leah by at least five inches, heavier by more than seventy pounds. She could snatch at the knife strapped to her ankle, the assorted cutlery spread across the table, but the odds were still against her. He could strangle her or fall on her body and suffocate her, and she would be virtually defenseless.

It would not be the first time he had tried to kill her.

It would not be the first time he had killed a woman.

Leah stared at him and he stared back at her, and she could read nothing in his face at all.

After a long moment, with a nod, he looked away. "So," he said. "As I always thought. It is not an action for which it is possible to seek forgiveness. Circumstances do not ameliorate the sin."

Moving slowly—perhaps so he did not frighten her into flight—Chandran pushed himself away from the table and drew himself up to his imposing height. "I will return to the harbor at dawn and book passage somewhere else," he said. "You need not fear hearing from me again."

He had crossed the floor and laid a hand on the doorknob before Leah was able to speak. "Wait," she said. Her voice scraped against her throat as the word fought its way out.

He paused and bowed his head, but did not turn around to face her. "There does not appear to be much point in waiting," he said.

Leah forced herself to stand, though her legs wobbled and she had to keep a hand on the table to maintain her balance. "Why did you come here tonight? Why did you come to Welce? Why did you want to see me?"

Slowly, still leaving a hand on the doorknob, he shifted his body around so he could see her. "Because the one thing in the past fifteen years that has brought me anything approximating joy has been meeting you," he said deliberately. "I thought I should see if I could recapture that emotion before I gave up on it forever."

She felt steady enough now to walk in his direction, though she came to a halt a few feet away. Just out of reach of a blow from his hand. "And why did you tell me the story about your wife? I never would have learned it on my own. You knew it would terrify me. So why tell me?"

"Because I never again want to attempt to build a life that has a lie at the core."

"I've missed you," she said. "So much."

"I cannot tell you how much I have missed you."

"But this frightens me."

"It would frighten anyone, I think."

"I don't know—I don't know what to tell you next. I don't know what to think."

"You do not have to think. I have already decided. I will leave Welce in the morning."

"No."

She blurted out the word without thinking. She could hardly say she'd thought the situation through. But . . . "No," she said again. "Give me time to absorb it. Give me time to—to understand it. Don't leave yet."

"Fear does not make a better foundation for a relationship than secrecy," Chandran replied.

"It doesn't," Leah said. "But maybe after I've thought about it, I won't be afraid."

He looked undecided. "And maybe you will. But you will be afraid to even mention the word 'fear' to me."

She couldn't help smiling in the near-dark. "I have some resources at my disposal," she said. "If I asked him for protection, the regent would give me a dozen soldiers to shield me from your violence."

"If you could predict when I would grow violent," Chandran pointed out. "Which you could not."

"We could add other safeguards," Leah said. "I could agree to see you only in public places. No more of this"—she swept a hand out to indicate the soft lighting in the shadowed store—"kind of setting," she ended lamely.

"That might do," he said. "For a time, at least. Until you decide, one way or another, if I can be trusted." He dropped his hand from the doorknob and turned to fully face her, though he did not step any closer. "Until you become convinced, absolutely and unwaveringly certain, that I will never do you any harm."

Leah tried for another smile, though it was rueful. "Unless I do something so dreadful that I deserve to be put to death."

"Even then," Chandran said. "I would not be the one to carry out the sentence. I have done with vengeance. I am not suited to the aftermath of regret."

Leah was chasing down an errant memory. "You told me once— back in Malinqua—you said that you would change the situation that led you to act but that you weren't sorry for what you actually did. Feeling as you do now, would you still have— Would you still have killed her? Or would you simply have left?"

He thought it over for a long time. "I would have tried to find some other way to disable her," he said at last. "But I could not have simply left her to operate at will." He glanced at her. "Perhaps I am not as reformed as I would like to think. But at any rate, I will never offer harm to you."

So you once thought about Dederra, Leah thought, *she of the pale cheeks and elegant hands.* "I have never been in a situation when I thought the world would be a better place if someone was dead," Leah said. "I don't know how I would act then."

"I hope you are never offered the opportunity to find out."

"But we have come to a decision? You will stay—for a while at least—and we will try to determine how to go forward? You will not simply pretend you have agreed to this scheme and then sail away tomorrow?"

"I promise to let you know if I plan to change my circumstances," he said.

"Then why don't you come back in the morning? *You* can work for *me* this time. See if you like that."

"Unless my presence here makes you uneasy."

"Annova will be here. And probably dozens of customers. We won't be alone."

"Then I will see you in the morning," he said, reaching for the door again.

She raised her voice to make sure she had his attention. "You realize," she said, "that there is no safety for you in Welce, either. There is a contingent of Karkans here—three that I have seen, and doubtless more acting as spies. Who knows how many others might be on the way? Some of them are from the royal house and might be familiar with your face if you and your wife ever spent much time in such circles."

Chandran nodded. "We did. And the thought occurred to me. But they have no reason to think I would come to this country—no reason to be looking for me here—and many other matters to occupy their minds. I will be reasonably vigilant and hope to escape notice."

Now he opened the door, but Leah kept coming up with more questions to ask, reasons to make him stay and talk for another minute, another five. "Have you found a place to stay? I could recommend certain parts of town."

"Thank you, I have taken rooms near the Plaza of Men."

"All right. Then I'll see you in the morning."

He nodded, glanced back at her one last time, and quietly exited the shop.

Leah stood there for a long moment, staring at the closed door.

Was she a fool for wanting to trust him or a cold-blooded cynic for not believing in him with her whole heart? Had he spun her a story calculated to stir her emotions or bravely presented her with his darkest secret, believing it to be safe in her hands? Was he a good man or a bad man? How could she possibly be expected to judge?

The hour was late, she was exhausted, and it was out of her way, but Leah went to the nearest temple in search of guidance. She was lucky that, only a few steps out of the shop district, she came upon one of the for-hire elaymotives and bargained with the driver not only to take her to the temple, but also to wait for her while she went in to draw her blessings. She was pretty sure she wouldn't have been able to make the entire trek on foot.

She had thought the place might be deserted, but no—three people were there already. An old man sat on the red sweela bench, meditating silently, not bothering to open his eyes when she stepped in. And a young couple cuddled together on the green torz bench, looking away from each other long enough to give her quick smiles. The man had his hand pressed against the woman's flat belly, and she had her fingers wrapped around the back of his neck. They could not make it any more obvious that they were deeply in love.

"I'll draw blessings for you if you'll draw some for me," Leah told them in a quiet voice, trying not to disturb the old man. But as soon as she spoke, he opened one eye, seemed to shake himself awake, and pushed himself to his feet. He was short, thin, and a little frail, but his eyes were fiercely alert. Had to be sweela.

"Let us all participate in the ritual," he said, approaching the blessing barrel in the middle of the room. The rest of them crowded around it alongside him.

"I'll go first, if no one else wants to," the woman said shyly. So the other three stirred the coins and chose blessings and handed them over. Fertility. Hope. Love. Each one made her smile grow a little wider. "Oh! This is so— I haven't even told my parents yet, but—my husband and I are having a baby!"

"You are to be congratulated," the old man said, and Leah couldn't stop herself from giving the woman a hug.

"How exciting!" Leah said. "Your first?"

The young man laughed. "I might not be so terrified if it were our second or third!" He didn't look terrified. He looked delighted.

"Let's see what blessings the father receives," Leah said. They were equally propitious: Steadfastness. Patience. And again love. "I foresee a happy life for this lucky child," Leah said.

"Oh, I hope so," the woman replied.

They drew a much different set of blessings for the sweela man: Clarity. Persistence. Triumph. The collection of coins made his thin mouth turn up in a small smile. Leah thought that, of the four of them gathered in the temple right now, he was probably leading the most interesting life.

Although her own had gotten decidedly more interesting in the past night and day.

"Now you!" the woman said gaily, searching through the barrel for just the right coin. "It's surprise," she said, showing Leah the glyph. "I hope it's a happy one!"

Had it been? "I hope so, too," Leah replied.

The young father presented her with the coin showing the sign for honor. One that Leah had carried throughout her lifetime, one that Chandran had recently claimed, one that could very well apply to the story he had told tonight. Or not. "I always think this is a good blessing to have," he said.

"It can be a bleak one," the sweela man demurred.

"Yes, but it is a good *starting* place," the father argued. "You can build on honor."

"You can build on happiness, too," the other man retorted.

Plainly hoping to head off a philosophical discussion, the pregnant woman gestured at the sweela man. "Then you pick the next one for her to build upon."

Leah was hoping for something comforting like certainty or kindness, but it seemed the temple had run out of comfort once it had painted a bright future for the young couple. The disk the other man handed to her was featureless, worn smooth from much handling. "Ghost coin, I'm afraid," he said. "Not much guidance there."

Leah tried not to sigh. "That's the way it's been going lately," she said. "I'll figure it out on my own."

The young man put his arm around his wife's shoulders and gave a squeeze. "Let's get you home. I know you're tired."

On the words, she yawned, then laughed. "If I can walk that far!"

"I hired an elaymotive," Leah said. "If anyone wants a ride." She looked at the old man. "You, too. There should be room for all of us."

"Only if you allow me to pay," he said.

Leah laughed out loud. "I'll split it with you," she offered. "I had a good day in terms of finances."

"Then I accept."

The young man seemed undecided, though his wife looked hopeful. Leah's deduction was that they didn't have much money, but he didn't want to shirk their responsibilities. He began, "Perhaps we should—" but the sweela man interrupted him.

"Our gift to the unborn child," he said. "You can't refuse."

So they all crowded into the elaymotive, and Leah asked what names they might be considering, and the wife chattered happily about nieces and nephews and how she'd always loved babies. It seemed like mere minutes before they were in front of Leah's lodgings and she was handing a few quint-silvers to the sweela man. "An unexpectedly pleasant ending to a day full of unexpected encounters," she said as she climbed out.

The wife waved to her through the window. "Like the coin said—surprise!" she called as the elaymotive sped off.

Leah smiled, waved, and turned toward her building, practically into the arms of Darien Serlast. She muffled a gasp and took a step back.

"Like the girl said," he repeated, "surprise."

She recovered her equilibrium. "It's been that kind of day."

"I hear you wanted to speak with me. I wasn't free till now."

Neither was I. "I'm so tired I'm not sure I'll be coherent, but if you have a few minutes, come upstairs with me," she invited. "I don't think this will take long."

He glanced over one shoulder, raising his hand in a signal to whatever driver or guard detail undoubtedly waited for him in the shadows, and then followed her inside. In a few moments, they were seated at her small table and Leah was sipping cold keerza to help herself stay awake. Darien waited with his usual imperturbability as she gathered her scattered thoughts.

"Last night near the Plaza of Men, I happened to come across three Karkans," she said. "One was Seka Mardis, whom I met at the palace the other day." Darien nodded. "Two were men I didn't know, though I'd recognize one of them if I saw him again. The other wore a hood and kept his face hidden. But he was a tall man, and I might know him again just by his shape. And his voice."

"Were they doing anything particularly noteworthy?" Darien asked.

"Not then. But something about them seemed furtive. I was curious, so I followed them when they took public transport south. And got off in the slums. At first I thought they might be lost, but then—I didn't think so. They seemed like they'd gone there for a reason. Like they were looking for something."

"I can think of a dozen things people might go southside to find," Darien said, "from drugs to prostitutes to unscrupulous individuals who would do anything for money."

"Oddly, what they seemed to be searching for was a young woman who looked more dead than alive. Not someone they already knew—someone they randomly found on the street."

Darien frowned. "What did they want with her?"

"I don't know. They took her into an abandoned building but I—Well, I was concerned. I interfered. They left her behind and disappeared into the night. I wasn't fast enough to see where they went." She shrugged. "I just thought you should know they are roaming around the city, being mysterious."

"Thank you. I'm not sure how to use the knowledge yet, but it's useful to have." He narrowed his gray eyes at her. "Have you had any other opportunities to speak to the Karkans? Or even the Soechins?"

"Not yet. Perhaps some of them will come by my shop. If not—" She shrugged. "I'll see if I can engineer an accidental meeting in one of the Plazas."

He nodded and rose to his feet. "Zoe tells me your first day was a rousing success," he said. "So even if you fail as a spy, you appear poised to succeed as a retailer."

She accompanied him to the door, unable to hold back her yawn. "I like to think I've already been somewhat successful as a spy," she retorted.

"Indeed you have. Then let us hope you are equally adept in every endeavor you undertake." He gave her another slight nod, she bowed in return, and he was out the door.

She didn't even go to the window to see him safely returned to his guards and driver. She merely pulled off her clothes and extinguished the lights as she crossed the room and fell into bed. She had a moment to think, *This was the strangest day,* and then she was asleep.

. . .

Leah's second day as a shopkeeper was almost as momentous as the first. Fewer people actually walked through the doors, but many of them required special handling or came with their own emotional weight.

As before, Annova was the first to arrive at the shop, and she was already hauling down fresh merchandise when Leah walked in that morning. "Do you *never* sleep?" Leah demanded. "Is that a function of being coru or of being older?"

Annova was amused. "I sleep when I'm tired. I sleep when I'm bored. I'm enjoying myself here."

"So once you start finding this job tedious, you'll show up late or not at all?"

Annova gave her a quick glance as she carefully arranged red scarves around scented candles in a sweela display. "I understood that the shop was just a temporary enterprise until Darien learns what he wants to know."

"Well, that's how it started."

"But you're thinking of continuing it once the Karkans sail away?"

Leah shrugged. She'd brought a pile of leftovers with her and was feeding them slowly to the reifarjin, and it gulped them down as if it hadn't a meal in a nineday. "Like you said. I'm enjoying myself so far."

There was a shadow outside and Annova murmured, "Customers already?" but Leah recognized the shape at the door.

"No," she said. "I'll explain."

Chandran stepped in and stood just over the threshold, looking around and awaiting an invitation. He probably figured she'd lain awake half the night, thinking things over; he wanted to make sure she hadn't changed her mind about allowing him even partway into her life. Leah motioned him closer, and he joined them in the middle of the room.

"Annova, this is Chandran. A merchant I worked for when I lived in Malinqua," Leah said in Coziquela. She tried to keep her tone casual, but there were so many layers to her relationship with Chandran that she wasn't able to achieve it. "I got in touch with him before I opened the shop, and he's the one who sent me some of the best merchandise. And now he's . . . here in Welce."

Annova was not easily fooled. She didn't attempt to hide her long, slow inspection of the stranger, or her sideways look at Leah once she was done. But "An unexpected visit?" was all she asked.

"Very unexpected," he answered.

"I asked him to come by and help us out," Leah went on, still floundering a little as she tried to convey just enough information to explain his presence. "Since we've been so busy and he's got so much experience working in a shop."

"I'm sure he'll be a great help," Annova answered.

"Chandran, Annova is— Well, some people think she's Zoe's maid, but she's really Zoe's friend. Zoe is the coru prime. Oh, and the regent's wife." Very well, *that* might have been the most incoherent introduction she'd ever attempted. But it seemed that Annova was no easier to sum up than Chandran was. And, of course, Zoe had so many roles that it could take forever to list them. "Annova's helping me out in the shop for as long as it holds her attention."

"You say that as if you expect her interest to quickly fade."

Annova smiled. "There are so many things to spend time on," she explained. "It is hard to concentrate on just one."

"She says that," Leah observed, "but she has been married to the same man for decades."

"Well, you'd have to know Calvin. He's never boring."

Leah gestured around the shop. "We sold a *lot* yesterday, so we're restocking—there's a storeroom upstairs. You could help with that."

"Gladly," he said. "But I thought of another way I could benefit you. I could write to my suppliers in Berringey and Cozique and ask them to deliver goods to me here. It will take some time, even so, for new shipments to arrive."

"Write the letters. I'll give them to Darien. He pays couriers and they're *very* fast."

"First let's display what we've already got," Annova said practically. "You look strong. Come upstairs and move boxes for me."

They disappeared through the door in the back of the shop. Leah stared after them and thought how odd it was to see the different halves of her life come together.

It would proceed to get odder.

The first customers arrived while Chandran and Annova were still putting fresh items on the display tables. The newcomers were two middle-aged women and three girls who might have been in their teens. All were wearing expensive clothing and giving off airs of entitlement that came only with great wealth and privilege.

"Oh, Seterre was right, it is a special place," one of the women said. "Look at those shawls! How do you pick among them?"

The youngest girl headed straight for the reifarjin and began tapping on the glass to get its attention. "He bites," Leah called over to her. "Don't put your fingers in the water."

The girl looked up. "Can I feed him?"

"There's food on the table in back. He eats anything."

One of the other two girls rolled her eyes and spoke to the third one. "Hundreds of beautiful things to look at and *she* wants to feed a fish."

The youngest girl cast her a look of scorn. "One live creature in the whole place and you'd rather play with dead things," she retorted.

Must be sisters, Leah thought. "There are six human beings here, too, unless we don't count as live creatures," she said.

The younger girl glanced at the older one with loathing. "*Some* of the humans count."

If Leah had really been a shop owner, dependent on the success of this operation, she would have made it her mission to sell this young girl something—to find an item that stirred her imagination and woke in her a covetous desire. Chandran had always been so good at that—determining exactly what might appeal to a total stranger and presenting it in a way that made it irresistible. For someone who normally gave away so little information about himself, he had always been good at guessing other people's secrets. He'd learned Leah's the day he met her.

But it had taken him years to guess his wife's secret.

"Now I like this," one of the women said, holding up a necklace from Dhonsho. "You'd never see Riana in something so wild!"

They were still debating what to purchase when three more customers came in, two women and a man. Before Leah had time to feel more than a surge of panic, Annova and Chandran were back downstairs, their arms full of packs and boxes. Leah met them in the middle of the room.

"You take over the counter. Annova and I will deal with customers, since we know everything in the shop," Leah said to Chandran in a low voice. Just in case anyone was close enough to overhear, she switched to Malinquese. "Most of the high-born Welchins will speak Coziquela, but not until you address them that way. But they'll like it. It will make them feel like they're very sophisticated."

Chandran transferred his bundles to her, his fingers lightly grazing her arm in the process. She suddenly wished she wasn't wearing a long-sleeved tunic, then she wished the thought hadn't crossed her mind. She kept her eyes down, trained on the items in her hands.

"Do they bargain?"

"Mostly not. They all have money."

"Ah. The best customers."

She laughed. "So I hope."

There was a voice behind her. "You— Are you Leah? I have a question."

She lifted her eyes to give Chandran one quick smile, then kept the smile as she turned to answer the customer. "I am! How can I help you?"

The next couple of hours flew by—still busy, but not as breathless as the day before. Chandran took advantage of a lunchtime lull to go out and forage for food.

"He knows his job, that's certain," Annova commented. "Everyone was comfortable with him, did you see that? Five or six people purchased scarves and stones because he made suggestions as they were ready to buy. That's a skill."

You were impressed by his salesmanship, but do you like him? Do you trust him? Leah didn't ask. "He's been selling luxury products for ten years. It would be pretty sad if he *wasn't* good at it."

"And before that?" Annova asked innocently. "What did he do?"

Leah wasn't prepared with an answer so she was silent a little too long. When she looked up, Annova was watching her closely. Leah shrugged. "Living a different life," she said lightly.

"How much do you know about that life?"

"Not as much as I thought I did."

At that, Annova raised her eyebrows but made no direct comment. "How much does he know about yours?"

"As much as is worth telling."

"You might try to make sure those two things balance out."

"That has occurred to me. But I appreciate the advice."

Annova smiled. "No one ever appreciates advice."

They had time to gobble down the fruit and meat pies that Chandran distributed upon his return, but five minutes later another group of women came chattering through the door. As smoothly as if they had worked together for quintiles, the three of them took their stations. Within the hour, they had rung up sales for eight more customers.

They had hit another quiet spell when the next set of visitors stepped in—Virrie and Mally. Leah exclaimed in delight and met them at the door.

"Come in! You have to see everything we've added since you were here yesterday."

"Considering how many people were here, I imagine half the shop must be new," Virrie commented.

Mally instantly turned her attention to the reifarjin. "How's your fish doing? Does he like having all the people here?"

Leah laid a hand casually on the girl's back and shepherded her over to the tank. "I think so. He seems to like watching the activity. Do you want to feed him?"

Mally nodded, never taking her gaze away from the reifarjin's gaudy frills. She bent a little to peer through the glass, and the fish stilled in its incessant circling to stare back at her with a single dark eye. "What's his name?"

"He doesn't have one. You can name him if you like."

Mally nodded again, but did not offer a quick suggestion. This was a child who liked to think things through. "He needs things to play with."

"He what?"

Mally laid her hand against the glass, keeping her fingers well away from the open top. "Things. In the water with him. Seashells or rocks. He could hide behind them if he didn't want people looking at him."

"Well, that makes sense," Virrie said. "I'd want things to hide behind if people were always looking at me."

Leah made a broad gesture. "You can pick anything you like to dress up his home. *You* can't put it in because he has a nasty set of teeth. But I think that's a lovely idea."

Mally glanced up at her. "Can I pick *expensive* things?"

"No," Virrie said, but Leah laughed out loud. She couldn't help herself. She stooped down and dropped a light kiss on the little girl's forehead.

"Yes," she corrected. "Anything you like."

"All right, then," Virrie said, taking Mally's hand. "Let's look around."

They moved through the shop, which had quickly grown crowded again during their brief conversation. Annova brushed up against Leah and murmured, "Where's Chandran?"

Which was when Leah remembered that Chandran was working in the shop today. Which was when she had a sudden spasm of horror: *Can I trust him around my daughter?* Which was when she realized why he was suddenly nowhere to be found.

He'd seen Mally come in—instantly guessed who she must be—and understood that this was the one person in all of Chialto that Leah would not want to expose to the slightest chance of risk. So he'd left.

Or maybe he'd left so he wouldn't have to see Leah's face when she discovered that she was afraid to have him near her daughter.

"I'm not sure," Leah said. She wanted to manufacture a better lie— *I sent him to make a deposit of today's cash; I asked him to take a message to Darien; he's meeting with a vendor who dropped by*—but she had formed the impression that it did no good to prevaricate with Annova. She always seemed to know when Leah was lying. Which then led Annova to be more interested in *why* Leah was concealing something than in what she was trying to hide.

"Will he be coming back?"

"I think so. Later this afternoon."

"Then I'll work at the counter until then."

Virrie and Mally amused themselves while Leah waited on customers and Annova rang up sales. It was near closing time before the place had emptied of buyers and Leah could check out the accoutrements Mally had assembled for the reifarjin. A pile of opaque blue stones (very cheap), a tiny gold box shaped like a treasure chest (rather more costly), and a red glass goblet (one of a set, but fairly inexpensive).

"You think he wants to sip out of the goblet?" Leah asked in amusement.

"No, it lies on its side so he can swim inside it and curl up."

"Do you think he'll actually do that?"

"Maybe," Mally said. "We could find out."

The trick with adding décor to the reifarjin's tank, of course, was keeping yourself from being bitten when you reached into the water. Mally distracted the fish by tapping on one end of the tank, while Leah outfitted herself with a long pair of gloves to provide some protection for herself. Then she carefully poured in the loose stones before situating the box and the goblet at the bottom of the tank. The reifarjin only nipped at her fingers twice, but he watched all of her incursions with anxious excitement, frilling his fins and fixing her with his unwinking eyes. After she withdrew her hands for the last time and stripped off the gloves, he made one quick, agitated lap around the interior of the tank, then came to a halt in the middle. His whole body was quivering, and his mouth opened and closed as if he was exhaling excess amounts of air.

"He doesn't like any of it," Mally said, disappointed.

Virrie patted her shoulder. "Give him a few minutes. He's just getting used to his new furniture."

"Feed him," Annova said. "That always makes him happy."

Mally trotted off to find some scraps. Virrie said, "She'll be absorbed in watching him for a while, don't you think? Could I leave her behind for about an hour while I run some errands?"

"Of course you can. Take as long as you like."

As she walked Virrie to the door, Leah glanced outside to see a few stragglers still strolling down the boulevard, peering into shop windows. *One or two more people might drop in before nightfall,* she thought. *Might as well keep the door unlocked.*

"Do you want to count money or run up and down the stairs replenishing stock?" she asked Annova.

"Stairs for me. Most anything is more interesting than money."

"Which is why you're one of the happiest people I know."

Annova laughed and disappeared through the back. Mally had returned to the fish tank, holding a handful of lunchtime leftovers—bread, scraps of fruit, even a couple of small chunks of chocolate.

"I'm not sure he eats sweets," Leah said.

"I want to see." She glanced at Leah. "If that's all right."

Leah spread her hands. "Only way to learn anything is to try it," she said. "Let's find out."

The reifarjin liked chocolate. He liked grapes and strawberries and orange slices, and they already knew he liked bread. "I think he'll eat *anything*," Mally said.

"So far that does appear to be true."

While Mally was occupied with the fish, Leah sat at the counter and began tallying the day's sales. She'd barely gotten through half the receipts when the door opened again. She glanced up to do a quick assessment of the new customers, and felt a quick spike of adrenaline.

Four people were stepping across the threshold—the four people, arguably, for whom the shop existed in the first place. Two were Soechin men, tall and pale and somehow odd-looking; two were Karkans. One was a stranger, but one was Seka Mardis.

Time to start spying for Darien.

ELEVEN

Leah put down her ledger, came to her feet, and smiled at the newcomers. "You're just in time," she said warmly. "I was about to close."

Seka Mardis was looking around with great interest, her intent gaze taking in the higher storage shelves as well as the more visible display tables. It seemed in character with her personality to be keenly aware of her surroundings. Today she was dressed a bit less ostentatiously than she had been when Leah first met her, though she still wore a closely fitting dress, a half dozen bracelets, and beads woven into her frosted hair. Her male companion also sported more accessories than Welchin men usually bothered with—several rings, a thick silver bracelet, a jeweled collar. If she'd had to guess, Leah would have said this was the man who had accompanied Seka Mardis on the visit to the palace, but not on the late-night excursion to the slums.

"We meant to come by yesterday, but events intervened," Seka Mardis said. "That was the day you first opened, was it not? How has business been so far?"

"Almost *too* good!" Leah said with a laugh. "We've scarcely managed to keep up. But I hesitate to complain because I would much rather be too busy than not busy enough."

Seka Mardis glanced around again. "'We,'" she repeated. "So you are not attempting to run this place all by yourself?"

"No—I have helpers," Leah began, then almost strangled on a surge of panic. *One of those helpers is Chandran! What if he comes back? What if they see him? What if they recognize him? I must not accidentally speak his name.*

"They seem to have abandoned you," Seka Mardis observed.

Leah forced herself to smile. Chandran was too astute to be caught unaware by visiting Karkans. He had absented himself the moment he recognized Mally. He would recognize Seka Mardis and her friend even more quickly. "One is upstairs going through stock and will probably reappear shortly," she said. "The other is running errands. I feel very well-attended."

Seka Mardis gestured. "So show me your most special items. I might buy something."

Leah glanced at Seka's companions. The other Karkan stood by the door in a pose that betrayed indifference and boredom. The Soechins had paused in front of the hunti table and were running their hands with sensuous delight over a collection of boxes made from highly polished ebony. A simple act, hardly sinister, and yet there was something off-putting about the intensity with which they were stroking the smooth dark wood. "Should I call Annova down to help your friends?" Leah asked.

"Oh, they're fine. If they need assistance, they'll ask for it."

Leah glanced at Mally, but she was still entranced by the fish. So Leah escorted Seka Mardis on a slow circuit of the shop, pointing out the most exotic pieces and explaining where they originated. The other woman wasn't interested in anything from Cozique—"Their goods are *littered* across the Karkades"—but the merchandise from Dhonsho appealed to her. The more colorful, the better.

"I like this scarf," Seka Mardis said, draping one of the bright shawls around her shoulders and nestling her chin in its folds. It was long enough, and she was short enough, that she probably could have wrapped herself in it twice over.

"I have a red shawl from Dhonsho that is one of the most beautiful things I own," Leah told her.

"Isn't it strange that something so lovely can come from a place so full of violence?" the other woman said, laying the scarf aside and moving to the next display. "Yet it is just that contradiction that I find so appealing."

When they reached the food table at the back of the shop, Seka Mardis consented to try a cup of fresh keerza, though she didn't like it much. "Bitter," she commented.

"It took me three years to come to appreciate it," Leah agreed.

Seka Mardis took another sip and grimaced. "That's right—you mentioned that you lived in Malinqua for some time," she said. "Five years, was it?"

Isn't that interesting? Leah thought, savoring her own keerza. *That she would remember such an unimportant fact let fall by an unimportant person during one very brief conversation?* "Five years," she confirmed. "It is where I developed my appreciation for all this." She gestured broadly to indicate the sumptuous variety throughout the shop. "It is where I learned that much of the world is so very different from Welce."

Seka Mardis leaned against the back wall and gamely tried another sip of keerza. By her expression, she still didn't like it. "I have been shocked, from time to time, at how very different the world is from the Karkades," she admitted. "It is odd to learn that something that seems very normal and natural to one person can be considered almost"—she searched for a word—"deviant to someone else."

She has to be talking about sex, Leah thought. *That's always what people are talking about when they're shocked by someone's behavior.* She nodded vigorously. "I know! In Malinqua, there was a scandal in the empress's court because one of her nephews was what the Coziquela call sublime. A man who loves other men. Whereas in Welce, that is not something that matters at all."

Seka Mardis looked intrigued. "Really? Such a thing is frowned upon in Malinqua? It seems like such a tame sort of sin."

Leah smiled faintly. "Even to call it a sin would imply that it is not acceptable in the Karkades," she pointed out.

Seka Mardis laughed lightly. "Oh, we Karkans take as our starting point the notion that all of us have desires and urges that are unhealthy. Unwise. Perhaps despicable. Even something so commonplace as eating a meal can be turned into an exercise in carnality, depending on what you've decided to consume."

Leah blinked at her. "That seems like a rather extreme way of looking at life," she said.

"Does it? Perhaps so. More exciting than some other philosophies I have encountered." She turned just enough to place the half-full cup of keerza on the table. "I have given up for the moment," she said. "I cannot learn to like it in one afternoon, I'm afraid."

"You don't ever have to like it," Leah said.

Seka Mardis laughed. "But now I want to. I like to overcome my—distaste—for things as an exercise in expanding my tolerances."

"Some things probably should remain distasteful," Leah said.

"Do you think so? I don't agree. I think we broaden our minds and our experiences if we can learn to embrace things that at one point filled us with revulsion."

Leah wanted to shudder, but instead she summoned a look of intrigue as she tilted her head and regarded her visitor. "Well, now you've stirred my curiosity," she remarked. "What sorts of things have you come to appreciate after initially finding them disgusting?"

Seka Mardis's laugh was airy and delighted. "Foodstuffs, mostly! In the Karkades, we have a delicacy called *tchiltsly*. It is made from the ugliest sea creature you ever saw. That alone was enough to make me never want to taste it, but the *smell*! As if dung and spoiled meat had been mixed together and left to rot in the sun for a nineday, then doused with rancid cooking oil. Repellent for so many reasons. And yet people rave about its taste, its texture, and its properties." She gave Leah a coy sideways glance. "For enhancing behavior in the bedroom," she clarified.

"So I surmised," Leah said dryly. "And have you been able to choke down enough of this delicacy to develop a taste for it?"

"A *passion* for it," Seka Mardis corrected. "I cannot get enough of it. If I am at a gathering where it is served, my hosts must forbid me the table or I will eat it all."

"Does it live up to its reputation for its other benefits?"

"It does. And then some."

"Then perhaps I should import some for my shop."

Seka Mardis laughed again, even more delighted. "My dear Leah, I will give you the name of a supplier!"

Leah laughed back. "I knew it would prove most beneficial to know you!"

"I feel the same way about you."

"Though I don't think I've done you any good so far," Leah said somewhat ruefully. "Since you don't like keerza and I don't have any of that—what did you call it? Shilsy?—on hand.

"*Tchiltsly*," Seka Mardis corrected. "And you don't have to be of use to me. It will just be nice to have someone in Welce I can consider a friend."

"Well, I'd be happy to be that person."

"Although—" Seka Mardis said thoughtfully and then paused.

"Although what? Ask me."

Seka Mardis eyed her uncertainly. "You're a woman of the world, obviously, and more sophisticated than many of the people I've met in Welce, but even so, you might be shocked."

Am I going to find out what they were doing in the slums two nights ago? Leah widened her eyes and tried to look both curious and nonjudgmental. "I suppose I might be, but I'll *try* to remain open-minded," she said.

"It is not illegal in the Karkades— Well, really, nothing is," Seka Mardis said. "But I understand that everywhere else it is."

"What is it?"

Seka Mardis dropped her voice. "Veneben."

Leah pursed her lips so she looked surprised instead of disappointed. This wasn't what Seka Mardis and her friends had been searching for southside. It was a very expensive hallucinogen with a high death rate for its addicts, and there was no possible way the half-dead girl in the streets had had any in her possession. In fact, it was the most predictable and the least interesting vice Seka Mardis could have claimed.

She's gauging my reaction, Leah decided. *She will start with small sins and work her way up.*

"Not something I've ever tried myself," Leah admitted. "But you want some?"

"*I* don't. One of my—traveling companions. He's become most distraught at being unable to secure any. And here in Welce, I don't even know where to start looking."

Leah nodded. "Give me a day or two. I have sources." She shrugged. *And they have sources. You know how these things go.*

"He'll pay anything," Seka Mardis said.

"Good, because I believe it's quite costly!"

The other woman studied her. "You're not shocked?" she said tentatively.

"I don't care what anyone else does as long as it doesn't hurt *me*," she said. Half true, anyway. *And as long as it doesn't hurt anybody else.* But she figured that coda was exactly the thing that would cause Seka Mardis to turn away and look for other friends.

For now, Seka Mardis seemed quite satisfied with the one she'd found so far. Her smile was wide and her eyes snapped with mischief. "He will be *so* pleased if I'm able to secure him a supply," she said. "I will most definitely be his favorite for a while."

Leah poured herself another cup of keerza. They had stood there talking so long that she wanted to suggest they pull up a couple of chairs, but then they couldn't pretend that this was just a casual conversation. Leah found it slightly odd that none of the other visitors had wandered over to join the discussion, but maybe the whole thing had been orchestrated in advance. *The three of you distract anyone else who might be in the shop so I can talk to Leah at length.* The other Karkan still stood by the front door, looking both bored and unpleasant; the Soechins had moved from the hunti station to the torz station and were now examining the sweela goods. Leah was sure they had picked up and handled every single item in the store. She would be tempted to go back through and wipe everything off just because there was something so disquieting about their intensity.

Annova was up on the second floor again, but she'd been downstairs twice since the conversation with Seka Mardis began. Each time she came through the door she glanced once at Leah and once at Mally, making sure neither one needed her. Mally still appeared to be engrossed in the reifarjin, but Leah saw her body turn slightly so she could keep track of the Soechins. Leah was willing to bet that Mally found them unnerving, too, though she probably couldn't articulate exactly how she felt. Annova was right to think she needed to watch over them all.

Leah sipped her keerza. "You will be his favorite for a while," she repeated. "So you are traveling with a group and there is some—politicking going on among you all?"

Seka Mardis nodded. "That is exactly it. If I prove myself worthy on this trip, I could greatly enhance my position once we return to the Karkades. I am determined to do whatever I must."

Leah nodded infinitesimally toward the door. "Are all your rivals men?"

"No," Seka Mardis said, "but I do not fear any of the other women."

Oh, it would be fascinating and frightening to someday learn exactly what Seka Mardis was capable of. Well, Leah already had a pretty good guess. *Anything.*

"I will help you as much as I can," Leah said.

"Does Darien Serlast do the same thing?" Seka Mardis asked. "Play the members of his court, one against the other, giving and withdrawing his favor?"

It sounded so unlike Darien that Leah wanted to laugh, but instead she feigned a look of dissatisfaction. "He doesn't favor *anyone*," she said. "You can't get close to him, you can't tell if you've pleased him, you can't figure out if he has a weakness. Good for *him*, I suppose, but very frustrating for the rest of us trying to figure out how to secure an advantage."

"His daughter," Seka Mardis suggested. "She might be a weakness."

"Corene?" Leah said. "Not if you've ever met her."

"Is that the older one? No, I meant the baby."

"Celia," Leah said. She nodded, but inwardly she felt a chill. "A weakness in what way?"

Seka Mardis waved a hand. "Oh, perhaps he indulges her. Showers her with gifts. He might favor someone who provided something special for his little girl."

"Maybe," Leah said, infusing heavy doubt in her voice. "But she's so young. I wouldn't even know what sorts of special things she might like."

"Or he might be grateful for someone who made a remarkable effort to keep her safe," Seka Mardis went on. "Who rescued her from danger—if danger somehow materialized."

If you manufactured that danger? Leah wondered. It was an alarming thought. "Maybe," she said again. "But the girl has guards around her night and day."

"And, of course, even to gain advantage, one would never want to see a child put in a perilous situation," Seka Mardis said lightly. Leah had the feeling that Seka Mardis didn't actually believe that. She had to fight back a shiver.

"I'll think about it some more," Leah promised, "but right now I couldn't name *any* weaknesses that Darien Serlast has."

She was a little distracted as she spoke, because her eyes were on the Soechin men. They had completed their circuit of the perimeter of the shop and turned casually toward the middle, where Mally still stood beside the fishbowl. One of them sank gracefully to his knees to put his head on Mally's level; one bent over to peer into her eyes. He lifted his hand as if to stroke her cheek, but never actually touched her. His face took on a beatific expression as his fingers hovered over her face, close enough to feel the heat of her skin through the inch of intervening air.

"Excuse me," Leah said to Seka Mardis, and crossed the shop floor in four steps. She arrived just in time to hear one of the men ask, "What's your name, then?" and Mally reply, "Odelia."

The Soechins straightened at Leah's approach, but still hovered uncomfortably close. Mally glanced up, her face pinched and worried, then she backed up against Leah's legs, as if taking shelter from a frightening world. Leah rested her hands on the girl's shoulders and smiled at them all with a wholly assumed cheerfulness.

"She's teasing. Her name is Mally," she told the men. "Sometimes she likes to pretend to be the youngest princess."

"Who doesn't like to pretend now and then?" one of the men said, smiling back. He watched Leah with a disconcerting intentness, focused on her mouth, as if imagining what it would be like to kiss it.

She strangled her unease and tried to make her voice friendly. "I've neglected the two of you ever since you set foot in the shop! Is there something you particularly like? Are there any questions I can answer?"

"We were just enjoying the many interesting items you have collected," the other answered in a smooth voice. He was staring at Leah, too, though he focused on her eyes and never seemed to blink. Both of them leaned forward very slightly, as if they were cold and Leah and Mally were radiating heat. Leah thought their mere presence might be even more unnerving than Seka Mardis's conversation.

"And admiring your young friend," the other one replied.

Seka Mardis had sauntered over to join them. "She's lovely," she said.

"Thank you. We all think so."

The Karkan at the front door raised his voice. "Seka. We need to be getting back. Have you gotten what you came for?"

I wonder what she came for? Leah thought, covering the thought by smiling at Seka Mardis. She didn't lift her hands from Mally's shoulders and Mally remained pressed against her as if unwilling to move even a step away. "We got so caught up in conversation that you had no time to shop!" she exclaimed. "Would you like to look around some more?"

"I would—but not today," Seka Mardis said. She held her hand up, palm facing out, and gave Leah a saucy smile. "You must indulge me with the standard Karkan ritual of hello and farewell," she said, "for I feel that we are well on our way to becoming friends."

Leah lifted one hand from Mally's shoulder and pressed her palm against Seka's. She was not surprised to find Seka's skin warm to the touch. "I hope so," she said.

"I am sure of it," Seka replied.

Another moment, another smile, and then the whole contingent was gone. Leah stepped away from Mally to lock the door behind them. "Well," she said, "those were some very odd people."

"I didn't like them," Mally said. "Not at *all*."

"I didn't, either."

Annova was pushing through the stairwell door, her hands full of more Dhonshon scarves. "No, and neither did I," she said. "I slipped out the back and alerted the guards that there could be trouble."

"The guards?" Leah repeated. "*Royal* guards?"

Annova couldn't discipline a smile. "They've been hovering nearby ever since the day that man came in and attacked you. You know Darien Serlast takes care of his own."

"I suppose I should be indignant," Leah said, "but I'm actually relieved."

"So did you learn anything useful from our unlikable guests?" Annova asked.

"I'm not sure. But I think Seka Mardis wants me to be an informant for her. Tell her about the court. About how Darien functions. What his weaknesses are."

Annova snorted. "He has none."

Leah glanced at Mally, who seemed to have recovered her equanimity. She'd gone to the hunti table and started arranging the new items Annova had brought down. "Seka Mardis seemed to think his family members might be weaknesses," she said softly.

Annova obviously reviewed the top candidates. *Corene—out of reach. Zoe—untouchable. Celia—* "Then you did learn something," she said.

Leah nodded. "I need to talk to him. About a couple of things."

"I'll let him know."

Leah felt suddenly exhausted. It had been a very long, very full couple of days. "I need a little more time to finish the accounts," she said. "But you can leave if you want. Virrie should be here soon, then I'll go home."

"Is Chandran coming back tomorrow?" Annova asked.

Leah kept her voice level. "I assume so."

"Then I'll see you both in the morning."

Virrie walked in just as Annova walked out. "Sorry I was gone so long. How was the rest of your day?"

"Odd," Leah answered. "We had some visitors from Soeche-Tas and the Karkades. The Soechins were so *strange*."

Mally spoke up from across the shop. "They *touched* everything. And they acted like they wanted to touch me, but Leah wouldn't let them."

So her protectiveness had been so obvious even a child had realized it. *Well, good.* "They were really disturbing," Leah added.

"I completely agree. Every time I meet one of them, I feel like I need to take a hot bath afterward. Even Navarr Ardelay—Zoe's father, you know, and a libertine who could put Nelson to shame—even he found them disgusting." Virrie shook her head. "I'm not surprised they wanted to touch Mally. They seem to have a craving to be around youth. It's quite unsettling."

"I wonder how Darien can stand to be around them for so many meals and meetings," Leah said. "I think I'd have a hard time choking down my food if they were sitting nearby."

That made Virrie laugh. "But that reminds me!" she exclaimed. "Will you have dinner with us tomorrow night? No Soechins at the table, but Taro is coming to town and he'd like to see you. Josetta will be there as well."

"I'd be happy to come. Why is Taro visiting?"

"He says he misses me, if you can believe that."

Leah kissed her plump cheek. "I do believe it. I'll see you tomorrow night."

"Excellent! Mally, grab your things, we're going."

A few minutes later, the shop was entirely empty. Leah finished adding up sales, then turned off the gaslight sign. She moved through the place one last time, making sure everything was in order for the morning. Then she stepped outside, locked the door, and started up the mostly deserted street. Chandran fell in step beside her. Even though she had been half-expecting him, she started slightly in surprise.

"There you are," she said. "I hope you managed to entertain yourself all afternoon."

"I did. I explored the Plaza of Men and met a young man who had sailed in from Malinqua yesterday and was trying to find buyers for some of his merchandise. I think you will like my purchases."

"Excellent!"

"I can describe them to you over dinner if you would like to get something to eat."

Because from now on we will only be alone together when we are in large public spaces. "Yes, I'm starving," Leah said. "There was hardly any time to eat all day."

"Ah, that is proof that you are working very hard."

They wandered toward the Plaza of Women and found a small, crowded café with a single open table. Once they had placed their orders, Leah poured fruited water for both of them from a carafe on the table.

"So, tell me," she said. "While you were living in the Karkades, did you ever try a delicacy called—I don't think I'm pronouncing it right—*shiltsy?*"

"*Tchiltsly,*" he corrected, though Leah still didn't think she'd ever manage all the consonants. "And I *tried* it," he went on, "but it made me sick enough to vomit. So I never tried it again."

"From the description," she said, "I think that would be my reaction as well."

He was watching her closely. "Who described it to you?"

"A Karkan woman who dropped by the shop this afternoon with some of her friends." Leah sipped her water. "I was glad you'd stepped out. I was worried that one of your countrymen might see you."

"They are not my countrymen," he said quietly. "I am Coziquela."

"I'm sorry. I misspoke. But I still didn't want them to see you."

"So how did *tchiltsly* come up in the conversation?"

"I had served her keerza, which she didn't like, but she seemed determined to keep trying it. She said she makes it a point of pride to overcome her aversion to certain kinds of food."

"She has probably overcome aversions to more disgusting things than food."

"Yes, I came to that conclusion as well." Leah took another sip from her glass. "I wonder if you know her. She calls herself Seka Mardis."

"There was a Mardis or two who enjoyed royal favor when I lived in the Karkades," said Chandran. "I might have met her, but it was fifteen years ago." He shrugged. "Doubtless she is like all the creatures at the Karkan court—ruthless, ambitious, and utterly without conscience."

Leah propped her chin on her hand, regarding him for a long moment. "You hate them all so much, not just your wife," she said slowly. "How did you endure the years that you lived in the Karkades?"

He spoke very deliberately. "As a man endures being flayed alive. In great agony and praying for death. I had almost determined to take my own life instead of hers."

She caught her breath. "What stopped you?"

A faint, bitter smile twisted his lips. "Strangely, the very thing that made my wife so terrible. The Karkan philosophy. I realized I had not made my atonement—I had not done the one great deed that would erase all my sins. If I killed myself, that deficit would always stand."

"Except for the murder of your wife," Leah said softly, "what sins have you committed?"

His bitter smile deepened. "Mundane ones. When I was younger, I stole a sum of money from my father. That was one of the reasons he was so insistent that I marry—he wanted to cement the relationship with the Karkades, yes, but he also wanted me out of his sight for a while."

"Then you *have* atoned for that sin," Leah pointed out. "The marriage wiped that debt clean."

Chandran shrugged and suddenly looked very tired. "I think my most monstrous sin was thinking so much about how I wanted to kill her. Even if I had never done it, the thoughts themselves had dirtied my mind to such a degree that I felt unclean. I am still trying to expiate."

"But you've led an exemplary life for fifteen years," Leah argued. "You were scrupulously honest in all your financial dealings in Malinqua. You worked hard to be an upright citizen. Doesn't that count for something?"

"I am not sure that many small, quiet virtues can ever accumulate to such an extent that they offset one great vice," he replied. "If I ever get a chance to make my grand gesture, I will take it. Until then"—he shrugged—"I will live as honestly as I can. And at the very least I will contract to bring no more harm into the world."

Their server brought their food and conversation lapsed as they took their first bites. "I have never thought of my life in terms of committing sins and earning absolution," Leah said after a few moments. "Mostly I've just tried to find my footing. Find my way. It's like I'm in a great forest, and I know there's a clearing somewhere, with a stream and a little cottage and a big garden. And if I can discover the way there, I can settle in and be safe and make my happiness." She took another bite. "But I keep stumbling and falling. I keep tripping over rocks and dead trees. I keep getting lost—choosing the wrong direction. I don't know if I'll ever find the cottage in the clearing."

Chandran busied himself cutting his meat. "Is anyone in the cottage with you?"

"Mally," Leah said instantly. "She's been waiting there all this time."

"Nobody else?"

Leah managed a breathless laugh. "I haven't thought that far ahead. But I like to think we wouldn't be there all alone."

They were both silent a moment. Leah toyed with the stem of her water glass. "It was thoughtful of you," she said at last, "to leave the shop when she arrived this afternoon."

"I did not want you to worry."

"I don't feel afraid for myself—at any rate, not right now—but everything changes when I think about Mally," Leah said. "I'm sorry that that's true."

"I would be surprised if it were not."

"Someday it might be different."

"Or it will not. I trust you will tell me, one way or the other."

She took a deep breath. "My hope is to be as honest with you as you've been with me. About the bad things as well as the good."

"Since your bad things cannot possibly be as bad as mine, I hope you will find honesty easier to come by."

"I'm out of the habit," she admitted. "I feel like the whole time I was in Malinqua, I was living a lie—yes, and even the last few years I was living in Welce, I was pretending to be someone I wasn't. Maybe I've never been truly open about who I am."

"I was open enough before I married Dederra, but I was as feckless and selfish as any young man," Chandran said. "The longer I lived in the Karkades, the more I withdrew into myself, the less I showed my true face. And while I lived in Malinqua, I had no incentive at all to be genuine."

"Do you have any incentive now?" she asked quietly.

He met her gaze, his dark eyes very serious. "Your friendship," he answered. "When I am with you, I find in myself a desire to throw off disguises and present myself as I truly am. I cannot explain why this would be, and yet that is how I feel."

"I feel the same way," she said, her voice very low. "And I can't explain it, either."

He offered her the smallest of smiles. "It is good to know, however," he said, "that we are both bewildered—and we are both willing to try."

A shadow fell across the table and Leah looked up, expecting to see that their server had returned. She had been so deeply engrossed in the conversation with Chandran that it took her a moment to realize the person standing there was Darien Serlast. During the time it took her to mentally regroup, he had borrowed a chair from another table and gracefully settled in next to her.

"I understand you want to talk to me," he said.

"Darien," she said blankly. "How did you even know where I *was*?"

"There are guards watching the shop," he said. "They saw you headed in this direction." He flicked a look at Chandran. "With a companion. I did not have to look too many places."

Annova was right, she thought. *Wish I'd known about the guards when I ended up southside two nights ago.* Aloud she said, "Darien, this is Chandran. A friend of mine from Malinqua. Chandran, Darien Serlast. Regent of Welce and soon to be king."

The two men eyed each other, not even trying to be subtle about the fact that they were trying to size each other up. Leah wished them both luck. She wasn't sure which one would be harder to read. Darien, probably. Chandran had already admitted a desire to peel back the layers of his own secrecy, but she couldn't imagine Darien ever would.

"Chandran," Darien repeated. "You're the merchant."

Chandran inclined his head. "Leah has trusted me to make some purchases for her."

"You're also the poisoner," Darien added.

Chandran nodded again, not losing an ounce of self-possession. "She had just expressed an interest in meeting *your* daughter for reasons she would not divulge," Chandran replied. "I wanted to disable her if her motives were dark."

"A man of justice, I see," Darien said.

"I try to be."

"What brings you to Welce? Are you merely overseeing the delivery of your purchases on Leah's behalf?"

"I was finding life in Malinqua less satisfactory than it had been in the past," Chandran replied. "There seemed to be no reason not to explore the rest of the world."

"Are you staying?"

"I have not decided yet. Circumstances will dictate my next course of action."

"As circumstances so often do."

At that point, the serving girl hurried up, carrying an extra glass and a fresh carafe of water. "Your pardon, I didn't see you come in," she apologized, sounding harried. But she didn't sound overawed, so Leah's guess was that she didn't recognize the regent. Well, who would expect him to just take a seat at a sidewalk café without announcing his presence? "Would you like to order something?"

"Thank you, no, I've eaten. But I appreciate the water," Darien said, smiling kindly at her. She bobbed her head and disappeared.

"You should smile more often. You actually look nice when you do," Leah told him.

"I don't always *want* to look nice," he retorted.

"Oh, in that case, just maintain your usual expression."

That amused him, though the smile he gave her was more sardonic than the one he'd bestowed on the waitress. "I'm wondering if it's your unconventional upbringing or your five years in Malinqua that make you think you can treat your regent with such disrespect."

Leah wrinkled her nose, trying to decide. "The time in Malinqua," she said. "I started to believe that everyone had a secret and everyone had a price. And anyone could be rattled if you pushed hard enough."

Darien lifted his elegant eyebrows. "Even you?"

She laughed. "*Especially* me. But since you already know my secrets—and my price—I don't think you need to try to push me off balance."

"So," he said. "Annova tells me you need to talk to me about something."

"I need some veneben."

Chandran inhaled sharply in surprise, but Darien merely raised his brows again. "Not something I keep handy in the palace, since I have no use for it myself," he said dryly. "And since, of course, I've endorsed harsh punishments for anyone caught selling it."

"I'm sure that's true," she said politely. "But I'd wager that *you* can obtain some more quickly than *I* can. Since, of course, you can do anything."

"I'll ask Annova's husband, Calvin. He's very enterprising."

She couldn't help laughing. "Annova's husband would have to be."

"I assume this has something to do with our visitors?"

"It does. One of them dropped by the shop today and made the request."

"How quickly do you need it?"

"I'm not sure. Within the next nineday, I think?"

"I'll see what I can arrange." He pushed his chair back from the table. "Anything else?"

"Maybe." She could tell her voice was troubled. "She asked about Celia. Well, it was odd, the way she put it. She was wondering if you

had any weaknesses, and speculated that Celia would be one of them."
She lifted her eyes to his hard gray ones. "It made me uneasy."

"It's an odd thing to say," he agreed. "I'll take steps to ensure she is
even more well-guarded. Anything else?"

"I don't think so. I'll let you know if something happens."

"Thank you." Darien rose to his feet and nodded briskly at Chandran. "I'm pleased to have met you. I expect we'll see each other again."
He strode off without another word.

Leah stared after him, then brought her gaze around to Chandran.
He wore a faint smile. "Now I understand," he said.

"Understand what?"

"Why you trusted him with your own secret. Why you were willing
to work for him at such a great distance. Why you would have done
anything to serve his daughter."

"He's cold and secretive and unyielding and absolutely hunti—
which is to say absolutely infuriating," Leah said. "But he's honorable.
I can't think of anyone I trust more. I think most people feel that way
about Darien."

"Welce is lucky."

"Very different from the Karkades," Leah said.

"On so many measures," Chandran said, "there is no comparison."

TWELVE

Leah's third day as a shop owner was smoother than the first two. Still busy, but not breathlessly so, and featuring fewer complicated visitors. No primes, no Karkans, no illegitimate daughters. Chandran again handled sales, Annova was responsible for restocking, and Leah waited on customers.

We make an excellent team, Leah thought, and then almost laughed out loud. *Until Annova gets bored and Chandran is overcome by guilt and I make some other mistake that sends my life careening off in a new direction.*

Well, she would enjoy the smooth unfolding of the days as long as they lasted.

In the evening, she headed to Darien's city house to have dinner with the people collected under his roof. Darien had lodged in spare bachelor quarters when Leah last lived in Chialto, so she was curious to see what kind of house he'd purchased once he married the coru prime. As she'd expected, the elegant, three-story building was situated in the most expensive part of town and looked quite forbidding from the outside, but the interior was something of a surprise. The kierten was a high, open column of space topped with a glass cupola; it must be an elay haven in daylight hours. Even now that dark had fallen, it exuded an air of deep peace that was instantly calming. She followed a well-mannered servant through a series of rooms and hallways that were all equally welcoming, even whimsical. *This has to be Zoe's taste, not Darien's,* Leah decided. It was heartening to think that even someone as hunti as Darien was susceptible to the effects of a coru lover.

She was eventually shown to a small dining room where Josetta, Rafe, Virrie, Taro, and Mally were already standing. "So sorry—am I late?" she asked, nodding at the others but giving Taro a swift kiss on the cheek. He responded with a hug that briefly made her feel as safe as a child in her father's arms.

"No, we're just an impatient group," Josetta said, signaling to the servant at the door. "I'm glad you could join us! We're getting sick of each other's company."

"Since I just arrived, I think I should be offended," Taro said.

Josetta bubbled with laughter. "Well, I didn't mean you. Everyone sit down. It'll just be a simple meal."

They took their places around the table, making no attempt to line up by rank or connection. Mally had chosen the chair between Virrie and Taro and was showing Taro pictures she'd drawn on a sheaf of papers. Leah tried not to be jealous. Children always wanted to sit by Taro.

Rafe was on Leah's left. "Josetta's meals are always pretty simple," he explained. "Down at the shelter, she's used to cooking dinners every night for twenty or thirty people who don't have anything except what she gives them, so she has a strong aversion to excess."

"I'm still so impressed that she does that," Leah said.

"Half the people in the Five Families think I'm more than a little mad," Josetta said. "They try to excuse my behavior by saying, 'Well, of course, she's *elay*,' but you can tell they're still baffled."

"Half the people in the Five Families are more than a little mad themselves," Taro said in his rumbling voice. "They just present themselves in the way they think others will find acceptable, because they don't want you to know."

"Nobody at *this* table is pretending to be somebody they aren't," Virrie said mildly. "So we'll do just fine."

Servants brought in platters of food—which *was* very plain, roasted meat and hearty vegetables, served with a side of bread—and instantly retreated, allowing the diners to serve themselves. Virrie was right. This was about as unpretentious a group as anyone could have hoped to assemble in all of Welce.

"So tell us how the retail business is going," Josetta invited, and Leah filled them in on all the activity of the past three days.

"Sounds like the worst job in the world," Taro grumbled. "Who would care about buying all that stuff? And who would want to stand around all day indoors, trying to sell it?"

"Now, if *you* were a merchant, you'd be selling fruit out of a wagon in the Plaza of Women," Josetta said. "Something harvested from the land that very day."

"That wouldn't be so bad," Taro admitted.

"Though I can't think the torz prime will ever be reduced to earning a living that way," Rafe observed.

"I could have been a farmer, though, and liked it," Taro said. "Thought that was where my life was headed. I'd taken over my grandfather's property and started making improvements." He nodded at Virrie. "Found myself a wife. Had a baby. Life looked pretty good."

"You didn't know you were going to be prime?" Leah asked.

He shook his head. "My uncle was prime before me. He had three daughters and a son, and everyone assumed one of them would take up the role after him. But it didn't work that way."

"How did you find out?" Leah asked. "How does *anyone* find out? Virrie said something the other day—that the elements themselves play a role in selecting the next prime?"

"That's right," Taro said. "And it's different for all of the elements."

"These are the sorts of conversations that make people think the Five Families are insane," Rafe said conversationally. He appeared to be enjoying himself.

"Didn't Zoe say she learned that she was the coru prime when she didn't drown in the Marisi?" Leah asked.

"Yes!" Josetta exclaimed. "It's such a terrifying story!"

Leah gestured at Taro. "So how does the torz prime find out the truth?"

"There's a patch of ground out on my property—or rather, the property that gets handed down from prime to prime. This part of the land doesn't look like much. A few bushes, a row of flower gardens that generally run to wild roses."

"You can't plant anything new there," Virrie interposed. "Nothing else will grow. And you can prune those bushes down to the topsoil, but the next day they're back. Even though they're just scraggly little shrubs with nothing special about them, except that they're too hardy to die."

Taro shrugged. "The story is that the old prime walks through the garden with whoever he thinks will be his heir. If he's right, those bushes start pushing out new green leaves and bright red flowers so fast it looks like they're exploding."

"Is that how it worked for you?" Josetta asked.

Taro nodded. "Pretty much. My uncle was as surprised as I was. He'd brought me out there to show me something on the other edge of the estate. We were just taking a shortcut."

"Of course, he was seventy years old before he identified Taro as his heir," Virrie said in her mild way. "I often wonder what would have happened if they hadn't taken that shortcut that afternoon and the old man had simply died."

"That's a good question," Leah said. "What *would* have happened?"

"I imagine every man or woman with a drop of Frothen blood would have tramped through that land hoping to make the bushes spring to life," Taro said. "Eventually I would have thought to try it."

"Is it always a Frothen?" Rafe wanted to know. "Does the power of the primes always follow bloodlines?"

"So far," Taro said. "It doesn't have to go from parent to child, but there's usually a close familial connection."

"Which leads to the next obvious question," Leah said. "Who's going to be your heir? You said you hadn't picked one yet." She remembered the conversation at Darien's lunch table. "In fact, I think Zoe said that only Nelson had done so."

"Which seems so unlike Nelson, doesn't it?" Josetta said. "Imagine having five people in the room and *Nelson* being the one who's most responsible."

"Although if Kayle and Zoe are two of your other choices, then it's not quite as surprising," Rafe said with a grin.

Virrie nudged Leah. "Ask him again," she said. "He never answers when *I* bring it up."

"Who's going to be your heir, Taro?" Leah repeated obediently.

Taro shrugged, unconcerned. "I don't know yet. No flaming bushes on my property so far. Maybe it's not time to know yet."

Rafe smiled at Leah. "Maybe it's you," he suggested. "It would fit with the poetry of the selection process."

Leah felt herself recoil. "*Me!* I don't think so."

"Why not?" Virrie said. "You're a purebred Frothen girl."

"I've crossed every inch of Taro's estate, including that spot that he's talking about, and nothing ever burst into bloom just because I walked by."

"Maybe the elements just weren't ready yet," Josetta said. Her blue eyes were sparkling; she was finding this very entertaining for a girl who, from all accounts, had felt overwhelming relief when she learned she was not going to inherit a crown. "Maybe they didn't think *you* were ready yet. But things have changed. You've been gone for five years, and you return just as the aging prime starts to decline—"

"I'm not *that* old."

"And when you visit the torz property, suddenly every tree and rosebush goes wild—"

"Even though it's the dead of winter," Rafe added.

"It could happen," Taro said. "Maybe Leah should come back with me when I leave Chialto."

"I don't think I'd make a very good prime," Leah said.

"You wouldn't think Kayle would, either," Virrie pointed out. "But, in fact, in some ways he's spectacular."

"It *is* very unsettling, though," Rafe agreed. "Suddenly finding out that you have a heritage you never knew about." He was fingering his right ear, and for the first time Leah noticed that it had been mutilated in a deliberate and oddly beautiful way—cut into five triangular points, each decorated with a small hoop earring. When he realized she was trying not to stare, he smiled and said, "A souvenir of my Berringey birthright. I usually wear my hair in such a way that you can't see it."

"It's quite impressive."

"I'll tell you the story sometime," he said. "But here's what I want to say. When you suddenly discover that you have a wholly unsuspected heritage, it makes you reassess everything you ever thought or felt in your entire life. And it makes you reconsider where your sense of self-worth comes from. Are you a valuable person because of what you do, what you achieve, who you're kind to, who you protect? Or are you a valuable person simply because of the blood that runs through your veins?"

"Can't you be both?" Virrie said.

"Maybe," Rafe said. "But I've never thought anyone could ever be valuable just because of bloodlines. You have to *do* something worthwhile, too."

"Being a prime seems pretty worthwhile," Virrie said with a smile.

"But I'm not a prime," Leah insisted.

Taro seemed intrigued by the possibility. "Like I said," he repeated, "maybe you should come back with me for a visit."

Mally looked up at that. This whole time she'd sat quietly by Taro, eating her food and playing with her sketches. "Could I come, too?" she asked.

Virrie looked dismayed. "Don't you like Chialto? I thought you were having a good time."

Mally nodded. "I'm having a *very* good time. But I'm worried about Natalie. Maybe she misses me."

"Do you miss her?" Leah asked quietly.

"A little bit."

"Maybe she could come here for a visit," Leah offered.

"Not a bad idea," Taro said. "Romelle could probably use a break. I'll suggest it when I get back." He glanced at Leah. "Though I still think you should come with me to the estate sometime."

Leah produced a strangled laugh. "To see if I'm prime? I'm *never* coming home with you if that's the reason."

Taro was smiling. "Well, we'll see."

Josetta picked up the meat platter and handed it to Virrie. "Come on, everybody, eat up. We don't want anything to go to waste."

After the meal, Mally took Leah on a tour of the house, which was full of quirky nooks and charming surprises. The best room was the lounge that Darien had had built for Zoe, a place full of huge windows, soft furniture, and a circular fountain that ringed the whole room like a bubbling brook.

"It's Zoe's favorite spot in the city, as you might imagine," said

Josetta, who had accompanied them. "Though I almost like her aunt Saronne's place better."

"What's special there?"

"She has an indoor pool that looks like a tiny lake you might find somewhere in the wild. The water is surrounded by rocks and plants and the whole space is enclosed with glass, so you can use it year-round. That's where I learned to swim."

Leah shook her head. "Coru folk. They do go to extremes."

Josetta looked over her shoulder. "Well, Taro isn't much better. He *hates* coming to Chialto. Everyone thinks it's because he doesn't like the politicking, but I think it's because he can't stand being so far from the land. He never bothers trying to explain it to Darien, but Zoe understands."

Leah nodded. "When I lived with Taro and Virrie, he was never so happy as when he was outside, kneeling in the garden or simply walking around the property. I used to think that, if he could do it, he'd plant his feet in the soil and simply sink into the earth—just let it absorb him."

Mally had taken a seat on a little bridge that arched over the fountain, and she was dangling her bare toes into the water. "Maybe that's what he'll do when he wants to die," she said.

"Mally!" Leah exclaimed. "What a sad thought!"

Mally shrugged. "I don't think *Taro* would be sad."

Josetta smiled at Leah. "I think she's right."

Leah held her hands up. "I can't think of a world without Taro. So no more of that talk."

Josetta swept an arm out to include the whole house. "Do you like it? There's plenty of room."

"Plenty of room for—?" Suddenly she remembered that afternoon at the palace, the day she'd first met her daughter. Darien had suggested that Leah could take up residence in his house along with Virrie and Mally. "For *me*?"

"Exactly! We'd love to have you."

Leah fixed her eyes on Mally and thought about it. She had been panicked—terrified, actually—when Darien first suggested it, but now the arrangement had a definite appeal. She would be able to see her daughter every day, casually, intimately, easily. Mally would get used to her, maybe even grow to love her, without any awkwardness or anxiety. But Leah would fall even deeper into Darien's debt, would be adhering even more closely to whatever script he'd laid out for her life. And she'd lose her independence, not a small consideration for a woman who'd been on her own for five years. She could not, for instance, easily bring a lover back to this house—

What lover? she thought, forcing her thoughts to pull up short. *You want to trust Chandran, but he is still a cipher. He is still the man who murdered his wife. He should not be the reason you turn away from something you want with all your heart.*

"I can see you have some reservations," Josetta said as Leah remained silent. "I have to tell you, I usually do everything I can to avoid falling in with Darien's schemes! He's so sure of himself and he's so often right that sometimes I'll refuse him just to be spiteful. He can bring out my most stubborn side. But in this case, I think Darien's plan has many advantages."

Leah frowned at her. "I can't remember," she said slowly. "Do you know—my situation?"

Josetta nodded seriously. "Virrie told me," she said. "*Not* Darien or Zoe."

"So the idea is attractive for many reasons. But I'm not sure—"

"Well, keep two things in mind," Josetta said. "One, it's a big house and it's a shame for it to stand half empty, staffed with servants. That's how Darien convinced me to move here in the first place, because he knows how much I hate things to go to waste! And two—" She spread her hands and smiled. "If you don't like it, you can always move out again. Just pack your things and go."

"That's an excellent point."

"And three," Josetta went on in an innocent voice, "you can always invite your friends here to visit."

"Friends?"

Josetta couldn't hold back a smile. "That Zoe *did* tell me. Annova told her."

Leah covered her face with her hand. She'd forgotten what it was like to be talked about, even by people she liked. Gossip was the primary occupation of the Five Families, of course, but this had been so *fast.* "It's a really complicated story," she said, dropping her hand.

"And you don't have to tell me—or Zoe or anyone. I just wanted to make the point that living here wouldn't mean—well. You know."

Leah laughed. "You're the most unconventional princess!"

Josetta beamed. "I *know*. I *try* to be. Corene is such a hellion, but she's far more proper than I am."

They turned to go and Josetta tapped Mally's shoulder as they approached her. "Come on, little girl, almost time for you to go to bed."

Mally held her hands up, and the two women hauled her to her feet. She didn't let go, so the three of them squeezed through the doorway together and continued down the hallway still handfast. Leah thought she had never felt anything so small and perfect against her palm.

"Have you heard from Corene?" she asked, to keep herself from getting overemotional.

"Oh yes. Letters on an erratic basis, full of *Melissande* and *the queen* and *Foley* and all these other people I don't know. She appears to be having a wonderful time. As well as winning her father some friends at court, so that pleases him greatly."

"I'm glad. I didn't know Corene that well, but I thought she was so—" Leah wasn't sure how to describe the redheaded princess. "I thought that if she had the desire and the skill to do something, she would be almost unstoppable," she said at last. "She just hadn't figured out yet what she wanted."

"Exactly right. Leaving Welce was probably the smartest thing she ever did for herself." Josetta sighed. "But I miss her."

Isn't that the best thing any of us can hope for? Leah wondered. *That someone will miss us when we're not around?*

Virrie and Rafe were still in the dining room when they returned. "Taro had to go outside and find a patch of dirt to stand in," Virrie said. "He'll be back in to say good night."

Mally dropped Josetta's hand but held on to Leah's and swung around to face her. "Are you going to come live here?" she asked.

Leah's heart managed one painful bound and then stopped beating altogether. "Do you think that's a good idea?" she asked.

Mally nodded. "It's very nice here," she said. "I think you'd like it."

"Maybe," Leah said, wrinkling her nose. "I've lived alone a long time."

"But you don't have to do that anymore," Mally said.

"Living alone isn't natural for a torz girl," Virrie said. "Elay, maybe, but not torz."

"I *never* had a chance to live by myself," Josetta said wistfully. "I think it sounds wonderful."

"Hey," Rafe protested.

She smiled at him. "Well, *now* I don't want to."

Mally was still looking up at Leah. "Do *you* want to?"

It took supreme effort to look down into those solemn eyes and not start crying. "I don't," she said, her voice just above a whisper. "I want to live here. With all of you."

So that would be a big change in a lifetime of big changes, but Leah was so busy she hardly had time to savor it. Things were so demanding at the shop for the next few days that she couldn't even think about packing her belongings and relocating. She would wait until firstday, when the whole world came to a brief halt. And then she would go live with her daughter.

It was the most exhilarating, frightening thing she had ever anticipated.

Chandran approved. She hadn't been sure exactly what to tell him—how to tell him—so she waited until Annova volunteered to fetch lunch and they were briefly alone in the shop.

"It's an excellent plan," he said immediately.

"I'll get to see Mally every day. I can hardly believe it. But I—well, I won't have as much freedom. People will know where I am all the time, and I—"

He smiled. "That is a good thing," he assured her. "I think it has been too long since there was someone who would know by morning if you had not survived the night."

Who will know if you *have survived the night?* she wanted to ask. *Who has known for the past fifteen years? You've been on your own longer than I have.* She was beginning to think that was what had drawn them together in the first place. A longing for connection between two isolated people who were not, by nature, creatures of solitude.

"But I still want— It is important to me— There are still things I need to learn about you," she floundered.

He nodded. "Good. We will proceed, just in a somewhat adjusted fashion."

"Lately it seems my life is nothing *but* adjustments."

"Life usually is."

Darien supplied a car and driver to help Leah make the transition from her rented room to his elegant house. She wouldn't have said that she had too many possessions, but it still took Leah, Yori, and Rafe multiple trips to transfer all her belongings to the elaymotive.

"This is the best part," Rafe said when they pulled up in front of the house late in the afternoon. "Darien's excellent servants can carry everything inside."

The elaymotive was speedily unpacked, but Leah stopped Yori before she drove away. "Would you be free next firstday to take me to the harbor?" she asked. "I need to make another buying trip."

Yori nodded. "The regent says I'm *always* free to take you where you need to go."

"Really? Then is there somewhere *you* would like to go? Because I would *instantly* find in myself an intense desire to visit that place."

Yori laughed and climbed back into the smoker car. "I'll keep that in mind."

Mally was waiting just inside the door. "I've picked your room," she said. "But Virrie says you can have a different one if you don't like it."

Is it close to yours? "Let me see what my options are," Leah answered. "I'm sure I'll like anything."

It turned out that the second story of the house had originally been intended for family members, and the third story for guests; even today, Rafe and Josetta had rooms on the second level, while Virrie and Mally were a floor above. The suite Mally had chosen for Leah was also on the third floor, on the opposite end of the hallway from the rooms that housed the other two. It was full of light, decorated in white and green, and overlooked a small garden that was almost completely dead at this time of year.

"Because you're torz," Mally explained. "You need to see the land, even when it's not very pretty."

Leah sank to the cushion of the window seat, and Mally climbed up beside her. "So do you, for the same reason."

"I keep some in my room."

"Land? *Dirt?*"

"Rocks. It's almost the same thing."

Mally stayed with her while Leah unpacked her bags and even offered an opinion, when asked, about what clothes Leah should change into for dinner.

"It's a special meal," she explained. "We're having company."

"Really? Who?"

"Nelson and Beccan and Rhan."

Leah felt a jolt of panic shiver down her bones. "The Ardelays. Really," she managed to say. "I wonder whose idea that was?"

"Taro wanted to see Nelson," Mally said.

That made sense. The two primes weren't often in the same city. "We do want to dress up for Nelson," Leah said. "Come on. Let's go find something pretty for you. Shall I fix your hair?"

"Can you braid it?"

"With *ribbons*."

"Then yes, please."

In a half hour, Mally and Leah were both suitably attired and heading downstairs for the evening meal. Even from the second-story landing, Leah could hear voices and laughter drifting up from the main floor. She tried to ease back her tension.

Mally patted her on the wrist. "It will be fine," she said.

The child was practically a mind reader. *That's certainly a sweela trait. She has her grandfather's sensitivity to other people's moods.* "Sometimes I get nervous when I have to make conversation with a lot of people," Leah said.

"Virrie says nobody else has to talk when Nelson's here," Mally said.

That made Leah laugh so hard she was still smiling when they entered the dining room.

"Mally!" Nelson roared and charged across the room to sweep her up in a tight embrace.

"Don't terrify the poor child," protested Beccan, who was trailing after him. She smiled at Mally over Nelson's shoulder. "Hello, there. We're so happy to see you again."

Mally, looking anything but terrified, laughed down at Beccan. "He's silly," she said.

"He is," Beccan agreed.

Rhan strolled up to join them, and suddenly they were a little family group, standing together casually. Mother, father, daughter, grandparents. Leah felt her breath turn to cinders in her throat.

"When my brother and I were little, my father would throw us into the air and catch us again," Rhan told Mally. He reached a hand up to her and she solemnly shook it. "My mother was always afraid he'd drop us, but he never did. It was the most fun ever. Saddest day of my life was when he told me I was too big to toss around."

"I don't want to be thrown in the air," Mally said.

"What if I twirl you around instead?" Nelson asked, holding her away from his body as he began spinning in circles. Mally's infectious laugh rang out; now everyone else in the little family group was smiling.

"Such a challenge raising children with such a childlike man," Beccan observed.

Rhan enveloped her in a bear hug and squeezed her so tightly she squealed. "But you managed to do a wonderful job anyway," he said.

Finally someone else came over to join them, breaking up the intimate tableau. It was Taro, looking like he'd just spent the afternoon weeding the garden. "You're here five minutes and already causing a commotion," was his greeting.

Nelson handed Mally to Beccan and gave the torz prime a critical inspection. "I'm glad you thought it was worthwhile to dress up for us," he said.

Taro laughed heartily. "I dress up for dinner at the palace and nowhere else."

"*Leah* put some effort into her appearance," Rhan said innocently. "She must have known we were coming."

"Yes, because I always want to impress you, Rhan," she snapped back. He merely grinned at her.

Taro waved everyone toward the table. "Come on, then. Let's eat."

Despite the fact that her bones buzzed with nervous energy and she was constantly squirming in her chair, Leah had a splendid time at the dinner party. Nelson was endlessly entertaining, Beccan and Rhan were almost as amusing, and it was clear that everybody in the room liked everybody else. Well, Leah and Rhan were edgy with each other. But the primes were obviously great friends, their wives enjoyed each other's company, and Josetta was at ease with the whole lot of them. Rafe didn't contribute much to the conversation, but his quick eyes darted from face to face as he listened closely and laughed along with the rest of them. It might have been the most relaxed meal Leah had had since she sailed back to Welce.

"Do you two have official business to discuss?" Josetta asked as they finished up with the course of sweets. "The rest of us can go somewhere else while you talk."

"That's an excellent plan," Nelson approved.

The seven of them ended up in the room with the circular fountain. Most of them disposed themselves on various chairs and sofas in the middle of the room, but Mally sat down at the edge of the water and was instantly barefoot. Rhan settled next to her and started unlacing his own shoes.

Leah was watching them enviously when Mally glanced around the room. "Leah," she said, holding her hand out. "Come sit with us."

Everyone else looked carefully in the other direction while Leah swallowed her heart, stiffened her spine, and made her way to the fountain. Rhan smiled up at her lazily. His feet were already in the stream.

"You'd think the water would be cold, but it's not," he said. "Trust Zoe to put in a *heated* fountain. Because, of course, she'd want to go wading in it."

"I'll sit here, but I'm not getting in the water," Leah said, dropping to the floor on the other side of Mally. "I put too much effort into trying to look elegant. I'm not going to ruin the effect."

Rhan made an exaggerated bow. "You look magnificent no matter how you're attired," he said, "but suit yourself."

"There's a fish!" Mally cried, pointing at a slim golden shape wriggling past. "Maybe we could bring the reifarjin here if it ever gets lonely."

"I think it eats other fish, so probably not," Leah answered.

"Mally was telling me about your little pet the other day. It sounds quite fierce."

"I like him," Mally said.

"He's exotic and strange," Leah said. "But I like him, too."

"So, Mally," Rhan said. "Tell me what else you like about Leah's shop. What should I look for if I go there?"

Mally obliged, talking about the striated rocks, the colorful scarves, the wooden boxes. Her voice slowed a couple of times and she paused to yawn, but then she kicked her feet in the water as if to wake herself up and continued in a slightly louder voice. Leah found herself smiling knowingly at Rhan over Mally's dark braids.

"Are you getting sleepy?" she asked, bending down to get a better look at the little girl's face.

"No," Mally said instantly.

"We could sit on a couch. It might be more comfortable," Rhan suggested.

"I like it here," Mally insisted. As if afraid they might abandon her for soft cushions and dry flooring, she grabbed one of Leah's hands and one of Rhan's and held on tight. "You stay, too."

Leah rearranged herself to relieve a slight strain in her back. "No one's going anywhere," she said.

"I feel like it's the time to tell sweet stories in a soft voice," Rhan said in low tones. "Soothing tales about bunnies and small children."

"Do you *know* any stories like that?"

"I was hoping you did."

Leah rolled her eyes. She'd never in her life tried to talk a child to sleep. But she would do anything to keep Mally nestled against her shoulder, her small hand curled trustingly around Leah's fingers. "My father was an actor," she said in a quiet singsong. "And there was a play his troupe would perform every year at Quinnelay changeday. It was about a little girl who left home to make her way in the world . . ."

It wasn't, actually. It featured a grown woman who got bored with her husband's lovemaking and snuck out of his house one afternoon to have a series of adventures. Leah thought she might be able to modify a few of the events to suit her audience. She'd just leave out the parts about the excessive alcohol and the foreign lovers.

Mally seemed to like it; at any rate, she grew increasingly still and listened without asking questions. Eventually, she rested her head so heavily against Leah's arm that Leah peered down to see if her eyes were still open. Yes, but barely.

"Are you sure you don't want to go sit on a couch?" Leah murmured.

"I like it here," Mally repeated, this time through a yawn.

"But you could put your head down on a pillow while you listen to me finish the story."

"I can put my head down *here*," Mally answered. And she crossed her arms—pulling Rhan's hand all the way to Leah's knee and Leah's hand toward Rhan's leg—and rested her head on top of her forearms. Her sigh was one of absolute contentment.

Leah stared down at the dark hair and was absolutely speechless. In the weave of hands and wrists, she could catch the rhythm of all three of their heartbeats, feel the specific and varying layers of heat rising from each of their bodies. She had never felt such a powerful, visceral connection with any other human beings.

We made this, she thought numbly. *Rhan and I—we* made *her. We are joined in her body. And we can never separate those component parts again as long as we live.*

She risked a look at Rhan, whose face was as serious as she'd ever seen it. He wasn't watching her, though. He was gazing down at Mally with an expression of confusion and longing that was wholly familiar to Leah. She thought the very same emotions must be on her own face.

She glanced at the other people in the room, none of them near enough to have overheard any of their exchanges. Virrie and Josetta and Rafe were engaged in a lively debate and paying no attention to anyone else, but Beccan was staring their way, her face equally sober. She didn't have to speak, didn't have to shout her words across the cheerful room, but Leah could guess what she was thinking. *Mine. The man and the girl, both mine. I made them.*

Leah hadn't expected this. Love—she'd thought she was prepared to feel that. Sorrow, at everything she'd missed so far. Eagerness, worry, hope, fear, determination—she'd figured she would run the gamut of emotions and maybe invent new ones. But she hadn't expected to look at this child and feel this sense of unmoored wonder that anything she had ever done with her hands, with her body, had produced anything so profound as this. She hadn't expected divinity.

THIRTEEN

L eah's second nineday as a shopkeeper proceeded as briskly as the first, but she had her rhythm down now and each day went a little more smoothly. Though sales continued to be strong, the crowds had fallen off enough that she and Chandran and Annova could each grab a break a couple of times a day, while still managing to keep stock replenished on an hourly basis. That meant Leah was locking up more quickly at the end of the day and having more free time at night.

She'd developed a rhythm for those early evenings, too. She and Chandran would walk to the Plaza of Women—or, on some of the increasingly colder days, take one of the transports—and wander around until they found a place that served food or drink. Leah never ate much on those outings, saving her appetite for dinner with Mally, but she looked forward to the hours spent alone with Chandran as her reward for the challenges of the day. They discussed shop business, of course, what was selling and what wasn't, but they talked about themselves, too. They had begun telling each other stories about their childhoods and young adult years—adventures and misadventures that occurred before the great calamities that had sent each of them, ten years apart, into exile in Malinqua.

But they never mentioned the calamities themselves—the circumstances, the occurrences, the conversations, the miscalculations, the emotions. It was as if each of them had excised crucial years from their lives and spliced the remaining parts together into one imperfect whole. Such a feat should have made them both seem younger, Leah thought, but the opposite was true. Each of them carried those missing years around as if they had spanned twice the allotted days; each of them had been aged by events. Each of them had been broken.

But we both want to be whole again, Leah thought one night as they shared a bottle of wine and talked over the day. *We're both hoping to find a way to make the future erase the tragedies of the past.*

During working hours, she rarely had time for such quiet, philosophical musings. While the crowds were smaller, the customers tended to be more demanding, and Leah often found herself waiting on some imperious matron from the Five Families who wanted Leah's undivided attention while she considered every piece of merchandise in the shop.

Worse still were the customers who assumed their wealth and class entitled them to any special service they desired. Which was how Leah found herself, one chilly day, accompanying an insistent Dochenza couple back to their house so she could advise them on where exactly to position the blown glass figurines they'd purchased to ornament their kierten. After spending an hour with them, trying every possible arrangement for the delicate statuary, Leah needed to walk back to the shop just to clear her head.

Right as she was crossing the Plaza of Women, the sun came out, chasing away some of the chill, and she paused a moment to feel the lick of heat along her cheekbones. That was when she spotted two Karkan men standing a few feet away, looking frustrated and indecisive. She didn't think she'd seen either one before, but they were expensively dressed and heavily bejeweled. Rich Karkans on the streets of Chialto. Surely they were connected to the prince.

Leah watched them a moment as they glared and argued, then she strode over and offered a cheerful smile. "You look lost," she said in Coziquela. "Can I help you?"

One of the men shook his head, but the other smiled back. "We would appreciate that," he said. "We had heard that there was a temple near the Plaza of Women, but we can't find it."

"It's not far, but it's not *right* here," Leah said. "I can take you there, if you like."

"We hate to trouble you," said the surlier man, but again his companion smiled.

"That would be kind," he said.

They fell in step beside her as she led the way. "I don't recognize your accent," she lied. "Are you visiting from somewhere else?"

"The Karkades," the friendly one answered.

"Oh, that's so far away!"

He laughed. "There are days that does seem true."

"Are you enjoying yourself so far? Why do you want to see the temple?"

The taciturn one turned his frown first on Leah, then his companion, but the second man answered anyway. "Just a ritual we like to observe when we visit new countries. Visit the shrines, make donations to the poor, offer some small thanks for the hospitality we've been given."

"What a lovely thought!" Leah exclaimed. "I'll have to remember that if I ever go traveling."

The talkative one glanced over at her. "Is a temple the best place to make such a donation?"

Leah nodded. "Most of the tithes go to cover upkeep on the temples themselves, but you can leave bigger offerings as well, and the money will get distributed to various charities."

He nodded. "Excellent."

Once they arrived at the small stone temple, Leah escorted them inside, showed them the tithing box, explained how the blessings worked, and offered to choose coins for them. "Not today, thank you very much," said the smiling man, pulling a small lumpy bag from his inner pocket. The contents were too thick to fit through the slot on the top of the box, so Leah pried up the lid and he settled the bag on the layer of coppers and quint-silvers already in place.

"Well, that's done," said his friend. "Now we have to get back."

They parted ways outside the temple door, Leah claiming she had business on the other end of town. She watched them hike back toward the Plaza, arguing again, then she set off in the other direction. When she judged they were out of sight, she returned to the temple. Two women had entered while she wasn't looking, so she had to sit patiently on the sweela bench, pretending to meditate, until they'd pulled their blessings and departed. Then she was back at the tithing box, pulling out the bag and peering inside.

And then staring.

Jewels. Of every color, every description. Some small and sparkling, even in the temple's dim light; others larger, darker, glowing with a buried radiance. She couldn't even calculate how much this treasure trove was worth, but it would be an astonishing sum. This was not just some thoughtful gesture, a token thanks for a host's hospitality. This was a form of reparation.

Leah replaced the bag, closed the lid, and left the temple, moving slowly, so deep in thought she almost wandered off the path twice. She kept remembering one specific phrase Chandran had used to describe the Karkan philosophy. *A woman who wants to cheat on her husband might buy him a very expensive gift to bank her forgiveness in advance.* This was a very expensive gift from the Karkades to Welce. What did the Karkans expect to be atoning for? What could they possibly be planning to do that would require such a lavish apology? And was there any way to stop them?

L eah had no time to brood over the Karkan donation once she returned to the shop, because Annova was at the door, greeting her with relief.

"A customer has just arrived and she only wants to deal with you," Annova said quietly. Leah brushed a hand through her hair, hoping it looked presentable, and glanced quickly around the shop to see if she could identify who had come calling.

In fact, there were two women browsing through the aisles, both finely dressed and reeking of money. One was tall, slender, and somewhat plain-featured, though her elaborate clothing and hairstyle added a great deal to her attractiveness. But it was the other woman who instantly caught Leah's attention. She was shorter and small-boned, with a heart-shaped face and masses of gorgeous red hair. Of course Leah recognized her. She was the old king's third wife, Corene's mother, and Darien's onetime lover: Alys.

Everyone knew the turbulent history of the sweela queen. Even when King Vernon was still alive, Alys had been notorious for her scheming, frequently creating scandals within the royal court. Corene's relationship with her had always been strained, and Darien made no secret of the fact that he despised her. The only person Leah knew who actually liked her was Rhan—and Rhan had a taste for vagrants and miscreants, so that was hardly a recommendation.

Leah glided over to greet her. "Majesty," she said, bowing deeply. "I'm so sorry I wasn't here the moment you arrived."

"Oh, are you Leah?" Alys replied in a light voice. "I have heard *such* things about your new place here. I couldn't let another day go by without seeing it for myself."

"I have gathered merchandise from across the kingdoms of the southern seas," Leah said, the phrase coming out a little more pompously than she'd planned. "Are you interested in items from anywhere in particular? Are you looking for a scarf, a jewel, or some other accessory? Perhaps an exotic food or beverage?"

"I am open to all possibilities," Alys replied, strolling slowly along the hunti display table and letting her fingers trail across the wooden boxes, the painted ceramic skulls. "Anything might catch my attention."

"Then I can just let you wander at your leisure."

"Oh, no, do accompany me and explain everything," Alys said, smiling at her prettily. It was odd, Leah thought, the queen and her daughter looked very similar, yet Leah's guess was that they were nothing alike. Corene could manage a regal, impassive bearing when she had to, but most of the time, she showed clearly what she was thinking or feeling; she could be impetuous, petulant, delightful, difficult, frightened, or fierce, all within the space of a few minutes. Alys looked like someone who would smile at you no matter what emotions raged behind her green eyes—and then slip a knife between your ribs the minute you weren't looking. She'd still be smiling when she did it.

"Gladly," Leah said. "Just tell me when I start to bore you."

The queen followed so closely behind Leah that Leah could smell her cinnamon perfume and hear the faint clatter of her beaded bracelet. It was hardly a surprise that Alys was drawn to the prettiest and most expensive items on the tables. She wrapped shawls around her shoulders, held earrings up to her cheeks, and sniffed at every jar of perfume in the store.

"Is *that* for sale?" she asked, pointing to the reifarjin.

"No, it's mine. But I could tell you where I purchased it. They might have more left."

"I'd probably have to feed it, though, wouldn't I? And make sure it always had enough water." The queen laughed. "I tend not to be very good at remembering to care for other creatures."

Her companion, who was a few paces away, looked up with a sardonic expression. "That's what servants are for," she said.

"I've never been very good at it, either," Leah said. *Though I'm getting better.* "So far I've managed to keep the fish alive. That seems like a good start."

"Next you could get a whole *school* of fish," the queen suggested, amused. "Then perhaps a stable of horses. And eventually, who knows? Children!"

Leah hoped her smile covered the painful contraction of her heart. "It might take a while to work up to that," she said.

Alys wandered over to the other side of the shop, still trailing her fingers over every surface. "Do you want children, Leah?" she asked. Her tone was idle and incurious, as if she was just trying to maintain a polite conversation with a stranger. But Leah felt another skip in her heartbeat. She had the sense that Alys never posed casual questions.

"I might," she said. "If the circumstances were right."

Alys lifted her eyebrows. "Circumstances?"

How had they gotten on this topic? So quickly, so smoothly? How could Leah get them off of it? "If I had enough money, a big house, a reliable husband—you know, if I thought I could give a child a good life."

"There are a lot of reasons it's important to have the right husband, but you don't need one to have a baby," Alys said, laughing.

Well, you were married when you had your daughter, though your husband didn't sire the child. And you were married the second time you got pregnant, too, though I understand you never brought that child to term. Naturally, Leah did not say either of these things. Instead, she smiled her agreement. "You're right, of course," she said. "But for the moment, I'll stick with fish."

Alys picked up a Dhonshon scarf—dark green, shot through with gold and yellow—and draped it over her red curls. She glanced in a mirror, then turned to Leah, her eyebrows up in a question. *How do I look?*

"A magnificent color for you, majesty," Leah said.

With a quick motion, Alys slipped the scarf off her own head and flipped it onto Leah's, coming close enough to tuck the ends into the top of Leah's tunic. "Even more suitable for you," the queen decided, tilting her head to one side. "It brings out the highlights in your hair, which is somewhat dark. A little more rouge, a bit of lightening right here—" She reached up a delicate forefinger to trace the curve of Leah's eyebrow. "You could be a *very* pretty woman."

"Thank you, majesty," Leah said.

The queen was still regarding her, tapping her own lip with one finger. "It's so odd," she said. "I feel like I've seen you before. More than once. Could that be?"

Welchin was not a good language for cursing, but Leah silently chanted a few satisfactory Coziquela obscenities she'd learned over the years. "I don't know. I grew up in Welce, but I've been living abroad for some time. I've only been back a few ninedays."

"Yes, my memory of you could easily be several years old," Alys said. She reached up to adjust the scarf, pushing it back to reveal more of Leah's hair. "We were at a dinner or a party or someplace fancy. And you were very well-dressed. Does that sound familiar?"

Indeed it did. "No, your majesty."

"Who were your parents?"

"My father was an actor, and my mother was a young woman who fell in love with him," Leah said, managing a wry smile. "From what I understand, it was something that happened a great deal."

The queen laughed. "Oh, I had a sweela father, so I understand that very well!" she exclaimed. "Perhaps I saw you in some theatrical production? Though that doesn't feel right."

Leah spread her hands helplessly. "I wouldn't think so."

"Well, I'll think of it. I always remember things when I want to."

Leah reached up and slowly pulled the scarf from her head, then folded it into neat thirds. Altogether, this day was proving to be a challenge to her nerves. "Is there anything else I can show you?"

Alys turned back toward the sweela displays. "I want to take another look at that ruby necklace."

Ten minutes and ten gold pieces later, the sweela queen and her friend were gone. Leah waited until they were lost among the crowd of other shoppers on the street, then turned to give Annova an expressive look. A smile was already lightening Annova's dark face.

"Of all the people I thought might recognize me, Queen Alys wasn't even on the list!" Leah exclaimed.

"Do you remember meeting her?"

"Oh yes. I was at a party at Nelson's and I was—" *I was arguing with Rhan. Mostly because he was flirting with Alys.* "And I wasn't having a particularly good time. But I don't remember doing anything so remarkable that the queen would have had any reason to notice me."

Annova shrugged. "Does it matter if she knows who you are? You're not trying to conceal the fact that you grew up in Welce, are you?"

It matters because she might remember that I was at the party with Rhan. Because she might figure out the truth about me. About Mally. Because someday I want everyone to know that Mally belongs to me, but I don't want them to learn that information from Alys.

Because I don't want her to find some way to hurt Mally.

"No, it doesn't matter at all," Leah said, trying to speak lightly. "Now let's decide what we can bring downstairs to replace that ruby necklace she bought! I can't say I like Alys very much, but she certainly has excellent taste."

On ninthday, Annova and Chandran and Leah reviewed their inventory and discussed what items Leah should look for when she drove to the harbor in the morning. When Annova headed out to pick up lunch, Leah invited Chandran to accompany her on the buying trip, and she was surprised and disappointed when he declined.

"It is is a very long ride to the harbor and back in very small quarters, and that is too much intimacy for a long day," he explained. "We must abide by the rules we ourselves have set."

"Yori will be with us the whole time. The driver."

He looked at her. "A large man might easily overcome two women. Especially on an extended journey down an often deserted road."

"I can defend myself better than you seem to realize," Leah said with mordant humor. "And Yori has never said so, but I'm sure she's one of Darien's guards, not just a driver. You might find us harder to disable than you think."

"I am glad to hear it," he said. "Maybe some other time."

She returned to Darien's house that night feeling confused and slightly depressed, though she tried to shake off the mood so she could enjoy the evening. Both Josetta and Rafe had been gone for most of the nineday—she to work in her southside shelter, he to do a stint flying test aeromotives for Kayle Dochenza.

"You might even run into him down at the harbor tomorrow," Virrie said. "Since that's where Kayle's factory is based. They say that sometimes the pilots fly over the harbor itself, and everyone runs outside and stares up at the sky, shouting and pointing."

"I admit, I'd like to see an aeromotive one day," Leah said. "Though I don't think I'd want to be *in* one." She appealed to Mally. "How about you? Would you like to go flying?"

"No," Mally said. "It's too far from the ground."

"That's exactly what Taro says," Virrie observed. "But someday I'd like to be in one. Just to see what it's like."

It was Leah's turn to tuck Mally into bed and, as usual, Mally requested a story. This time she was specific. "Tell me about when you were a little girl."

How much of *this* actual tale should she truthfully relate? "My mother was a rich young woman who fell in love with a poor young actor," Leah said. "They didn't have a house of their own. They lived in a big wooden wagon that was part of a caravan with seven or eight other wagons, and they traveled all across the western provinces, putting on plays. When I was born, they just kept traveling, so I grew up in that wagon."

Mally was fascinated. "There was no kitchen? What did you eat?"

"Mostly we bought prepared or dried food when we stopped in little towns. Sometimes we made campfires and cooked outdoors."

"Did you sleep in the wagon?"

"Mostly. Sometimes in the summer we'd sleep outside under the stars."

"Right on the *ground*?" The idea seemed to please her.

"Well, we had blankets. But yes. On the ground."

"That would be the best," Mally decided. "I want to do that."

Leah tilted her head. "You've never slept outside? That surprises me. I have to believe Taro does it with some regularity. Or rather, that some nights he's out walking the estates and just forgets to come home."

"I don't know about Taro," Mally said. "But *I* want to."

"Then we'll do it sometime," Leah promised. "When it's warmer. You and me." She smiled. "It will be the most fun I've ever had."

FOURTEEN

Yori picked Leah up in the morning, so early that the whole world still looked black and white. The sky was nothing but a promise of light over a landscape of stark shadows, and frost added a pale gilding to the dark patterns of houses and trees.

"It's *cold*," Leah complained as she slid into the front seat.

Yori grinned. "It's Quinnasweela."

They were down the Cinque and across the canal bridge before most of the city had woken up. Yori drove with her usual calm competence, but Leah couldn't stop yawning for the first thirty minutes of the drive. It was her own fault that they'd set off at such an early hour. She wanted to get back tonight, no matter how late, because she had a shop to run in the morning. She needed to take advantage of every daylight hour available.

They arrived in the harbor while it was still mid-morning, and the first thing Leah spotted was a heavy freighter tying up at the southernmost dock. It was flying a bold red flag divided by crossed swords and covered with a field of white flowers. "Look at that," Leah said in satisfaction. "A Malinquese ship has just sailed into port. Let's see what it has for sale."

The captain was a slim, hollow-eyed woman who looked frail

enough to blow overboard in a high wind, but she had an eye for merchandise and a stubborn streak when it came to negotiating prices. Still, Leah bought three trunks of specialty foods, high-quality linens, and whimsical musical instruments and was convinced that she'd made a good deal.

She was less successful with the next two ships she tried, both from Berringey, walking away completely empty-handed from the second one. But the fourth ship was the real prize. Not only did it hail from Cozique, but the captain had swung by the Karkades on his way to Welce. Half his crew was Karkan, and he had a hold full of merchandise Leah hadn't seen anywhere else.

"I have a few Karkan expatriates as customers, and I think they're getting homesick," she told him. "What could you sell me that would make them eternally grateful? What's something they can't get anywhere else but home?"

Captain Demeset was a weathered old sailor with leathery skin, wild white hair, and a reprobate's smile. That smile lit his face as he considered her question. "Let me check with the cook in the galley," he said. "We brought treats for the crew—nothing we planned to sell, you understand—but there might be enough left to make up a special gift for a friend. If you would be willing to wait—?"

Leah settled back in the hard chair in his tiny office. "I would."

"I'll be back in a bit."

He was gone for fifteen minutes, during which time Leah tallied up what she'd purchased so far and how much money she had left to spend. Once she factored in the items she'd already committed to here, the answers were *quite a lot* and *not too much*. Well, she'd wrap up her business with Captain Demeset and then be on her way back to Chialto. It would be nightfall before they were home, but she considered it a good day's work.

Captain Demeset returned with an armload of small metal canisters that were stained with grease and dented from much use. "Cook says these are the three things Karkan sailors appreciate the most," he told her, setting them on the small table. "Not too much left of any of them, but might be worth your money anyway."

Leah scooted closer, smiling broadly. She liked Captain Demeset's attitude. "Let's see."

He pried the lid off a small container, and the tiny office instantly filled with a dark and sweetly wistful scent that made Leah think of funeral feasts and mourning sachets. "I love that," she said, inhaling deeply. "But it has an air of sadness to it. Is that an odd thing to say?"

"I had the same thought," the captain admitted. "Cook says it's a spice that only the very wealthy can afford. He put it in a dinner pudding for a special occasion, and the Karkans went wild for it."

Leah nodded. "All right. And the next item?"

This canister, when opened, released an odor so foul that both of them exclaimed aloud and Demeset recapped it as quickly as possible. "Cook said I wouldn't like this one, but I think it's gone bad," he said. "Your pardon."

"Maybe not," Leah said. "Did he put a name to it?"

"Shilly—shilty—something unpronounceable," Demeset replied.

"From the way it was described to me, I believe that's what it's supposed to smell like," she said. "But it's even worse than I expected."

Demeset looked doubtfully at the canister. "I think it's gone bad," he repeated. "You can't want this."

Leah smiled. "I think I do, though. But let's see what's in the last container."

The items in the final tin were hard, round candies with no particular scent, though both Leah and Captain Demeset were wary when the lid first came off. They peered in to try to get a rough count of the pieces inside—maybe thirty, Leah thought.

"Cook says these are dessert treats, but they come with a little kick," Demeset said. "More potent than wine, so he'll only dole out one or two to a man."

"Easier to transport than liquor," Leah observed. "But I hate to deprive your crew of a special indulgence."

Demeset grinned. "These are leftover bits. Cook says he's got full tins of all three—though if he has any more of that shilly stuff in the galley, I'd be tempted to throw it overboard."

Leah laughed. "I don't blame you. But my friend spoke of it so longingly that I've got to try to give her a supply."

"So you want all three?"

"I do."

They haggled amiably over the price since, for Demeset, this was an add-on sale and he didn't need to make much of a profit. When they were done, Leah had arranged to buy such a large quantity of merchandise that the captain wondered if she had enough room to transport it home.

"I do," she answered. "But my driver and I might need help getting it all in the elaymotive."

"Ah, now that's something I'd like to get a closer look at," Demeset answered.

"Then come on down with me," Leah invited. "And my driver will take you around the harbor."

Once a couple of sailors had helped Leah and Yori pack all the goods into the smoker car, Yori took Captain Demeset on a quick tour through the nearest streets. He returned looking both delighted and unnerved.

"It doesn't seem right that anything can travel like that, with nothing pulling it or pushing it along," he said as he climbed out. "But I can think of ten lords in Cozique right now who might want to own such a thing."

"The elaymotives are built in a factory near here," Leah told him. "I know the owner and I'm sure I could find the address."

"I know right where it is," said Yori, who was lounging against the car and listening with interest. "I've taken the regent there a dozen times."

Demeset looked undecided. "Probably more than I could afford as a speculative investment."

"Maybe," Leah said. "But it might be worth the conversation to find out."

Demeset nodded. "Let's go talk to the owner." He glanced at Leah. "If you have time to make the introduction?"

She was eager to get back on the road, but she wouldn't often have the chance to broker a deal between a Welchin prime and a Coziquela merchant, so she nodded and squeezed in next to Demeset in the front seat. Yori drove carefully through the crowded and poorly maintained streets until they arrived at a huge, featureless building with a bright yellow roof. Once they unfolded themselves from the smoker car, Demeset sniffed cautiously at the air, which was heavy with a bitter, oily odor.

"It smells almost as bad as the shilly," he remarked.

"I was thinking the same thing."

As they headed for the door, Leah was wondering if she should warn Captain Demeset about Kayle Dochenza. She'd known the elay prime fairly well when she lived with Taro and Virrie, and people weren't entirely joking when they described him as a madman. Kayle Dochenza didn't seem to move through the world with the same solidity as most people did; he appeared to be far more focused on thoughts and ideas than on living creatures occupying corporeal space. Strangers tended to find that unsettling the first time they met him.

The door opened before she could reach for it, and Rafe Adova stepped out.

"Leah!" he exclaimed. "What are you doing here?"

She had completely forgotten Rafe might be at the harbor. She smiled at him. "I'm shopping for merchandise, of course."

He laughed. "I didn't think you had enough floor space to sell elaymotives."

"No, but I just concluded my business with Captain Demeset of Cozique and he expressed an interest in learning more about elaymotives—and so here we are."

She knew that Rafe had never been in the retail business, but he used to make his living by convincing strangers to play cards with him for money, so he had an effortless charm designed to put anyone at ease. "Then he's come to the right place," Rafe said. "Kayle Dochenza isn't here, but his agent is. Why don't I take you up to meet him?"

Captain Demeset turned to give Leah a slight bow. "Thank you. I'll be happy to do business with you next time I'm in port."

"And I with you. You can find your own way back to your ship?"

"Easily."

"Then I'll be on my way."

"You're going back to the house tonight?" Rafe asked.

"Yes—are you? You can ride with us if you like."

"That would be perfect. Josetta's supposed to be there, and she said

Zoe was coming over for dinner. Let me just make quick introductions, and I'll be right back."

While he was gone, Yori and Leah moved some of their recent acquisitions to the front seat so Leah and Rafe could sit in the back compartment more or less in comfort. Rafe still laughed when he came downstairs a few minutes later.

"Are you sure there's room for me?"

"More room than there is in a pilot's box in an aeromotive, from what I understand," she retorted. "And much less danger of crashing."

They climbed inside and situated themselves as best they could before Yori eased the car back into traffic. Rafe said, "Hey, I haven't crashed an aeromotive in—let's see—almost a quintile."

"And how many times did you crash one before that?"

"Four. But the last two were more like uncontrolled landings. I didn't even get bruises."

"So tell me what it's like to pilot an aeromotive."

Rafe was a good storyteller, with an attractive voice and an excellent sense of the dramatic, so Leah found herself enthralled by his descriptions of flying. "It almost makes me want to go up in one with you someday," she said.

"You couldn't—not yet. So far Kayle's only built machines that can hold one person and a small bit of cargo. But he has grander plans. He thinks someday they'll be like transport buses and carry twenty or thirty people at a time."

"That'll be bad when the first one goes down," Leah commented. "Unless you think they'll be completely safe by then."

"I doubt it. But elaymotives aren't danger-free, either. Neither is riding a horse. Nothing is."

"I suppose not," Leah said on a sigh.

"Even your time in Malinqua had to be hazardous now and then," he said. "So tell me what your life was like while you were there spying for Darien."

She regaled him with a few stories, then spent twenty minutes describing the customs and peculiarities of the Malinquese people. "But you should go see for yourself," she finished up. "I'm sure your brother would love to show you off to the court."

"Ah, I can't leave Welce," Rafe said with a smile. He absently fingered the strange design sculpted into his right ear. "My cousin Ghyaneth, the prince of Berringey, made it clear that he would kill me if I ever left the country. He's afraid I would try to usurp his crown. To ensure peace between our nations, we made all sorts of promises to each other, and one of mine was that I'd never set foot off Welchin soil."

Leah had a feeling there was far more to the tale but this was all Rafe was prepared to divulge. She didn't want people poking into her secrets, either, so she let it go. "He doesn't sound like he's a very nice person."

Rafe laughed. "I don't believe he is."

Full dark had fallen by the time they crossed the canal and turned onto the Cinque. Leah saw Rafe's eyes cut toward the slums as they passed the shadows and silhouettes of those dark streets. Thinking about Josetta at her shelter, she supposed, or remembering his old life as a gambler in a southside tavern. He might not have crossed the boundaries of Welce, but in his way he'd traveled even farther than Leah.

Yori called to them from the front seat. "Should we swing by the regent's house to drop off our passenger before going to the shop?"

"Of course not!" Rafe exclaimed before Leah could answer. "You saved me a long, dull trip on public transportation. The least I can do is help you unload all of your purchases."

"Glad you feel that way," Leah said, "because I was going to tell Yori no."

The whole street was eerily dark by the time Yori pulled up in front of Leah's. What illumination there was filtered down from the upper-story windows of the buildings where the owners lived above their shops. The gas-powered streetlamps lining the road marched mournfully into the distance, cold, dark, and unhelpful.

"A problem in the line," Yori said when Leah expressed dismay. "It happens all the time. It'll be fixed by morning."

Leah gestured at the upper stories. "But the gas seems to be working in *some* places."

"Candlelight," Rafe guessed. "See how it's flickering?"

When Leah looked more closely, she could tell that the illumination behind the windows was being supplied by a capricious and uneven source. She sighed. "Well, there are boxes of decorative candles on the sweela tables," she said. "We ought to be able to see well enough to carry this all inside."

It took them five trips each to transfer everything to the shop. After a single foray to the upper level—Yori lighting their way with a candle while Leah and Rafe wrestled a trunk up the narrow stairwell—they decided everything else could be left downstairs and dealt with in the morning.

"If customers stumble over boxes and bundles, so be it," Leah said, trying to strangle a yawn. "Maybe they'll find something they wouldn't have looked at otherwise."

They all stepped outside and Leah bent close to the door so she could see to set the lock. When she straightened, she found both Rafe and Yori standing motionless beside the elaymotive, staring hard at a shadow pooled on the ground against a nearby building.

Leah stepped noiselessly up to Rafe and whispered, "What is it?"

"Person," he breathed.

Yori crept forward on silent feet, waving the other two back when they started to follow. Leah was more convinced than ever that the other woman was one of Darien's guards. Yori approached the figure cautiously, her left hand close to her hip where Leah assumed she kept a weapon. A moment later, Leah realized Rafe had also shaken free a knife. He might consort with primes and princesses these days, but Rafe was a man who had lived in the slums and knew how to defend himself in a street fight.

Yori had gotten close enough to the shadowy shape that she could get a sense of whether or not it offered danger. Leah felt Rafe grow even more tense as Yori leaned over to ask a question—and then, a moment later, drop to her knees. That was signal enough for Rafe, who instantly jogged over to her. Leah trailed a half step behind.

"It's a young man," Yori said in a low voice as they crouched beside her. "He's covered in blood."

"Alive?" Rafe murmured.

"Barely."

"Can we move him inside?" Leah asked.

"Very carefully."

Leah ran back to the shop to fetch a heavy woolen shawl that she could spread on the ground next to the injured man. Yori and Rafe gently moved him onto the fabric, causing him to groan in pain, and slowly, delicately, carried him into the building.

"I'll get candles. And water," Leah said, hurrying to collect supplies while the other two settled the young man on the floor. Not until a lit ring of candles threw some illumination on the victim did Leah get a good look at his condition. And then she gasped.

The man looked as if he had been deliberately and precisely cut in a half dozen places—along his wrists, his femurs, his throat. Each wound was shallow and short, only an inch or so long, and crusted with dried blood, but the area around each incision was smeared and blurry with a pale fluid that might be blood mixed with some unidentifiable substance. Against the pink and red, his skin was marble white, and his flesh beneath Leah's hand was chilly. He lay motionless on the floor and only the twitching of his face, drawn tight against pain, gave any indication that he was still alive.

"Looks like he's almost bled to death," Rafe said grimly. "He might not recover."

"Is he conscious?" Leah asked.

Yori shook her head. "I don't think so. And—he might be drugged."

"I don't know if there's much we can do for him," Leah said. "Except clean him off and bind him up and hope."

Rafe came swiftly to his feet. "I'm getting Josetta," he said.

Leah stared up at him. "Why?"

"She's got some sickroom training. And I'm sure there are medical supplies at the house." He appealed to Yori. "Can I drive the car?"

In reply, the guard tossed him the key. "We'll do what we can for him while you're gone."

Leah barely paid attention as Rafe strode through the door. She was following Yori's instructions as they carefully cleaned the wounds and turned the body. It was impossible to miss the fact that the man was wearing plain and tattered clothing, which hadn't been clean even before it was streaked with blood. Judging by the condition of his hair and the odor of his body, he might not have bathed in a nineday. Or two.

"Slum boy," Yori said, after they had cleaned the last cut and covered the broken body with another shawl.

"How did he make it this far with these kinds of injuries?" Leah demanded.

"Probably didn't," Yori said. "Someone brought him to this part of town and whatever happened to him happened not too far from here."

Leah couldn't help shuddering. "Jugular, femoral arteries," she said. "That's where you'd cut if you wanted a lot of blood really fast. I can hardly believe he's still alive."

"There was some kind of paste on every wound," Yori said. "I'm guessing every time an incision was made, it was quickly covered up to stop the bleeding. Then another incision was made somewhere else."

"Do you think— Would it be possible— Could he have done this to himself?"

"Seems unlikely," Yori said. "The blood would have been pumping out pretty fast. He would have had a hard time getting the salve on before he passed out. But I guess he could have done it."

"Though not before he was covered with blood," Leah said quietly. "And there's hardly any of it on his clothes."

Yori's eyes lifted to meet hers. "No," she said. "I noticed that."

"Then—where did it go? Was he dressed in different clothing *after* all this occurred?"

Yori spread her hands in a broad *I don't know* gesture. "That doesn't make sense," she said.

"None of this makes sense."

It was a relief to hear the growl of the elaymotive returning, the sharp crack of doors slamming shut, the musical jumble of women's voices growing louder as a group of people pushed into the shop.

"It's worse than I thought!" Josetta exclaimed, hurrying over and dropping to her knees beside the victim.

Leah glanced over at the rest of the newcomers—astonished to recognize Zoe locking the door behind her and horrified to see Mally resting sleepily in Rafe's arms.

Zoe read her expression. "Virrie's gone for the night, the servants have firstday off, and we couldn't leave her alone in the house," she said.

"I'll take her upstairs," Rafe said. "She tells me you keep a box of stones that are just for her to play with."

"In the chest by the window," Leah said distractedly.

"I want to stay down here," Mally said.

Rafe exchanged glances with Leah and she just shrugged. This wasn't a sight Mally should see, but saving the victim seemed more urgent than arguing about it. She turned back to join the other women clustered around the injured man. Josetta, moving with businesslike efficiency, was opening a medical kit and pulling out strips of gauze and jars of muddy-yellow paste.

"He seems to have stopped bleeding," Josetta said, "but infection's the next thing to worry about. I want to use antiseptic salve and then bind his wounds. If he wakes up enough, I can give him some medicines that will help with the pain."

"Not sure he'll live long enough to develop an infection," Yori said. "I hardly think there's enough blood in his body to keep his heart pumping."

"That's why Zoe's here," Josetta replied.

What? Leah almost said, but Yori nodded. And while the princess and the guard worked together to smear him with ointment and bind his wounds, Zoe settled beside the unconscious man and simply took his hand in hers. She didn't whisper incantations or even focus with any particular intensity on his face. In fact, she appeared lost in thought, as if trying to decide the best seating arrangements for a dinner she wasn't looking forward to. Five minutes passed while Yori and Josetta worked and Zoe merely sat and thought.

The coru prime. A woman of blood and water. *Is it possible?* Leah marveled, feeling a little dizzy. *With just her touch, is she helping him rebuild and replace all the blood he lost tonight?*

Leah watched the man's colorless face and thought it showed the faintest flush of pink.

There was a rustle behind her, and she looked over to find that Mally had abandoned the window seat and crept over to the group gathered on the floor. Rafe was behind her, his hands spread in apology.

"Mally!" Leah exclaimed. "Please go sit down with Rafe."

"I want to see him," Mally said. "I want to see the hurt man."

Leah got to her feet, prepared to carry Mally away herself if Rafe couldn't be firm with the child. "I don't want you to look at him and be upset."

"But I'm worried," Mally said. "I think he must be cold."

"What?" Leah said helplessly. Then, "Darling, we'll take care of him. You go sit down with Rafe."

Of course, Leah hadn't reckoned with Josetta, the crusading princess who probably thought it was a splendid idea for a girl to grow a social conscience at a very young age. "I think he probably *is* cold," Josetta said. "Maybe you could rub his feet?"

"His feet are filthy!" Leah exclaimed.

"Then she can wash her hands afterward."

Leah glanced at Zoe—surely the mother of a young daughter would realize this was a terrible plan—but Zoe still seemed absorbed in her own private meditations. And Leah had no rights here. She couldn't say, *I'm her mother and I forbid her to touch this southside scum.* She had to simply watch while Mally knelt down at the young man's feet and solemnly began chafing his toes.

Leah raised her eyes to shoot Rafe a look that clearly said, *This is all your fault.* He smiled faintly. "So what else can I do to help?" he asked.

"You can figure out where we're going to take this young man once we've fixed him up," Josetta said.

Leah's attention swung back to her. "Is he well enough to be moved?"

Josetta nodded toward her sister. "He will be once Zoe's finished." She glanced around the shop. "I guess we could leave him here all night. I'd stay with him."

"Not unless I stayed, too," Rafe said.

"It's my place—I can be the one to watch him," Leah responded, though it was probably the last thing in the world she wanted to do. No, the last thing after watching Mally rub the feet of a street urchin who'd nearly been murdered.

Yori shook her head. "I'm taking him back to the palace. The regent will want to talk to him."

That caught Josetta's attention. "Why?"

Yori seemed to debate before answering. "Because the regent wants to know everything."

"Why?" Josetta asked more insistently.

Zoe seemed to shake herself awake, though she still didn't let go of the young man's hand. Leah couldn't help but notice that his face had gained even more color, though he still looked far paler than he should. Though, maybe not. Given his lifestyle, his cheeks might always have an unhealthy pallor.

"Because this isn't the first poor soul who's showed up on the streets of Chialto, cut up in precisely this fashion," Zoe said softly. "But all the rest of them have been dead. Not able to answer questions."

Josetta sighed and sat back on her heels, folding her hands in her lap as if there was no more she could do for the victim. "That's what I was afraid of. I've seen a few cases like this near the shelter, too, in the past couple of ninedays. I've been wondering if there's some new kind of—diversion—that's been making the rounds."

"You haven't mentioned it to Darien?" Zoe asked.

"Never crossed my mind that I should."

A smile flickered across Zoe's face. "But, Josetta," she said softly. "Don't you realize the regent wants to know everything?"

"My mistake," Josetta said. "I thought he already did."

Rafe bent down to peer critically at their patient. "He looks a lot better than before," he said.

"His feet are warm now," Mally announced.

"Yes, thanks to all of you, I think he's tremendously improved," Josetta said. "I'm a little concerned that he's still unconscious, though."

"Yori thinks he's been drugged," Leah offered.

Zoe pushed herself to her feet. "Just as well," she said. "That'll make it easier for him to endure the ride back to the palace."

The rest of them stood up, too, rubbing their knees and fighting back yawns. It couldn't be much past the dinner hour, Leah thought, and yet it seemed like midnight must have passed an hour ago. She took Mally upstairs to wash her hands; when they returned, the others were discussing logistics.

"I can ride back to the palace with Yori and our friend here, then return with the elaymotive to drive the rest of you home," Rafe offered.

Zoe exchanged a droll look with Yori. "I have to think there are closer options."

Yori grinned and ducked her head. "I'll be right back," she said, heading out the front door.

Rafe burst out laughing. "Darien's ubiquitous guards!" he exclaimed. "Following me or Josetta or Zoe?"

"Darien gave up protecting *you* a long time ago," Zoe retorted. "Since you were always so ungrateful. But it's rare there's not an escort trailing me even when I don't want one." She gestured at Leah. "And I believe the shop is also watched, though I'm not sure it's under constant observation."

"I suppose I should be glad of that," Leah said.

"You can be indignant," Josetta encouraged her. "I always am."

In a few moments, Yori was back, trailed by two brawny guards in severe black uniforms ornamented only with the Welchin rosette. Mally looked up at them in slight alarm, so Leah casually stepped over and swung the little girl into her arms. Mally rested her head against Leah's throat, watching as the soldiers hoisted up the injured man and carried him outside. Leah assumed they must have a vehicle nearby.

"You can keep the elaymotive for tonight," Yori told Rafe. "I'll swing by in the morning to get it."

"Thank you for everything," Leah told her. "This has been a long day."

Yori just grinned at her. "Interesting, though. The kind I like," she said, turning for the door.

"Oh, wait— Is there room for me to ride with the guards?" Zoe asked.

Yori nodded. "Sure. You might want to sit up front with the driver, though."

"I'll be out in a minute."

As soon as she left, Zoe said quietly, "Before you discuss this evening with anyone else, you might let me talk to Darien. I have the feeling he doesn't want the news to spread very far—that people are getting cut up and bleeding to death."

"It might be news that people *need* to know," Josetta pointed out.

"I realize that. But maybe you could let Darien choose when to tell it."

Josetta shrugged, and Zoe didn't press the issue. The rest of them nodded. Leah couldn't help wondering if this unfortunate young man had fallen afoul of the Karkans. Maybe whatever they'd done to him tonight they'd also intended to do to the young woman in the slums a couple of ninedays ago. But if that thought had occurred to Leah, it would no doubt occur to Darien Serlast as well. At any rate, she would be just as happy not to discuss the specifics of this evening with anyone. She only hoped it didn't give Mally nightmares.

She gave the little girl a gentle squeeze, then gazed over her head to look ruefully around. Between the merchandise they'd simply dumped on the floor and the bloodied rags from their medical ministrations—not to mention the decorative candles now guttering in their own pools of wax—the shop was in pretty extensive disarray. "I'd better get here *especially* early tomorrow morning," she said.

"You sleep in," Zoe ordered. "I'll send Annova here early. And tell her to open late." She waved and slipped through the door.

Josetta surveyed the mess. "We could stay and clean up," she said doubtfully.

Rafe took her arm and pulled her toward the door. "We're all tired," he said. "Zoe was right. This can wait till the morning."

In a few minutes, they were back in the elaymotive, and Rafe was driving them home. Josetta sat beside him in the front seat, turned toward him, talking with great animation. Leah could hear the rising and falling tones of their voices, though she couldn't make out words and sentences.

It didn't matter. She wasn't interested. She wished the ride would take forever. She sat in a perfect bubble of warmth and dark and quiet, holding her slumbering daughter in her arms.

FIFTEEN

By the time Leah made it to the shop the next morning, it was in utterly pristine condition. Every recent purchase whisked out of sight, every candle stub disposed of, every drop of blood wiped away. There were three visitors browsing the merchandise while Chandran helped a fourth one at the sales counter and Annova moved between customers.

"You really are a treasure," Leah murmured to Annova when she had a moment. Annova only laughed.

It was another hour before Leah had a chance to talk to Chandran for a few minutes. "I understand there was some excitement here last night," he said.

Mindful of Zoe's instructions, Leah answered vaguely. "Yes—some poor man who looked to be both injured and in a narcotic haze," she said. "We brought him in and patched him up and sent him on his way, but it made for quite a thrilling end to what had already been an eventful day."

"I would be interested in hearing all the details."

"Did you take a look through everything I bought?"

He nodded toward the door, where three new customers were just now entering. "There has been no time."

"After we close, maybe."

"I will look forward to it."

As Leah had observed many times in her life, the busier she was, the faster the hours skipped by. This day was no exception. Sooner than she would have believed possible, Annova was stretching her arms over her head and releasing a satisfied sigh. "Closing time," the older woman said. "Another good day."

"I think we'll have to restock half the floor!" Leah exclaimed. It was an exaggeration, but barely.

"I can't stay," Annova said. "Zoe has a formal dinner to attend and I promised to get back in time to help her dress."

Leah made shooing motions toward the street. "You should have told me! You could have left hours ago!"

Annova grinned and ambled toward the door. "Don't worry so much. Everything is fine."

Leah laughed and locked up behind her. "I never used to think of myself as much of a worrier," she said to Chandran. "But then I met Annova. *Nothing* seems to weigh on her. It makes me want to be coru."

"I am not sure you should envy her," he said. "I think she might have earned her light heart through heaviness and grief."

Leah nodded. She had come to the same conclusion herself. "So, let me show you everything I picked up yesterday and we can figure out what to put on display for tomorrow."

They passed an agreeable hour sorting through the new acquisitions. Chandran was highly complimentary about the purchases she'd made, giving her background information on some of the Malinquese and Coziquela items that she had bought just because she liked the way they looked or felt.

"Ah—that is a bride's wedding shawl," he said, fingering a heavily embroidered length of blue silk from the Karkades. "Very finely made. And look, a groom's sash to match. These should fetch a handsome price."

"Yet another prize from Captain Demeset," Leah said, because she'd already described the man to Chandran in great detail. "I feel certain he will become my favorite supplier."

"And you his favorite buyer," he replied with a smile. "Especially since you took him to the elaymotive factory. He will always reserve his best for you."

Once they had restocked the display tables, Leah invited Chandran back upstairs to give his opinion on the three canisters she'd purchased specifically to appeal to Seka Mardis. "I want you to tell me if Seka Mardis will love them as much as Captain Demeset's cook seemed to think."

Chandran glanced out the front door, where gaslamps carved cones of light in the deepening night shadows. They had already violated their pact to avoid being alone in quiet, intimate settings. "Perhaps tomorrow?" he suggested.

She knew she should be more wary, but she just couldn't bring herself to be afraid of Chandran. If he intended her harm, surely *he* would be the one who wanted to stay? "It won't take that long," she said. "And who knows when Seka Mardis might drop by again? I need to be prepared."

He nodded and followed her up the stairs. They had just stepped into the big, open storeroom—well, "open" except for the stacks of boxes everywhere—when the interior gaslight flickered alarmingly.

"Quick—there are matches and candles by the door," Leah said. Chandran barely had time to light two tapers before the gaslight sparked again and then went out completely.

Leah sighed. "It did this last night, too. Yori said there's a problem in the line. Too bad I don't know anyone who can relay my dissatisfaction to the regent."

Chandran smiled and moved to the center of the room, where there was a small table, three chairs, and a collection of dishes and carafes of water. Whenever any of them had a free moment during the hectic workdays, they would sneak up here to take a quick break. "I imagine he has a great deal invested in the happiness of the merchants on this particular street," Chandran said. "Someone will be addressing the problem very soon."

She collected the canisters and sat across from him at the table. "So let's see what we have here," she said, prying off the lid to the first one.

It happened to hold the colorful pieces of hard round candy. "Keitzees," Chandran said with satisfaction. "They are prized the way a very fine wine would be. Anyone with any pretense of sophistication would be delighted to receive them."

"Well, now I'm curious," Leah said, dipping her hand in and pulling out a yellow piece. "What will happen to me if I eat one?"

"You will feel very much as if you have had a glass or two of that expensive wine," he said. "Though you will not have the aftereffects in the morning that sometimes occur with alcohol."

She popped the candy in her mouth. It tasted both sweet and tart, like lemon saturated with sugar. But it left a tingling sensation on her tongue that she couldn't quite describe. "Do the different colors have different flavors?"

Chandran watched her a moment by the friendly candlelight, shrugged infinitesimally, then took a piece of candy for himself. His was red. "Slightly," he said. "But not enough that you should try all the different hues just to see."

She laughed. "Should I crunch down on it with my teeth or just let it melt away?"

"It will dissolve sooner than you think," he told her. "Just be patient."

Already she could feel the tingle tickling down the back of her throat and fluttering in her stomach. It was a highly pleasant sensation. "I like the way it tastes," she said. "I might want more than one."

"I would start with one tonight," Chandran said.

"Maybe I won't give all of them to Seka Mardis," she said. "Maybe I won't give *any* of them to her."

Chandran looked amused. "She does seem unlikable enough to be denied any special pleasures," he agreed.

As Chandran had predicted, the keitzee disintegrated all of a sudden on Leah's tongue, leaving behind a taste of citrus and mischief. She leaned her elbows on the table, feeling relaxed for the first time all day. "Well, I'll be supplying her with veneben," she said dryly. "That seems like a special enough treat for someone like her."

"Has the regent secured it for you yet?" When she shook her head, he added, "Perhaps he'll find it difficult to obtain."

"Difficult, maybe. Impossible, no. He's *Darien.*"

"You have a great deal of faith in his infallibility."

"Oh, I think Darien has made plenty of mistakes. But I truly believe there's almost nothing he can't do. It's not just that he's so intelligent. It's not just that he's so determined. It's that he has all these people around him who believe in him. From the guards and servants to all five of the primes. High and low. Of *course* he can get things done."

She gestured a little too broadly, almost knocking one of the candles to the floor. Chandran rescued it as it wobbled in its metal holder. "I am sure you are correct."

"Anyway, it's just veneben. I could have found someone else to supply it if I had to."

Chandran smiled at her. "Yes, I truly believe there is almost nothing you are unable to do," he echoed. "Because you are intelligent and determined and have many people who believe in you."

Leah threw her head back and laughed, but that made her so dizzy she straightened up quickly and spread her hands on the table to aid her balance. "I never used to," she said. "I mean, I never had many people around who seemed to be on my side. Virrie and Taro, yes. But they were such a small part of my life until I was sixteen. I had been raised under such strange circumstances—I was half wild—I had no idea how to behave at public functions with members of the Five Families. I felt so odd and out of place. Isolated. Different from everyone else."

She gazed down at the table and consciously relaxed her fingers. "I think that's why I was so drawn to Rhan," she said. "He seemed to *like* that I was different from all the other girls. He didn't think I was awkward or strange—he thought I was funny and endearing." She glanced up at Chandran, feeling the wry expression on her face. "He used that word. Endearing."

"It is a good word for you."

"*Then* it might have been," she agreed. "But now I'm harder. I'm suspicious. And I'm—" She tapped her thumb against her forefinger, trying to pluck the word out of the air. "I'm self-sufficient. I don't care whether or not people like me." She laughed again, more carefully this time. "And now that I don't care, more people seem to like me."

"I think all of us care, all the time, whether we are liked or not. Loved or not," Chandran said. "It is the primal human drive—to seek connection. It is the only way we can tell whether we actually exist."

Now she leaned her cheek on one hand, since her head was just a tiny bit too heavy to hold itself up unsupported. "Did you? Seek those connections? When you were in Malinqua?" she asked. Even she could tell that the question was obscurely phrased. "I mean, the whole time you lived there, did you ever—well—I mean, your wife was dead—"

"I had a few people I could consider friends," he said quietly. "I did not allow my emotions to engage more deeply than that. I did not feel it was— I could not in good conscience— My secrets and my crimes were too great for me to pursue deep relationships. But I was not entirely solitary, and I allowed myself to believe that was enough."

Until you met me, she wanted to say. The keitzee had loosened her tongue to an alarming degree, but she retained enough sense not to make that comment out loud. "I didn't. Not really. In Malinqua," Leah said. "I mean, not *true* friends. I had plenty of people I would talk to, but we weren't close. I didn't tell them things." *Until I met you,* she added silently.

"Any lovers?" he asked, so lightly that it took her a moment to realize what he'd said. And that it had probably cost him something to phrase it so casually and that she definitely shouldn't answer him.

"Two," she replied recklessly. "But I wouldn't have said I was close to either of them. I didn't even tell them my real name."

"Is that how you gauge whether you have truly connected with another soul?" he asked, and this time he sounded deeply curious. "By whether or not he knows your name?"

Leah brought up her other hand, so now she was supporting her head with both closed fists. "You mean, what information do I only share when I trust someone entirely?"

Chandran made a small, elegant gesture. Leah noticed that *he* didn't almost knock over a candle when he did so. The keitzee had not gone to his head nearly as fast as it had gone to hers. "For some people, the ultimate mark of trust is to give their bodies to someone else. For others, the body is easily shared, but the heart is kept always in reserve. I suspect that for every man and woman, the gift is different."

"My gift would be— I don't know what my gift would be," Leah said. She had honestly never thought about it before, and her mind was too fuzzy at the moment to solve complex ideological puzzles. "Staying, maybe."

"Staying?"

Leah nodded. "I never have, not since my mother died. I left my father. I left Rhan. I left Virrie and Taro. I left Mally. I left Malinqua." She glanced around the room, a collection of dark, indeterminate shapes crouched around the small circle of light where she and Chandran sat. "Now I've come back and I want to stay—with Mally, at any rate. But I don't know if I can. I've never done it." She gave him a quick sideways glance. "What about you? What would your gift be?"

He poured a glass of water from the half-empty carafe on the table, pushed the glass over to her, and poured another one for himself. "Sacrificing, I think," he said. "Making a grand gesture at great personal cost."

She sipped from her glass and thought that over. "Not something you could do very often," she said. "If *sacrificing* means giving away all your money or cutting off a limb or even dying for someone else."

He smiled. "Right. But I do not think I will find too many occasions, during the rest of my life, to make such a gesture. I do not think I will find too many people for whom I would give up so much."

Am I one of them? she wanted to ask. She didn't need to, of course. They both knew they were talking about themselves, talking about each other. *If I ever decide I love you, this is how I will prove it.* The conversation made her head hum almost as much as the keitzee did.

"Well, before you do anything too drastic, you should make sure your friends would appreciate the gesture," Leah advised. "I mean, maybe your friends wouldn't *want* you to die for them. They'd rather still have you in their lives."

Chandran grinned. "If the opportunity arises," he said, "I will definitely inquire."

She laughed and reached for the second canister. "Well, we've settled *that*," she said. "Let's see what else I can offer Seka Mardis."

This container, when opened, released the foul scent of tchiltsly. Leah let Chandran get one good whiff and then quickly put the cap back on. "Demeset was afraid it had gone bad," she said. "I couldn't tell."

"No, that is what it is supposed to smell like," Chandran said, waving his hand to brush the lingering odor from the air. "It is putrid. But your Karkan friend will gobble it up with joy."

Leah pulled a marker from her pocket and wrote a sloppy X on the top of the can. "I do *not* want to forget which one this is," she said. "I don't want to open it again by accident until I hand it over."

"Very wise."

Leah reached for the third canister and said, "Tell me what you think about this one." When she opened it, the dreamy scent of the winter spice drifted out like the memory of love and loss. Leah closed her eyes and inhaled deeply. "It has such a mournful feel to it and yet I just love it," she said.

The sound of Chandran's chair toppling over jerked her eyes open. He was on his feet, staring down at the tin with a look of revulsion on his face. His hands were knotted into fists, and she thought he might be shaking.

"Chandran—" she exclaimed, dumbfounded. Hurriedly, she shoved the lid back on and jumped to her feet. "What is it?"

"Lotziel," he said bleakly.

"Why do you hate it so much?" Because he was backing away from the table as if the lingering fumes were a fatal poison.

"It is—my wife—she often smelled of lotziel," he stammered. "When she went to visit—the sick and the dying—the stench in that town was overwhelming. She would sift lotziel over her clothing to combat the odor. She would brush it on her nostrils to mask the foul scent every time she inhaled. I came to hate the smell of lotziel so much that I could not eat anything made with it. I could walk into a house where the cooks had been baking some holiday dessert, and as soon as I caught the aroma of lotziel, I would walk back out." He paused to take a deep breath, to visibly force himself back to a state of calm. "I have smelled it only once in the past fifteen years," he said. "A trader came to my booth in the Great Market and tried to sell some to me. I nearly fainted from despair."

Leah stuffed the canister into a pile of boxes and circled the table to put a comforting hand on Chandran's arm. Through the layers of silk and wool, she could feel him trembling. "I'm so sorry. I didn't know. I'll throw it out tomorrow the first chance I get. Or I'll go to the canal and toss it into the water. Pretty soon it'll be swept all the way to the ocean."

He was shaking his head in small, deliberate motions. "I am the one who should apologize," he said, his voice formal. "I have upset you with my behavior. You could not possibly have expected such a grim tale to arise from such an innocent purchase. And I should not, all these years later, react with such disgraceful weakness to such a simple reminder."

She clutched his arm tighter and gave him a little shake. "Don't say such things! It is a terrible reminder of a terrible time. And of a terrible woman."

He looked down at her. He was a big man, heavily bearded, and in the poorly lit space he was all bulk and shadows. She should never forget his capacity for violence; she should always remember that the wife who perfumed herself with lotziel was a woman he had murdered. But all she could see was his grief. All she could feel was the shiver in his bones. She brought her free hand up to grip his other arm.

"Only if you believe me," he said, his voice low and hoarse. "Only if I am telling you the truth."

She met his eyes squarely. "And are you?"

"Yes," he breathed. "Oh, what I would not give for these stories to be lies."

"Then I believe you. And my heart breaks for you. And we shouldn't stay here another minute with that terrible box of poison sitting right beside us. Come on. Let's close up the shop and go find something to eat."

Chandran said he wasn't hungry, and Leah didn't have much appetite herself, so they just set out on foot and wandered into the night. Leah kept one hand in the crook of Chandran's arm, and he allowed it, but neither of them remarked upon the contact. She was still a little giddy from the keitzee, but steadier than Chandran; she could feel him, now and then, leaning into her as if only her light touch kept him upright. She found herself standing taller, stiffening her spine, gathering her determination to prop him up, keep him strong. It was an odd sensation. Most of her life, she'd only focused on keeping *herself* strong. She hadn't had the reserves to support someone else.

No surprise that they eventually ended up at the Plaza of Men, which, as always, was nearly as active in the evening as it was during the day. It was also the only place in the city where the gaslight seemed to be functioning properly, because the whole place was cheerfully lit. "Would you like to buy a horse?" Leah asked in a teasing voice, trying to lighten the mood. "Make a legal transaction? This is the place to do it."

"No, thank you. These are not services or acquisitions I am interested in at this time." She could tell he put some effort into making his tone match hers.

The booth of promises appealed to him, though. He came to a halt in front of the open awning and considered the tables of ink and parchment. "I recorded a promise of my own the day before I opened the shop," Leah said, in case he needed encouragement. "I found it a very satisfying experience."

Chandran turned away. "Some other time," he said, "when I have thought through more precisely what kind of oath I might want to keep."

A few yards beyond the booth of promises they found an enterprising young boy who had overturned a wheelbarrow to create a makeshift table and set a small pail on top. "Don't have time to get to a temple? Draw your blessings here!" he called out as they strolled past.

Leah laughed and tugged Chandran to a halt. "Have you? Since you've been to Welce? Have you drawn blessings?"

He shook his head. "As I told you, while I was in Malinqua I visited a Welchin temple. Do those blessings not cover me for the rest of my life?"

She waggled her head from side to side. "Well, your lifelong blessings really need to be chosen for you a few hours after you're born. Any other time you draw blessings, they're just giving you direction at that particular moment."

"Then perhaps I need another set."

The young entrepreneur looked delighted when they approached. "Looking for guidance? You've come to the right place. I've got all the blessings in this little barrel. A full set—nothing missing."

Leah instantly suspected that that was a lie. Just by glancing into his weathered bucket, she could see that he'd collected an odd assortment of tokens. Some looked like charms or pendants that had once hung from a lady's necklace; others looked like they might have been filched from an actual temple; and a few appeared to be quint-coppers and quint-silvers that he'd thrown in just to make the pile more impressive. "This should be an adventure," she said.

The boy held out a battered metal cup and rattled it hopefully. "You have to tithe first," he said.

That made her laugh out loud, but there was something charming about his effrontery, so she dropped in a pair of silvers. "To cover both of us," she said.

The boy nodded. "Do you want to select your own coins, or shall I draw for each of you so that you have three different hands to pull blessings?"

"Oh, I definitely think we want you to join in!" Leah said, bubbling with laughter. She wished Zoe were here. This young fellow would appeal to the coru prime, though she suspected he had a sweela man's conniving heart. "Let's pick my coins first."

She couldn't say the blessings provided her with any insights—she ended up with hope and health, as well as a quint-copper that the temple-master insisted represented wealth—but they didn't foretell any disasters, either. Chandran's coins were more interesting: honesty, honor, and grace. Leah supposed that there could hardly be a better set of attributes bestowed on a man you would like to believe in with your whole heart.

"Does that make you feel better?" she asked him as they moved away. Behind them, she could hear the boy repeating his patter to the next couple who drifted across his path.

He glanced down at her and she was relieved to see some of the humor back in his expression. "I am not convinced that the ritual we just participated in was a wholly accurate representation of reality."

She laughed. "Well, no. But I have learned over the years that wisdom can be acquired in unexpected places. Everyone has something to teach you." She jerked her thumb back toward the young man at the impromptu temple. "Even him."

Now his eyes were shadowed again. "What did you learn from the experience we just had?"

She met his gaze with a serious look of her own. "That you come away with the glyph for honor every time you touch a blessing barrel."

"Only twice," he reminded her. "Once in Malinqua, and once just now."

"We'll go to a temple again tomorrow, or the day after that, and try again," she said.

"And if 'honor' never reappears on any coin I draw?"

She shrugged. "Then we'll see what other blessings have been showered on you instead."

He was silent a moment. "And if it does?"

She tightened her grip on his arm and pressed a little closer. "Then I will start to feel I have some justification."

"For what?"

Her voice was almost a whisper. "For believing in you."

SIXTEEN

There was no time to look for a temple on the following day; too many other things were happening. The weather was rainy and cold, and Leah expected customers to stay away. Instead, they lingered in the shop longer than they ordinarily would, loathe to step back out into the miserable damp.

Just past noon, Yori arrived unexpectedly. "I have something for you," she said when Leah was able to break free from a group of wealthy buyers.

"What might that be?"

Yori nodded toward the stairwell and they climbed to the upper story. There the driver pulled a small leather pouch from an inner pocket and handed it over. "From the regent."

Leah untied the flap and poked inside. The packet was filled with coarse dried leaves of a peculiar reddish-orange color; they gave off a faint odor that reminded her of mint, but darker. "Veneben," she said. "And quite a lot of it."

Yori nodded. "Worth at least a couple of gold coins."

Leah took a pinch between her thumb and forefinger, rubbing the leaves together until they crumbled to dust. She sniffed at her fingertip. "I wouldn't know. I've never traded in it. Or *tried* it, even. Have you?"

Yori grinned. "It's illegal," she said.

Leah eyed her. "But?"

"I've always been the curious type," Yori said, still grinning.

So that means you have, Leah thought. "I know it's a hallucinogen," she said. "What's it like?"

"It gives you visions—makes you see the world through a kind of prism. Turns the sky funny colors. Sets the world to spinning when you turn your head."

"Sounds disorienting," Leah said. "Why do people like it?"

"Some people like to be disoriented. Plus there's a *rush* to it. The world might be spinning, but you feel like you're in control of it. Things are moving really fast, but you feel like you're moving just as fast. It's exhilarating."

"But it's dangerous, right?"

"Yep," Yori said, nodding. "If you don't take enough, you don't get any of the effects. Take too much, and it kills you."

Leah gave Yori a stern look. "I hope you were careful."

Yori opened her eyes wide. "I'm always careful."

"I think there's a lot more to you than shows on the surface."

"Isn't that true of everybody?"

Leah laughed. "I suppose."

That was the only moment of calm in the whole day. The rest of the time Leah and her staff were waiting on buyers, dashing upstairs to bring down additional items, and wiping up the wet footprints that visitors tracked in. Leah had never been so happy to see a workday come to an end.

"*Now* the rain stops," she said bitterly as sundown ushered in clear skies. "Maybe everyone will celebrate good weather tomorrow by staying home."

Chandran had closed the cash box and set it on the shelf below the counter. "But now that the weather has improved, I have an errand I must run," he said. "I will return in the morning."

"Of course," Leah said, disappointed. After yesterday's emotional twists and turns, she had looked forward to spending a quiet hour with Chandran. She suspected that he was leaving abruptly for that very reason—to avoid a repeat of last night's confessions and affirmations. "We'll see you then."

Annova waited until he'd closed the door behind him and they'd watched him pick his way through the nearby puddles on the street. "I can stay late if you like," she offered. "Help you prepare for the morning."

Leah waved a hand. "I'll be fine. I won't mind being alone for a few hours after the day we've just had."

Leah moved slowly but with a certain contentment after Annova left and she had the shop to herself. Now that she was living in Darien's house, she rarely had time alone, and she missed the solitude. She couldn't always think clearly when there were people nearby, laughing and talking and asking her questions. Though she liked those people very much. *And if you ever do get a chance to keep Mally as your own, you'll give up your solitude forever,* she reminded herself. The trade-off seemed eminently worthwhile.

She had just come downstairs for the third time, a bundle of Soechin shawls in her arms, when she saw a shadow at the front door. Her heart bounded in anticipation; had Chandran returned? And then it squeezed down in a moment of panic. There were three shapes at the door, none of them right for Chandran. She could drop the shawls to the floor and grab her knife, but she could hardly fight off that many assailants—

Then the first shadow knocked on the door and called through the glass, "Leah! Are you there? It's Seka!"

Relief flooded her veins with a third potent emotion in less than a minute. Depositing the cloths on a display table, she hurried over to unlock the door. Seka stepped inside but motioned for her escorts— two heavily cloaked men with the stance of soldiers—to stay outside.

"I tried to get here all day, but it was just one emergency after another," Seka said in her overly friendly way. "I hope it is not too late to stop by."

"Not at all! I'm just straightening everything up. Did you come to shop? Or merely to talk? I can brew you a cup of keerza and you can try again to make yourself like it."

Seka laughed. "I would very much enjoy that! Do you have time?"

"I do."

They pulled chairs up to the table of treats against the back wall, and Leah set the kettle on to boil. "But I have something else you'll like better than the keerza," she said with a smile.

"Ah," Seka said. "The veneben I asked for? It is the real reason I dropped by tonight."

"That's for your traveling companion—the one you would like to please," Leah said. "I have something else for *you*."

"Now I'm intrigued!"

"Watch the kettle for me. I'll be right back."

Moments later, Leah was settling into her chair again, laying out three separate items for Seka's pleasure. "Inside the pouch is the veneben. It was very dear, I'm afraid—three gold coins."

Seka nodded, her hand going instantly to a small jeweled purse slung over her shoulder. "I told you no price was too high. That's actually reasonable."

Leah smiled. "Should I raise it?"

"No, no! That leaves me extra money to buy more if I need to."

They swapped coins for leather, and Seka opened the pouch to sniff the contents. "Very high grade," she commented. "He will be *so* pleased."

"I hope he shows that pleasure in some suitable fashion."

"I am certain he will." Seka's eyes had already gone to the next two items Leah had placed on the table. One was a metal canister—the other a small net bag tied with a green ribbon.

"Keitzees!" Seka exclaimed. "Wherever did you find any? I *love* them!"

Leah presented her with the bag. Inside were about ten of the candy drops, since Leah had decided she liked them enough to reserve the rest for herself. She knew it was a mistake for the dealer of a drug to develop a fondness for it—but she figured in this case, with such a limited supply, she could take the risk.

"I met a sea captain who'd just sailed in from Cozique in a ship half-crewed by Karkans," Leah said. "He sold me a few items his cook had brought for the sailors, swearing to me that anyone from the Karkades would be delighted."

"Oh, I am! How much did he charge you?"

"I'm not telling. They're a gift from me to you."

"Aren't you the generous one! *Thank* you!"

Now Leah handed over the metal canister. "Another gift. You might be able to guess what's inside."

"Tchiltsly?" When Leah nodded, Seka practically hugged the tin to her heart. "I can't wait! I have been pining for some for the past nineday."

"Well, don't have any until you've left my shop," Leah said. "It smells *horrible*. The captain wanted to throw it away, but I was sure you would want it."

"Oh, I do, I do! You must let me pay you for this, at least. It can be very pricey."

Leah laughed. "Not at all! The captain practically paid *me* to get it off of his ship. It's another gift."

"The fates were generous when they introduced me to you," Seka said. "I intend to make many, many purchases at your shop."

Leah swept a hand out to indicate the shelves and tables. "We just put out a new shipment today. Let me know if you see anything you like."

Seka jumped up. "I will!"

She spent fifteen minutes browsing through the merchandise, fingering scarves and holding rings up to the light to check the clarity of the gems. But she didn't get truly excited about anything until she came across three small jeweled flutelike instruments prominently displayed on the elay table. "Darnish pipes!" she exclaimed, picking one up with some reverence. "Oh, aren't they *beautiful*?"

"They are. But none of them play, I'm afraid," Leah said. "They look like they *should*, but my assistants and I blew into each one, and we couldn't produce a note."

"That's because they're Darnish pipes," Seka said again, as if that was a perfectly reasonable explanation.

"What does that mean?"

Seka was giving a thorough examination to the one she held, touching each separate garnet and amethyst and stroking the slim gold body. "Exquisite workmanship," she murmured. "See the little ring welded to the back? You can slip it on a chain and wear the piece as a necklace. It's beautiful enough." She looked over at Leah. "Every pipe is different, crafted to special frequencies. There might be a hundred people in the world who could blow on this pipe and produce music and a hundred *different* people who could hear the music being played. But there must be one of each in the same vicinity or there will be only silence."

"That's sort of romantic," Leah said.

Seka nodded vigorously. "Yes, a Darnish pipe is the most treasured of wedding gifts! But it has to be custom-made, of course, and then it is very expensive."

"These aren't exactly cheap."

"No, I imagine not." Seka lifted the flute to her lips and blew softly into the mouthpiece, then looked hopefully at Leah. "Did you hear anything?"

Leah shook her head. "Sorry. Nothing."

Seka set that one aside and picked up the second pipe. It was crafted of silver and ebony, with an opal inlay around the mouthpiece. "I've never been able to hear one, either," she said. "I keep hoping that someday—" She set her lips to the ring of opal. Leah heard her breath hiss out, but no other sound.

"Nothing this time, either, I'm afraid."

Seka picked up the last and finest pipe. It was even smaller than the other two, the size of Leah's index finger, and constructed entirely of mother-of-pearl. "Look at that—it practically glows in the dark," Seka murmured. "Have you ever seen anything so beautiful?" She lifted it to her mouth and produced three distinct tones.

Leah gasped and put her hands to her ears. "I heard that!" she exclaimed.

Seka's eyes snapped with delight. "You did? Truly?"

Leah hummed back the notes Seka had played. "Right?"

Seka fairly vibrated with excitement. "Yes! Yes! You heard me!" She put the pipe back to her mouth and produced a longer melody, but still a simple one. The music was sweet and piercing, tinged with wistfulness. Leah stood transfixed until Seka dropped her hand. "I have no musical training," she apologized. "I wish I could play a more beautiful song so you could hear how the pipe really sounds."

"I'm still amazed I could hear it at all," Leah said. "If what you say is true, the odds against that happening are impossible to calculate."

Seka stepped forward, her bright face earnest. "It means we are soulmates," she said. "It means there is a bond between us. I feel it, don't you?"

Leah managed not to recoil, but she did allow herself to look uncertain. "I'm not the kind of person who develops close bonds very quickly," she apologized. "But I do feel like—there's something special about you. Something different. I can't explain."

Seka smiled. "Yes—I could tell that about you. You like people, but you keep them at arm's length. I am not that way. I'm passionate and I *fling* myself into relationships. But I will not fling myself at you." She took a step backward and winked. "Not yet, anyway."

Leah laughed a little shakily. "But I am very glad that you could play the Darnish pipe—and that I could hear you."

"So am I! I must have it, of course. Let me buy it—and then, sadly, I must be on my way."

As soon as they had completed the transaction, Seka said, "I was going to ask you about something anyway, but now that you're my *soulmate* I have to."

"You're not going to keep saying that, are you?"

Seka laughed. "I promise! Not another word! But I do want to invite you to a very select get-together that will be held on firstday. You might have heard that the crown prince of the Karkades has come to Chialto to meet with your regent."

Leah nodded. "Yes! Most of my customers can talk about nothing else."

"And you may have guessed that I am here with his entourage. In fact"—Seka tapped the leather pouch—"the veneben is for him."

"This is so exciting!" Leah exclaimed. "I've had a chance to do a favor for foreign royalty!"

Seka smiled. "I'm sure he would enjoy an opportunity to thank you in person at this event. It will be quite casual and have nothing to do with politics. There will be entertainment. And exceptional food. I think you would enjoy it, I really do."

Leah had to confess to having equal parts curiosity and horror when she contemplated Seka Mardis's notions of "entertainment." But, of course, this was too marvelous an opportunity to pass up. "I wouldn't miss it. Just tell me when and where."

Seka rattled off an address in the wealthy district and said, "Festivities will start around eight and continue until everyone is exhausted."

"Maybe sooner for me," Leah said regretfully. "Since I will have a shop to run in the morning."

"Then stay merely an hour or two."

"May I bring someone with me?" Because she wasn't going by herself to any entertainment of Seka Mardis's devising.

"Of course! That will make it all the more fun." Seka held up her hand, palm out, and Leah pressed her own against it. "Then I will see you in a few days," Seka said.

"I'm looking forward to it."

Since Leah obviously couldn't bring Chandran to Seka's party, her first choice was Rafe Adova. She figured he had had plenty of experience reading strangers and keeping himself out of trouble in all kinds of dicey situations. So that night, once Virrie had taken Mally up to bed, Leah told Rafe and Josetta about Seka's invitation and asked if Rafe would be willing to escort her.

"I wish I could," he said. "But the Karkans met me the first time Darien had a formal dinner for them. I even sat next to Seka at the table. She'll remember me."

"What did you think of her?" she asked.

He absentmindedly shuffled a deck of cards as he considered his answer. "I thought that I wouldn't want to make her an enemy," he said. "I got the sense that there were no limits on what she would be willing to do."

"I had the same impression," she answered.

"I was seated by the prince that night," Josetta said. "He was— odd. A tall, thin man with a very delicate way of moving. I thought he could have been a dancer. Or a singer. His voice was beautiful."

"Did you like him?" Leah asked.

"No. In fact, it's more accurate to say I hated him. I couldn't put my finger on why, though. He was extremely polite."

Rafe glanced at Josetta. "Tell her what Nelson said."

"Nelson said he'd always thought the viceroy of Soeche-Tas was the most unsettling man he'd ever met, until the Karkan prince walked into the room. And you know, it's rare that Nelson finds people frightening instead of fascinating."

"I'm not certain you should go to this party after all," Rafe said.

"Well, I'm definitely not going alone. But if you can't escort me—"

"We'll come up with somebody," Josetta said. "We need to keep you safe from the crown prince."

Rafe exchanged a look with Leah. He said, "And Seka Mardis."

. . .

Chandran's opinion was that the event wouldn't be as debauched as Leah expected. "It might be vulgar and ostentatious, but as a somewhat public event in a foreign capital, it will be relatively sedate," he said. "You might even enjoy yourself."

"I think I'll be too nervous to enjoy myself," she said doubtfully, "but maybe."

"You might want to bring a gift for your host," he suggested. "That is a common practice."

"What kind of gift?"

"I am sure he would be happy with another supply of veneben."

"I'll see what I can do."

Leah sent a message to the palace, and the very next day, Yori arrived with another pouch.

"I'm going to start thinking that Darien is dealing in the stuff," Leah said. "Or that *you* are."

Yori laughed. "In a different life, I might have," she admitted. "But I think I like this life better."

Leah stared at her, almost dropping the pouch to the floor. "I don't know why I didn't think of this already! You'd be *perfect*!" she exclaimed. "Do you want to come with me on firstday?"

"Sure. Where?"

"To a party hosted by the Karkan prince and his friends. I don't know what exactly will be on offer, but I imagine it includes drugs—" She waved at the leather packet. "And alcohol. And people without a whole lot of inhibitions. I'm afraid to go alone."

"Sure," Yori said again. "Sounds like fun."

SEVENTEEN

When Yori arrived at Darien's house on the evening of first-day, for a moment Leah didn't recognize her. The guard had left off her usual severe livery and instead sported more traditional Welchin clothing—a navy-colored tunic and trousers accented at neck, cuff, and hem with rows of turquoise buttons. She was wearing shoes with spiky heels that added at least four inches to her short frame, and she'd applied enough cosmetics to turn her friendly face sultry. Leah was pretty sure the guard had concealed knives under the flowing fabric at her ankles and hips, and she demonstrated another neat weapon: a thick gold bracelet with a hidden blade that snapped out with a single twist.

"Can gouge a man's eye out in ten seconds," Yori said with satisfaction. She might look like a merchant's daughter planning a wild night, but she still had a soldier's heart.

Leah herself had gone for color. Her tunic and leggings were dyed a bright purple, and she'd added a Dhonshon shawl shot through with violet, green, and sapphire. She wore her emerald necklace and the matching earrings Chandran had given her, as well as three amethyst rings. Mindful of Seka's usual style, she had braided a few matching jewels into her hair as well, and was a little embarrassed at how much she liked the look. She wasn't used to either vanity or excess. But they seemed eminently appropriate for an evening out with the Karkans.

"I think you both look lovely," Rafe told them. "And I hope you're both armed."

Yori showed him the dagger-hearted bracelet, while Leah peeled back her left sleeve to reveal a sheathed knife. "And I have to think Darien will have soldiers trailing us there and back," she added.

Yori looked innocent. "Soldiers? Following us?"

"No doubt," Josetta said. "Have a good time. I think. But be careful."

It was a short drive to the address Seka Mardis had supplied. They arrived at a well-maintained three-story structure of white stone with black accents and a small front garden that looked bare and forlorn in the winter chill. Curtains were drawn across all the windows, but brilliant light seeped out past the ones on the bottom level. The illumination on the second floor was paler and gentler, and almost nonexistent on the upper story.

Yori tilted her head to gaze for a minute at that top level. "You think they've rented the whole house for the night?" she asked.

"I think it's where they're living for their entire stay here in Chialto," Leah answered.

"Huh," Yori said. She didn't explain what had caught her attention and Leah decided not to ask.

At the door, which opened before they knocked, they were met by a man wearing tailored black livery and a close-fitting hood that concealed everything but his eyes and mouth. "Come in," he said in Coziquela, and they stepped inside.

The kierten was hung with streamers of many different colors and textures—fabric, metal, flowering vines—and lit by a profusion of lamps and candles. It was also perfumed with some kind of heavy, sweet scent that appeared to emanate from a brazier near the door. Yori took a couple of sniffs and raised her eyebrows in surprise, but when Leah looked alarmed, Yori just grinned and shook her head. Leah interpreted that to mean: *It's some kind of illegal drug, but it's not potent enough to knock you out or turn you into a madwoman. You'll be fine.* The perfect start.

Most kiertens opened onto short hallways with rooms on either side, but someone had hung heavy velvet curtains over the archway to the left, so they were clearly meant to turn toward the well-lit space on their right. Here they found a scene of almost chaotic gaiety. Maybe twenty people moved through the room, most of them dressed with far more opulence than Leah—in brightly colored dresses and jackets that sparkled with jewels and gold thread; they wore beads and tiaras and feathered head-bands in their hair. Many were holding drinks or lifting pomanders to their noses or smoking pipes filled with fragrant substances. Light spilled down from dozens of sources—candles, lamps, sconces, mirrors—and the sweet drug-laden scent was even stronger here. Some kind of stringed instruments were playing a lively, swooping tune that seemed to glance off the walls and bounce through the swaying bodies.

Everyone appeared to be in motion. Gesturing, twirling, or simply sauntering around the room. Leah suspected that the perfumed smoke contained a stimulant of some kind because she could already sense an impatience building in her body. She wanted to snap her fingers or tap out a few dance steps. She could feel her shoulders shake slightly, back and forth, in time with the frenetic music.

Wouldn't it be funny if I actually enjoyed myself tonight? she thought. Out loud, she said to Yori, "I wonder where we start."

Yori nodded to a figure heading in their direction. "I think some-body has recognized you."

Indeed, Seka Mardis was breaking through the crowd to join them. "Leah! I'm so glad you could make it!" she exclaimed, holding out her palm for Leah to press. Seka was attired even more sumptuously than usual, with a collar of jewels encircling her throat and heavy bracelets around her wrists. Her hair was braided with strands of pearls and slim gold chains, and the shimmering Darnish pipe hung from her neck like an overlarge pendant. "This is your friend?" Seka asked.

Leah introduced them, but Seka didn't offer her hand to Yori. She merely nodded and said, "Let me take you around! Have you had any-thing to eat or drink?"

"We just stepped in."

"I'll show you all the *best* things." She flagged down a passing woman who was carrying a tray full of glasses; like the man at the

door, the server was dressed all in black and wore a hood that completely covered her head. "Start with this. Soechin wine. Unmatched."

Trying not to seem obvious about it, Leah waited until Yori had
taken her first cautious taste and then a second more relaxed sip. "I
can't indulge too much," Leah said with a smile. "I will need to have a
clear head in the morning."

"I understand. But it would be a sin not to try Soechin wine."

Leah wasn't much of a connoisseur, but even she could tell the vin-
tage was superior: sweet and fiery at the same time, smooth as ice against
her tongue. "So who are all these people?" she asked, raising her voice
slightly over the music. "I didn't realize you'd brought so many in your
delegation."

"Oh, only a few are from the Karkades or Soeche-Tas. The rest are
friends we have made since we've been here." She sipped at her wine.
"Merchants and traders, mostly." She took another swallow. "It did
not seem like *quite* the venue where your regent and his wife would feel
at ease."

Leah laughed. "No, indeed." *Though Rhan would be very much at
home here. In fact, I might run into him before the night is over.* "So
what can we expect?"

Seka gestured at the room. "Here people are simply gathering to talk
and listen to music and sample the wine. In the next room is dancing. In
the room beyond that is entertainment. And beyond that, there are two
rooms set up for dining. One is loud and boisterous and one is more quiet
and refined. You may choose where you feel most comfortable."

Yori spoke up. "What about the chambers upstairs?"

Seka smiled. "Those are set aside for anyone who wants to carry on
a conversation in privacy."

Leah spoke with mock bewilderment "I can always find privacy
without going to someone else's house," she said.

"Yes, but sometimes the person with whom you wish to have an
intimate talk can only be found at events like these," Seka replied with
a laugh. "Or you meet someone you've never encountered before and
you'd like the chance to get better acquainted."

Leah glanced around. "There do seem to be a lot of interesting
people here."

"So are you hungry?"

"Not yet."

"Then let's go see the other rooms."

They made their way through the jittering, nervous crowd and into a room that was larger, darker, and louder. This was the place where the musicians were actually situated, five of them sitting on a small round dais and sawing away with maniacal energy at their violins and cellos. Equally maniacal were the couples on the dance floor, romping up and down the room and spinning into frenzied dips and whirls, then laughing almost hysterically. Leah could hardly blame them; the combination of bright music, dramatic lighting, and seductive scent was making her want to fling herself into motion as well.

"Would you like to dance?" Seka Mardis called over the music.

Leah set down her glass. "Yes! But I don't know the steps."

"I'll show you," Seka said, gripping Leah's hands with surprising strength and pulling her into the stream of dancers.

It wasn't hard to follow Seka's lead as she tugged or pushed Leah in the direction she was supposed to go—and, anyway, the motion of the crowd carried them first in one direction and then another. There was something exhilarating about the movement, the color, the insistent music. Leah felt a bubble of pure joy form in her chest and break loose in a carefree laugh.

"It is great fun, is it not?" Seka shouted.

"It really is!"

They galloped up and down, sideways and back, always at a breakneck pace. Leah could feel a film of perspiration forming across her forehead and under her arms. *Maybe the smoke is just to mask the smell of sweat,* she thought. When the music abruptly halted, she skidded to a surprised stop and found herself staring into Seka's intense face. Seka still had both of Leah's hands in hers, and Seka flexed her fingers to tighten her grip. Leah scarcely noticed.

"It's over?" she asked blankly. She felt heavy and slightly unbalanced, as if she had pulled herself to the shore after hours spent in the water. *The motion itself is part of the drug,* she thought somewhat hazily. *And it starts to dissipate once you come to a halt.*

"No, no. Just a short break."

In less than thirty seconds the music started up again, and they plunged back into motion. If this particular dance had a different set of steps, Leah couldn't discern them; it seemed to be the same giddy frolic. One difference, though: They hadn't been dancing more than a minute when Seka practically careened them into another couple, and before Leah knew it, she was partnered up with a stranger. He was about as tall as Rafe, but burlier. She spared a moment to be anxious, but then he swept her into the stream of revelers and she was delighted again. At one point he set his hands on her waist, lifted her in the air, and spun her in a complete revolution. She clutched his shoulders, threw her head back, and laughed.

Three more times she changed partners on no signal that she could detect, twice dancing with other men and once with another woman. She was pretty sure the second man was Soechin, though he was as gaudily dressed and broadly smiling as any Karkan in the room. But there was something spindly about him, and he was even clumsier with the dance steps than Leah. She suspected he was no more native to this party than she was.

The next time she changed partners, she was paired up with Yori.

"I'm *so* glad to see you," Leah murmured, clutching Yori's cool fingers as if to catch her balance.

"You look like you're having a good time," the guard commented with a grin.

"I *am*. That's the scary thing. I'm supposed to be observing behavior and gathering information, but instead I'm *cavorting*."

"It's the sineshee," Yori said. "It makes you lose your inhibitions."

"Is that the incense that's burning in all the rooms?" When Yori nodded, Leah said, "It doesn't seem to be affecting *you* so much."

Yori laughed. "I've probably been exposed to it more often. Built up my tolerance."

"Well, make sure I don't become so lighthearted that I do something stupid."

"Like take a stranger to an upstairs room?"

"*Yori!*"

"Don't worry. It's not strong enough to turn you into someone you're not. Just to make you worry a little less about who you are."

"Who I am is suddenly so exhausted that I think I need to sit down."

Yori guided them toward the wall, where various other couples had paused to fan themselves or take refreshments. As if she had been watching Leah's every move, Seka Mardis suddenly descended on them in a swirl of clattering beads.

"That was fun, was it not? Would you like to move on?"

"Of course."

The next room was even more dramatically lit—mostly in darkness, with a raised stage along one wall. *The entertainment*, thought Leah. The performers were lithe and muscular, dressed in flesh-colored clothing that fit so tightly they appeared, at first glance, to be naked. Some were executing impossible leaps and poses across the stage; others clung to colorful rings and streamers hung from the ceiling as they spun around upside down in dizzying circles. While Leah watched, openmouthed, one of the spinning women released her grip and dove with an artist's precision into a thicket of waiting hands. As the crowd gasped, she sank out of view, shielded by their bodies, before flying upward again as the others flung her back into the air. Casually, with one hand, she caught a narrow ring suspended over the stage and leaned into an accelerating pirouette.

"That's pretty impressive," Yori murmured in her ear.

"I saw something like this in Palminera once," Leah replied. "I wonder if this troupe was hired from Malinqua?"

Suddenly the music changed into something more like a call to arms—sharp, decisive measures punctuated with percussive clashes. Leah wasn't the only one who was startled, but the performers had obviously been expecting the signal. Almost as one, they leapt off the stage in all directions, eliciting shrieks from the audience. Then they grabbed whoever was nearest and drew them into a demented dance, sometimes flinging their partners into wild spins, sometimes using them as springboards for cartwheels and backflips and other gyrations.

Leah saw one performer rest his fingers on a man's shoulders, then coil into a handstand so that he was upside down over the other man's body, their heads just an inch apart. A push, another leap, and he had flipped himself over so that his feet were on the man's shoulders instead. As everyone pointed and stared, he began dashing through the crowd, his quick feet landing on a shoulder here, a head there, as if all the partygoers were just cobblestones along his morning run. Leah held her breath, certain he would miss a foothold as someone shrank out of his way or collapsed beneath his weight, but he ran lightly as a deer through a magical forest before he somersaulted back onto the stage. Everyone applauded madly.

Leah looked around for Seka, but she was nowhere in sight. So she leaned over and said to Yori, "She was right. This is pretty entertaining."

Yori shrugged. "I'm disappointed, though."

"You *are*?"

"Well, this is all fairly tame. I mean, it's excessive, but it's not—" She searched for a word. "Sinful."

"For which I am grateful," Leah murmured. "I'm not sure I'd be up for anything more outrageous."

Yori smirked and looked like she was going to say something, but then her eyes sharpened and her gaze fixed on something over Leah's shoulder. "What is it?" Leah asked, suddenly fearful.

"Someone here I didn't expect to see."

Casually, not wanting to draw attention to herself, Leah turned around and scanned the room. It wasn't hard to guess who had caught Yori's eye—an attractive redhead from the highest echelon of Welchin society. Not Rhan Ardelay, oh no. Someone whose presence here was even more scandalous: Queen Alys.

"*She* has made friends with the Karkans?" Leah murmured. "That can only mean she's trying to stir up trouble."

"We'll have to tell the regent," Yori said. "But he won't even be surprised."

Just then, Seka Mardis found them again. "I'm parched," she said. "Let's find something to drink. And eat."

"An excellent idea," Leah said. "And a quiet place to sit, if such a thing can be found?"

"Of course! Come with me."

They made their way through a maze of corridors, passing more of the hooded servants carrying trays of food and drink, and found themselves in another large room with low, restful lighting. The place was set up like a dining hall, with a buffet laid out along one wall and a profusion of draped tables scattered throughout the room. Pillar candles sat in the center of each table, providing smoky illumination, but the spaces between tables were so dark Leah could hear people stumbling and apologizing as they tried to navigate the room. She was relieved to find this chamber free of the heavy incense, though the smoke still clung to her tunic. It was also much quieter, though the muted music could still be heard through the intervening doors and hallways.

Leah followed Yori through the buffet, taking only items the guard put on her plate, and choosing the same beverage Yori favored. Really, she would have been lost if she'd come here alone. She suspected that Rafe's knowledge would have been almost as extensive as Yori's, though, and that he, too, would have known what was safe to consume and what wasn't.

They found seats at an unoccupied table and immediately dug in. Her drink, Leah discovered, was nothing more sinister than fruited water; she could identify most of the foods, too, once she tried them, though they had been seasoned and prepared in unfamiliar ways.

"What a delightful party you've put together," Leah said.

Seka Mardis pouted for a moment. "Not *my* party," she said. "It was all Borner's idea."

"Borner?"

"One of the prince's other advisors. He thought such an event might make us—more popular with some of the people of Chialto. The prince has been very pleased with Borner as a result." She brooded for a moment.

Leah tried to cheer her up. "Yes, but you've brought him veneben!"

"I have," Seka said with a sigh. "But he's used most of it already."

"Then you will be happy to see the gift I've brought with me tonight."

The smile was back on Seka's face. "Truly? You have more? Oh, thank you *so* much. You have no idea what this—*thank* you."

"Do you want it now? I don't know the etiquette of such things."

"No, I think— Why don't *you* give it to him? You may say I suggested it, or some such thing, but—I have told him about you and he said he would enjoy meeting you."

Leah glanced down at her purple tunic and feigned worry. "Am I dressed finely enough to meet a *prince*?"

"Oh, he doesn't care about such things. Especially at an event like this! But finish your food first."

"It's very good," Yori said.

"I'm glad you like it! Borner had the idea for the party, but *all* the work was mine."

The exercise or the sineshee or the stress of the evening had left Leah famished, so she ate every scrap on her plate and had to resist the notion of going back for more. Seka and Yori ate just as heartily, and Leah had to assume everyone else in the house would be equally hungry. In fact, as she watched, servants carried in a dozen more trays, all mounded high with breads and fruits and meats. The Karkans might be spending as much on food tonight as they were on entertainment.

The minute Leah finished her water, Seka jumped to her feet. "The prince is alone at the moment, for a wonder. Quickly, before anyone else approaches."

Leah and Yori both stood up, but Seka frowned at Yori. "I'm sorry," she said, "you must stay behind. I am certain he would like to speak to Leah in private."

There was a frozen moment while Yori and Leah stared at each other. Leah thought she could read the question on Yori's face: *Do you feel safe enough to talk to him if I am not nearby?* Leah gave the slightest nod, and Yori turned back to Seka with her usual amiable expression.

"Sure," she said easily. "I'll check out the entertainment again."

"Excellent," Seka said, turning away without another word. She set off through the darkened room, Leah closely following. She only looked back once, but Yori had already disappeared.

In the farthest corner of the room, at a small table set apart from all the others by a broad and unlit swath of space, a single man sat in solitude. The lone candle on his table had burned so low that it barely illuminated the gold goblet that sat beside it or the glittering rings on his folded hands. His face was a ghostly blur and his exact shape was lost to shadow, but Leah formed the impression that he was both tall and thin. She was also convinced that this was the man she had followed to the southside slums three ninedays ago.

"My prince," Seka said in an obsequious voice, "I would like to introduce to you one of the friends I have made here in Chialto. She runs the shop where I have acquired such delicious items in recent days. Her name is Leah."

"Welcome, Leah," the prince responded, his voice very low and musical. Leah was pretty sure it was the same voice she had heard speaking briefly that night in the ghetto. She bowed deeply, as she would have to the regent, but the prince held out his palm in the traditional Karkan greeting, so Leah laid her hand against his. Like Seka's, his skin was shockingly warm to the touch. "I trust you have enjoyed your time under my rented roof."

"Very much so. I have never seen anything quite like those dancers."

He gestured at the seat across from him and she sat down. Seka drew back, out of the faint circle of light, though still close enough to hear. "They come from Berringey, though they were trained in Malinqua," he said. "I am always captivated by grace, and so I enjoy the poetry of their movements."

"I am impressed by anyone who is willing to get up on a stage," Leah said. "My father was an actor and so I realize that only a certain kind of personality is meant for performance."

"Ah, I greatly enjoy theater," the prince said. "I have seen two productions since I have been in Chialto. The themes and the styles of performance were much different from the ones we put on in the Karkades, but I enjoyed them nonetheless."

"How did they differ? If it's possible to explain," Leah asked.

There was a short silence while he took a sip from his goblet and seemed to consider his answer. "Your plays seemed lighter in spirit," he finally answered.

Since at least half of the Welchin dramatic productions were heavy tragedies, Leah decided she didn't want to pursue that line of inquiry. "I hope you have enjoyed everything else you've sampled of Welchin culture," she said.

"I have," he said. "Though I was confounded by my visit to one of your temples."

"You were? Why?"

"I did not understand how I was supposed to fit into one of five preconceived molds. Surely there is more variety among the people of the world? Might not a man contain within himself all of those elements? Be spiritual one day, carnal the next? As wayward as water, as stern as wood, as lush as the earth? In my country, we are very aware that a man may be a certain thing at the same time he is its exact opposite. It is this contradiction that makes life so varied and rich."

"Such sentiments would make you seem coru," Leah said with a smile. "For the coru reserve the right to be constantly inconstant."

"Coru—that is your word for the element of water, is it not? If I had to confine myself to one category, that is the one I would choose. Water and blood."

She assumed it was her imagination that he emphasized the last word. "Did you draw blessings for yourself while you were at the temple?"

"Yes, but they provided me with little guidance. Two indicated travel and one was blank. I did not learn very much."

"It's true that foreigners sometimes do not draw very useful blessings," Leah admitted. "It is as if the Welchin elements only have an affinity for Welchin souls." She smiled. "Or perhaps it is just that you are very mysterious and not easily scanned."

She thought she saw him smiling in response. "I like the idea of being mysterious."

She wondered if she could get him to reveal anything interesting and tried a general gambit. "Have you enjoyed your visit so far? What has caught your attention in the city of Chialto?"

"The city appears to be very well-regulated, which surprises me."

Which surprised *her*. "Oh? Why?"

"Your regent does not seem to display a firm hand. He is not decisive. From what I can tell, he seeks advice from others on almost every topic of any importance."

Leah was childishly delighted to hear someone insinuate that Darien was weak. It was the last adjective she would have attached to him. But. "It is true he surrounds himself with trusted counselors," she said cautiously. "But I think that's why Welce has always been such a peaceful nation—because so many participate in its government."

"That is not how things are done in the Karkades," the prince said a bit scornfully. "The king's word is law. His power is infinite and immediate. If he wants something done, it is done."

"An excellent life for the king," Leah murmured. "Perhaps not so excellent for the people he rules."

The prince shrugged, as if those people didn't matter. *They probably don't—to him.* He leaned forward over the table, which brought his face closer to the light. She was surprised to see that his features were coarse, his skin blotched, his look altogether unrefined and at odds with his cultured way of speaking. He was also wearing an expression of dissatisfaction.

"But the Karkan king does not have *absolute* power, because he still must abase himself before and answer to the whore-bitch queen of Cozique," he said. His measured voice made the epithet even more shocking. "It is time the Karkades freed themselves of this restrictive and humiliating arrangement. We would seek the support of your regent in this goal—but he professes himself unable to make such a commitment without the input of too many ministers to count."

Ah. Leah could guess Darien's strategy now. He didn't want to anger the Karkans—or their Soechin allies—by refusing outright to pledge support, so he was blaming his reluctance on the primes and his other advisors. "Unfortunately, that is the way the Welchin court operates," she said regretfully.

The prince settled back in his chair, sipped from his goblet again, and set it carefully on the table. Leah thought she could discern a faint raspberry residue along the rim. "I understand that this was not the case when the old king was still on the throne," he said. "I understand that Vernon would act swiftly and with no debate."

Who did you hear that from? she wanted to ask. It wasn't true, of course; for the last several years of his life, Vernon had relied heavily on Darien Serlast's counsel. And even before that, he had had to factor in the opinions of the primes before he made any sweeping decisions. In fact, Vernon had been far *less* autocratic than Darien, though Leah wasn't going to say so. "Yes, things were different when Vernon was king," she offered instead. "But perhaps things will be different again once Darien is officially crowned."

"You mean when he usurps the throne."

What? "Sire?" she said faintly.

The prince made a broad gesture. "Vernon's daughter still lives! A direct descendant! Yet Darien Serlast, who is no relation at all to the king, will be the next to wear the crown. To the Karkan mind, this is unfathomable."

She had no idea how to answer this, so to buy time, she asked a question instead. "Does the Karkan throne always pass from parent to child, then?"

"Always. Since the beginning of time. It is an unbroken dynasty."

"Then I must suppose you are the son of the current king."

"I am. My father has ruled for thirty years and two quintiles."

"That's impressive," Leah said. "Are you his only heir?"

"I have two sisters and a brother still living."

The phrasing was so odd she found herself echoing him. "'Still living'?"

He nodded. "One brother and one sister who died."

"I'm sorry to hear that." Here was another line of inquiry she didn't want to pursue. Some of the other nations of the southern seas were famous for the bloody intrigue that accompanied any change in the monarchy; she didn't want to ask how exactly his siblings had passed away. "Do you have children of your own?"

"Three, all of them quite promising," he said. There might have been a note of pride in his voice; it was hard to tell. "One of them will take the crown after me."

"Many years from now, of course," she said lightly.

He smiled in response. "So I should hope."

"You are fortunate," she said. "In Welchin history, there have been several instances of the throne passing to another family when there were no living heirs."

"Perhaps that is unavoidable under certain tragic circumstances. And yet, in this case, there *is* an heir. She is young, but she is of the royal lineage."

"She is damaged," Leah said gravely. "Her head cannot bear the weight of the crown."

The prince leaned closer again. Now Leah was able to trace the network of veins in his nose, see the intensity in his narrowed brown eyes. And she could catch a whiff of whatever he'd been drinking, though she couldn't identify it. Something salty and warm, with an undercurrent of rot. She tried not to inhale too deeply. "So you have been *told*," he said. "By the upstart regent. Can you prove it? Do you know it for certain?"

She stared at him. Well, now that he asked—no. Leah had never met Odelia, she of the fragile mind, the strange and insular way of looking at the world. How *could* she be certain that the child had the condition that was ascribed to her? How *could* she know Odelia was unfit to rule?

She would have staked her life on Darien's integrity, but she didn't have to. Taro—Zoe—Nelson—*all* the primes had come together in agreement. Odelia would be put aside and Darien raised to power in her place. At some point in the history of Welce there might have been primes who could not be trusted, but Leah didn't believe a single one of those perfidious creatures was alive right now.

"I am convinced it is true, sire," she said quietly. "It is not just Darien, but all of his ministers, who think the throne is better off in other hands."

"Or that is what they *say*," the prince responded. "Perhaps they merely wish to turn attention away from the girl until she attains maturity. Perhaps they have some reason to fear for her safety, and they believe this fiction will keep her out of danger until she is old enough to rule."

"That never occurred to me!" Leah exclaimed. "It would be a very clever ruse."

The prince pushed himself back in his chair, but she fancied she could see his look of dissatisfaction intensify. "And yet I am left with a pretend regent and a squabbling band of advisors who will not give me definitive answers," he said.

"Perhaps they will," she said. "If you give them enough time."

He held up a bejeweled finger, as if he had had a sudden idea. "But I am led to believe that if the situation was dire enough—if he had cause enough—even this charlatan regent would make a drastic response," he said. "And he would not wait to survey his ministers before he took action."

That was certainly an ominous thing to say. How to respond in a way that satisfied but did not encourage this perverse prince? "I do believe Darien is more decisive than you might think at first," Leah replied. "Can he be driven to extreme action? I suppose so. Who couldn't be? Would it be the action you hoped for? In my experience, Darien rarely does what you think he will. It's one of the most frustrating things about him."

She thought the prince might be smiling again. "I don't always do what people expect, either," he said.

She bowed her head. "Sire, even this brief conversation with you makes that very clear."

He laughed, pleased at her answer. "But we have talked far too long about me and my impressions of your royal court! Tell me something about yourself. I have met only a few ordinary Welchins, and I would be greatly interested to hear more of your story."

So she rattled off a quick and highly edited biography, focusing largely on her new life as a shop owner. "I have developed connections that enable me to procure almost any item I desire," she said at the end, reaching into a pocket of her tunic to pull out the leather pouch. "And when Seka Mardis mentioned that you had a fondness for a certain item, I was happy to think I might supply it to you this evening. I wasn't sure I would get a chance to talk to you, but Seka thought you would enjoy our conversation. And my gift."

He took the packet with pleasure, opened it, and sniffed at the contents with a connoisseur's rapture. "Superb," he murmured. "Nothing could please me more." He gazed at her with a calculating expression. "I wonder if there is something I might offer you in return."

"Oh, I have been paid in advance by the marvelous entertainment of the evening! There's nothing else I require."

"What one *requires* and what one *desires* are often not the same thing," he replied with a lingering smile. "I am sure that somewhere in this house is something that would provide you with a great deal of pleasure."

Yet again, she struggled to frame a reply. The best she could come up with was, "A most generous offer! But I am meeting a Dhonshon buyer at dawn tomorrow morning, and I've already stayed later than I planned. I don't have time to sample any of the other delights you might have available tonight."

The prince expressed his regret, they exchanged a few more pleasantries, and then *finally* the conversation was over. A few minutes later, Seka was leading her through the curtained hallways toward what Leah devoutly hoped was the exit. She was confused by the layout of the house, so Seka might be escorting her to a chamber of horrors instead.

But they arrived without incident at the front entrance, where Leah was relieved to see Yori already waiting. Seka opened the door for them herself. "That went very well, I think," she said ebulliently. "And you took *just* the right tone when you handed him the veneben. I think you are my favorite person in all of Welce!"

"I'm glad to hear that. You're my favorite Karkan," Leah replied with a laugh.

"Soulmates!"

"It does seem that way," Leah agreed.

She wasn't prepared for Seka throwing her arms around her and kissing her full on the mouth. She managed not to jerk away from the embrace and to wipe the shock from her face before Seka pulled back and gave her a mischievous grin.

"I know, I know, your affections are otherwise engaged, and you Welchins seem to set some store by fidelity," Seka rattled off, her gaze darting to Yori's face and back to Leah's. "But it was a lovely evening. I'm so glad you came!"

"So am I," Leah said, setting off down the walk at a determined pace and waving a cheery goodbye. "Thank you for inviting me!"

They were in the car and pulling into traffic before Yori allowed herself to start laughing. Leah punched her lightly on the arm.

"I don't mind being kissed by a woman, but I don't want to be kissed by *Seka Mardis*," Leah said.

"Would a kiss from the prince have been better?" Yori asked between chuckles.

"Worse! I don't know what he was drinking, but it had a strange smell and I wouldn't have wanted to get any of it on me."

Yori gave her a quick glance. "What did it look like?"

"Red and kind of sticky."

Yori nodded. "Might have been blood. I saw a pitcher of it on the buffet. Cow's blood or pig's blood. Something like that."

"That's disgusting."

"No more than eating meat, when you think about it."

"Then I'm not going to think about it."

Yori just shrugged in reply. Leah studied her a moment by the faint gaslight filtering in through the windows as she drove. "So, what were *you* doing while I was having a polite conversation with the prince?"

Now Yori was grinning. "Took a tour of the upstairs rooms."

"Bringing a new friend with you? I didn't even see you flirting with anyone."

That made Yori laugh, but she instantly sobered. "I didn't go to the second floor. Went to the third."

Leah felt a little chill dance along her shoulder blades. "Why? What were you looking for?"

"Wanted to make sure anyone who was on the premises actually wanted to be there."

Leah's chill intensified as she thought that over. "And— *Was* anyone there against their will?"

Yori gave her a quick glance, then returned her attention to the road. "Not anymore."

"But you— What was— I don't even know—"

"Don't worry about it," Yori said. "I'll tell the regent."

Leah continued to stare at Yori a few more moments, not sure what to say, what to think. She couldn't bring herself to ask for details about what, exactly, Yori had found in those upstairs rooms, so she finally shook her head and leaned back into her seat. "I suppose," she said at last, "we'll both have a lot to tell the regent the next time we see him."

"I suppose we will."

In Leah's case, that was a great deal sooner than she expected, because he was waiting for her when she got home.

One of the servants met her at the door and took her directly to Zoe's lounge, where she found Darien Serlast relaxing in a chair and staring meditatively at the merry little brook that ran around the perimeter.

"Darien," she said blankly. "What are you doing here?"

"It's my house," he said mildly.

She dropped into a seat across from him. "Yes, but you don't *live* here," she pointed out. "So you must want something."

"Just to hear how your evening went. I happened to be nearby and decided I would drop in and wait for you."

"Had I known, I would have come back sooner. I'm sorry if you were bored."

"Not at all. I had a lovely visit with Virrie and Mally until they went upstairs. And then I had a few minutes of utter quiet, which I enjoyed immensely. Such moments are rare in the life of anyone who aspires to be king." He glanced around the room. "I was remembering what it was like to be an ordinary man with no particular ambitions or responsibilities."

"You were never that man," she challenged. "Your father was prime and you were serving at the court from the day you were old enough to say 'Yes, sire' and 'No, sire.' You have no idea what the life of an ordinary man is like— No, and you'd hate such a life if it was forced on you."

His gray eyes showed faint amusement. "Maybe. It seems unlikely I will ever find out. So, tell me about your party tonight. Was it as debauched as you feared?"

"No—Yori called it tame, and I'm inclined to agree. At least, the parts that I was privileged to see were far from shocking. Yori will tell you about other activities she stumbled upon."

He raised his eyebrows but didn't comment on that. "Well, it couldn't have been *entirely* proper," he said, "since you reek of sineshee."

She grinned. "And I offered my host a gift of veneben, which he was delighted to receive. I did not mention that I got it from you, though maybe I should have. Maybe he would like you better."

Darien raised his eyebrows. "He dislikes me? I thought I had been most agreeable in my dealings with him."

Leah kicked off her shoes, slouched back in her chair, and prepared to enjoy herself as she related the conversation. "I'm not sure he dislikes *you* so much as the way Welce is governed," she said. "First, he expressed a low opinion of a ruler who has to seek the approval of his ministers before he can take any actions."

Darien smiled slightly. "I might have overemphasized my reliance on the primes so I could avoid giving him direct answers."

"Very smart," she approved. "Next, he seemed suspicious of any country that couldn't provide an unbroken series of kings and queens all descended from the same progenitor. Apparently every ruler in the Karkades has produced the next one since the day the place was founded."

"I had heard that," Darien said, "and wondered if it could possibly be true. I would guess that here and there history has glossed over an impotent king or a barren queen."

She grinned. "As Welce tried to do?"

"With disastrous results, as you know."

"At any rate, that was something else that displeased him. But the worst thing is that he thinks of you as a pretender. Or a usurper. He isn't sure which."

Darien cocked his head to one side. "You'll have to explain that."

"He doesn't understand why you will be named king when there's a living heir of Vernon's own bloodline. So he thinks you've either snatched the crown away from Odelia—or you and the primes have cooked up this story as a way to shield Odelia from attention until she's old enough to rule."

She had the satisfaction of seeing Darien nonplussed. "But these are— Both stories are too far-fetched to be believed," he said. "Clearly, he's been researching the Welchin royal family, but key pieces of his knowledge are wrong."

She smiled broadly. "And that's the most interesting thing I learned tonight. I think I figured out where he got his information."

Darien's gaze sharpened and fixed on her face. "Which was where?"

"From someone who happened to be at this event. One of Vernon's former queens."

For a split second, fury and disgust roughened Darien's face, and then he resumed his habitual calm mask. "Alys. Of course. I should have expected her to be on the scene."

"She could have filled his head with all sorts of tales about how you betrayed Vernon by stealing the crown from his daughter," Leah said. "I don't know why she would bother, though."

"Merely to cause me difficulties, no matter how slight. If the prince does not trust me, he will not negotiate with me in good conscience. Even if it merely costs me a trade agreement, Alys will feel her meddling achieved her goal."

"Apparently she also told him that Vernon was a strong, decisive king who didn't need the steadying hands of his primes," Leah said. "Unlike you—the weakling or the pretender or whatever you are."

"Interesting. Alys might have done me a favor, not intending to. I do not want to make alliances with the Karkan prince, but I also do not want to anger our Soechin neighbors. If they believe I am ineffectual as opposed to obstructive, I suppose it is not a bad thing."

"What did you think of him?" Leah asked abruptly. "The prince?"

"I thought he was so focused on himself and his own desires that he would be easy to manipulate," Darien answered promptly. "Except that he was also very intelligent, which would make him difficult to outwit. My guess is that he is a man without boundaries, which makes him dangerous."

"Josetta said she hated him."

He smiled. "Josetta has hated most of the foreign royalty who have visited Chialto, so you can't judge by that."

"I didn't like him, either," Leah said, "but I'm not sure I could say why. He just seemed—like someone I wouldn't want to be alone with."

"Well, that's not much of a standard," Darien said, unimpressed. "The list of people with whom I would not want to be left alone is almost as long as the list of people I know."

That sent Leah into a fit of the giggles. "I *meant*," she said, when she was able to speak again, "that I would not feel *safe* around him."

Darien hadn't even cracked a smile. "You think he would offer you bodily harm?"

"No. I don't know. Maybe. I think it comes back to what you said earlier. He seems to have no boundaries. So if I was alone with him, he might do anything he pleased. Things I wouldn't even think of."

Darien came slowly to his feet and Leah more reluctantly followed suit. She was so tired she thought she could probably fall asleep right there in the river-rimmed room. "Well, it seems unlikely you ever will be left alone with him," the regent said. "So there is no need to fear."

"I feel somewhat the same about all the Karkans I've met," she confessed. "Even Seka Mardis."

Darien crossed the bridge, Leah at his heels, and they strolled together toward the kierten. "Even your friend the poisoner?" he asked.

She should have expected that swift dagger thrust. "He's Coziquela. His wife was Karkan," she said calmly. "So that makes him different."

He paused with a hand on the door and looked down at her. "That didn't actually answer the question," he said softly. "Would you be afraid to be alone with him?"

She stared up at him defiantly. No one else had thought to ask her this question—but then, nobody else knew why Leah might have a reason to fear Chandran. "We were alone in the shop just the other day," she said. "At night. Upstairs. Not visible from the street. If he'd wanted to harm me, he had ample opportunity."

"Maybe his harming days are done."

She noticed Darien didn't say, *Maybe he'd never harm anyone*. For the second time tonight, she felt a shiver down her back. "I suppose any of us can hurt someone else if we have enough incentive," she said.

"That has been my experience," he said. "The trick is to know those incentives in advance."

"Your own or the other person's?" she retorted.

"I know my own," he said. "I am always interested in other people's motivations."

She crossed her arms and leaned against the doorframe, her head tilted up so she could watch him. The leaded glass cupola overhead was spattered with starlight, but there was only pale gaslight to illuminate the kierten, and Darien's face was almost as hard to see as the prince's had been. "Now I have to ask," she said. "What would motivate *you* to take violent action?"

His faint smile was back. "A serious threat to the people and things I love," he said. "My wife. My daughters. My country. I don't think that makes me particularly unusual."

"It's probably the *way* you'd respond that makes you unusual," she agreed. "You wouldn't punch a man in the face. If he tried to hurt your family, you'd sell his house out from under him and ruin his credit with the bank. I don't know how you'd punish a foreign country that tried to harm Welce."

He pulled the door open. "Let's hope we never have to find out," he said, stepping into the night. Leah watched him through the windows just long enough to see two Welchin guards materialize in the street. Then, fighting back a yawn, she headed for the stairwell.

"I believe everyone is in for the night," she told the footman hovering in the hall. "You can lock up the house."

She was exhausted and a bit light-headed and she smelled like she'd bathed in incense, but she had to make one quick stop before she readied herself for bed. She tiptoed into Mally's room and stood for a moment beside the bed, watching her daughter sleep. Her small face looked perfectly smooth, perfectly peaceful, perfectly beautiful, perfect. Mally's breath was even, her hands lax on the blankets, her dark hair spread in tangles on the pillow. Just looking at her made Leah want to cry.

There is nothing I wouldn't do to protect you, Leah thought. *No action would be too violent, no sacrifice would be too great.* The next words to surface in her mind were, oddly, the last ones that Darien Serlast had spoken. *Let's hope we never have to find out.*

EIGHTEEN

Chandran wanted to hear the details about her evening at the prince's house but didn't seem surprised by anything Leah described. "What did you think of the prince?" he asked.

"He was intelligent and well-spoken and said nothing remotely threatening, and yet I was uneasy the whole time I was talking to him," she replied. "I can't explain why."

"Many people feel that way about him."

"Have you ever met him?"

"Several times."

"And did you feel unnerved in his presence?"

"Abundantly."

She eyed him a moment. They were having dinner together after the rush of business on secondday. She had enjoyed being back in her normal routine and had spent much of the day looking forward to the meal with Chandran. She had been too tired to want to go out, though, and he'd agreed to fetch food and bring it back to the shop. So once again they were sitting together upstairs, amid the welter of exotic goods, in the friendly candlelight. They each had their own water glass but were eating from the same plate, and the table was so small their knees touched whenever one of them moved.

It was the second time they'd broken their own rule against solitude and intimacy. Leah knew she should be more worried than she was. She couldn't tell, from Chandran's grave expression, whether he was worried or pleased. Probably a little of both.

"So what crimes is the *prince* atoning for?" she asked.

"Many, I would presume."

"You don't know them? I'm disappointed. I thought they'd be common gossip."

"One rumor is that when his mother was pregnant with her— fourth? fifth?—child, he mixed an abortifacient into her food to make her miscarry. He was quite young then—eleven or twelve."

Leah felt her eyes widen in shock. "He didn't want any more competitors for the throne?"

"That was only part of it. Apparently his father had taken him aside for a stern talk. Telling him that he would have to start showing how much he wanted to be named heir. He couldn't just assume the crown would be his—he had to prove he was worthy."

"And that was the kind of action that convinced his father?"

"That and some other things."

"Which you don't want to tell me."

Chandran sipped his water. "These are ugly people who do ugly things," he said gently. "I would talk of more pleasant topics."

"I'm still curious about him, though," she confessed. "Did he ever try to kill off his other brothers and sisters?"

"You might expect that, but no," Chandran said. "They were all oddly close. Two of them died from other causes when they were older, and by all accounts, everyone in the royal house truly grieved. They say that when the youngest boy died, the oldest princess went down to the mausoleum and slept on his coffin for three days, weeping uncontrollably. Not until she fainted from weakness were they able to carry her up to her room and nurse her back to health."

"That's sweet. Sort of," Leah said. "It's also excessive."

Chandran smiled. "They are a people of extremes."

Once they had finished the meal, Leah pushed the plate to one side and fished around among the boxes at her feet before triumphantly producing the tin of keitzees. "I saved some for us," she said. She poked at the candies before selecting a purple one, then offered the container to Chandran.

He hesitated. "I should not."

Leah's was already in her mouth. "I can't resist. Probably a good thing there aren't that many of them. Though I'm hopeful that Captain Demeset will return soon and bring *pounds* of the stuff."

With a slight gesture of capitulation, Chandran picked out his own candy, a transparent green. "At that point, perhaps you should sell some instead of hoarding them all for yourself," he suggested solemnly. But she could tell he was teasing.

As before, the keitzee seemed to tingle in her mouth, down her throat, all the way through her veins. "I will most definitely sell *some* of them," she said. "But I'll keep some, too." She turned her chair away slightly so she could stretch her legs out without kicking Chandran in the ankle. "I didn't see you at all yesterday. Tell me how you spent your time."

"Mostly touring your city," he said, "visiting all the spots a foreigner might want to see. The royal palace is lovely."

"Not as big or as striking as the one in Malinqua," she said. "But still impressive."

"Particularly situated next to the waterfall. Quite dramatic."

"What else?"

As he recounted his activities, Leah listened with pleasure, less to the content of his words than to the even cadence of his voice. He spoke with such measured precision, such easy eloquence; just the rhythm of his sentences was soothing to her, reassuring, like a lullaby or a promise. She would like him to read her a story sometime, a whole book, perhaps a collection of poems. Every stanza would cup her heart in a comforting embrace, every rhyme would find an echo in her pulse. She closed her eyes, still listening to him speak.

"Ah, I have talked too long. You are falling asleep," Chandran said, self-reproach in his voice.

Leah forced her eyes open. "I'm not! I'm tired, but I love listening to you."

He came to his feet, gesturing at her to stand up. "Keitzee does not pair well with exhaustion," he said. "You had better get home. Tomorrow will be another long day."

She wanted to protest—she was not ready for the evening to end— but it was obvious he was right. She yawned and shook her head to clear it, then they spent ten minutes closing everything up for the night. It was a shock to step outside and find that the temperature had dropped by at least twenty degrees.

"Quinnasweela now and no mistake," Leah said, shivering a little.

Chandran regarded her with concern. "Are you steady enough to make it home on your own?"

"Of course I am! I'll just head to the Cinque and catch a transport. Darien's house isn't a very far walk from the stop."

He looked undecided. Leah didn't think it was on purpose that she produced another yawn. "I believe I should accompany you," he said. "I do not want you falling asleep on the omnibus and riding endlessly around the Cinque all night."

"That won't happen," she said with a laugh, "but I don't mind you coming with me if you like. You can see Darien's house."

"From the outside, at least," he said.

It wasn't as late as Leah's exhaustion made it seem, and the transport was crowded with people heading home from work or out to appointments. Chandran and Leah found seats on a back bench, but the press of nearby bodies squeezed them together, shoulder to shoulder and thigh to thigh. Leah didn't mind; she didn't think Chandran did, either.

By the time they disembarked at the stop nearest to Darien's house, she was so overheated from the crowd on the omnibus that she welcomed the cold air outside. She had thought the keitzee would have worn off by now, but she still felt half dizzy with its irresistible mix of euphoria and recklessness.

"I should invite you in," she said when they paused outside the elegant silhouette of Darien's house. Lights showed in various windows on every level, but the two of them stood in the street, away from direct illumination. Leah had her hands in her pockets to keep them warm, and she could feel the chill starting to paint color on her cheeks. But she didn't want to go inside.

"I do not believe I would accept the invitation."

She peered at him in the dark. "You'll have to meet them sometime. The people in my life. If you're going to—if you'll be—if you decide to stay in Welce."

"I do not think either of us has made that decision yet," he said seriously.

"You're afraid to meet Mally," she said suddenly. "Or you're afraid what *my* face will look like the first time I see you with her."

"There is some truth to that," he acknowledged. "I think we have a little ground to cover before either of us will be comfortable with that moment."

"It doesn't seem fair," she said on a sigh. "*I've* had to meet and pretend I like all those odd Karkans. *You* should have to meet and pretend you like a few Welchins."

"The difference is that you love these Welchins and I despise those Karkans," he replied.

"I don't like the Karkans, either," she said in a confiding way. "Intense and nasty and much too familiar. Oh! I forgot! The worst part! Do you know what happened last night?"

Amusement was back on his face. "I cannot guess."

"When I was leaving the party. Seka Mardis *kissed* me! I wasn't expecting that at all."

He didn't look surprised. "They tend to be far more affectionate physically than the people of Welce or Malinqua, or even Cozique," Chandran said. "It took me a while to get used to their habits once I relocated there. But there are times such physicality can be—quite nourishing."

Leah slipped her fists out of her pockets and took hold of Chandran's hands. His were so much bigger than hers, slightly more calloused, warm even on this chilly night. He pulled free as if to withdraw from her grip, but instead he folded her hands together then wrapped both of his around hers, as if enclosing them in a safe space with his own to stand guard. "You miss it," she said, "that physical contact."

"I do," he said. "The craving for touch can be as strong as the craving for wine or veneben. It can create addicts of any of us. It does not matter if it is palm to palm or breast to breast—skin delights in skin. It is as if there is no membrane between them—each body soaks up the essence of the other and converts it to a kind of narcotic for the senses."

She drew their entwined hands upward, nursed them under her chin, felt his hands unfold to resettle around her face, his palms against her cheeks. She turned her own hands outward to hook her fingers over his wrists. "You should not have gone so many years without allowing yourself this simple drug," she said.

"I did not feel like I deserved it," he said.

"And now you do?"

"No. Now my craving is stronger than my scruples. But I will only transgress so far."

"Do you know why I slept with those men in Malinqua?" she asked in a low voice.

"No."

"Not because I cared about them. Either of them. Not because I was lonely or bored—not because I was hungry for someone else's touch. But because I didn't want Rhan to be my last lover. Or—how could I know? If I died, my *only* lover. I took them to bed to make *him* less important. I didn't want him to be the last man who had his hands upon my body."

His face was very grave as he stared down at her in the dark. She could feel his thumbs tracing the line of her cheekbone, down toward her mouth, up toward her hairline. "You think I need a body to intervene between my own and the ghost of my wife."

She smiled up at him, half flirting, half reassuring. Slipping her hands from his wrists, she slid them all the way up his arms to his shoulders, feeling the wrinkled wool of his jacket against her fingertips and her palms. "Well, I do," she said, "but I wasn't even thinking about what *you* need. I was thinking that Seka Mardis kissed me yesterday, and what if I die in the night? I don't want her to be the last person whose lips touched mine."

"That is a most excellent argument," Chandran said soberly, but she could hear the underscore of laughter. "That is something all of us should review as we prepare ourselves for bed every evening. What were the last words I spoke? Were they cruel or kind? What was the final action I took? Did it help someone or harm someone? Who was the last person I kissed? Is that the memory I want to take with me into eternity?"

"I'm afraid I might have to ask for your cooperation here," she whispered. Now she curled her fingers around the back of his neck, pushed herself up to the tips of her toes, leaning into him, offering herself up to him. "I want a different memory. I want a different final kiss. And you're the only one around."

He resisted but only, she was sure, to prolong the game. "You would ask me to sacrifice my long-held principles merely so you could sleep easy tonight?"

Her mouth was only an inch from his. "Well, that's what you say you want, isn't it?" she murmured. "To make a great sacrifice to atone for your sins?"

"I did not expect it to be as immense as this one," he said, bending his head and kissing her.

She flushed with heat, she fizzed with excitement, she tilted into him to keep her balance. His mouth was heavy on hers, hungry, but she could feel him holding back, taking only so much, limiting himself to just a taste. She wanted more—she wanted to fling her arms around his body and draw him so close it almost hurt to breathe—but she held back, too. Just this much. This little bit. This touch. This kiss. Soaking up his essence through the pores of her skin.

Chandran was the one who lifted his head, who pulled back, though he kept his hands against her face. "I would like to say that was the fault of the keitzee, but I have wanted to kiss you for some time now."

She managed a shaky laugh. "How long, exactly?"

"Since before you left Malinqua, certainly."

"I know *that*. But when? Between the time you tried to poison me and the time I sailed for Welce. When did you start thinking about me—that way?"

He considered. He had started that motion again, brushing his thumbs over her cheekbones. The delicate touch made her shiver, or maybe she was finally starting to feel the cold. "When you rescued that girl," he said at last.

"Who, Alette? That was all Corene's doing. Not mine."

"It was Corene's idea," he said. "But you arranged everything. You took advantage of your many contacts and put yourself at considerable risk to save her life."

"Think well of me if you like," she said. "But I only did it to keep in Corene's good graces."

He smiled down at her. "That is untrue. You did it because you knew you could save that girl and without your help she would die."

She felt her mouth twist. "Maybe," she said. "But that still doesn't make me an admirable person. Someone you should care about. It just means I'm atoning. Like you. Trying to do something good now and then to negate all the bad things I've done."

His own smile went awry. "That is when I knew you would leave Malinqua. When I knew you would want to go home. Because you were finally finding within yourself the strength to change. To atone. To make everything right again."

"What about you?" she asked softly. "When will you realize you *have* atoned? That by living a solitary and thoughtful life, you have made up for whatever sins you've committed?"

He dropped his hands but did not turn away. "I do not know that I ever will," he said.

She put a hand on his arm and he didn't shake her off. "But you want to. You want to believe you're good enough for an ordinary man's existence—surrounded by friends, loved ones, maybe a family. You want that, or you wouldn't be here. Tonight, with me. You wouldn't be in Welce at all."

"Maybe," he admitted. "But just because I want to be with you does not mean I believe I deserve to be." When she started to speak, he gave her a stern look. "And just because you kissed me tonight does not mean you trust me enough to take up that life at my side."

"Maybe not," she echoed him. "But I want to."

He spread his arms and her hand dropped back to her side. "I do not want to go backward from here—back to loneliness and isolation," he said. "But I do not know how to go forward."

She leaned up and gave him one quick kiss on the mouth, a reminder, a promise, a reassurance that she wasn't afraid. "Slowly," she said. "As we both find our footing."

He bowed his head and nodded. "Slowly," he agreed. "But I am not ready for any of the rest of it yet. Your friends, your daughter. Both of us must be more certain before we take a step down that particular road."

"I agree," she said. "But I hope the journey starts before long."

"I hope for the same thing."

She squeezed his arm, said, "I'm freezing," and ran lightly up the walk. At the door, she paused to blow him a kiss before stepping inside.

Josetta was standing in the kierten, trying not to smirk. "I swear I wasn't spying," she said. "I thought I heard voices so I looked outside and then I realized it was you and so I—well—you *could* bring him inside, you know."

Leah laughed and threw her arms around Josetta, who laughed and hugged her back. "Not quite yet," she said. "Soon. But not quite yet."

"In my experience, *soon* arrives when you're not expecting it," Josetta said. "Don't think you can play too many games with fate."

Leah laughed again. "Not this time," she said. "I almost think I know what I'm doing."

B ut Josetta was right. *Soon* came the very next day, when Chandran met Mally.

It was thirdday, never as busy as secondday, so Annova, Chandran, and Leah had a few quiet moments between customers to straighten the cash box and replenish stock. They were clustered around the front counter, debating which new pieces of merchandise to put out next, when Leah heard the door open and felt cold air swirling in. She had already donned her professional smile when she turned to greet the new visitors, but that warmed to an expression of real pleasure when she saw who had entered.

"Virrie! Mally! I didn't know we were expecting you!"

Mally ran up to hug her—a mark of favor so great it still practically drove Leah to her knees—while Virrie offered her usual placid smile. "Josetta asked me to come with her to the shelter this morning and I didn't think it was the place for a child," Virrie said. "I hoped you wouldn't mind watching her for the day."

It took a second before Leah put those pieces together. Mally—here all day—with Chandran. At Josetta's request. It required no great stretch of the imagination to guess that the princess had done this on purpose to engineer a meeting between Leah's daughter and her admirer. *And she thinks* Darien *is a meddler,* Leah thought somewhat hysterically. *She's worse than he is.*

"Of course—we're always delighted to have her," Leah said. She smiled down at Mally and patted the girl's dark curls, but her mind was racing. In fact, her heart was racing. Was Josetta right? Was it time for Chandran to meet Mally? He would leave if she asked him to. In fact, she could sense him behind her, folding up his papers, stepping away from the cash box, preparing to announce he had some errand to run.

"I want to play with the rocks," Mally said. "And feed the fish."

"Then that's what you'll do," Leah said.

Virrie waved and headed out the door. "Josetta sent an elaymotive for me, so I've got to go. I'll be back tonight."

Chandran's voice sounded, right behind Leah. "I need to leave, too."

She didn't think about it too hard; she just turned toward him and placed a hand on his arm. Her other hand was still resting on Mally's head and she felt like a conduit between them, a living connection. She could bind them together, she could keep them apart, and any consequence would be directly attributable to her actions.

"Oh, surely that other chore can wait," she said. "You at least should stay long enough to say hello to Mally."

Annova could always be counted on to know when a situation was volatile. "I'm going upstairs," she said, and disappeared.

Then it was just the three of them. Still standing a few feet from the door. Still tied together by the placement of Leah's hands. Chandran, she could tell by his corded muscles, was almost too tense to breathe. He stared down at Mally in absolute silence.

By contrast, Mally seemed at ease, deeply curious. She stared, too, but in a friendly way, taking in the details of Chandran's face and clothing. In her role as decoy princess, she'd probably met dozens of foreigners, Leah realized, or at least had seen them at close range. She wasn't frightened or shy, but she wasn't simpering and obsequious, either. Merely, she was Mally. Interested in everything.

Leah dropped her hands to her sides as she began introductions. "Mally, this is Chandran. I knew him in Malinqua, where he traded in very fine merchandise, but he's originally from Cozique. Chandran, this is Mally. She lives with the torz prime and his wife, Virrie. The one who just left."

Leah had spoken in Welchin, since Chandran could manage it with reasonable fluency and she wanted this to be as easy as possible for Mally. Chandran offered the sort of bow he would give a high-ranking noblewoman, and Mally responded in kind.

"Do you speak Coziquela?" Mally asked.

"I do," Chandran said.

"So do I," Mally said, switching to that language, "but I'm not very good."

Chandran bowed again and said, "I think you sound quite respectable."

"It's easier than Soechin," Mally said. "Maybe because Soechin isn't very pretty."

"I agree," Chandran said. "There is no language more beautiful than Coziquela—and no language spoken by more people. If you learn it, you will never be at a loss for conversation, no matter who you meet."

"Were you born in Cozique?"

"I was."

"Why did you leave?"

Leah sucked in her breath, but Chandran answered without hesitation. "My father arranged for me to marry a woman from the Karkades, so I went there to live. But I did not like it, so after a while I moved to Malinqua."

"And now you're here."

"And now I am here."

"Is this where you're going to stay?"

"I do not know yet. How about you? Are you going to stay in Welce for your whole life?"

Mally gave the question a moment's thought. "I don't know yet," she said, giving him back his own answer.

"There are a lot of other countries to see," Chandran said. "You might find one you like better."

"I might find one I *like*," Mally said. "But probably not one that's *better*."

Chandran smiled for the first time during this conversation. "So I understand that in Welce you all have elemental affiliations," he said. "What is yours?"

"I'm torz. Like Taro and Virrie and Leah. What about you?"

"I do not seem to have an affiliation."

Leah interposed. "Sometimes people from other countries don't. Not the way we do."

Mally regarded him a moment. "I don't think you'd be torz, anyway," she said.

"Is that a bad thing?" Chandran asked.

Now Mally smiled for the first time. "No, don't be silly. You can be anything and it's good. Unless you're Rafe."

Chandran raised his eyebrows. "He is not good?"

Mally laughed and Leah tried to explain. "He's half Malinquese and half Berringese, and whenever he draws blessings he always ends up with ghost coins. Or so Josetta tells me."

"Do *you* get ghost coins?" Mally asked him.

"No, indeed. I have tried it twice, and each time I have ended up with real blessings."

"Like what?"

"Honor, travel, resolve. Honesty. Grace."

Mally listened closely. "Which one did you get twice?" She didn't miss anything, this girl.

"Honor," he said.

"Maybe you're elay. Like Josetta."

"Maybe."

Mally looked at Leah. "Taro could probably tell him."

Leah was amused. "Why do you think that?"

"Because he's the torz prime. He always knows what people are before they tell him." She thought about that for a minute. "Well, he knows after he shakes their hands." She turned back to Chandran to expand on her answer. "Zoe and Taro have to touch people to understand them. So does Mirti. Nelson has to hear them talking and Kayle just has to be nearby. All the primes are different."

"I see," Chandran said. He was obviously trying to hide his amusement.

"It sounds a little crazy, but she's actually right," Leah said. "Nelson can practically read people's minds. Zoe can put her hands on people and analyze their blood—she can tell if they're related to each other, just by touching them. It's fascinating and a little unnerving to watch."

"So you should ask Taro," Mally said.

"Perhaps I will. If I meet him."

"You'd like him," Mally said. "Everybody does."

"She's right about that, too."

Mally looked around the shop. "Do you still have the box of stones for me? Can I play with them?"

"Yes I do, and yes you can. Do you want to go upstairs with Annova or do you want to stay down here? You can set up in the window again. There's a display table there now, but you can sit on the floor next to it. There's lots of light."

"I want to be in the window. I can watch the people walk by." She looked at Chandran. "Do you want to sit with me?"

He glanced at Leah and she gave the briefest of nods. "That would be delightful," he said. "There is nothing I would like better."

NINETEEN

For the next hour, the shop was eerily quiet, existing in a strangely peaceful and undisturbed space. Leah sat behind the counter, tallying receipts; Annova moved between the upper and lower levels, carrying down merchandise and tidying displays; and Chandran and Mally sat in the window embrasure, talking in low voices. No customers walked in. There didn't even seem to be any traffic down the boulevard. No one appeared to be alive in all of Chialto except the four of them.

Despite the calm, Leah was far from relaxed. She sat on a stool, counting money and reconciling accounts, and felt her whole body clench with tension as she strained to overhear what Mally and Chandran were saying. It appeared to be simple and random—he told her about the Great Market in Malinqua, she described Taro's estate and Darien's house—and yet they both seemed wholly engrossed in their conversation. Or maybe they were engrossed in their activity. Mally had hauled out the box of multicolored stones and dumped them on the floor between them. This time she wasn't arranging them into patterns; this time she was balancing one on top of the other to create fantastical towers. She chose and placed her rocks with great care, laying a smooth, flat specimen across one that was more conical in shape, then placing another flat one on top of that. Leah was astonished to see how skillfully and solidly she was assembling these structures. She had already created one that was nearly two feet tall and showed no signs of toppling over, and she'd started a second one a few inches away. It looked as sturdy as the first.

Chandran sat beside her, building something of his own. He didn't appear to be aiming for height so much as dimensionality. From what Leah could see without craning her neck, he had used a couple dozen rocks to define a honeycombed space about the size of a large dinner plate, and now he was essentially roofing this bottom level with a thin layer of wide, flat stones. He had a pile of chunkier rocks next to him; Leah thought he might be planning to use them to build a second level. So far, his construction didn't appear to be any more likely to fall over than either of Mally's.

Annova came back downstairs, glanced at the two builders, and headed to the sales counter to drop off some papers for Leah. "That looks like fun," she said.

"I think I'd manage to put three rocks together before they all came tumbling down."

"And you call yourself torz," Annova scoffed.

Before Leah could answer, three women stepped inside the shop. She put on her professional smile and stepped up to greet them. "Welcome to Leah's! Is there anything you're looking for?"

The women wandered from display to display, asking questions and testing various items against their cheeks or hair. In the end, they only bought small trinkets and Leah was just as glad to escort them back to the door.

Before anyone else could walk in, she stopped by the window to admire the progress of the two artists. Mally had completed her second sculpture, almost exactly the size of the first and apparently just as steady. Chandran was working on the fourth layer of his building.

"Well, you two have certainly been busy," Leah said. "Mally, I can't believe how tall you've made those stacks of stones. Why don't they fall over?"

"Because I put them together just the right way," Mally said seriously.

"She has a great sense of weight and balance and center of gravity," Chandran said. "Remarkable, really."

"I see your own creation is just as ambitious, but not as high," Leah said. "It looks like you've created a palace with many, many rooms."

"He's building the Great Market and I'm building both of the towers," Mally explained.

They were landmarks from Malinqua. "Ah," Leah said. "I suppose Chandran's been telling you about the royal city of Palminera."

"He says the red tower is for the sun and the white tower is for the moon. And the red tower is fire and the white tower is ice."

"Yes, and they're both really high. Each one has a stairwell inside and you can climb to the top, but you're out of breath by the time you make it," Leah said.

"Did you ever do that? Climb all the way up?"

"A few times." The last time with Chandran. On the night of a citywide celebration. They'd brought food with them, and laughed and talked while they consumed their meal, then they'd stood at the railing and looked out at all the color and gaiety in the streets below. She'd planned to tell him she was leaving Malinqua, but he'd already guessed. She hadn't known how to tell him goodbye; she hadn't known how much she'd miss him once she was gone.

There were so many things she still didn't know, but at least they were different things.

"Did you ever go to the Great Market?"

"*Go* there? I *worked* there. For a while, anyway, at Chandran's booth. That's how I learned so much about being a shopkeeper."

"Maybe I'd like to see it someday," Mally allowed.

"If you ever leave Welce," Chandran said.

"If I ever do."

Annova had come up to peer over Leah's shoulder. "Look at that. Those piles are almost as tall as the girl herself."

"I think you should build something," Mally said.

Annova grinned. "I think I should."

So Annova sat with Mally while Chandran and Leah minded the shop. And then it was Leah's turn to sit with Mally while the other two waited on customers and kept everything in order.

"I don't even know what to try to build," Leah said, picking up pieces and setting them down again.

"I'll help you," Mally offered. She scooted closer. "Choose a rock."

Leah sorted through the pieces on the floor and selected one that was a lopsided cube, rough on the edges but showing a certain defiant coppery spirit.

"That's very good," Mally said approvingly. "Now you want a flat one. But not too flat. See how your rock is a little taller on one side? You want one that fits it. The same but the opposite. And you put that on top."

"Oh, I think I get it. Like puzzle pieces."

"Except your puzzle is going up."

Even with Mally to help build it, Leah's tower fell over twice before she managed to make it more than six stones tall. Still, there was something unexpectedly absorbing about the exercise as Leah attempted to judge size and weight and counterweight. Absorbing and soothing. Leah had been jumpy and a little on edge ever since Mally had entered the shop, but this tranquil, focused task was calming her jangled nerves.

"I wonder if hunti people do something like this with sticks and tree branches," Leah said. "Maybe they build little huts out in the forest and then sit inside and meditate."

"I would if I was hunti," Mally said.

Leah smiled. "What would coru people build things out of?"

Mally thought for a moment. "Ice?"

"Oh, I bet you're right. And sweela people?"

"I don't know!"

"Hot coals," Leah suggested.

"They'd get pretty dirty."

"I can't even guess what elay people would use."

Mally shook her head. "They're elay. They don't need houses."

Less than an hour later, Virrie showed up at the door, an elay-motive idling outside. "Back from my adventure in the slums," she said, grimacing when Leah asked her how the day had gone. "I don't know how Josetta stands it there. All those people—all that suffering. And yet there's a serenity that flows from her so powerfully you can almost see it. I still can't imagine how she can live there five days out of nine."

Leah glanced at Mally. "She's elay," Leah said. "She doesn't need a house."

A few minutes later, Virrie and Mally were gone and Annova was gathering her things. That was when Leah realized it was closing time—the entire day had gone by while she had been focused on receipts and rocks and a little girl.

"No need to get here especially early tomorrow," Annova said. "Everything's in good shape."

On her way out the door, Annova passed two men who had arrived in a horse-drawn cart loaded down with shipping trunks. One stayed with the wagon while the other entered. He wore the excessive personal adornments she associated with Karkan natives.

"I'm looking for Leah Frothen?" he said hopefully, glancing over at the lighted sign.

"That's me," she answered. "Are you making a delivery?"

Chandran joined them. "One of my suppliers," he said, launching into an animated exchange with the visitor, all conducted in Karkan. When he turned back to Leah, he looked satisfied. "He was able to bring everything I requested. I think you will find your foreign customers very pleased indeed."

It took almost an hour for the four of them to unload the cart and carry everything upstairs, and then Leah raided the cash box to settle the bill. "Be a few ninedays before we're back in Welce," one of the men said as he pocketed the money. "But we can come back with more then."

"Please do," Leah said.

It was full dark before she locked the door behind the Karkan traders. "So?" she asked, turning to Chandran. "Which of these new bits of merchandise will be the most thrilling to Seka Mardis?"

"The spice you'll find in the red tins. It is called fillichie. Her prince will be equally delighted."

"Delighted enough to come here to get it? Or will I have to go to him?"

"Having met you, he might be curious to see you here in this setting," Chandran said. "Make sure that your guard is on hand if he comes to visit, though."

Leah laughed. "I will, but I think Yori might be even more uninhibited than the Karkan prince."

"No," said Chandran. "She is not."

That gave her a chill, but she covered it with a yawn, then sank to the floor right where she stood. Since she happened to be by the sales counter, she leaned her back against it and said, "I'm exhausted."

Chandran settled on the floor in front of her, dropping down with unexpected grace for such a big man. "I admit the day was not an easy one," he said.

"Physical labor late in the day. Always hard."

"Physical effort combined with emotional effort," he said softly. "They both take their toll."

She gave him a tired smile. So they were going to talk about it. "What did you think of Mally?"

"Like all children, she has a curious, sideways wisdom—a way of looking at the world that is so much fresher than the way we adults see it. It makes complex things seem simple and simple things complex."

"You were nervous at first."

"As were you," he retorted.

"I was," she admitted. "But I—I'm glad you got to meet her. I wanted you to. I'm glad it went so well."

"As am I."

She drew her knees up and linked her hands around her ankles. "I was watching you with her," she said. "And I thought— You've been around children before. Did you have any of your own?"

"No," he said, and there was a note in his voice much darker than regret. "At first I wanted children and my wife did not. Then Dederra wanted children. But I did not."

"Why did you change your mind?"

He spoke with great deliberation. "I did not think she should be anyone's mother."

Hardly a surprise, given what he'd said about his wife before, but the words still sent a shiver down Leah's back.

"But by the natural way you acted with Mally, you must have had children in your life at some point," Leah said.

Chandran nodded. "There were servants in our house and among them they had several children. One was a girl about Mally's age. Blond, though, and thinner than Mally. A laughing girl. Sweet." He fell silent a moment before adding in an almost inaudible voice, "She died."

Leah felt a burning uneasiness gnawing at her gut. *Don't ask the question you don't want to know. Don't ask the question you don't want to know.* She could hear the warning in her head, but she couldn't heed it. "What happened to her?"

"My wife killed her."

The silence in the shop was so deep it built up like geological layers. The air was thick as a sandstorm, impossible to breathe. They sat there so long without speaking that Leah thought a whole quintile might have passed, each nineday compressed into an impenetrably dense moment.

"Killed her?" she finally managed to say, barely choking out the words. "But how did— What happened?"

"When I lived in the Karkades, some members of the wealthy class had developed a new—appetite," Chandran said. He was trying to keep his voice to its usual steady measures, but Leah could hear the pain and repressed emotion underlying the calm tones. "They liked to drink blood."

Leah swallowed against a tight throat. "When I was at the party the other night. The prince was drinking a red liquid. Yori said it was blood."

"I would not be surprised."

"I thought—I mean, I just assumed—I mean, animal blood?"

"I do not know what the prince was drinking," Chandran said, "but in the Karkan court, the fashion was to drink human blood. At first, it was a game—often part of sexual play. A knife, a thin slice in the skin, a few drops of blood or maybe more than a few drops. Exciting, a little dangerous, but everyone was willing."

Now Leah's throat was so thick she couldn't swallow or speak. This was going to be worse than she had imagined. She nodded at him to go on.

"But for a select few among the nobility," Chandran said, "these sips of human ambrosia were insufficient. They wanted more. A glassful. A carafe. A keg, a barrel. More blood than one body could contain. For some of them it became practically their sole sustenance."

That's disgusting, Leah wanted to say. In her head, she heard Yori's response: *No more than meat, when you think about it.* But it was. It felt like it was.

"Among the poor of the royal city, it became a new source of income," Chandran said. "They could come to certain collection houses, cut open a vein, and squeeze out as much blood as they thought they could live without. They were paid handsomely." He made a sharp gesture and his voice changed, assumed sardonic overtones. "A few of them miscalculated and gave too much. They would be found collapsed in the street, pale and chilled, too weak to move. Some of them recovered. Some did not. Those who died near enough to one of the collection houses would be brought back in for their blood to be harvested while it was still warm."

"I'm going to be sick," Leah managed to say, pressing a hand to her mouth.

Chandran, usually so solicitous, did not even pause to ask if she wanted him to abbreviate the tale. He just went on, unheeding. "But there were those among the nobility who found the taste of the donated blood to be too bland. They argued that it lost some of its flavor, some of its—its—potency if it did not flow straight from another person's vein into their own bodies. And, as you can imagine, there were still volunteers who, for a great sum of money, would present their wrists or throats to the hungry mouths of the wealthy and depraved."

Leah could see where this was going—but surely not—but how else? She stirred on the floor, pushing herself to a kneeling position, and bent over a little, hoping to relieve the building nausea. It didn't help much.

"The *tastiest* blood, or so I was given to understand, consisted of the last few ounces, the final drops that a body would yield before it could no longer sustain its own life," Chandran continued. "So for even more fabulously huge sums of money, very poor individuals who wanted to ensure the well-being of their families—"

"No."

"Would agree to open their veins and be sucked dry."

"No."

"It was a legal compact," Chandran said in a hard voice. "Everyone benefited, and no one objected. But, of course, for some people, that was not enough."

I can't hear any more, Leah said. Or wanted to say. She couldn't get the words out.

"The blood with the freshest, sweetest, richest taste came from children."

Leah flung herself across the floor, trying to find a receptacle for the vomit that rose violently up her throat. A hunti bowl shaped like a grinning skull—perfect. She threw up twice. When she felt Chandran loom behind her, she extended one hand as if to hold him off. Even she wasn't sure if she was saying, *Don't come near me* or *Don't say another word.*

They stayed like that, Chandran motionless, Leah bent over, panting slightly, awaiting the decision of her roiling stomach. When a couple of minutes had passed, Leah thought it was safe to straighten up.

"Don't," she said, when Chandran stepped forward and opened his mouth. *Don't speak. Don't touch me.* "I need to clean this up. Wait for me down here."

She went upstairs to the water room, rinsed out the skull bowl, washed her face, cupped her hands and slurped down so much water she thought she'd throw up again. Then she stood over the spigots for a long time, bent forward, resting her head against the cold tile of the wall.

It all made sense now. Chandran didn't have to supply the coda for Leah to understand what had happened next. Dederra was one of the reckless nobles with an insatiable taste for blood; the servant's daughter had died to satisfy that craving. Maybe Chandran had even caught his wife with the girl's lifeless body in her arms. Leah wasn't surprised he'd killed her. She was surprised he hadn't gone on a rampage to murder every bloodthirsty noble in the city. She wanted to send a fleet of warships to the country right now and burn the whole place down.

She dried her face, smoothed back her hair, and stepped into the storage area to rummage around for a piece of candy. Not keitzee, oh no. She needed her head clear for this. But she wanted to chase the taste of vomit from her tongue. She found a bar of creamy chocolate and ate half of it with one bite. Then she snatched up her coat and headed back downstairs.

Chandran was standing by the hunti display, rearranging merchandise, but she thought he was just trying to find something to occupy his hands. He looked up when she stepped through the stairwell door, but he didn't speak. His face was troubled, riled by old memories, but she knew he was glad he had told her. *That is the very worst of me.* She could only hope that was true.

"Get your coat," she said. "We're going to the palace."

Chandran raised his eyebrows. "Why?"

"Because we have to talk to Darien."

They hired a private elaymotive to take them around the Cinque and up the hill to the palace, sparkling like a fairy castle against the chilly winter evening. Traffic was heavy enough along their route that

Leah suspected their timing was bad—there was a dinner or some other event going on at the palace and their arrival would be inconvenient. She didn't much care.

Indeed, as soon as they entered the huge, booming, cavernous space of the kierten, she could tell she was right. Servants hurried in all directions, carrying platters and decorations and cleaning supplies. She could smell complex and delicious aromas wafting out from the kitchens in back. The whole staff was so busy that none of the footmen approached to ask her business and she guessed even the palace steward would be reluctant to disturb Darien as he prepared for a state dinner. And she was in no mood to wait.

So she headed straight for the corridor leading to the king's quarters. Chandran trailed behind her. None of the servants stopped them, but they hadn't gotten within five yards of the doorway before three guards deployed around them, faces stern and weapons drawn.

"You can't enter here," said the fiercest-looking one.

"I need to speak to the regent," Leah said. "And I need to speak to him now. I'm the niece of the torz prime, and Darien Serlast will want to hear what I have to say."

Ten minutes later, Darien and Zoe joined Leah and Chandran in Darien's small, quiet study. They were both in formal attire, wearing dark severe clothing and discreet jewels, though the effect was more transformational on Zoe than Darien. The regent always dressed as if he was about to speak to a crowd of funeral mourners.

If Darien was annoyed at being interrupted right before his dinner, he showed no sign. "What have you discovered?" he asked.

Zoe showed more concern for the talebearer than the tale. "Are you all right? You look so pale," she said, coming over to lay a hand on Leah's arm. Instantly, Leah felt uplifted, as if Zoe's touch had energized her lethargic blood. *Blood.* Leah pulled away.

"Chandran has just been telling me something that might explain a few of the bodies that have turned up in Chialto lately," she said.

Darien remained impassive. "What bodies?"

Leah felt a wave of irrational anger at his pretense. "Oh, for once, see what it gets you when you share information!" she exclaimed. "You might learn that other people have knowledge that can help you!"

Chandran touched her arm. On his face was a look of mingled concern and horror. "What bodies?" he asked urgently.

Leah pointed at Darien. "I overheard something. The first day I was here. About someone who was cut and bleeding and found dead at the river flats. And then about a nineday ago, right outside my shop, Yori and Rafe and I found a young man who was all sliced up—his throat, his wrists, his legs—"

Leah heard Chandran whisper a Coziquela curse but she didn't even try to interpret it. "And Yori said you'd want to know about it and Zoe said we shouldn't tell anybody else about it, so I didn't, not even Chandran—although if I had told him, we'd have learned about this a lot sooner—"

"This is Chandran?" Zoe murmured. "I've been wanting to meet you."

Leah ignored her. "So *apparently* what's been *happening* but you haven't *told* anybody is that someone is going through Chialto and taking people off the streets and cutting them open and siphoning off all their blood. And *apparently* from what Chandran just told me, this is a common practice among the Karkan nobility. So I'm guessing that the loathsome prince you've brought in is responsible for all those corpses. And who knows what other disgusting things."

Darien's gray eyes sharpened, but otherwise he showed no change of expression. "I didn't bring in the loathsome prince, he invited himself," he said in a mild voice. "But this is very interesting." He looked at Chandran. "Are you willing to talk to me about the details of this practice?"

"I had no idea they had imported their activities when they arrived," Chandran said. He looked more upset there in Darien's office than he had in Leah's shop when he was recounting his story. Maybe because his wife's predations were familiar to him, and this situation was new. Maybe because he felt obscurely responsible. *I hate those Karkans,* he had said. But in some way, he was still connected to them.

"I had begun to suspect the Karkans were responsible for the mutilated bodies, but I had no proof," Darien said. "And the timing seemed off, because the first few cases occurred before the prince was officially in Chialto. So I have been hesitant to lay these crimes at his door."

Suddenly, Leah's anger fled, leaving her exhausted. She flapped a hand in Chandran's direction. "Tell them," she said, and collapsed in a chair.

"For the past fifteen years or so, wealthy Karkans have considered human blood a delicacy," Chandran told the other two, who drew closer to listen. "Most of them pay for willing donors. It is possible your corpses received money for their transactions." He spread his hands. "But it is possible the prince simply took from them what he wanted."

Darien was watching him very closely. "How do I make him stop?"

"It is very hard to dissuade Karkans from any course of action," Chandran said. "They are never embarrassed and rarely chastened. They recognize only their own personal code of honor. Nothing is wrong unless *they* think it is wrong."

"Then my only option is to withhold," Darien said.

Chandran inclined his head. "You are exactly right. You have discovered the trick to negotiating with the Karkans."

"But it only works if I have control over something they want," Darien said.

Leah lifted her head. "An alliance against Cozique," she said. "Isn't that what they're here for?"

"A defensive alliance with the Karkades?" Chandran repeated. "That seems like a bad bargain." When Darien gave him a swift look, Chandran bowed his head. "I apologize. I am not here to advise you on statecraft."

"No, but I agree with you," Darien said. "I wouldn't even be meeting with them, pretending I am considering their terms, if I wasn't trying to placate Soeche-Tas."

Leah leaned her head back against the chair. Darien had the most comfortable furniture. Since she had never seen him relax for even five minutes, she had to assume someone else had picked it out. "Since when do you care so much about Soeche-Tas?" she demanded.

Darien shared a look with Zoe. Leah straightened up fast. "What?" she said. "What else is going on that you probably haven't told anybody else because you're so secretive?"

"I'm not secretive, I'm careful."

Zoe's voice was regretful. "Relations with Soeche-Tas have been strained for several years, ever since the viceroy's engagement to Corene was—interrupted," she said. "Earlier this year, when the prince of Berringey came visiting, he spent a good deal of time in Soeche-Tas—and *he* has reason to dislike us as well."

"Oddly," Darien murmured, "in both cases, actions by Zoe have led to the estrangement between Welce and other nations."

"That's so unfair," Zoe said. She was laughing.

Leah knew what Zoe had done to anger the Soechin ambassadors. She had no idea what Zoe had done to alienate the Berringese, but she imagined it had to have been equally spectacular.

"At any rate, Soeche-Tas has expressed its dissatisfaction with Welce, so far, in small ways," Darien went on. "Merchant ships that sail to the northern ports have been harassed. Towns on the northern border, up by the mountains, have been raided. We have sent more ships to patrol the waters and more troops to patrol the land, and so far we have seen nothing but skirmishes. But I admit to a certain nervousness."

"So if you make a deal with the Karkans—"

"The Soechins are placated," Darien finished. "Yet I find myself allied with two nations that I neither like nor trust."

"If the Karkans wish you to promise military assistance against Cozique, then perhaps the answer is to ally with Cozique instead," Chandran said.

"An excellent strategy—if Cozique was only a one-day journey away," Darien answered. "And if Cozique hadn't made enough enemies of its own."

Leah groaned. "Malinqua," she said. Cozique had invaded the smaller country just a few days before Leah left, and she supposed it would take a long time before good relations were restored between the two governments.

"And Dhonsho," Darien added. He walked to his desk and spun a small painted globe that sat on the corner, stopping it when it showed the expanse of the southern seas dotted with islands and small continents. "If Dhonsho, Berringey, the Karkades, Malinqua, and Soeche-Tas all form a single alliance, Cozique will be very lonely. Will the queen be willing to shore up Welce's military if her own country could be attacked at any minute by five other nations? Or would she be better served guarding her own borders and not worrying too much about overmatched friends on the other side of the ocean?"

Zoe gave them all an apologetic smile. "Nothing is ever as simple and straightforward as it seems," she said.

"So I am in a precarious situation," Darien said. "I do not like the Soechins—not a single one that I've ever encountered—and I have developed a deep distaste for the Karkans. And yet I do not want either one as an enemy, which means I must maintain them as friends or at least neutral parties." He paused a moment, then added grimly, "And yet I do not want them murdering Welchin citizens, whether or not they pay for the privilege. And I am not certain precisely how to dissuade them from pursuing that particular pastime while we negotiate our relationship."

Zoe had tilted her head to one side and appeared to be thinking something over. "I wonder if I might be able to help them understand how unacceptable such behavior is by Welchin standards," she said.

Darien regarded her for a long moment. At last he said, "I wonder if you might."

She was trying not to smile. "Tonight?"

"Too public," he said. "There will be forty people in the room. Maybe we can arrange a private luncheon in a day or two."

Leah almost bounced in her comfortable chair. "No! Come to the shop! I just got a shipment of Karkan goods. Chandran says the prince will be so excited about them that he'll come to me if I invite him."

"Perfect," Darien said. "Of course, you'll have to clear everyone else out."

"That's easy enough."

Chandran spoke up. "And provide guards for protection."

Zoe waved a hand at him. "You don't even need to mention that."

Chandran was still watching her. "But what will you do?"

Zoe was smiling widely. "I'm the coru prime," she said. "I'll think of something."

Darien sent them back in one of the royal elaymotives, though neither one of them wanted to go home. It had been a strange day—*even measured against all the other strange days lately,* Leah thought—and they were both still sorting through the ramifications. So they had the driver drop them off at the Plaza of Men and they wandered through the booths along with the other restless nighttime visitors who weren't deterred by the cold. As they strolled along, Leah casually reached for Chandran's hand, and he casually laced his fingers with hers. She was worn out from the stresses of the day, and a little achy from carrying heavy boxes up the stairs, but she figured she could walk another hour or two, just so she didn't have to let go of Chandran.

Neither of them had any interest in buying a horse, but they stopped in front of the horse trader's stall anyway to listen to the breeder explain the good points of his animals to a group of young men gathered in front.

"How did you find out about the little girl?" she asked as the trader prattled on about muscle and wind and length of leg. "The servant's daughter?"

"I discovered her," Chandran said. "In my wife's bedchamber. Her mother had been looking for her all afternoon. As soon as I heard that, I knew where she would be."

Leah squeezed his hand so hard her own bones protested. "I'm so sorry."

"That was the day," he said. "That was the day I killed her."

She didn't know how to answer that. She lifted their linked hands and kissed his knuckles, one after the other. Then she touched the back of his hand to her cheek, so he could feel her tears.

"I do not know how something that happened so long ago can still feel so raw," he said.

"Which thing?" she murmured. Now the horse trader was talking speed and endurance and the various merits of two different breeds. "Finding or killing?"

"Both," he said. "Grief and rage."

"You need to fill your head with other pictures," she said. "Fill your heart with other memories."

He pulled their linked hands to his own face so that she could feel the stubble of his cheek. She couldn't tell if the traces of moisture there had been transferred from her own skin or if Chandran was crying, too. "I am trying," he said. "It is hard."

The gawkers at the horse trader's stall were beginning to disperse, so Leah and Chandran moved on. Just past a booth where a scribe was selling his services they found a familiar sight.

"There he is," Leah said, irrationally pleased. "I thought that boy would have closed up his makeshift temple by now."

"Clearly too many people need blessings and are too lazy to go searching for the real thing."

"Shall we try again?"

"I can always use a little guidance."

"Get your blessings here! Full set—nothing missing!" the boy called out to the passing crowd, then he beamed at them as he realized they were approaching. Leah already had a few quint-silvers in her hand and dropped them into his tithing box.

He gave no sign that he recognized them, so Leah supposed he'd done a brisk business in the past nineday. "Do you want to pull your own coins, or do you want me to help you pick?" he asked.

"Oh, we need three hands in the barrel," Leah said. "So you have to help."

As before, Leah's blessings were a little fuzzy—one quint-copper, one disk that looked like the button off a soldier's coat, and one battered temple coin stamped with the glyph for certainty. *Wouldn't that be nice?* she thought. As before, Chandran's were more illuminating: courage, clarity, and honor.

"Again," Leah murmured when she saw the coin in his hand. "It follows you. Maybe we should go to a jeweler's and buy you a charm with this blessing."

"You can keep that coin," the temple-master said eagerly, "but you have to pay."

Chandran dropped it back in his bucket. "Oh, no," he said, "I would hate to make you break up your set." They were both laughing as they strolled away.

TWENTY

Two days later, Leah hosted a small, private party for Karkan royalty.

The day after the meeting with Darien, she had sent a note to Seka Mardis, describing a few of her new purchases and hinting at others, wondering coyly if the prince could be persuaded to come to the shop "some evening when we would have the place entirely to ourselves." On Chandran's instructions, she'd sprinkled the note with grains of an aromatic spice that had arrived in the most recent shipment.

"It is the scent of promises for the future," he said. "A woman might tuck a sachet of it into the pocket of a man she wants to become her lover. One of our famous historical adventurers sent some to his sworn enemy as a way to let him know he would exact his revenge."

"I don't want to give Seka Mardis the wrong impression," Leah objected.

He smiled. "You have gone to some trouble to give her the wrong impression," he pointed out. "But this gesture will do no more than intrigue her. And by all indications, she is a woman who loves to be intrigued."

Whether she was intrigued, curious, or merely bored, Seka Mardis answered within the hour and offered to bring the prince to the shop on fifthday. *It will be quite delightful!* she wrote. *We are looking forward to it.*

Naturally, Leah had to arrange for food and drink and comfortable chairs for her visitors, and naturally this was the day dozens of customers chose to drop by, requiring Leah's personal attention. But by nightfall, she was more or less prepared. She had created a cozy seating area in the back of the shop, shadowy enough to let the prince hide his face if he wished, but illuminated with candles for a welcoming ambiance. She had thought Chandran would leave the premises altogether, but he wanted to remain upstairs, along with any royal guards Darien elected to send.

"What if he insists on a tour of the whole building? He'll see you. What if he recognizes you?"

"I would rather run that risk than worry about what might be happening while he is here with you."

"I'll have a half dozen protectors."

"Well, now you will have one more."

She figured it was safe to allow both Yori and Annova to have free run of the shop, since Yori would be viewed as Leah's intimate friend and Annova would be seen as hired help.

"They might look twice at Yori, but they won't think *you're* a threat of any kind," she said to Annova. "They'll think you're a bit frail and elderly. But I've always had a feeling that you could defend yourself if the necessity ever arose."

Annova was grinning. "I'll be unobtrusive unless the situation gets out of hand."

Zoe would show up later.

Yori arrived with three guards shortly after the shop had been tidied up from the day's business and organized for the night's visitors. Chandran and the soldiers went upstairs, but Leah and Yori and Annova were left with little to do but stare at each other. Leah thought about fetching Mally's box of stones, but Yori pulled out a pack of cards and asked, "Does anybody play penta?"

Leah laughed. "Are you joking? I share a house with Rafe Adova. Apparently, everyone who's ever known him longer than five minutes is forced to learn it."

"I knew the game long before I met Rafe," Annova said.

"Then let's play a few hands," Yori said. "Low stakes, of course."

Leah eyed her. "I have a feeling I shouldn't play you for money." She looked at Annova. "*Either* of you."

Annova was smiling. "Quint-coppers," she said.

If there had been a lower denomination of coins, Leah would have been better served holding out for that, because she lost every hand. The other two women were fairly evenly matched, though their styles differed wildly. Annova would win huge pots on spectacularly risky plays, while Yori devised masterful strategies that relied on a perfect memory and iron nerve. "You both ought to be down in a southside tavern, earning a living by fleecing tourists," Leah said in disgust as she threw down her last cards.

"That's not a life that would keep my interest very long," Annova said.

Yori yawned. "Not enough action."

Almost on the words, there was a clatter in the streets and a figure hurried toward the shop. Yori swept up the cards and faded toward a side wall while Annova slipped behind the sales counter. Leah opened the door, extending her palm and smiling widely.

"Seka! You're here!" she exclaimed. "But where's the prince?"

Seka pressed Leah's hand, kissed her cheek, and gestured toward the street. "Outside while I come in to look around and make sure—" She shrugged eloquently. "Everything is in order."

"Absolutely. I just have a couple of friends on hand to assist me, if necessary. You remember Yori from the other night?" Yori waved but didn't come any closer. "And Annova works with me here in the shop. She's utterly trustworthy."

"Oh, and how important it is to have one or two people you can rely on even when the rest of the world is failing!" Seka remarked. "We have brought attendants as well—three of them—though the others can stay outside if you like."

"Inside or out, it doesn't matter to me."

"It's a cool night," Seka said. "I will bring them in as long as they keep out of the way."

In a few minutes the shop was filled with the scent and the restlessness and the glittering presence of five Karkans. Three men who were clearly guards, though they were dressed like courtiers, clustered by the door, trying to be unobtrusive while still maintaining constant readiness. The prince entered last, stooping a little at the low door, pausing to place his warm palm against Leah's. His face was shadowed and his clothes were completely covered by his dark, hooded cloak, but when he touched his hand to hers she felt the metal of rings on every one of his fingers. She thought she also caught a flash of gold braid on the clothing under the cloak.

"How very pleasant to see you again," he purred in his rich, cultured voice. "Seka has teased me with hints of the treasures you have laid in for our visit. I admit I am quite wrought up with curiosity."

Wrought up with something, at any rate. What she could see of his face under the hood looked flushed and ruddy; his breathing seemed a little too fast. Sometime within the past hour he had enjoyed *something* very much.

"I hope you are pleased with my offerings," she replied, her voice demure but her smile provocative. "When one makes new friends, one is never sure what will—captivate them."

"That is why new friends are so exciting."

She urged him to the back of the shop, where she had arranged a table of refreshments and four chairs. The fourth chair was for Zoe, although the prince wouldn't know that; he was supposed to think she was just being hospitable, in case he brought other high-ranking friends.

Seka Mardis had followed close behind, and the three of them sank into their seats, Leah closest to the steamer trunk that had been stuffed with goods. "May I get you something to eat or drink? I have cans of tchiltsly to send home with you, but for now I thought we might sample some traditional Welchin pastries while we look over the merchandise."

"I would take keerza, if you have any," Seka Mardis said.

Leah laughed. "Have you managed to acquire a taste for it?"

"Not yet, but I'm still trying."

"Wine for me," the prince said, moving restlessly in his chair. He resettled himself, crossed his arms, uncrossed them, and began tapping his fingers against his knee.

Annova had trailed soundlessly behind them, and now she busied herself with the refreshments. It made Leah a little less nervous to have Annova's calm presence nearby.

Once they were all served, Leah leaned over, opened the trunk, and pulled out the first item. Not a Karkan import, but something she knew would be welcome, anyway. "More veneben, of course," she said, handing the pouch directly to the prince. "In case you don't like anything else I have on hand, I know you will still leave here happy!"

"You are the most generous of hostesses," the prince said. He held the pouch to his nose, inhaled deeply, then laid it in his lap, but his fingers kept toying with the clasp. The man couldn't sit entirely still.

After that, Leah brought out a series of items—the fillichie, the tchiltsly, a tin of keitzees, a box of caramel-like candies that had small hard cores of poison. "Eating them is a game," Chandran had told her. "Can you suck off all the sweetness before you get to the kernel of venom at the center?"

"I would spit it out long before I got too close," she'd said.

"Not if you had ever had one," he'd replied. "They have an exquisite taste. You would hate to give up even the smallest amount."

"Then why bother making them toxic? Why not just make them wonderful?"

"Because that would be too simple. Because only risk makes you savor the reward."

"Karkans are insane."

"That is not a statement with which I can argue."

Seka Mardis almost moaned with pleasure when Leah offered her the caramel candies. "I didn't dare to *hope* your supplier would be so good!" she exclaimed, hugging the container to her chest. Leah found herself wondering if anyone else, even the prince, would get a chance to sample those delights. "Who advises you on your purchases? It must be someone who spent a great deal of time in my country."

"The trader himself was from the Karkades," Leah said. "I merely asked for his suggestions."

"If I am in your city much longer, I might want this trader's name for myself so I can deal with him directly," said the prince.

Leah showed a face of hurt, exaggerated so that he knew she was joking. "Depriving me of the pleasure of your company?"

He smiled. "I would not want to deprive you of any pleasure at all," he said, and his low, musical voice made her skin crawl.

But she managed to giggle. "Now these next items," she said. "They're not really for you. I don't know if you'll want them. But you mentioned that you had children and I thought they might enjoy puzzles."

She handed over a series of wooden balls in various sizes. Each one was made of interlocking pieces of wood that snapped together so smoothly they created one seamless whole. But disassemble them and you would find it almost impossible to put them back together. At least, Leah hadn't been able to do it. Rafe had, but he admitted that it had taken him more hours than a rational man would waste on such a project. Josetta and Annova had refused to even try.

"I'm going to put them out on the hunti tables, because they're wood," Leah said. "But if you wanted a couple—"

The prince was examining them with every sign of fascination, sliding out one of the pieces just enough to see how the puzzle worked, not enough to make the whole object come apart in his hands. "Very cunning," he approved. "My oldest daughter and my son will be intrigued."

"But not Elsita," Seka said with a laugh.

The prince shook his head. "No, she is not the type to sit down and bend her mind to a difficult problem." He mimed throwing the ball against the floor. "She is more likely to smash it in a tantrum and run away."

Hard to know what kind of platitude to offer in response to that. "And yet I'm sure you love her very much," Leah ventured.

"Indeed," he said with a sigh. He placed the sphere on the table. "Do you have children, Leah?"

She found it impossible to offer a flat negative to his question, even in a situation as delicate as this. It would be like denying Mally's existence, and she had done that for far too long. "Oh, I've been a wanderer for so many years that I didn't think it was a good idea for me to try to raise a child," she said. "But now that I am more settled—who knows? I think I would like to be a mother."

Seka's face wore a slight frown, as if she were chasing an errant memory. "But there was a little girl here when I was at the shop before," she said. "Wasn't there? With dark hair and a solemn expression. Not yours?"

Even harder to lie this time. "She's the ward of the torz prime," Leah managed. "I believe he and his wife have raised her from infancy."

"Someone asked her name and she said . . . Odelia, that was it," Seka ended on a triumphant note.

"I thought Odelia was the name of the youngest princess," the prince said. "Is that who was visiting you?"

How had they gotten on this topic? How could they get back to safer ones like gifts and commerce? Leah covered her face and groaned in frustration. "Oh, she *always* says that!" she exclaimed. "Someone told her once that she looked like Vernon's daughter, and she was so taken with the idea that she started pretending she was the princess. But she's really just an ordinary girl named Mally. I'll have to tell Taro and Virrie that she's making up stories again."

"Well, I might have told people I was a princess if I thought they would believe me," Seka Mardis confessed. "Unfortunately, I look *nothing* like royalty."

"I would be too afraid that I would get caught in the deception!" Leah said. "I don't think, in general, it's a good idea to impersonate the crown."

The prince laughed a little too loudly. "No," he said. "In my experience, princes and princesses are not eager to allow anyone else to be as special as they are."

"Speaking of special," Leah said, leaning over the trunk and hoping to change the subject. "I have something else I think you'll like. The trader told me—"

Annova interrupted her. "Someone's at the door."

Now they all heard it—a knock, a rattle, a woman's voice calling, "Leah?" through the thick glass. The Karkan guards jumped to attention, but they offered no threat, just waited to see what would happen next. Yori had drifted over toward the door, too, appearing to be merely curious. But Leah saw her hands hovering near her hidden knives.

"Oh, dear. It's probably somebody who saw the lights on inside and doesn't realize we're closed for business," Leah said apologetically. "Annova, could you send them away and tell them when we open in the morning?"

"Of course," Annova said, heading across the shop.

Seka Mardis tittered. "We were having so much fun that, for a moment, I forgot there might be other people in the world."

I doubt you ever forget there are other people who must be placated, outwitted, or overcome, Leah thought. She merely smiled. "It *has* been very enjoyable," she agreed.

Seka was watching Annova at the door. "It looks like she's having trouble convincing your visitor to leave," she said.

Now Annova turned to face the group at the back of the shop. Her face showed uneasiness, and she spread her hands helplessly. "Leah—it's Zoe Lalindar," she said. "And she's brought the sweela prime."

Nelson? Leah thought. *What's he doing here?* It was easy to summon a look of bafflement for the benefit of the Karkans. "Prince— perhaps you have been here long enough to understand—the primes . . . That is, in Welce, the primes wield almost as much influence as the regent—"

The prince waved a magnanimous hand. "Yes, of course you must allow them entry. You must allow them to shop in privacy. Or—" He shrugged. "I have no objection to letting them join us for casual discussion. I have met them both and am happy to further my acquaintance."

Leah rose to her feet. "Thank you. That is so generous."

Her eyes glittering as much as the gems in her hair, Seka grinned up at Leah and tucked one of the tins under her chair. "You can even show them some of our treats," she said, "but they cannot have the tchiltsly."

Leah laughed. "Trust me, they won't want it."

She hurried to the doorway, where Zoe and Nelson were just now taking off their overcoats and shaking away the chill of the night air. "Leah! I had no idea you were keeping evening hours!" Zoe greeted her. "But when I saw the lights on inside, I made Nelson stop—" She caught sight of the visitors and paused mid-sentence, her expression becoming rueful. "Oh, but I see I've interrupted something! I'm so sorry! We can just leave—"

Leah caught her arm. "Do stay," she urged. "It's the prince of the Karkades, and he just said he would enjoy the opportunity to see you in a more informal setting."

"I'd like that, too," Nelson said frankly. "It's too difficult to get to know someone when there are a hundred people in the room."

Leah thought she could interpret that: *It's harder for me to read people, especially foreigners, if there's too much bustle and interference.* Though she imagined even Nelson would have a hard time sifting through the mind of the Karkan prince.

"I'll get another chair," Annova said, heading for the stairwell.

Leah shepherded the new arrivals to the back of the shop, where she introduced Seka to the primes, and the Welchins pressed the palms of the Karkans, and everyone claimed to feel pleasure at the chance encounter. Annova returned with a fifth chair and they all took their seats.

"How enterprising of Leah to host private parties for special guests," Zoe said. "I shall have to arrange something for my own particular friends."

"I imported merchandise especially for the prince and his advisors," Leah said. "I'm not sure you'd like any of it."

"Surely keitzee must be a universal favorite," the prince said.

"It's candy with a kick," Leah informed the primes. "It makes you feel as if you've had a couple of glasses of wine. But better than that."

"You must have sampled it," Nelson observed.

Leah made her smile demure. "I had to understand its effects if I wanted to be able to sell it."

"I'm willing to try it," Zoe declared. She leaned forward confidingly. "Alcohol tends not to have much effect on me," she said. "Something to do with being the coru prime. But it will be interesting to see if a concoction from another country overcomes the baffles in my blood."

Leah had no idea if this was true or if Zoe was just making it up on the spot. Nelson, by contrast, was laughing. "Well, every sweela man will tell you alcohol has too *much* effect on him," he said. "But I love it just the same. I'll be happy to sample your doctored candy."

Since someone had to keep their wits about them, Leah passed on the opportunity, but promised herself a keitzee treat once this nerve-racking evening was over. Leah wasn't surprised to see both Seka and the prince take two candies at once, since they seemed likely to have built up a tolerance for the stuff, but Zoe and Nelson started more cautiously with one apiece.

"Oh yes, this is quite tasty," Zoe said, speaking around the keitzee. "And it almost feels like it's—*humming* in my mouth."

"'Humming'! That is exactly the way I describe it!" Seka told her.

"How soon before it takes effect?" Zoe wanted to know.

"Almost instantly, in my experience," Leah said. "You can't feel it?"

Zoe shrugged. "Maybe a tiny bit."

Nelson waggled his head from side to side. "I can. That's a fun sensation."

Zoe sighed and manufactured a pout. "The life of the coru prime. Full of so many disappointments."

Nelson hooted with laughter, but the prince hitched his chair closer. "We hear so much about the primes and their powers," he said. "But I confess I do not fully understand what you can and cannot do."

Zoe waved a hand at Nelson, who had sprawled back in his chair as if relaxing under the effects of alcohol. Leah couldn't tell whether or not he was acting. "As the sweela prime, Nelson has an affinity with fire. He could take one of these candles here and coax it into a conflagration. Or he could make the flame die down to nothing."

Leah had seen him do both of those things that night in Malinqua when one of the city's celebrated towers had gone up in a spectacular blaze. To be fair, Corene had set the place on fire to begin with. Although, to be even more fair, she'd done it to save herself from soldiers who were trying to kill her.

"But there's more," Zoe went on. "We believe that the element of fire corresponds with the physical attribute of the brain. Nelson says he can't read minds, but he has an uncanny way of knowing whether or not someone is lying—he can assess the true essence of another person better than anyone I've ever met."

"Even if that person comes from a different country?" Seka asked. Leah wondered if she was unnerved by the idea. Or—being Seka—intrigued.

Nelson gave her one of his broad, happy smiles. "*Some* people," he said. "*You* I can scan with some accuracy, I think. You're ambitious and driven—you're not easily frightened—and you don't have too many moral boundaries. But you're loyal. That shines out of you like sunlight."

Seka loosed a small sound that tried to be a laugh and sounded more like a gasp. "Well, I don't suppose I'd quarrel with any of that," she said. "It feels very odd, though, to have a stranger say such things to me."

"What about the prince?" Leah asked.

Nelson's smile grew a little sardonic. "He is impenetrable to me," he said. "Nothing but darkness."

Not so impenetrable, Leah thought, guessing that Nelson was fully aware of the irony. *You have described him with perfect precision.*

But Nelson's words pleased the prince. "A man likes to believe he can maintain his secrets," he said, "especially a man treating with foreign representatives."

Especially a man who has secrets, Leah thought.

Seka gestured toward Zoe. "And you? The coru prime works with water, does she not?"

"Water and blood," Zoe said, nodding. "I can tame rivers or bring the rain or draw groundwater up to a dry well."

"That's useful," the prince said.

"But I have found my work with blood to be even more beneficial in some situations," she said.

The prince leaned forward. They were finally on a topic of deep interest to him. "In what way?" he asked. "How can you manipulate blood?"

"I could, if I wanted, bring a bruise to your body," Zoe said, "merely by calling the blood to the surface of your skin."

The prince immediately held out his arm. "Do it. I would like to see."

"Majesty. I cannot, even in such a small way, harm you."

He nodded at his advisor. "Then do it to Seka."

"Only if she is willing."

Without hesitation, Seka extended her hand, palm up, and pushed back her close-fitting sleeve. "I'm not easily frightened, remember?" she said, flashing a smile at Nelson.

Zoe touched her fingertip gently to Seka's wrist, right where one of the blue veins pulsed against the skin. They all bent closer to watch, in the flickering candlelight, as a purple stain spilled out slowly from the place where Zoe's finger rested against her flesh. When the bruise was about twice as big as a quint-gold, Zoe lifted her hand and the stain stopped spreading.

Seka did not look at all discomposed. She lifted her arm to get a closer look at the mark, turning her hand this way and that as if checking for the extent of pain. The prince was sitting up straighter in his chair and there was no other word for it: He appeared enthralled.

"That is remarkable," he said. "Is there a limit on how much damage you can do?"

"I don't know," Zoe drawled, "since I've always stopped myself before I went too far. But I'm fairly certain I could sit here and cause all of her blood to mutiny in her veins. I wouldn't even have to touch her, and I could pull every drop out of her body."

The prince gave a considering look to Seka, who finally appeared somewhat nervous. It was clear he would love to see such a demonstration. Zoe added, "I'm not going to do it, of course."

"Of course," the prince echoed.

"But I have skills that are even more useful," Zoe went on. "I can touch someone—even a stranger from another country—and learn his heritage. I could take hold of your hand, and hers, and determine if you were related, merely by the composition of your blood."

The prince was fascinated by this revelation as well. "We are not related, Seka and I," he said, "but one of the guards is a distant cousin of hers." His sentence ended on an interrogative note.

Zoe smiled. "You would like me to prove my abilities?"

"It would be very interesting to see."

"Then call them over."

The guards were summoned and, one by one, they allowed Zoe to wrap her fingers around their wrists. "This one," Zoe said as soon as she laid hands on the second man. She took the hand of the third man, then nodded over at the first guard. "And these two are related in some fashion, though I am not convinced they're brothers."

"Half brothers," the third guard said.

"Remarkable!" the prince said. "Most impressive." He made a gesture and the three Karkan soldiers quickly retreated to their posts at the front of the shop.

"I cannot tell you the number of times that skill has come in handy," Zoe said. "I could probably detail for you every indiscretion committed among the Five Families in the past thirty years."

The prince extended his arm, palm up, fingers spread, almost the pose of a supplicant. "I wonder what you would read in my blood," he said.

"If you are not related to anyone else in the room, not much, I think. But I would be happy to take your hand and see what information I can uncover."

"Please do."

Zoe placed his hand between both of hers, applying a little pressure as if she wanted to sink through the calloused barrier of flesh. Leah held her breath and watched closely; she had a sense that this was where the trouble was about to start. Zoe wore a look of intense concentration, which changed quickly to one of surprise, then curiosity, then something darker. Disbelief. Anger. Disgust. She released him abruptly, flinging her fingers wide as if to flick away drops of tainted water, then began rubbing her palms against her trousers.

"Well," she said in a hard voice. "I was not expecting that."

The prince looked bewildered. "Expecting what? What did you read in my body?"

Zoe came abruptly to her feet. Nelson scrambled up next to her, looking somewhat unsteady, and the rest of them more slowly stood up. "I don't want to ruin your lovely evening with harsh words," she said in a grim voice. "Leah, I'm sorry to have disturbed you. Perhaps we can talk in the morning."

"But— What's wrong? What have I done?" Leah asked. It wasn't difficult to make her voice sound shaky and uncertain.

"Nothing *you* have done," Zoe said, turning to go.

The prince held up a hand. "Please. Something in the pattern of my blood disturbed you. I think I deserve to know what it was."

Zoe turned back to him, her face cold with fury. "Do you? Then very well. There is blood in your body that does not belong to you. Welchin blood. It doesn't run through your veins and arteries, but through your stomach and your guts. You have *ingested* it."

Nelson appeared astonished. "What? How could something like that even happen?"

"Only one way," Zoe said, still coldly. "If the honored prince of the Karkades was somehow acquiring the blood of Welchin people and drinking it like water."

"Well, that's revolting," Nelson said.

The prince tried to look surprised, but his face more truly showed uneasiness. "Is such a thing a crime in your country? That is not the case in the Karkades."

Zoe took a step closer to him. She was a tall, slender woman without much body mass, yet she exuded so much rage that it was hard not to be a little afraid of her. "Is it a crime in the Karkades to sip so much blood from a man's body that he dies?" she hissed. "Because in the ninedays since you have been in our city, ten corpses have shown up in our streets and alleys, sucked almost dry. My husband used the word *exsanguinated*. We could not imagine who was performing such acts. But now, given the evidence of your body, I have to assume it was you. So, yes. Murder is a crime in my country. Is it not in yours?"

"It was not my intent to murder anyone," the prince said. Now he tried to appear shocked. "Perhaps my advisors—who have sought to meet my specific needs—have been too zealous on my behalf. I can speak with them."

"*Speak* with them," Zoe repeated. As if she couldn't help herself, she reached out with one hand and shoved the prince in the chest. "I will *speak* with you. I do not know how much longer you intend to remain in my country, but you will not drink the blood of one more Welchin citizen."

Seka Mardis tried to push herself between Zoe and the prince. "Prime," she said in a placating voice.

Zoe knocked her aside with a swipe of her hand. All her attention was focused on the prince. "If one more body shows up in the slums or the river flats—if one more man is found staggering through the streets, broken and bleeding—I will come for you. You want to see if I can cause your blood to riot against you? You want to know what it feels like to have every inch of your skin raw and bruised? Continue this foul practice, and you will very quickly find out."

Seka had righted herself, and now she looked almost as angry as Zoe. "Prime!" she snarled. "Do not speak to the prince in such a fashion!"

Zoe shot her a look of venomous contempt. "Oh, don't think *you* have any hope of stopping me, whatever I choose to do."

Seka's head snapped back. "Guards!" she called. "Come quickly! Help the prince!"

Leah almost knocked over her chair as she scrambled out of the way, gathering her breath so she could scream for Darien's soldiers. The Karkan guards were hurtling in their direction, Yori running in at an angle to cut them off, and Seka was yelling something in her own language.

Then Nelson slashed his hand through the air with one impatient gesture. All three of the rushing guards grabbed their heads and sank to their knees, moaning and rocking in pain. Yori skidded to a halt and looked down on them, then glanced up and caught Leah's eye. She was grinning.

"Call them off," Nelson said calmly to Seka. "Or they will not easily recover." He did not sound remotely drunk.

Seka stared at him. "What did you do?"

"I enflamed their brains. Would you like to discover what that feels like?" His voice was as polite as if he was offering her keerza.

She pressed her lips together, trying to bite back fury. "Release them. I will order them to stand down."

He cocked his head, eyeing her with some mistrust, then he swept his hand upward. Instantly, the three guards collapsed to the floor as if freed from crippling vises. Two of them just remained there, panting; one pushed himself to his hands and knees, but he didn't seem to have the strength to rise. Yori stood over them, a blade in her hand, but she didn't look too worried.

"Stay where you are," Seka called. "We'll sort this out."

"There's nothing to *sort out*," Zoe flashed. "Your prince will restrain himself for the duration of his stay, or I will bring him to the point of agony. That seems clear enough to me."

All this time, the prince had not spoken; he had scarcely moved. Judging by the brightness of his eyes, barely visible beneath his hooded cloak, he was excited rather than dismayed by the sudden eruption of violence. Aroused, even. "Entirely clear," he answered in his beautiful voice. "I will abide by your restrictions."

"I am glad to hear it," Zoe said. She looked at Leah. "Is there somewhere in this building where I can wash my hands?" The implication was impossible to miss. *I want to scrub away any memory of this prince's rotten blood.*

"Yes—upstairs—I can show you—"

"I will find my way." She favored all of them with a minatory look before heading to the back stairwell—where, Leah assumed, Chandran and the Welchin guards were crowded into the narrow space behind the door. Annova silently followed Zoe.

"As soon as she's back, we'll be on our way," Nelson told Leah.

"No," the prince said. He smoothed down the folds of his cloak. "It is we who must be going." He nodded at Leah and held out his palm to her. "Thank you for an unexpectedly entertaining evening."

Somewhat unnerved, she pressed her hand to his, then helped Seka gather up the items that the Karkans had liked the most. "I am so sorry—if I had known—tonight of all nights!" she whispered to Seka as she handed over a bag stuffed full of tins. "Please don't be angry with me!"

"I am too confused and unbalanced to be angry," Seka whispered back. "But it's not your fault. She is—they are—this was a strange evening."

"When they leave," Leah said, "I am going to eat half a can of keitzees."

Seka laughed. "When I get back to our rooms," she said, "I will do the same." She kissed Leah on the cheek, then ushered the prince to the door. The guards had recovered enough to escort them outside, and the last one pulled the door shut behind them.

Nelson, Yori, and Leah stayed frozen in place while they watched the shadows of the street resolve as the prince's entourage pulled away. Another moment of silence—another—and just to be sure, another— and then Nelson doubled over and began laughing.

"Oh, it's a rare treat to see Zoe in a fury!" he exclaimed when he straightened up. "She looks like a peasant's daughter with hardly a thought in her head, and then suddenly she's making people weep blood from their eyeballs and threatening to kill them where they stand! I can't tell you how much I love that girl."

He was only halfway through his rant before Zoe pushed through the back doorway, trailed by Annova, Chandran, and the Welchin guards. "I find it disappointing that it is for my violent qualities that you admire me most," she said. She was grinning. "I would rather be loved for my sweet disposition and the goodness of my heart."

Yori motioned to the soldiers and they followed her out the front door, no doubt to reconnoiter. The remaining five clustered in the middle of the room, Chandran hanging back a little.

"Anybody can have a good heart," Nelson said, unimpressed. "But who else can promise to bruise a man from head to toe without ever laying a hand on his body?"

"So is that more or less how you intended the meeting to go?" Leah said. "I didn't have any idea what you were planning. I was almost as shocked as the prince."

"Pretty much," Zoe said. "It helped that he kept asking questions. Now he can blame himself for how the evening turned out."

Annova asked the question at the back of Leah's mind. "Could you really sort out the blood that he had swallowed from the blood that ran in his veins?"

"If I hadn't known what he'd done? I might not have been able to figure it out. But I could tell there was something odd in his body. Something that didn't belong."

"You ought to be an actress," Nelson said. "Ask Josetta's mother if she'll cast you in one of her theatricals. Preferably a melodrama."

"You'd be perfect for the stage," Leah said. "And trust me, I've seen more than my share of productions."

"I do think it would be fun," Zoe said.

"So what happens now?" Annova asked. "I only got a glimpse of him, but the prince does not seem like the type to meekly obey someone else's orders."

"No, and that worries me a little," Zoe said thoughtfully. "I have no idea what he'll do next."

Nelson pointed at Chandran. "Let's ask this fellow. He's the one who knows all about the Karkans, isn't he?"

That was the point at which Leah realized that Chandran was meeting yet another member of her small circle of family and friends. She hadn't done a very good job of keeping him partitioned from the rest of her life. Maybe she hadn't wanted to. She hastily made introductions.

"How much of our little brawl were you able to overhear?" Nelson demanded.

"Most of it," Chandran said. "We were all camped out in the stairwell."

"What's your assessment?"

"The prince respects a strong will," Chandran said. "I would guess he was more infatuated with the prime's powers than chastised by her anger. He will either leave off his current habit—or be much more careful about leaving evidence behind."

"That's what I'm afraid of," Zoe said glumly. "He'll just start burying bodies in the garden of his rented house."

"Maybe it's time to simply send the Karkans and the Soechins packing," Nelson said. "Refuse to make the deal, and live with the consequences."

"I think Darien is almost at that point," Zoe said. "But you know Darien prefers to keep all his options open for as long as possible."

"I have to say, I don't know how they manage to run a government in the Karkades," Annova said. "This man is the heir to the throne?"

"That's right," said Nelson.

"From what I've seen, all he wants to do is smoke veneben and drink other people's blood," Annova said. "Doesn't sound like he'll be a very good king."

They all looked at Chandran, who shrugged slightly. "He is not simply the wastrel hedonist he presented himself as tonight. He would tell you that his vices are in exact proportion to his virtues—that he is wise, dedicated, and insightful in matters of state, so that he may be foolish, fickle, and indulgent in matters of personal recreation."

"That's not exactly reassuring," Zoe said.

"No," Chandran agreed. "Very little about the Karkan royal family is."

Nelson glanced around the room. "I'm parched. What do you have to drink? And I'm hungry. Also—I liked that candy a great deal! Can we just sit for a few minutes and talk?"

Why don't you want to go home? Leah thought, but they were all keyed up. Certainly there was a lot of appeal in the idea of a glass of wine or a piece of keitzee.

"Yes, of course—I had a whole spread laid out for my guests, but we didn't get to half of it," Leah said, leading them all to the back of the room where the chairs were still set before the refreshment table. "We may as well finish it off."

Soon they were a much more relaxed group as they sampled Karkan and Welchin delicacies and discussed the evening. Neither Nelson nor Zoe showed the slightest hesitation in taking second helpings of keitzee, but Leah figured if any individuals could accurately judge their tolerance for stimulants, it would be two primes. She was still feeling a bit unsteady, so she confined herself to keerza, as did Chandran; Annova dissolved a keitzee ball in her cup of keerza and sipped it like liqueur. *That's what I'm going to try next time I feel safe enough to lose my head a little,* Leah thought. She wondered if such a day would ever come.

"If you're still feeling adventurous once you've finished the keitzees," Leah said to the group at large, "you can try these other candies. Seka was pretty excited that I had some on hand."

"What makes them an adventure?" Zoe wanted to know.

"Chandran tells me that they have an addictive taste—but there's a core of poison in the middle. You need to judge how long it's safe enough to keep the candy in your mouth."

"Is the dose fatal?" Nelson asked.

"Sometimes. For the young or frail," Chandran answered. "But in most cases it just makes you violently ill."

"I don't mind a little risk," Annova said. "But not for candy."

"I'll try a couple," Nelson said, holding out his hand. Leah dropped a few cubes into his palm. "Though I think I'll wait till I get home in case I miscalculate."

"Which is easy to do," Chandran said. "Since the toxic core differs from piece to piece."

If anything, Nelson just looked more intrigued. "Well, I'm curious now," he said. "It better taste like the distillation of life itself."

"It does," Chandran said.

Nelson leaned back in his chair and gave Chandran a friendly inspection. "You know a great deal about these people, and yet you're not Karkan," he said. "Coziquela, I'm assuming?"

"That is correct."

"So why are you so familiar with their customs?"

"I was married for a period of time to a Karkan woman." When Nelson continued to wait, as if expecting more information, Chandran added, "Our fathers had been trading partners. They arranged the marriage between them."

"Even though you hated her?" Nelson asked.

Chandran glanced quickly at Leah, but she shook her head. *I haven't told Nelson anything about you. He's picking this up just by eavesdropping on your thoughts.* She should have warned Chandran about the sweela prime. Then again, she had never envisioned them sitting down to have a conversation.

"I did not hate her at the beginning," Chandran said.

Nelson narrowed his eyes, openly scanning Chandran's face, his mind, for clues as to the kind of man he was. Leah wanted to punch Nelson in the shoulder, break his concentration, insist that he leave Chandran in peace, but she didn't think it would do any good; it was impossible to turn Nelson aside once his attention had been engaged. Neither Zoe nor Annova seemed discomposed by the long examination, but then, they were both changeable coru creatures who didn't care what anybody else thought of them. You could spend all day trying to figure them out, and maybe succeed, but the next day they would be altogether different people.

Leah and Chandran each had made themselves over at various points in their lives. But the efforts had cost them. And to someone who could read souls as if they were printed pages, each of them wore the evidence of their previous lives like angry red scars.

At least that seemed to be Nelson's assessment. "And now you hate yourself," said the sweela prime. "Though in your heart you believe you are still an honorable man."

Chandran bowed his head. "That is not proof that I am indeed honorable," he said in a low voice. "The Karkan prince would also use that word to describe himself, though all of us might disagree."

"It's a tangle," Nelson agreed, instantly diverted by the prospect of debating philosophy. "Which measure is more accurate? The opinion of others or the verdict of your own heart? Can you be reviled by the rest of the world and still be justified in your actions—be, in fact, a virtuous and admirable man? As you say, a villain often believes he is a hero, so I don't think it's possible to entirely discount the judgment of the outside world. We must agree on common definitions of *good* and *evil*, or the world devolves into chaos. But I believe that extraordinary behavior can be condemned by the majority—and still be the correct course of action. The trick then is to keep up your courage. To husband your certainty. To reward yourself, not punish yourself, for the depth of your conviction."

Now Chandran lifted his eyes and gazed straight at Nelson. "You do not know what I have done," he said.

"No," Nelson admitted. "But I know that you would do it again, even though you suffer for it now. So I have to believe that *you* believe you made the right choice, impossible though it seemed."

Zoe sipped from a glass of fruited water as if to wash down the last traces of keitzee. "You could *tell* us what you did," she said in a chatty tone. "And we could let you know whether or not we think you can be redeemed."

"I am not sure," he said, "that I will accept anybody's judgment but my own."

"You could tell us anyway," she said with a laugh, "just because we're dying to know."

That did elicit a small, painful smile from Chandran. "Someday, perhaps," he said, "when the whole world trades secrets."

"Ah, well—secrets," said Nelson, stretching his arms over his head and fighting off a yawn. "I'm of a mind that we all have them, and it's a good thing."

"*You* have secrets, but you're always trying to uncover everybody else's," Zoe retorted.

"Why is it a good thing?" Annova wanted to know.

"Because we learn something about ourselves when we choose to share them," Nelson said. "Do we tell the stranger we'll never meet again? Do we tell the friend we believe will never betray us? Do we confess to the parent or the person in authority, hoping for absolution?" He glanced casually from Chandran to Leah and back to Chandran. "Do we tell the one we love, offering that secret as a gift, an element of courtship?"

"Do we tell no one?" Chandran said.

"Harder to do than you might think," Nelson said.

Zoe stood up, brushing crumbs from the front of her tunic. "Here's my secret—I'm exhausted," she informed them. "Leah, thank you for creating this opportunity. I think Darien will be pleased with how the evening turned out."

The rest of them came to their feet with varying degrees of steadiness. Leah was annoyed to see that Zoe, Annova, and Nelson all seemed to maintain perfect equilibrium, whereas she felt dizzy enough to tumble over, and she hadn't had so much as a drop of wine or a lick of keitzee. "The only repercussion I can see is that Seka may no longer consider me reliable," Leah said. "She *appeared* to believe you dropped by without an invitation—but she's not stupid. She might figure it out."

"If she does, she does," said Zoe, unconcerned. "Even if you never provide another scrap of information about the Karkans, I think Darien will still think this venture has been completely worthwhile."

Leah feigned alarm. "So will he then cease to fund me? If I'm no longer useful to him?"

"Judging by our receipts these past two ninedays," Annova said, "you don't need the regent's backing."

Zoe put one hand on Annova's arm and one on Nelson's and started pulling them toward the door. "And if you conclude that you don't want to run the shop at all, whether for yourself or Darien, you still have a decision to make," Zoe said over her shoulder. "Which is, what exactly *do* you want to do with your time?"

Leah opened the door for them, shivering as the cold air rushed in. "Thank you for reminding me," she said. "I had forgotten that I still need to figure that out."

Zoe laughed. "It's the great work of our lives," she said. "Determining what we want our lives to be."

"My answer keeps changing," Annova said.

Zoe laughed again. "So does mine."

Nelson freed himself from Zoe's hold so he could give Leah a hug. She couldn't help leaning into the embrace; even when she was most irritated with Nelson, she could take comfort from his warmth and presence, and right now she was feeling sorely in need of comfort.

He squeezed her tighter and spoke quietly in her ear. "That Chandran. He's a better man than he thinks he is. Make sure he knows that you know that." He kissed her cheek and followed Zoe and Annova into the night.

Leah switched off the glowing sign in the window and cut the power to the gaslight; the whole shop was plunged into darkness except for the candles burning in the back of the shop, where Chandran was still standing. She headed toward him in an utterly straight line. When she was close enough, he held his hands out, and she collapsed into his arms.

"What a night," she whispered into his shoulder. She felt him nuzzle the side of her neck. "I feel like I've just climbed off the deck of a ship that was caught in a storm at sea."

"What very strong personalities your primes have, to be sure," he murmured into her hair.

"*And* strong powers," she said with a shaky laugh.

"Yes, but it is the personalities that put those abilities in play."

"I don't know why Zoe brought Nelson. The way it turned out, I'm glad he was here—though Zoe could have defended herself without his help."

Chandran pulled back enough to look down at her, though he kept his arms wrapped around her waist. "She seems to be very interested in your well-being and aware of the fact that I have become a part of your life," he said in his precise way. "Might she have brought him for no greater purpose than a chance to meet me?"

"Yes! That's what I'm afraid of!" Leah wailed. "First Darien—then Josetta—and now Zoe and Nelson—they're all meddling in my life! Or *trying* to."

Chandran freed a hand so he could trace the outline of her face, from the corner of her left eye, to the edge of her ear, down along her jaw. He ended by tapping his fingertip lightly on her mouth. "Those are the choices you make," he said gently. "Either you live all alone someplace like Malinqua with no one to care if you are well and if your heart is whole. Or you live in Chialto, surrounded by family and friends who care very much about those things. You are alone and free, or surrounded and connected. You choose."

She pursed her lips to kiss his fingertip. "*You* are alone and free," she said in a low voice. "Is that the choice you wanted to make?"

Slowly, he shook his head. "If my life had unfolded otherwise, I would be at the center of a loving circle. In my moments of weakness, I would be able to call on others' strength. In moments of triumph, I would have hands to clasp in celebration. I would have strength of my own to lend. I would savor the victories of my friends. I would give gladly and receive gratefully, and I would fear many things, but not one of them would be lonely solitude at the end of an empty day."

She couldn't stand it. She pulled his hand away so she could kiss him urgently on the mouth. For a moment she could feel him resist—try to resist—drawing his battered honor around him like dented armor. But then he swept her closer, held her tighter, kissed her with the desperate hunger of a man on the verge of drowning who had finally fought his way clear of the sea. She could feel the battle raging in his soul as his powerful will was overcome by his burning, inextinguishable desire for human connection.

With a gasp he tore himself away and stood there, panting. "I am sorry," he managed to say. "I think I am not to be trusted alone with you."

She reached for his hand—reached for it a second time when he pulled it away. That time he let her keep it, though she could feel him trembling. "And I think you are," she said. "I think I can trust you with my heart. With all the random fragments of my life that make no discernible pattern and make no rational sense. I think you can help me put them together again, just as I can help you with yours."

"But I am not—you cannot be sure—the things I have done . . ."

She kissed him gently. "The sweela prime told me you were safe to love," she whispered. "But I had already decided that on my own."

He cast his eyes down a moment, too moved to even look at her. "I am humbled by your trust," he said.

She tugged him closer, put her arms around him, nudged her face against his chest. "I don't want you humble," she said. "I want you joyful."

She felt his mouth as he kissed the top of her head. "I might manage thunderstruck," he murmured. She could hear the beginnings of a smile in his voice. "It is not quite the same thing."

She laughed. "I'll take it."

She lifted her face and he obligingly kissed her. She kissed him back, but her mind was already turning on practical matters. "I obviously can't bring you to Darien's house," she said. "The room you're renting—what's it like?"

"Cramped and noisy and impossible to beautify," he said promptly. "Not a place conducive to transcendent experiences."

That made her giggle. She could feel a rising excitement in her blood, the first euphoric edge of passion. "Well, then," she said, looking around. "Here we are."

"Windows," he said.

She took his hand. "Upstairs."

With her free hand she grabbed one of the candles, and he did the same, so they made their way up the back stairwell by wavering yellow light. Once they were upstairs, they lit a few more candles and assessed the possibilities. The scrubbed wooden floor wasn't very inviting, but they dug through boxes to find fleece rugs from Berringey, brightly woven wool blankets from Dhonsho, and embroidered pillows from Welce. Leah arranged cushions and fabrics while Chandran knelt beside her and sorted through one of the trunks that had recently arrived from Cozique.

"What are you looking for?" Leah asked, stripping off her overtunic and laying it aside.

He turned to her with a smile, his hands full of small glass jars. "Items I thought I saw in this shipment the other day."

She reclined against a pile of pillows and smiled up at him. "And those items are?"

He set down all of the jars but one and unscrewed the lid. Immediately the air was filled with a smoky scent, half sweet, half seductive. "Perfumes," he said. "Elixirs."

He used his fingers to scoop out a cinnamon-colored cream. Moving closer, he applied it in gentle strokes across her cheekbones, to the tip of her nose, from her chin all the way down her neck, to the hollow in her throat, to the fabric that edged the neckline of her undertunic. She shivered with restrained delight at the scent, at his touch, at the way the cream felt cool against her skin and slowly heated to a temperature hotter than her own body.

"I love that," she whispered.

"I thought you might."

She slipped off her undertunic and her trousers, everything except thin undergarments so sheer they hid none of her curves. Chandran scooped out more cream, rubbed it slowly into her shoulders, her arms, the palms of her hands, pausing to kiss her fingertips. Another handful, and he was smoothing it down the insides of her thighs, the long lean lines of her calves. He pressed his mouth to her kneecap.

"My whole body is on fire," she said, taking the jar away from him. "Now you."

He shook his head and handed her a different container. "This one," he said.

She pried off the lid, then made an impatient gesture. "Your tunic. Take it off."

She sniffed at the jar in her hand while she watched him disrobe, his motions as deliberate as always. He was not only heavily bearded, he was covered with dark hair on his arms and chest; in the uneven candlelight he appeared to be almost equal parts flesh and shadow. She sniffed at the jar again.

"This smells like a forest," she said, dipping out a fingerful of pale green paste. "I like it." She touched the high ridges of his cheekbones, rubbed the cream into the ruddy skin at the join of his neck and shoulders, down the central corridor of his torso where the dark hair was sparse. He sucked in his breath as her fingers approached the waistband of his trousers.

She set the jar aside, pushed him down onto the blanket, and lay on top of him, feeling every inch of his body where it pressed against hers. He buried his fingers in her hair, drawing her into a kiss, and she gripped his shoulders, rocked against him, feeling desire rip through her like a form of starvation. She had to have him, she had to; she was full of a hollow craving that could not be sated any other way. She moved aside just enough to pull off the rest of her clothes and he did the same.

Now they were naked and clinging to each other, kissing with passion so intense it was almost mindless, their hands exploring each other, their bodies repositioning themselves—their bodies conjoined, striving, slippery with cream and drenched in the scents of desire. Leah rolled onto her back and Chandran rolled with her. They rocked together, clung together, gasped and drove together again. Her hands were curled tightly over his shoulders, her body arched up to his; he moved inside her and she moved with him and there was no room for any other thought, any other sensation. They were surrounded by the scents and textures and colors of the entire world, and yet they were their own world. All of existence came down to this.

TWENTY-ONE

Taro wanted Leah to host a party.

She learned this much too early the following morning when she stumbled downstairs after about four hours' sleep, fighting a headache and already late for work. Virrie and Mally were nowhere in sight, but Josetta and Rafe were still lingering at the breakfast table, talking with Taro, whose presence came as a surprise to Leah.

"When did you get here?" she asked, stuffing a piece of buttered bread in her mouth without even bothering to sit down.

"Yesterday evening," he said, motioning her over so he could kiss her cheek. "I did try to wait up for you, but Josetta said you had some kind of mysterious meeting set up at the shop and you might be home late."

Leah glanced at Josetta, who was trying to maintain a demure expression as she sipped a glass of juice. Clearly the princess had guessed that something in addition to the "mysterious meeting" had kept Leah away from the house long past midnight. She hoped she wasn't blushing. "And it was quite the exciting evening," she agreed. "The Karkans were there, and Zoe and Nelson showed up. I actually thought there was going to be bloodshed."

Now Josetta's smile disappeared. "What happened?"

Leah hesitated. "I'm not sure how much I'm supposed to tell. This was something Darien and Zoe came up with. I just provided the venue."

Rafe pushed himself to his feet, flashing his easy grin. "Surely you can tell the *prime*. I'll give you some privacy."

Josetta stayed put. "*I* want to hear everything," she said. She flicked a look at Leah. "*All* the details."

Leah bit her lip to keep from laughing, but she quickly grew serious again as she gave Josetta and Taro a brief synopsis of the evening. She obviously wasn't going to escape from the house anytime soon, so she sank to a chair as she finished her recitation. She could only hope Annova was at the shop with her usual punctuality. "I don't know if there will be repercussions," she finished up. "But Zoe seemed satisfied with how everything turned out."

"Nelson *and* Zoe offering violence to foreign royals," Josetta said on a sigh. "Good thing Taro wasn't there to add his own threats."

"Not me. I'm a peaceable man," Taro rumbled.

Leah took a bite of fruit and studied him for a moment. "I've never *seen* you tumble boulders or shake the earth," she said, "but I have to believe you could do it."

"But how would you stop assailants?" Josetta wanted to know. "Mirti could break their bones, and Kayle could drive the breath right out of their lungs. What would *you* do?"

"I could flay them alive," he said softly. "Strip the flesh right off of their bodies. At least that's what my uncle told me. I've never had cause to do it."

Josetta shivered. "And I hope you never do."

"Ugh. Me, too," Leah said. She finished her hasty breakfast and gulped the last of the juice. "I want to get to the shop, but I have to ask— Why are you here? Did something happen?"

"Merely that Natalie was bored and lonely, so I offered to bring her to the city for a few days so that Romelle could get some peace," Taro answered. "Mally was delighted to see her, and the two girls went off somewhere with my wife early this morning. I hope it's not too much of an imposition."

"Not an imposition on *me*," Leah said. "It's Josetta's house."

"It's Darien's," Josetta said. "And of course it's not an imposition! We're delighted to have you."

"I thought we could have a dinner or reception one night," Taro said. "Bring in all the Frothen relatives who live in Chialto so they have a chance to get reacquainted with Leah." He shrugged. "And to meet Mally by her true name. It's been more than a quintile since the primes announced that Odelia would be put aside, and we've made no move to formally introduce Mally as herself. But she's a Frothen, too, and her aunts and uncles and cousins should get to know her."

Leah's chest was tight. "I'm not sure—is she ready—how do you plan to introduce her?"

Taro smiled at her kindly. "Someday I hope you will be willing to tell Mally—and the world—that she belongs to you," he said. "I would like to claim her, and I believe Nelson would as well. But for now, I can merely call her a Frothen. Everyone will believe me. That should be good enough."

Leah nodded dumbly, trying to absorb that, but Josetta was already making plans. "Do you only want Frothens here?" she asked. "Or should we invite all the primes? What about Darien? If Romelle isn't here, we don't need to invite any of Vernon's other wives, though I'm sure my mother would love to be included."

"I'll let you and Virrie make up a guest list," Taro said. "But we don't want Leah to be *too* overwhelmed."

Josetta turned to Leah with an artless smile. "Is there anyone in particular you'd like to invite?" she inquired.

I suppose I can't kill a princess, Leah thought. "Um—I don't know. I'll think about it. Maybe."

Taro arched his heavy eyebrows, but didn't ask any questions. "Let's have it as soon as we can," he said. "I can't stand to be in the city too long."

"But, Taro," Josetta said in a sweet voice, "it's almost Quinnelay changeday. Don't you want to stay for the celebrations?"

He snorted. "It's eleven days before the celebrations start, and, no, I do not! Who would hold a regatta in the dead of winter? Not that I would go to a boat race if it were summertime, which is when any reasonable person would schedule such a thing."

Josetta laughed. "We'll try to get your party planned by firstday," she promised. "Virrie and I will get started this morning."

Leah stood up. "I *have* to get going. I'll see you all tonight."

"I'll walk you to the door," Josetta said brightly, jumping to her feet and following Leah from the room. They were scarcely out of Taro's earshot before the princess whispered, "*Well?* You were out so late everyone started to get worried. Rafe wanted to go down to the shop to make sure you were all right, but I persuaded him not to."

Leah groaned and stepped through the kierten, out into the brisk morning air. She drew her jacket tighter; Josetta just hugged her arms around her body for warmth. "Thank you for that, at least. Doesn't he realize—don't you *all* realize—that I lived on my own in Malinqua for five years? I can take care of myself."

Josetta unwrapped one of her arms so she could touch Leah briefly on the shoulder. "Yes, but now you don't *have* to," she said. "That's what it means to be part of a family."

It was very much along the lines of what Chandran had said last night. Leah wanted to say, *You're not really my family.* But she supposed, in some convoluted way, the princess *was* related to her. Well, Josetta was Nelson's niece and Mally was Nelson's granddaughter, so they were connected by Ardelay blood. And Ardelays, Leah was beginning to understand, never let go of their own.

"I'm still not quite used to being watched over so closely," was all she could think to say.

"Well, *I* am quite used to having many sisters, who all are very interested in my life," Josetta said, hugging herself again. "So, before I freeze to death, tell me! Last night? You were—" She paused, as if trying to think of a delicate way to phrase her question. "Spending time with your friend?"

"You mean *after* the confrontation with the Karkans and the little demonstration that the primes put on?"

Josetta laughed. "There is *no* way those activities took up all the time allotted."

Leah ducked her head and tried to fight down the blush, but she could feel it heating up her cheeks. For a moment she was swept with a mad, girlish desire to huddle in a corner of the house, out of the wind, and pour all her thoughts and worries into Josetta's sympathetic ears. *Honestly, I don't know him that well and some of the things I do know are frightening. So why do I feel such a powerful bond with him? How has he become so necessary to my well-being? And last night— Oh, I can't even begin to describe what happened last night . . .*

"Yes. I was with Chandran," Leah said at last. "It was— I am— I don't remember feeling like this before. Even with Rhan. I don't know if Chandran is good for me. I think I'm good for *him*, but I'm not even sure about that. And I can't clearly see a way forward."

"But you want him in your life?"

"I do. Oh, I really do."

Josetta gave a happy squeal and threw her arms around Leah. "Then you'll find a way to make it work. I'll help you. And you should invite him to the party!"

Leah laughed and pulled back. "I don't think so. Not yet. But maybe I wouldn't mind if *you* met him."

"Maybe not in the next few days, with so much to do for Taro," Josetta said, reaching behind her to open the door. "But soon."

"See you tonight," Leah said, waving and turning away to head into the wind. She could feel the faint grit of ice in the air, but it was strange. She felt warm all over, and the cold didn't bother her at all.

When she arrived at the shop, Leah burst through the door as if she had nothing but tardiness on her mind. The only person immediately visible was Annova, who was in the back of the room, sweeping up the evidence of last night's eventful meeting. Not until this moment did it occur to Leah that it might be awkward to see Chandran again for the first time with Annova hovering nearby.

"I'm so sorry! Taro was at the house and I couldn't get away," she apologized.

"It's fine," Annova said with her usual serenity. "We're still cleaning up."

Now Leah felt fresh color burning in her cheeks. She and Chandran had folded up the blankets and put away the jars of spice before they left last night—well, early this morning—but anyone with a passing familiarity with the upstairs storeroom would realize *someone* had been using the space for a social activity. "Last night was much more dramatic than I expected it to be," she observed, just to have something to say. "Though, I suppose, with both Nelson and Zoe on hand, I shouldn't have been surprised."

"I was past sixty before I met my first prime, and now I'm acquainted with them all," said Annova. "It's been fun."

Leah laughed. "I'd have said *terrifying*, I think."

Annova smiled. "And that's the difference between coru and torz."

Leah clapped her hands together like someone who needed to get busy. "Well. I'll carry those extra chairs upstairs and then bring down fresh merchandise," she said. "Time to get ready for the day."

The chairs were cumbersome burdens to carry up the steps, but the effort was worth it, because once Leah made it to the second story, she found Chandran there before her. As soon as she crossed the threshold with her ungainly burdens, he turned to her with a smile, holding his arms out. She dropped the chairs and flung herself across the room, into his embrace.

"I *missed* you," she exclaimed, her voice muffled against the fabric of his jacket. She could feel him kissing the top of her head, the side of her face.

"It has scarcely been six hours since you have seen me," he said.

She looked up indignantly, and he dropped a kiss on her mouth. "That should have been plenty of time for you to miss *me*!"

He laughed and kissed her again. "But then, I have missed you ever since you left Malinqua," he pointed out. "It has just become one of the constant emotions of my life."

"I can't figure out how to improve the logistics," she said. "I could move back into my own apartment—but I don't want to give up the closeness to Mally."

"You should never compromise your relationship with her, certainly not for me," he said.

"But I don't see how I can bring you back to my room at night, despite what Josetta says."

"That does not appear to be a solution at this time," he agreed.

"Although maybe—sometime—if you feel like it—you could join us for dinner," she said tentatively. "You've met Virrie and Mally, and you'd like Josetta and Rafe—it would be strange, probably, at first, but maybe not so bad—"

"I would like that," he said gravely.

"But it still doesn't solve the problem of how we get private time together," she finished up. She glanced around the room, then gave him a coquette's smile. "Though it *was* lovely here last night."

"I think the simplest solution is for me to acquire more hospitable quarters," Chandran said. "I have not bothered to look for more comfortable rooms because I was not sure how long I would be staying. But if I am to remain in Chialto for the foreseeable future, which now seems likely—"

"Very likely."

"Then the investment is worth it."

A question occurred to her for the first time since his arrival. She pulled back enough to search his face. "Do you have the money to cover your expenses?" she asked bluntly. "You left Malinqua so abruptly—I can't imagine you had time to liquidate your assets."

"I did not," he admitted. "But you forget I have been a fugitive for many years. I made sure I always had large amounts of cash at my disposal, and I set other protocols in place. Since I have been in Welce, I have been able to contact my bankers in Malinqua and recover most of my investments. Everything at my booth in the Great Market was forfeit, and those items represented a considerable sum, but I am able to withstand the loss." He kissed her once more and released her. "And, of course, you pay me for my work here."

She laughed. "Yes, barely enough to cover the rent on your squalid little room, I'm sure," she retorted. "But I'm glad you have *some* resources."

"Like you," he said quietly, "I am always prepared to take care of myself, if an emergency arises."

She sighed and turned away to survey the room. "Yes, we're both aware of how quickly life can push us to extremes," she said. "Now. What's left to be done up here, and what have you decided should go on display this morning?"

The three of them worked companionably for the next half hour, at which point the first customers arrived. Leah was tired from lack of sleep and she couldn't shake the headache, so she moved through the day in a lax and dreamy state. That made her thoughts duller and her decisions slower, but wore away her usual somewhat anxious edge. *Not entirely a bad thing,* she thought.

She perked up late in the afternoon when it turned out that the two men who strolled through the door were not buyers, but sellers—Jaker and Barlow back from a long, meandering trip through the countryside.

"Did you bring me treasures?" she demanded as they hauled three big trunks through the door and set them up in the back of the shop.

"*We* certainly think so," said Barlow, always the more boastful one. "We were up at the northwestern ports where the smaller ships come in."

"And ships from some of the northern countries that don't like to sail all the way south to the Chialto harbor," Jaker added.

"Almost all the Soechin captains use the northern port," Barlow put in. "Saw some Karkan flags when we were there, too."

Those vessels probably belonged to the prince and his attendants, Leah thought, if they'd sailed down to Welce after making treaties with Soeche-Tas. She pretended to be disappointed. "I expected you two to bring me goods from places more exotic than Soeche-Tas and the Karkades."

"Oh, we did," Jaker assured her. "I don't think you'll find this stuff anywhere else in the country."

She introduced them to Chandran, and the four of them went through the items in the trunks while Annova waited on customers. Jaker was right—they'd brought back items Leah hadn't seen in any other shop in the city, from countries she had only heard of in passing. There were necklaces of brilliant black gems mined only in Botchka, fabrics spun from the fur of horselike creatures in Milvendris, spices from Loelle, seeds from Kelk. Jaker carefully unrolled a colorful shawl woven of hundreds of feathers in bright blue, brilliant pink, and jaunty yellow, and draped it over Leah's shoulders.

"You could charge anything you wanted for something like that," he said. "There won't be another one like it anywhere in Welce."

She watched herself in the mirror, turning this way and that. It was gaudy, impractical, ridiculous, and gorgeous. She could name three of her regular customers who would buy it in an instant. "It's not the sort of thing you could wear too many places," she demurred.

"You've got a coronation coming up," Barlow pointed out. "Seems like just the thing to wear to an event like that."

Leah slipped the shawl off her shoulders. "Obviously, I have to have it," she said. "And everything else you brought. You're my best suppliers by far."

They spent a few minutes haggling amiably about prices, but since they were all determined to be fair, negotiations went quickly. Still, Leah laughed when they agreed on a final number.

"If I wasn't so tired and didn't have a headache, I'd argue a little longer," she said. "Next time, I'll be more stubborn. You'll see."

"Headache? That's too bad," Barlow said with easy sympathy. "Jaker gets them, too."

"It was a late night with a lot of—drama."

"I can give you some corvier for it if you want," Jaker said. "Mine are frequent enough that I always carry some with me."

"Corvier?" she repeated. "That was pretty well-known in Malinqua. But it was always sold as a poison."

"That's one of its uses," said Jaker. "If you take enough, it'll kill you. But just a couple of drops can have a miraculous effect on pain."

"Jaker's always been interested in medicinals," Barlow said with a certain pride. "Won't deal in anything that's not legal, but he knows about every drug you can find between here and Cozique."

"So if you want something—" Jaker said.

"I think a good night's sleep is all I need to cure my headache," Leah said. "But I'll let you know if that changes. How long are you going to be in town?"

"Maybe a nineday," Barlow said. "We both have family to visit."

"And more goods to deliver," Jaker added.

"What? You didn't bring me everything?"

Barlow grinned. "We have other clients we have been supplying for a lot longer than we've been supplying you," he said.

"But if you keep buying as freely as you did today, we'll keep saving some of our best merchandise for your shop," Jaker added.

"Good. I like a mutually profitable relationship."

Jaker and Barlow slipped out only a few minutes before closing time, and Annova was right behind them.

"Can you two close up?" she asked, managing to hold back her smile. "I need to get back to the palace."

"Yes. We'll manage. Thank you," Leah replied, hoping she sounded dignified instead of flustered, but pretty sure she didn't. "See you in the morning."

Annova was scarcely out the door before Leah turned to find Chandran, and they fell into each other's arms. She loved the specific shape of his body against hers, his size and height and utter solidity. She loved the spicy smell that seemed to be woven into the crisp fabric of his jacket—or, maybe it was the particular smell of his own warm skin. She loved the feel of his arms enclosing her, tightening around her body as she drew him even closer. She stood there a moment, simply burrowing into him, and then lifted her head for his kiss.

"That wasn't easy," she said after a while. "Being so close to you all day and not even being able to touch you."

"I felt the hardship myself," he said solemnly, but his dark eyes were laughing.

"Though Annova wouldn't care. I don't think. I mean, I'm sure she suspects something anyway. It's just that—I don't know that this is the right time—"

"It is too new," Chandran said. "Too young to be shared with anyone else."

She rested her head against his chest and thought that over. "That might be it," she said. "Or maybe I'm just a coward."

He freed a hand so he could tilt her head up. "In what way?"

She half shrugged. "I haven't had the nerve to claim Mally as my own. I'm not ready to tell the world about you. Maybe I just don't know how to be public about my feelings."

"Maybe your last relationship conditioned you to think that feelings do not last," he countered. "So you hide them, hoping that the loss will not seem so great if the rest of the world does not know."

His words hurt—not because he said them, but because they seemed true. Because they exposed her heart as a small, sad, shivering thing crouching in a dark corner. "Maybe I need to get braver," she said. "And not care about pain."

"Everybody cares about pain," he said. "But it is a matter of degree."

She tilted her head to look up at him. "What about you?" she challenged. "You haven't trusted yourself to have a real relationship in fifteen years. And your last one ended more badly than mine."

"By any measure," he acknowledged.

"So? Will *you* be able to trust again? Will *you* be able to walk back into the daylight?"

There was a small padded divan in a corner of the store where visitors could rest for a few minutes, recovering from the exertions of shopping. Chandran tugged her over there and sat down, drawing her onto his lap. "I do not know," he said, his voice raw with honesty. "I know that I trust you as I have trusted no one I have met since I left Cozique. I do not know why this would be so. Could I have misjudged you? Could you be someone other than the person I believe? Could you turn against me, betray me, take a literal or metaphorical dagger and plunge it into my heart?"

"No," she said.

"I have to believe that the possibility of disaster exists, because the possibility of disaster always exists," he said. "But I want this too much. I want *you* too much. I am willing to risk myself again, wholly and completely, because the chance of having you in my life offers me so much joy. It outweighs the risk of annihilation."

She put her hands on either side of his face. "Chandran," she said urgently. "I will never willingly hurt you. I will never consciously betray you. We might— This might— Maybe we won't be able to make this work. But I won't harm you or turn against you. I won't—I couldn't possibly—"

She couldn't summon the right words. She didn't know the right vows. She just kissed him frantically, wrapping her arms around him, clinging to him, trying to make her body the oath, the promise. He returned her fervor, made his own pledge with his mouth, his hands, his body. They had lost the gift of language, but they remembered even older skills, and those were what they called upon as they signed a binding contract.

Leah was home for dinner, but barely—everyone else was just taking their final bites of food or sipping from a last glass of fruited water.

"Sorry," she said. "I've been running late the whole day."

Virrie kissed her cheek. "It's just dinner," she said. "Don't apologize."

Mally ran up to give her a hug and settled on Leah's lap as she sat at the table. One of the servants instantly appeared, carrying a plate loaded with steaming food. "Did you have a *good* day?" Mally asked.

Leah couldn't resist kissing the top of Mally's head. She refused to look in Josetta's direction. "I *did*. Two friends came by with three trunkloads of new merchandise to show me and I bought it all. You'll have to drop by the shop soon and see everything."

"Can Natalie come?"

Leah lifted her gaze to glance around the table. Sitting between Virrie and Taro was a slim girl about seven or eight years old. She had dark hair, narrow cheeks, and an expression of bright curiosity. And she was watching Leah with great interest. She and Mally looked enough alike that they could pass for sisters. *Which they've done for five years.*

"I'm Leah," she said. "Are you Natalie?"

The girl nodded. "You're the one from Malinqua, aren't you?" Natalie asked.

"Well, I'm from Welce, but I lived in Malinqua for five years," Leah answered.

"Why?"

"Because I didn't like the way my life was going in Welce and I thought it might be better somewhere else."

"Was it?"

"It was, actually," Leah said. "I met a lot of interesting people—and I found interesting work—and I came closer to figuring out the person I wanted to be."

"Isn't everybody already a person?" Natalie wanted to know.

"You'll find that she can ask more questions than anyone else in all of Chialto," Taro said.

"You told me it was good to ask questions," Natalie shot at him. "You said that it was one of the things you liked about me."

Taro rested a hand on the top of her head. "It *is* one of the things I like about you." He looked at Leah. "Also, she never forgets anything you ever say."

"But you didn't answer me," Natalie said. "Isn't everybody already a person?"

"Yes," Leah said, not sure how to explain. Her headache, which had abated somewhat during the interlude with Chandran, was returning full force. "But maybe some people wish they were different. For instance, if you're someone who gets mad easily, maybe you want to be someone who can stay calm."

"When I get mad, I want to hit people," Natalie informed her. "But Taro says I shouldn't."

"When I get mad, I cry," said Mally.

Josetta leaned her elbows on the table. "When something makes me mad, I go out and do something about it," she said. "I try to fix things."

Natalie liked that. "What things? How do you fix them?"

"Things that are unfair. For instance, if there's a neighborhood in the southside where people can't get fresh water, I have Zoe come in and help me build a well."

"I'd like to be that kind of person," Natalie decided. She looked at Leah. "What kind of person did *you* want to be?"

Goodness, you're exhausting, Leah thought. No wonder Romelle wanted Natalie to come to the city for a few days. "Someone who was more sure of herself. Someone who made better choices. Someone who wasn't afraid."

It was clear Natalie didn't think much of these goals. "Why did you decide to come back to Welce?"

Taro snorted. "Because Nelson Ardelay went and fetched her."

"Is that why?" Natalie asked.

Leah was laughing at Taro. "He did show up and say he wanted to bring me home," she admitted. "But I only came back because I was ready."

"Are you glad you did?"

"I am."

"Do you think you'll go back to Malinqua?"

Unexpectedly, Mally turned in her lap and put her arms around Leah's neck. "I think you should stay," Mally said.

Leah drew her daughter closer, refusing to let the tears rise. She leaned over and whispered into Mally's dark curls, "I think I should stay, too."

Taro and Rafe went off together for a card game, while the women followed Natalie and Mally into the room with the indoor river. The two girls played happily in the water, tossing rocks, poking at fish, and making up games on the spot. Natalie was clearly the one in charge, ordering Mally to stand here or move there or *stop* splashing so much.

"She's a little bossy," Leah said as the women reclined lazily on the sofas. Leah didn't know about Josetta and Virrie, but she could fall asleep right here. *Long day. Long couple of days.* Good days, though. *Very.* She had to hide a smile.

"A *little* bossy?" Virrie repeated. "She tries to tell everyone what to do, even Taro. Mally mostly goes along with her because Mally just likes to be included in whatever's happening. But other times Mally has a will of her own. It's funny to watch. Natalie will get so impatient and *demand* that Mally pay attention, and Mally just goes on doing whatever she's decided to do."

"How does Natalie behave with Odelia?" Josetta asked.

"Pretty much the way she behaves with everyone else," Virrie said. "For a long time, we tried to keep Odelia separated from the others. We didn't want Natalie to be confused—having *two* sisters, both called by the same name—so we thought it would be easier to keep them apart. But Natalie has a mind of her own, and she kept finding ways into Odelia's quarters. And we'd find them playing together, Natalie ordering her about, and Odelia mostly ignoring her. But Odelia never seemed to mind having Natalie nearby. Other people would make her anxious, but not Natalie." Virrie shrugged. "So now we let them be together whenever they want."

"And Natalie doesn't have any trouble telling the two girls apart?" Leah asked.

Before Virrie could answer, Natalie's voice carried clearly across the room. "O*del*ia. Don't put sticks in the *water*. I mean, Mally. Put them *here*."

"As you see," Virrie said with a faint smile. "I'm convinced she always knows which one is which, but for years we wouldn't let her call Mally anything but Odelia, because we never knew when there might be other people around to hear. So now she slips up from time to time—as do all of us who have been around both girls since birth. But it's getting easier to think of her as Mally."

Josetta stirred on her couch. "I always wondered," she said. "Is Mally short for something?"

"*Mallarinda*," Leah said.

"That's pretty."

Leah leaned back against her cushions and tried to crush down the pain. The ache in her head, the ache in her heart. "I didn't name her," she said. "But I agreed when Taro suggested it."

"That was his sister's name—Leah's mother, of course," Virrie said softly. "Everybody called her Rinda. It was a way to honor her without making it obvious who Mally really was."

"Has anybody ever figured it out?" Josetta asked.

"Nelson always knew," Virrie said. "And Beccan, of course. I assume that Zoe and the other primes used their abilities to read blood and bone. But none of them said anything, and as far as I know, no one else ever learned the truth."

"Not even Alys?" Josetta asked.

Leah pushed herself to a more upright position so she could stare at Josetta. "Why would Queen Alys be more likely to know than anyone else?"

"First, because she's a troublemaker," Virrie said.

"And second, because she knows other things Darien wishes she didn't," Josetta answered. "For instance, Romelle confided in her—in Alys! of all people!—the truth about Odelia's condition. So Alys knew before anyone else in court that Odelia would never take the throne, and she started scheming immediately."

"And third, because she and Rhan are close friends," Virrie said. Her voice was compassionate, since she knew Leah would flinch at the sound of his name, but she spoke up anyway. "He may have told her at some point. Although, if he did, she's never found a way to use that information for her own benefit."

"And it can't matter anymore," Leah said. "So, even if she knows, there's no harm done."

Josetta was watching her. "Unless you don't want anyone else to know that Mally's your daughter."

Leah turned her head to watch the two girls. They were squatting on either side of the little river and skipping a stone back and forth across the placid water. "I want everyone to know," she said. "As soon as I think it's right for Mally."

Virrie said, "I think that day will come very soon."

TWENTY-TWO

They scheduled the party for firstday and spent the entire day getting ready for it. "Just a small group," Virrie said. "Maybe forty or fifty people. Still, I think we need more chairs."

Taro managed to stay out of sight while the women arranged furniture and consulted with the cooks, but Rafe was always available to move heavy objects or hold up an end of a decorative rope of greenery.

"You like parties," Leah said to him in an accusing voice. She'd already confided that she was experiencing low-grade terror at the thought of interacting with so many people at once.

Rafe laughed. "I like being around people. I like trying to figure out what a man is thinking or how to put a woman at ease."

"*You* should be the torz one, then."

"Well, it will certainly be a torz sort of gathering."

It certainly would. More than half would be Frothens by blood or marriage. Most of them were people Leah had known fairly well five years ago—cousins and second cousins and assorted aunts and uncles—though Taro's sons were all significantly older than she was and she'd never been close to them or their children. Josetta and Virrie had also invited a host of sweela folks—Nelson and his entire family, down to Kurtis's children—as well as Darien, Zoe, and a handful of other court perennials. Leah was already worried about trying to keep all the names straight, though Josetta told her not to even bother.

"Just say, 'It's so good to see you again, what have you been doing lately?' and they'll be happy to talk about themselves," said the princess.

"No they won't, they'll ask me what *I've* been doing, and I don't know what to say!"

"Tell them you were in Malinqua conducting business for Darien and you're not supposed to talk about it," Josetta advised. "That solves everything."

Leah laughed. "You are so much more devious than you appear to be."

"Lifelong training. So have you invited Chandran to attend?"

"No, and I'm not going to."

"Then maybe one night during the next nineday," Josetta suggested. "Please? Because I need to go spend time at the shelter, but I'd like to meet him before I go."

"Come by the shop."

"You need to bring him *here*," Josetta said. "So he can see your real life."

Leah let her eyes wander around the room with its high ceilings and beautiful proportions and great bundles of scented flowers set out in advance of the festivities. "I don't think this *is* my real life," she said.

Natalie and Mally came running through, squealing and chasing each other, then disappeared into a hallway. Down another hallway floated Virrie's voice, raised in a question, and Rafe's quick reply. The front door opened and they heard Taro in the kierten, calling out for one of the servants. Josetta raised her eyebrows as if to say, *You see?*

"It's *part* of your life," Josetta said. "Or at least the people are. You have to figure out how to bring all of the parts together in one whole."

"I know. I'm not sure how, though."

Josetta nodded. "I'm still working on that myself."

The evening was long, chaotic, and overwhelming, but Leah had to admit later that she sort of enjoyed herself. Almost. Generally speaking, the Five Families weren't particularly demonstrative; they were more likely to nod or bow in greeting than touch a person's hand as the Karkans did. But that reserve didn't hold for anyone with torz blood, and a hug was the standard opening gambit. Leah was surprised at how many times she was actually happy to see a familiar face, how much pleasure she felt when aunts and cousins threw their arms around her. Each kiss on the cheek was like a droplet of water falling on parched ground; under the patting hands and the warm embraces she felt herself turn from a rough-edged flinty lump of stone to a patch of mixed earth flowering into spring.

Even Rhan's presence didn't bother her—brought her, she had to confess, the slightest bit of pleasure. "You look like a little girl who's been run over by a parade on Quinnahunti changeday," he informed her as he brought her a glass of fruited water and stood beside her to contemplate the crowd. "Dazed but happy."

She laughed and gratefully gulped down half the glass. "*Happy* might be too strong a word, but it's a pretty incredible group," she said. "Hard not to like everybody."

He sipped at his own drink, which was wine instead of water, and watched her closely. "Have you decided yet? When you're going to tell the truth about Mally?"

Not even that question filled her with guilt and panic. Maybe she was too glutted with affection at the moment to have room for anxiety. "It seems like there's no reason to keep the secret anymore," she said. "But I have to tell Mally first. She has to have time to adjust to the notion."

"Should I be there when you tell her?"

She hadn't expected that offer, and she tilted her head to survey him. "Do you want to be?"

He lifted his shoulders in a shrug. "I want her to know. I want to be more to her than I am now." He exhaled on a laugh. "But I admit I'm a little afraid of the conversation."

"Then let me tell her about me first. And then, if she wants to know, you. Then you can come over and the three of us can talk."

"Like a family," he said.

"We're not a family," she said, the words coming out so easily and so painlessly that she wondered how long they had been curled there, under her tongue, awaiting the chance to be heard. "We're connected— we always will be—but we're not a family."

"To me connection *is* family," he said. "And family is much wider and more complicated than I used to realize. We're just not a household."

"All right," she said, laughing. "I'll accept that."

Before she knew what he intended, he bent down and kissed her on the cheek. "Good," he said. "Let me know when you tell her. Make it soon."

He slipped away and she stood there a moment, waiting to be slammed by the old despair, but it didn't come. Instead, she lifted a hand to her cheek to touch the spot where he'd kissed her, and all she felt was peace.

"Well, I *don't* think you should be flirting with Rhan," Josetta said from behind her. Leah turned with a smile.

"We were just talking. It's nice to be able to do that casually without wanting to go somewhere afterward to cry."

"Are you having a good time?"

"Much better than I thought I would. Though I've lost track of the number of people who asked if I was going to the regatta on changeday."

"It's a lot of fun," Josetta said. "Unless you almost drown."

Leah laughed. "I imagine that *would* make it a little less delightful!"

"Mally would probably enjoy it," Josetta said. "Taro doesn't usually come to town for the event, so I'm not sure she's ever been to one."

"She seemed to do well—didn't she?—I kept being swept off by Frothen relatives, so I didn't have much chance to monitor her."

"Taro took her around and introduced her to everybody," Josetta said. "A lot of people were still saying, 'Is that Odelia?' and anytime someone *called* her Odelia, she would answer. And then Natalie would say, 'Her *name* is Mally.' So I think it was a little confusing, but everyone made her feel welcome. She seemed to have fun. She and Natalie and about six other children all ended up in the river room for most of the night."

"So I guess we count the evening as a success."

Josetta laughed. "I guess we do. By the way, I came looking for you because Darien wants to talk to you. Come on. He's in his old study down the hall."

The study was the one room in the house that most of the current occupants avoided; it still had such a strong sense of Darien's presence that it didn't encourage relaxation. Its central feature was an enormous desk that had made Leah feel like a child the one time she sat behind it. Anyone else would have been swallowed by its size, but she was pretty sure that Darien always managed to command the room whenever he was seated there.

This evening he was standing beside the desk when Josetta ushered her in. He nodded at them and said, "It's been a most enjoyable evening, thanks for inviting me. I have to leave soon, but I have one commission to carry out before I go." He pulled an envelope out of a pocket and handed it to Leah. It was made of a thick, rough paper that was folded and smudged as if it had been in transit for a very long time.

She took it with some bewilderment. "What is this?"

"A letter that came to me at the palace, addressed to Corene. You can imagine how pleased I am to be acting as postal courier these days for my daughter and all her friends."

She grinned at that comment but she was still confused. "If it's for Corene, why are you giving it to me?"

"Because she told me that if any letters arrived from exotic locations, I should show them to you before forwarding them on."

"That's so unfair," Josetta said. "She writes Darien *all the time* and I've only gotten two notes from her."

Leah was turning the envelope over in her hand. "'Exotic locations'?" she repeated. But there it was, on the back, the stamp of a port city far west of Cozique, and the letter *A* drawn in a painstakingly beautiful script. Leah felt her heart stop.

"It's from Alette?" she whispered.

"That's my assumption."

"Who is Alette?" Josetta wanted to know. "Is that the Dhonshon princess you told me about?"

Clumsily, hastily, trying not to rip the paper, Leah pried open the envelope and unfolded the letter inside. It was brief, written in a precise, flowing hand.

My dearest Corene,

It is with great gladness I am able to inform you that Cheelio and I have made it about halfway to our destina-

tion. We have had many adventures along the way, and indeed at first it seemed unlikely that we would make it out of Palminera harbor, but we won our way to freedom. The voyage has been very long, and we are still some ninedays from Yorramol, but we feel confident that we will make it safely there. We have fallen in with a group of Dhonshon natives who have made their homes in Yorramol and who are returning there after a long visit to my homeland. They assure me that Yorramol is much more colonized than I had expected and that we will be welcomed by the other Dhonshons who have fled my father's regime. There is so much more I have to tell you, but a ship captain is leaving for Welce within the hour, and I am determined that this letter will go with him. Please share my news with Liramelli, Melissande, Leah, and Teyta, all of whom generously risked themselves for someone so insignificant as me. I do not have words to express my gratitude.

Know that I will always keep all of you faithfully in my heart.

Alette

Leah was almost crying by the end of the letter, she was so happy. Josetta put her arm around Leah's shoulders. "Is it bad news?" she asked.

"No—no—the *best* news," Leah said. "I told you how Alette needed to escape from her father—"

Josetta nodded. "He wanted her dead."

"So Corene helped her run away. Well, we all helped, but it was Corene's idea. We weren't sure she had even gotten safely out of Malinqua, but she did, and she's on her way to Yorramol. She sounds so happy. Darien, you have to put this letter on the *fastest* ship to Cozique."

Darien looked amused. "It will go out tonight. I suppose Corene can then write to her fellow conspirators in Malinqua. It is a rare privilege to be the bearer of glad tidings. I shall savor the feeling."

. . .

Darien and Zoe left the house about five minutes later, but everyone else seemed set to stay all night. "Maybe we should roll out mats in the kierten and allow them to bed down," Virrie said with a rare flash of irritability. But finally, a couple of hours after midnight, they were able to escort the last Frothens to the door and set the locks behind them.

"We can clean up in the morning," Josetta said, heading straight for the stairwell. "Good night!"

On the way to her own room, Leah paused to peek inside of Mally's. She fully expected the little girl to be asleep, but the form under the covers moved restlessly as soon as the door opened.

"Leah?" Mally asked.

Leah stepped inside the room, which was illuminated only by the faint light filtering in from hall sconces. "How did you know it was me?"

"I just did. Is the party over?"

Leah perched on the side of the bed and brushed the hair away from Mally's forehead before folding her hands in her lap. "Finally. Why are you still awake?"

"Just thinking about things."

"Good things?"

"Mostly."

"Did you have a nice time tonight meeting everybody?"

Mally took one of Leah's hands in hers and started playing with her fingers. "Yes. I have a lot of cousins."

"Well, you're related to Taro, and *he* is related to dozens of people, so you do indeed have a lot of cousins."

"But Natalie isn't my cousin. She isn't my sister, either."

Leah felt her heart cramp down. "She isn't. But that doesn't mean you can't be as close as sisters. That doesn't mean you can't love her as much as you ever love anybody."

"She's going home pretty soon."

"Is she? Back to Taro's?"

"Yes."

Leah took a deep breath, though she tried to speak casually. "Are you thinking that you want to go back, too? You've been gone a long time."

Mally was silent. For a moment, she continued to toy with Leah's fingers, then she flattened her palms around Leah's hand. "I don't belong there," she said at last.

Leah placed her free hand on Mally's shoulder and leaned down to gently kiss her cheek. "I wish you'd stay here," she whispered. "With me."

Mally's hands pushed together, putting pressure on Leah's. "I belong with you," Mally said gravely. "Your skin is like my skin."

"And your face is like my face," Leah murmured. "Do you know why that is?"

"I think so."

"I'm your mother."

Suddenly Mally lifted both arms and held them out in a silent request for a hug. Leah swept her into her arms, holding the small body against her own, desperately trying not to cry. Not letting go for an instant, she levered her body onto the bed, stretching out next to her daughter and drawing her even closer. Mally buried her face in Leah's chest and clung to her neck even tighter.

"I'm so sorry I didn't tell you sooner," Leah said, whispering into the dark hair. "I'm so sorry I was gone for such a long time. I didn't know how to take care of you. I didn't know how to take care of anybody. But I'm trying to figure it out. I want to do it. I love you so much. So much."

"Stay with me," Mally begged, moving over to make more room in the bed.

Leah settled closer, twitching the top quilt so it fell over both of their bodies. "I will," she said. "I'm here now and I'll never leave you again."

TWENTY-THREE

When Leah opened her eyes in the morning, she and Mally were sharing a pillow, face-to-face, and Mally was awake and watching her. Leah's body felt cramped and stiff from the night spent in an unfamiliar bed, and her arm was asleep from where it was stretched under Mally's shoulders. But she didn't move. She didn't speak. She just stared back.

"We have to tell everybody," Mally said, picking up the conversation from the night before. She didn't seem worried or excited or angry or unsure. If her new reality had come as a shock to her, she was handling it with grace.

Maybe she'd figured it out, Leah thought. *Though I don't know how.* "Most everybody else knows," she confessed. "At least, everybody else who lives in this house. And Darien. And Zoe. Oh, and Nelson and Beccan."

"And Rhan?"

Leah took a deep breath. "And Rhan."

Mally didn't say why she'd asked after Rhan, she just nodded. "If I live with you," she said, "can I still go stay with Taro sometimes?"

Leah leaned in to kiss her forehead. "As often as you like."

"But Virrie won't be here with us."

Leah shifted to a more comfortable position, and Mally adjusted herself alongside her. "No," Leah said. "I think it's almost time for her to go home to her own life."

"Will I stay here by myself when you're at the shop?"

"Absolutely not! Little girls don't stay alone in big houses. Maybe I'll bring you with me every day. Maybe I'll find a tutor. Or a school! We'll figure it out."

"That's good," Mally said, sounding a little relieved. "I don't like to be alone all day."

Leah kissed her again. "I don't, either," she said. "I *used* to. Or at least, I told myself I did. But once I moved in here with you and Virrie and Josetta and Rafe, I realized I like to have people around me. All the time."

"Well, you'll have me," Mally said.

"That sounds pretty wonderful."

The door opened and Virrie poked her head in. "Mally, are you awake yet— Oh! Leah! Josetta was just wondering if you'd left early, but I see—well. The rest of us are going down to breakfast."

"We'll be there in a minute," Leah said, sitting up and shaking away the last of her drowsiness. That was the moment she realized she was still wearing her party clothes. She laughed and gestured down at her colorfully embroidered tunic. "Obviously, I need to get cleaned up and changed," she said to Mally. "Do you need any help getting ready?"

"I can help you and you can help me," Mally offered.

"Let's do it. Pick out your clothes and come with me to my room and we'll get ready together."

Josetta couldn't have looked more delighted when Mally and Leah made it to the breakfast table, dressed in tunics and trousers of very similar shades of blue. "Look at the two of you! You match!" she exclaimed.

"Mally chose what we should wear," Leah said. This was ridiculous; her heart was pounding at the thought of speaking these words out loud. "Because we had a long talk last night and I told her that— told her I'm her mother."

Everyone exclaimed out loud at that, and Rafe even came over to give them each a hug. "Exciting news!" he said.

"But very good news," Taro said in his rumbling voice.

"Leah says you already knew," Mally said to him somewhat sternly.

He laughed. "Well, I did. But I'm glad you know now, too."

"If you're her mother, why have you been gone so long?" Natalie wanted to know.

"Because I didn't know how to be anybody's mother."

"Do you know *now*?"

"Nobody knows how to be a mother," Virrie put in. "You just do your best and try to recover from the mistakes and love the children as much as you possibly can."

"That's what I'm going to do," Leah said.

Natalie was frowning. "I don't like to make mistakes. I don't think I want to be a mother."

"You don't have to be," Virrie said. "But you *do* have to eat your breakfast, so stop asking questions and finish your meal."

"This is proving to be a very interesting morning all around," Taro said.

"Why? What else has happened?" Josetta asked.

Taro heaved himself to his feet. "I'll show you. Just stay right here."

He left the room and the rest of them glanced at each other, mystified. Virrie just shrugged. "He gets this way sometimes. I just humor him."

When Taro returned, he was carrying a sad little potted plant with a single forlorn branch. It appeared to have been stripped from some woody hedge that had lost all its summer greenery before it was stuck in this container in the hopes that it would flourish. And, indeed, incongruously, a slim twig right in the middle of the branch had sent out a few tendrils of timid green and one bright-red five-petaled flower. The rest of the limb looked completely dead.

"He wanted to put that out on the sideboard last night," Virrie said. "I told him he has no aesthetic sense and to leave the decorating to people who do. But when I looked again, there it was, right next to all the food."

"I wanted everyone to see it," Taro said with satisfaction.

Josetta looked puzzled and Rafe looked incredulous, but Leah felt as if all the air had been sucked out of her body. Her toes and fingertips tingled with premonition. "That's from your estate, isn't it?" she said. "From that bush?"

Taro nodded, regarding the branch fondly. "It is. And I thought— why not try it and see? I knew that half the Frothens in Chialto would be here last night. I wondered if the presence of my heir could bring the thing to blossom." He held out his hand. "And you see, it did." .

A moment of silence was followed by a chorus of questions. *But who—? How could that be? If everyone in the room was a Frothen—*

"So were you watching it all night?" Virrie managed to raise her voice above the rest. "Do you know whose presence had this effect?"

"No," he admitted. "I tried to stay in the dining room, but I kept getting pulled away. I checked last night before I went to bed, and the whole thing just looked dead." He beamed at the rest of them. "But this morning, leaves and a flower."

"So then you don't actually know who your heir is," Rafe pointed out.

"No, but I know he or she was in the house last night," Taro said. "I can start narrowing it down."

"I don't think that's very many flowers," Natalie said. "I think there should be a *lot* of flowers. Don't you?"

"Maybe," Taro acknowledged. "But maybe when I bring my heir back to the estate, the whole property will burst into bloom."

"You must have your suspicions," Leah said carefully.

He looked her straight in the eye. "I do. But it's a burden, being heir to a prime. A gift, but a burden. Maybe this person isn't ready for the role yet." He glanced at Natalie. "And that's why there's only one blossom."

"If I was the prime, I'd want a hundred flowers," said Natalie.

Taro laughed and ruffled her hair. "Then when you come back with me to the estate, we'll go to the wild hedge and see what you can do," he said.

Leah took her last sip of water and rose briskly to her feet. "Time for me to get to work," she said. She smiled down at her daughter. "Mally, do you want to come with me? You can play with the rocks and feed the fish."

Mally looked undecided. "I do," she said, "but I'm supposed to go with Taro and Natalie today."

"I told them I'd take them to the Plaza of Men," he said. "They want to make oaths at the booth of promises."

"Now, those are a couple of promises I'd like to hear," Rafe observed.

"We're not going to tell you what they are," Natalie told him primly. "They're *secrets*."

"And I'll bet they're good ones," he answered.

"I can come tomorrow," Mally said to Leah a little anxiously.

Leah swooped down to kiss her cheek. "Darling, you can come any day you like. But you should absolutely go off on your adventure with Taro and Natalie! Have a wonderful day and I'll see you this evening." She straightened up and waved at the table. "I'll see you *all* this evening."

"And then we can gossip about the party," said Josetta.

Leah was halfway out the door, but she heard Natalie's reply. "It isn't nice to gossip." She was laughing for the next five minutes.

Chandran was alone in the shop when she arrived, so Leah was able to give him a quick kiss without anybody seeing. "Where's Annova?" she asked, still standing within the circle of his arms.

"She only came by to unlock the door and stock the cash box," he answered. "She has errands to run for Zoe and will be gone the rest of the day. I told her we could manage without her."

"For a day we can," Leah agreed. "But I dread the morning she comes in and says she's bored with retail work! I'll never find anyone else as competent as she is."

"It is something to consider for the future," he said. "Finding someone you trust to replace her." He set his mouth against her forehead and she briefly closed her eyes with pleasure. "So how was your party last night?"

"Good—crowded—exhausting—and *long*. I didn't think people would ever leave. But, Chandran, the most amazing thing happened after the party."

"What?"

"I *told* her! I told Mally. I stopped by her room and she was still awake and she wanted to talk and I— She mentioned that Taro and

Natalie are going home in a few days and she— I asked her if she might want to stay with me, and she said—she said she *belonged* to me. How did she know that? But it's true! And she wanted me to stay with her all night and I did and I think— Chandran, I think—I think it's going to be all right."

By the time she finished this speech she had started to tremble; her emotions were so high that she couldn't contain them. He drew her closer, tighter, as if attempting to hold her bones in place so they wouldn't vibrate right out of her body. She felt him kiss the top of her head. "Most excellent news," he said gravely. "She will become the core and center of your life, and all that old heartache will melt away."

"I still haven't told her everything," she confessed. "I didn't tell her about Rhan. But she mentioned his name and I wondered—maybe she's guessed that, too." She looked up at him and she could feel the intensity, the earnestness of her expression. "And I didn't tell her about you, either, but I will. I want to. Someday soon. Because you're at the core of my life, too. I've gone too long without having anybody I cared about. Now I have a lot of people, but I can't pick and choose. I want them *all*."

"There is time," he said. "We can move slowly. You know that I am here waiting. And I have learned the subtle and taxing art of patience."

She laughed shakily. "I *used* to know it," she said. "Now I've developed the mad curse of *im*patience. I want it all and I want it right now."

He kissed her again and let her go. "But that in itself is a gift," he told her. "To know what you want and to see it take shape right in front of you. Some people never get that much."

She nodded. "There are days," she said, "when I realize how lucky I truly have been."

She was feeling less fortunate and less grateful by closing time. The day's customers had included two demanding and unpleasant women who took an hour of her time and left without making a purchase. During the afternoon, a small, excitable girl had knocked over an entire table of elay glassware, breaking half the pieces; her mother ushered her out of the shop without even offering to pay for the damage. There was a leak upstairs that Chandran could only fix temporarily by shutting off the water altogether. They managed to gobble down a hasty luncheon

Chandran had bought from a street vendor, but the meat smelled off and the bread was stale.

"It's one of those days that you'd like to have the chance to start over from the beginning," Leah observed as she turned off the lighted sign in the window to indicate that the shop was closing.

"It is best to group your bad luck in one miserable stretch," he said solemnly, but she could tell he was amused. "Then it is all done with at once."

"Well, here comes good news," she said, as the door opened and Jaker and Barlow stepped in. "Have you reconsidered?" she asked them. "You've come to sell me the rest of your goods?"

"Nope—we've unloaded every last item," Barlow said with a grin. "We dropped by to say we'll be on our way tomorrow and to see if you have anything in particular you'd like us to pick up on our next trip."

"Those black jewels from Botchka were very well-received," Chandran said. "We could sell any number of items featuring those."

"I think we can arrange to get more," Jaker said.

"And the feathered shawl sold in an hour," Leah said, "if you happened to find something like that."

"Not likely," Jaker said. "But we'll look."

Leah didn't have a chance to make any more requests because a small elaymotive came racing down the street so fast it almost jumped the curb as it slammed to a halt. Yori leapt out and ran for the shop door. Leah felt her whole body flood with panic as the guard burst inside.

"Get to Darien's *right now*," she said sharply. "Natalie's been hurt—Taro is half dead—and Mally's been taken."

At first, Leah couldn't make sense of the words. "Taro—Mally—*what*?" she said, stumbling forward.

The guard was already halfway out the door. "I have to track down Zoe."

Leah clutched at Yori's shoulder. "No, you have to drive me to Darien's!" she cried, her voice rising. *Mally's been taken? Mally's been taken? Who took her? What's happening?* "I have to go— I have to see—"

Yori jerked free. "I'm sorry! I have to find Zoe." And she vaulted into the elaymotive and was gone before Leah could even turn back to the others.

Who all looked stunned and puzzled. "What did she mean? Who is Mally?" Barlow asked.

"My daughter," Leah said. Her lips felt so numb she could hardly speak the words. Terror was building in her chest, taking up so much space she couldn't draw in air. *Where's Mally? What's happened to Taro?*

"Why would anyone take her?"

"I don't know! This doesn't make any sense! She's— I can't— Chandran, we have to get to the house— Maybe you can find an elaymotive for hire—"

"We've got a smoker car parked in the alley," Jaker said. "We'll drive you."

Nothing made any sense once they arrived at Darien's house, either. All the doors were open, so anyone could walk in off the street, but no one was available to answer questions. Servants were rushing around on urgent and mysterious tasks, and an air of palpable dread filtered through the hallways like rotting incense.

"Should we leave?" Leah heard Barlow ask in a low voice.

"Perhaps you might sit in some quiet corner," Chandran suggested, "in case there is need for quick transport. If you have the time."

"We'll be happy to," Jaker said.

Leah didn't stay to get them settled or to show Chandran around the house. She bounded up the stairs and headed toward the room that Taro shared with Virrie when he was in residence. She'd only made it halfway down the hall when Rafe rose from a chair outside the door and came toward her with his arms outstretched.

"What *happened*?" she demanded from the safety of his hug. "What's going on?"

"We're not entirely sure," he admitted, pulling her into a small seating area near the second-floor landing. "Taro and the girls were in the Plaza of Men shortly after noon. They didn't have any guards with them because—because Taro's a prime. He can protect himself and anybody who's with him."

Leah sank to a spindly chair that hardly looked solid enough to bear her weight. "But he couldn't," she breathed.

Rafe shook his head. "They were just leaving the booth of promises when four men came up behind them— This is what witnesses say, but the scene was very chaotic. Three of the men attacked Taro, apparently knocking him out before he even knew they were there, and continued to beat him once he'd gone down. Natalie tried to stop them and was shoved aside." He took a deep breath. "The fourth man snatched Mally."

Her stomach was clenched so hard she thought she would vomit on her shoes. "But why? Who? I don't understand!"

"Nobody understands," he said gravely. "But the witnesses say these men spoke to each other in a language that was neither Welchin nor Coziquela."

She stared at him, uncomprehending.

He spoke in a low and compassionate voice. "It seems mostly likely that she was taken by the Karkans or the Soechins."

Her stomach clenched again and she put a hand across her mouth to hold back the bile. "Seka Mardis," she whispered. "And the prince. But *why?*"

"An attempt to force Darien's hand, I suppose," said Rafe. "To make him agree to terms that do not appeal to him. But the question remains. Why Mally? Why not Natalie, too? Or Natalie instead? It makes no sense."

But Leah knew. All of a sudden, the pieces came together in her head—all of Seka's questions, all the prince's insinuations. She knew why they wanted Mally and knew that they had kidnapped the wrong girl. What would they do to Mally when they realized their mistake?

"Where's Darien?" she asked abruptly. "Is he here yet?"

"In his study downstairs," Rafe answered. "He's calling in his spies from all over the city to see if they can figure out where they might have taken her."

Leah came to her feet, surprised she could manage it. "And Taro? How badly is he hurt?"

Rafe stood up next to her and looked, if possible, even more worried. "Very," he said. "He appears to have a concussion and a dozen broken bones, and he's lost a lot of blood. Virrie and Josetta are with him, and we've sent for Nelson and Mirti. Darien even sent a car to the harbor, but it'll be late before Kayle can get here."

The primes. Darien was gathering all the primes to Taro's bedside. *I have to track down Zoe,* Yori had said. Taro was so close to death that only elemental magic could anchor his body to this world. Leah tried to swallow and found it impossible.

"And Natalie?"

"Frightened and a little bruised, but she'll be fine. She gave us our best description of the men who attacked Taro."

Leah nodded. "I have to talk to Darien," she said. "We can't— This is—"

"I know," he said. "There are not enough words to describe this day."

Leah was halfway down the stairs when she heard the front door slam open and Zoe's voice demand, "Where is he?" Seconds later, footsteps came pounding up the steps. Leah shrank to one side to provide clear passage. Zoe paused only long enough to give her a grim look and a touch on the arm before she rushed past on her way to Taro's room.

Leah stumbled downstairs and through the hallways, resting her hand on the walls for physical support, and went straight to Darien's study. He was sitting behind his great desk, issuing a series of orders to a slim, stone-faced man wearing royal livery, but he broke off as soon as Leah stepped in.

"That's all for now," he said, rising to his feet and striding around the corner of the desk. "Check back with me later."

The man bowed and exited the room just as Darien reached Leah's side. He took hold of her shoulders with both hands, gazed down at her with his hard gray eyes, and said, "We'll find her."

She stared back up at him. "They think she's Odelia," she said.

His grip tightened and then he dropped his hands. "What?"

"They think she's Odelia. That's what she called herself the one time she met Seka Mardis. That's what Natalie calls her when she slips up—even Virrie does. Anyone in Welce who's ever met Mally thinks she's Odelia, except the people who met her at the party last night."

"So? Why would any of our foreign visitors want Odelia?"

"Because the Karkan prince thinks you're just putting on a cha-rade," Leah said. "He doesn't think you really *are* going to be crowned king. He thinks she's the true heir—and that he's just captured the future queen of Welce."

Darien let out a long groan and backed up a few paces so he could lean against the desk. He put the heel of his hand against his forehead and shut his eyes, as if trying to think this through.

"But then what do they intend to do with her?" he said. "This makes me more hopeful that they won't actually harm her—but are they hold-ing her for some kind of political ransom? Will they only release her if I agree to terms?"

"I don't know," Leah said. "And was it the Soechins who took her, or the Karkans? Just from what I know about the Karkans, I'm hoping for the Soechins."

"You wouldn't, if you knew much about the Soechins," Darien retorted, dropping his hand. "But they're not behind this."

"How can you be so sure?"

He looked as if he was trying to decide how much he should tell her. "We've been talking. Privately. Without the knowledge of the Karkans," he said finally. "We appear to be coming to agreement on some—issues—that have divided our nations. They wouldn't jeopardize our fragile détente by pulling a stunt like this."

"Then it was Seka Mardis and the prince," Leah said, trying to keep her voice steady. "They took her."

"Probably. And we have to figure out how to get her back."

"We need Chandran," Leah said. "He knows them better than any of us do."

"Is he nearby?"

"He's in the house."

Darien strode to the door, spoke to a servant, and then stood there, unmoving, until Chandran crossed the threshold. Leah immediately put her arms around him, desperate for comfort, and heard him speak over her head to Darien.

"What can you tell me?"

Darien gave a succinct recitation of events. "Since you have knowledge about the Karkan court," he added, "we wondered if you might have any insights."

Leah felt Chandran urge her across the room, so she reluctantly pulled free of his arms. The three of them sat in a small grouping of chairs by the window, though it was past sunset by now and the sky showed nothing but dark skies faintly streaked with red.

"I told Darien that they think Mally is Odelia—Vernon's true daughter," Leah said. "If that explains anything. And they believe Odelia is still destined for the throne."

Chandran nodded. "What you must understand is that the Karkans believe a great wrong has been done to them—the Coziquela occupation—and that any actions they may take are justified if those actions lead to a righting of that wrong. They want your aid in ousting Cozique from their shores. They have taken what they believe is most precious to you—your future queen—because they believe you will do anything to get her back. Including agreeing to a treaty that you might otherwise refuse."

"Will they harm her?"

"Almost certainly not," Chandran said, and Leah sagged against his arm in relief so great that it almost dissolved her bones. He went on, "She is too valuable a prize to damage. If they want your cooperation, they will have to keep her whole. But that's not the only reason. They fetishize royalty. They believe in the divinity of the blood heir. They won't hurt her."

"How do we get her back? Since we obviously are not going to be blackmailed into a treaty that we would break at the first opportunity."

"They will set off for the Karkades as soon as possible," Chandran said. "Despite the fact that the country was overrun by Cozique many years ago, the royal city itself is highly defensible. Once they get her inside the palace walls, it will be virtually impossible to get her out."

"They are a few hours ahead of us already, and I don't even know where they've gone," said Darien, the frustration evident in his voice. "Will they try to sail out of the southern harbor? Will they cross the mountains to take refuge in Soeche-Tas? I have sent men in both directions, but so far there have been no reports of any travelers matching their descriptions."

Leah stirred on her chair and sat up straighter. "No," she said, her mind racing. "They'll take her to the northwestern port. That's where their ships are lying at anchor." When Darien narrowed his eyes at her, she added, "That's what Jaker and Barlow told me. That's where the Soechin merchant ships always come in, and the Karkans sailed here directly from Soeche-Tas."

"It makes sense," Darien said. "So if we send soldiers to the harbor—though we're still almost half a day behind—"

"Do you not have some faster method of transport?" Chandran asked. "I understand the elay prime has perfected flying machines."

"They're not perfected, and I already asked Rafe if they could be used for reconnaissance," Darien replied in a regretful voice. "He said their range wasn't far enough to do us any good, since they can barely make it a few miles past their home facility."

Leah jumped to her feet. "I know! Let's ask Jaker and Barlow! They might know a faster way to the port. They know every road in Welce."

Darien and Chandran stood up more slowly, but Darien's expression had sharpened. "That's a good idea. Do you know where to find them?"

"Here! In the house! They brought us here!" She turned to Chandran. "Please. Go get them."

But he made no move for the door. Instead, he gazed at her a moment, and there was something in his dark eyes that made her breath tangle in her throat. "Just a minute," he said softly, turning his attention back to Darien. "Once you catch up with the Karkans," he said, "you have to be prepared to negotiate."

"I'll negotiate with soldiers and weapons," Darien said. "They cannot possibly muster as many men as I can. If I find them, I can contain them."

"But Mally," Leah said. She couldn't manage any more words.

Darien looked at Chandran. "You said they wouldn't hurt her."

"If they were under attack," Chandran said, "they might take desperate measures."

"Then how do I deal with them?"

"Offer them something they want even more than they want Mally. Even more than they want a treaty."

"And what might that be?"

"Me."

TWENTY-FOUR

Once again, Leah felt as if the language being spoken around her, even the simplest words, made no sense. But dread rose in a toxic tide; every vein in her body tingled with poison. She placed her hand on his arm. "Why would they want you?" she whispered.

He smiled down at her very kindly. "Because I murdered the prince's sister."

She shook her head. "I don't understand."

"He was married to the king's youngest daughter," Darien filled in. "He killed her and then he fled."

"Ah," Chandran said. "Your spies are as good as everyone says."

Even more confused, Leah looked at Darien. "What? How do you *know* that?"

Darien met her eyes. "You had given me enough clues that I was able to figure out who he was. And Corene supplied part of the story. His family is prominent in Cozique, and she was able to learn a great deal about him."

"The Karkans have been looking for me for fifteen years," Chandran explained. "They want to bring me to justice."

Leah's hand tightened on his arm. "No."

Darien looked unconvinced. "They may hate you, but do they hate you enough?" he said. "By their reckoning, Mally is a valuable prize. She could be the key to achieving a treaty that will change the course of their history. Will they give that up just to wreak vengeance on you?"

"Yes," said Chandran.

"No," Leah said again. "No no no no no no! You can't do this! We'll find another way— Darien has *thousands* of soldiers—we'll make them give her back—"

Chandran put his hands on her shoulders and drew her closer. She was frantic, she was shaking, but she couldn't help seeing that his own expression was serene. He looked at peace for perhaps the first time since she'd known him. "I did a great wrong fifteen years ago, and ever since that time I have been looking for a chance to atone," he said. "Now I have found it. If my act of contrition ensures your happiness, I will make the sacrifice with an even lighter heart."

"But, Chandran," she said, and she could feel the tears welling up and spilling down her face, "I don't want you to die."

"Everybody dies," he said. "At least I will have a death with meaning."

"I'm going to look for Barlow and Jaker," Darien said and strode from the room.

Leah dimly heard the door shut behind him as he gave them privacy, but the truth was, she didn't care. She didn't care if Darien witnessed this wrenching scene, she didn't care if every resident of the house, every servant, every visitor, watched her fling herself into Chandran's arms and sob, and beat her hands against his shoulders, and beg, and sob some more.

"I have just *found* you," she wailed. "We have just found each *other*. Please don't throw your life away—"

"I am not throwing it away," he said. "I am trading it for something of greater value. I am merchant enough to recognize a good bargain."

"We'll find another way to get her back! We have to!"

"And if Mally is not recovered, how could you and I ever have a life together?" he demanded, though his voice was still kind. "Every time you looked at me, you would think, 'If not for this man, I would have my daughter.'"

She stared up at him hopelessly. "And when I look at her, I will think, 'The man I love died on her behalf.'"

He smiled. "Yes. And you will be grateful every day that I was able to give you such an amazing gift."

"But, Chandran—"

He kissed her forehead with an air of finality. "You cannot stop me," he said. "I will do this thing, and I will be glad of it."

For the moment, there was no more to say. She rested her head against his chest and felt his arms come around her waist, and she briefly wondered if it was possible for a person's body to break apart because of such intolerable pain. *No,* the dreary thought came to her instantly. *You have endured pain before. You know how stubborn the body is, how it clings to life when all you want is oblivion. You will survive this, too. You have more to live for. But you will never again be whole.*

She heard the study door open again, and she lifted her head. "I'm sorry," Darien said. "But the only maps are in this room."

She forced herself upright and took a step away from Chandran. After all, she would have to learn to stand without his support. "Come on in," she said.

Darien was followed by the two traders. Barlow only gave her a quick, embarrassed glance; he was not good with displays of raw emotion. But Jaker came over and squeezed her shoulder. She nodded because she couldn't muster a smile.

Darien was sorting through oversize volumes on one of his bookshelves, and he pulled out a long leather-bound portfolio. "The land surveys are a little out of date," he said, "but no more than three or four years old."

"Should be good enough," Jaker said.

The men all dropped to their knees, opened the portfolio, and began unfolding nested sheaves of paper. Fairly soon, nearly a third of the open floor was covered with a meticulously detailed map of the entire country of Welce. Barlow was down toward the southeastern edge and Jaker knelt diagonally from him, at the northwestern border that ended at the ocean.

"This is Chialto, of course," Barlow said, tapping at the colorful concentration of streets and landmarks close to the southern border. "Anyone headed to the northwestern ports would start out on this road." He traced a route that crossed one of the canal bridges and angled upward.

"And that's good for the first day, day and a half," Jaker took up. "But then they'll hit a roadblock. The main bridge washed out just a nineday ago, and when they went to fix it, they found rot on the supports at both banks. It won't be repaired for maybe a quintile."

Barlow stretched himself out to indicate a different route on the map. "Most people, especially those with big vehicles, will turn north to get around the impasse," he said. "Those roads are good, but they meander, and they double back east before going west again. Travelers will lose a day."

"At least," Jaker agreed. He pointed at the place where the obstruction had occurred. "But there's a southern route. Narrow road, not very well-maintained. Only the locals use it. But it hooks up with the main road a lot quicker than the northern way. Problem is, you can't send anything bigger than a one-horse cart or a two-man elaymotive over that ground. If you wanted to send a hundred soldiers that way, you'd need fifty cars."

"I can conscript any vehicle in the city, if I want to," Darien said, his voice like ice. "I could send a thousand cars."

"Then that's the way you should go," said Jaker.

Darien glanced at the window, which showed nothing but inky black; even the last pink traces of sunset had disappeared. "Will they travel through the night?"

"Unlikely," Jaker said. "Twenty miles outside of the city, the road gets rough enough that it's tricky to travel if you can't gauge the conditions. Even seasoned travelers wait till sunrise to go on. *We* do."

"Then I have time to assemble my troops and I can wait till first light to send them out."

"That's what I'd do," Jaker said.

Darien nodded and sat back on his heels. For a moment, he surveyed the traders. "Is there somewhere else you need to be?" he asked. "Or can you come with us and serve as guides? I'll pay you."

"We'll come, of course," Jaker said quietly.

"No need for pay," Barlow added.

"Good," said Darien. "The servants will get you settled. If you'll excuse me, I have an army to organize."

. . .

The next few hours were controlled chaos. Josetta and Virrie were still in the sickroom, and the servants were overwhelmed, so Leah found herself de facto head of household. She conferred with the house-keeper to determine where each new visitor would sleep, gave the cook instructions about what food to prepare and when to serve it, and made sure messengers found Darien and medical supplies made their way to Taro's room. The incessant activity served to distract her, just the tiniest bit, from the continual anguished wailing in her head. She was terrified for Mally, heartbroken over Chandran, breathless with panic, and numb with fear. So she moved through the house answering questions, making decisions, trying to maintain some scrap of sanity, but it was the hardest stretch of time she had ever endured.

Once she got Jaker and Barlow established in a room, she went to check on Taro. Her quiet knock was immediately followed by an invitation to enter, but she paused from sheer shock the minute she stepped across the threshold. It was as if she'd passed through an invisible curtain humming with life and into a chamber of crackling energy. She felt her scalp prickle as her hair lifted; her skin seemed to carry a static charge. The very air of the room seemed to buzz with activity just below the level of sound. The lighting was muted, just a few wall sconces turned to a low setting, but a faint phosphorescent glow seemed to cling to the walls, the furniture, the bodies of the people bending over the bed.

Leah blinked twice trying to focus on the six individuals in the room. Taro was a large, unmoving shape under the thin covers; the slow, labored breathing had to be coming from him, though his chest barely rose with each inhalation. Leah was not surprised to see Josetta acting as nurse, checking his pulse and smoothing down a bandage; and, of course, she'd known Virrie would be sitting right beside Taro, clutching his hand. But they weren't the ones whose presence had filled the room with that strange light, that tingling energy. Those traces of evanescent magic were coming from the three primes.

Zoe hovered near the middle of the bed, her hand flattened on Taro's chest, as if she was forcing blood into his heart and back out through every compromised vein and artery. Nelson, who must have arrived while Leah was closeted with Darien, had pulled up a chair near the headboard; he had laid his hands on either side of Taro's skull, and he stared down at Taro's face in fierce concentration. Calling back Taro's wandering mind, perhaps, reminding Taro of who he was, where he was, how intensely he was loved. Securing his consciousness to the living world, not letting it slip away into the realm of death.

Mirti Serlast stood near the foot of the bed, one hand wrapped around Taro's ankle. She was a thin, spare woman of no particular grace or beauty, but she looked strong as an oak and as intransigent as bone. Leah had never had many dealings with the hunti prime, but there was something indomitable about her, something absolutely unbreakable. If Taro could be made whole again by touch alone, Mirti would be the one to work the miracle.

Only Josetta looked up when Leah stepped in, and she gave the slighest nod in recognition. Leah moved quietly through the room so she could fold Virrie in a hug. The older woman sagged against her for a moment, her hand coming up to clutch Leah's arm.

"How is he?" Leah murmured into her ear.

"Holding on," Virrie answered in a low voice. "But only because of *them*."

"Is Kayle Dochenza coming?"

"We believe he's on his way," Josetta answered. "But it might be midnight or later before he arrives." She adjusted a blanket over Taro's shoulders. "I think he may have a punctured lung," she added. "Mirti has healed the broken rib, but we need Kayle to ease his breathing."

"Is there anything I can do?" Leah asked. "Bring you food? Water? Anything?"

"The servants have kept us well-supplied," Josetta answered.

Virrie stirred in her arms. "Mally?" she asked urgently. "Is there any news?"

Leah fought down the panic that threatened to rise again. "No news," she said, "but a plan of sorts. We think the Karkans have taken her and are heading to a northwestern port. Zoe's trader friends Jaker and Barlow know a faster route there. We'll take soldiers at dawn and follow them."

Now Zoe wrenched her attention away from Taro. "Jaker and Barlow—you couldn't be in better hands," she said. "But if you show up with soldiers, won't they—aren't you afraid—"

It was such an effort to speak calmly. "They might hurt Mally. Yes," she answered. "But my friend Chandran. The one who's been working in the shop with me. He—it turns out he—there is some history between him and the Karkans. He believes he can be—he says—" She had to pause for a moment to get her voice under control. "He believes they will trade Mally for him."

Now Josetta gave her a sharp look. "*What? Why* would they do that?"

Leah just shook her head. "It's too complicated to explain right now. But he'll come with us in the morning."

Virrie leaned her head against Leah. "You're going with them, of course."

"I have to be the first one to see Mally," she said. *I have to be the last one to see Chandran.*

"But I don't understand. About Chandran," Josetta said urgently. "You can't— He can't—"

"I know," Leah interrupted. "But he is insisting."

Just then, Taro gave a low groan and tried to resettle himself on the bed. Instantly, everyone's focus was on him. Leah gave Virrie another squeeze and released her, then she quietly let herself out of the room. It was amazing how strange she felt once she closed the door behind her, as if her limbs had gained fifty pounds and her mind was suddenly clouded over. She took a moment to steady herself, then headed downstairs to see what new arrival was causing a small commotion at the front door.

She had just made it to the bottom story when two people surged in from the kierten. Rhan and Beccan. Without thinking, she ran to them with her arms outstretched, and the three of them came together in one long, hard embrace.

"Tell us quickly—Taro? And Mally! What's happening?" Beccan demanded while they still stood with their arms around each other.

"All the primes but Kayle are with Taro, and he is still alive," Leah said. "Darien is sending out a force tomorrow morning to try to rescue Mally."

"I'm going with him," Rhan said immediately.

Leah just nodded. "So am I."

"How can I help?" Beccan asked.

Leah pressed her cheek against Beccan's, then pulled back. They all dropped their arms, though they still stood close enough to touch. "Stay here and run the house," Leah said.

Beccan nodded briskly. "That I can do."

"And—I think—make sure the primes are fed," she added. "I can't describe it, but it seems as if they're all just *pouring* their energy into Taro. I have to think they're burning through their own physical resources without much regard to the consequences."

"Yes," Beccan said. "I've seen what they can do. I'll look after them."

"Good. Now, let's see what we can find for you in the way of rooms."

Dinner was a strange affair, attended by a broad assortment of people. Beccan had persuaded Josetta and Virrie to come down for the meal, and they were joined by Natalie, Rhan, Chandran, Rafe, Jaker, Barlow, Darien, and one of Darien's high-ranking soldiers, who looked ill-at-ease and ate as quickly as he could before abruptly rising from the table. Beccan and Virrie talked quietly to each other for the whole meal, while Rhan, improbably enough, seemed to enjoy a wide-ranging conversation with the itinerant traders. Leah took care of Natalie, who alternated between being even more sharp-tongued than usual and breaking into sudden tears. Rafe and Darien appeared to be talking defensive strategies, moving plates and silverware around as if deploying troops on the terrain of the tablecloth. Josetta devoted herself to Chandran and never once looked in Leah's direction.

Leah ate only because she had to. She had to have the strength to make the journey tomorrow, to endure the travel, to be prepared to deal with whatever had been done to Mally. To say goodbye to Chandran. She didn't think she could do it. When Natalie broke down for the fourth or fifth time, Leah just drew the girl onto her lap, buried her face in the dark hair, and cried along with her. It was Rhan who reached over and patted Leah's back, never even breaking off his discussion with Jaker. Leah took three deep breaths, hugged Natalie tighter, and raised her head. She took another bite of fruit. She would be strong. She would make herself strong. She would find her way through the coming days.

. . .

After all, Leah and Chandran spent the night together in Darien's house. Almost everyone Leah knew in the world was under that same roof, and a day ago she couldn't have imagined taking her lover into her bedroom with such an audience ranged around her, but tonight she didn't care who saw her or what any of them thought. She might never get another chance to hold him, tell him she loved him, tell him she believed in him.

She clung to him, she wept in his arms, she begged him to reconsider, to let Darien look for any other way to save Mally, but in the end what she did was love him. She had not thought she would sleep at all, but she was so exhausted by the terrors of the day that, some hours past midnight, she fell into a light and unrefreshing slumber. When she woke, Chandran's arms were wrapped around her and his mouth was pressed against her hair.

"Almost dawn," he whispered as soon as he felt her stir. "Time to go."

TWENTY-FIVE

Darien had indeed mustered close to a hundred elaymotives and maybe three times that many soldiers, and they all set out from the northern edge of Chialto just as the sun was edging above the horizon line. The majority of the vehicles were slim racer-style smoker cars barely big enough to hold two people; the rest were larger transports designed to carry ten or twenty.

"The smaller cars will take the faster southern route," Darien explained. "The bigger ones will follow the northern track, to block the Karkans if they think to double back."

Only soldiers rode in the large transports. Everyone who had some role to play in the negotiations—Darien, Leah, Rhan, Chandran—traveled with the smaller vehicles. There wasn't room for three people in those cramped elaymotives, but Leah managed to squeeze in beside Chandran and Jaker anyway. If she only had one day left with Chandran, she was spending every minute at his side, no matter how uncomfortable the journey was.

They made good time, speeding over the northwestern route as fast as road conditions would allow. Primarily, she supposed, to distract her, Jaker pointed out sights and described the cargos he and Barlow had bought or delivered at many of the small towns and sprawling estates they passed on the way. Leah could barely concentrate on his words, but Chandran listened with genuine interest, asking about local buying patterns and typical exchange rates as if he might someday have a use for the knowledge. The thought made her want to scream out loud.

By nightfall, they had reached the turning point of their journey, the ruined bridge and the forked road. Although Leah would have plunged on through the darkness, jouncing mindlessly over the narrow, rutted track that curved away to the south, Darien ordered everyone to pull over and bivouac. His scouts came back with the news that they seemed to have gained ground on the Karkan caravan, which was now only a few hours ahead of them.

"We should catch them sometime around noon," Jaker predicted.

"Good," said Darien. "Then we must all fortify ourselves tonight."

Barlow pitched a tent for himself and Jaker, Jaker pitched a tent for Leah and Chandran, and everywhere around them, soldiers fell easily into the other camp tasks of building fires, cooking food, and digging latrines. Darien requested Chandran's presence, leaving Leah to move aimlessly through the campsite, trying to stay out of everyone's way, trying to shut down the endless circling of her mind. The day had been cold and relentlessly gray, and she was sure her toes and feet would never be warm again, but she couldn't bring herself to sit quietly before a fire. She had to exhaust her body or her brain would never settle. She kept walking.

She had passed the perimeter of the camp and embarked on a slow excursion down the rocky slope of the unlit road when she heard someone jogging up behind her. She turned, but in the darkness she couldn't make out more than the shape of a man. Only when he was close enough to put a hand on her shoulder did she recognize Rhan.

"You shouldn't be hiking alone at night," he said. "Anything could be out here. Wild animals. Karkan soldiers. You need to be careful."

She turned away from him and resumed walking. Rhan fell in step beside her. "I feel safe enough," she said. "Or rather—nowhere is safe, so I may as well be here as anywhere else."

He couldn't dispute that, or at least he didn't try, so for a few moments they walked in silence. "I wish I'd had a chance to tell her," Rhan said at last. "If something happens to her—"

"Nothing will happen to her."

"But I want her to know," he persisted. "I want her to know why I couldn't claim her before. But I can now, and I'm going to. I'm going to tell everybody she's mine. If we get her back—"

"*When* we get her back."

"I want her to see that I'm here, waiting for her. I want her to know that I'll always be waiting for her. Anytime she needs me. Anywhere."

Leah just nodded, though she wasn't sure he could see the movement in the dark. They walked on a few more paces before he said, "You'll let me, won't you? You'll let me be a part of her life?"

That stopped her. She swung around to face him, though all she could see was his shadow before her; she supposed that was all he could see of her. "Yes," she said. "I want her life to be full of people who love her. I want every Frothen and Ardelay in the city to know she belongs to them, to take her in and soak her in adoration. I want her to have so much love that she almost can't hold it all, except there's always room for more love. I want her to have *everything.*" Her voice started to shake, and she tried desperately to keep it steady. "I want nothing bad to happen to her, *ever.* I don't want her to be afraid or lonely or hurt. I don't want cruel strangers to abduct her—and terrify her—and carry her away to—"

The words knotted up in her throat; she couldn't force them out. She was crying, she was sobbing, and Rhan had stepped forward to take her in his arms. She didn't want him holding her, she didn't want him comforting her, but there was no other comfort anywhere in the world, and she wasn't strong enough, at that precise moment, to exist without some external support. Even when he said it, she couldn't believe that *everything will be all right*; but she needed to hear it, she needed the promise. She needed to fashion some slim tether of hope to lash her sanity in place. It was a lie, she knew it was a lie—Rhan had always lied to her—but tonight, right now, she needed the lie, and she chose to believe it. She rested her head against his chest, felt his arms around her waist, and gave him the lie right back.

Chandran was in their tent when Leah returned. He had unrolled their sleeping mats, found a candle somewhere, and scrounged up a couple plates of food, so she entered a scene of domestic tranquility when she crawled in through the narrow flap. He didn't ask where she had been, merely kissed her cheek and handed her a plate.

"How did your conversation with Darien go?" she asked.

"Good. We plotted strategy for tomorrow."

"Such as?"

"What he might say to the prince. When he would reveal that he has me. How we might manage the exchange so the Karkans do not break their word."

She forced herself to swallow the food, which she could barely taste. *I need to stay strong.* "What will they do to you?" she asked.

Chandran merely looked at her. She nerved herself and said, "I know you believe they will kill you. Will they do it here, or wait until they get you back to the Karkades?"

"I believe they will wait. The prince's remaining siblings would no doubt enjoy a chance to express to me their unwavering hatred."

"Will they—" She couldn't say the word *torture.* "Will they hurt you?"

"Possibly."

"Are you afraid?"

"A little," he acknowledged. "But still absolutely convinced this is the right decision. I am wholly at peace." He made an uncertain motion with one hand. "Except for the knowledge that the manner of my departure will cause you some pain."

She nodded, because there didn't seem to be any way to explain how *much* pain. "There are drugs you could take," she said. "Pills. They'd kill you quickly if that seemed better than—what you were enduring."

"There are," he said. "Unfortunately, I do not have any of those with me."

"Jaker sometimes deals in pharmaceuticals," she said. "We could ask him in the morning."

"We could," Chandran agreed. "Although—" He shrugged.

"Although what?"

"The prince might search me for evidence of such a thing. If he wants me to suffer, he will not want me to slip away from him so easily."

She had to sip from the water jug, twice, because her mouth was so dry she couldn't speak. "Some drugs," she said at last, "take a long time to do their work. You could swallow them before you even left the camp, and it would be a day or two before they took effect." She gulped more water. "Corvier works slowly. I know Jaker has some of that."

He managed a smile. "You lived in Malinqua too long," he said. "You are thinking of some of their more infamous murders."

"Yes," she admitted. "If I learned nothing more from my time in Palminera, it's how useful a good poison could be."

He had nothing to say to that. Leah choked down a few more bites and then asked, "So, tomorrow afternoon? We will catch up with them by then?"

Chandran nodded. "That is what Darien's scouts have told him. And then we will need time to discuss terms and make the exchange."

"So we might have tomorrow night together as well."

"Possibly," he said. He smiled again and lifted a hand to push a strand of hair behind her ear. "Or by tomorrow night, you may have Mally in here with you instead."

"I want you both," she whispered.

"You will have had us both," he said. "Just not at the same time."

She fought back a sob and he reached over and drew her into his arms. Such warmth and comfort in his embrace—how was it possible that after today, he might never hold her again? If she could force herself to truly believe that, she would be howling like a mad thing instead of quietly sniffling into his chest.

"So, Seka Mardis," he said after a while, speaking over her head.

She rubbed her sleeve across her runny nose and said, "What about her?"

"I might have known her somewhat better than I allowed you to believe."

She wiped her nose again and pulled back to gaze up at him. "What does that mean?"

"She was at court when I lived there. She was one of my wife's best friends."

"Is she of noble birth?"

"Not quite. Sub-noble. You do not seem to have a similar caste in Welce. She and persons of her ilk can be very powerful, but they need patrons—the wealthy members of the aristocracy—to give them cachet. And then they can be dangerous indeed."

"In what way?"

"They are considered facilitators. Procurers. They learn what it is that their patrons desire and find ways to fulfill those desires."

"She supplied your wife with victims," Leah guessed.

"Precisely. She was, in some ways, even more amoral than my wife. Even more extreme."

Leah trembled a little, remembering Seka's intense attentions, her fervent kiss, her seemingly unappeasable appetite for novelty. For *life.* "And how has she atoned for the terrible things she did?"

"As far as I know, she has not. As far as I know, she considered her work for my wife to be her *good* deeds. They are what she banked against any heinous actions of the future."

"She must hate you."

"I find it hard to imagine that anyone anywhere in the southern nations hates someone else as much as Seka Mardis hates me."

"Then you really need those drugs, if Jaker has them."

"Yes," said Chandran. "I probably do."

Morning came too soon, if Leah gauged it by how quickly Chandran might leave her. Not soon enough, if she concentrated on retrieving Mally. They were on their way by daybreak, the bigger, heavier vehicles lumbering away on the northern route, the smaller, sleeker ones navigating the poorly maintained road that angled to the south.

Today, Yori was their driver, and she was small enough that the three of them fit more comfortably in the elaymotive. She wasn't as talkative as Jaker, though, and concentrated almost wholly on maneuvering down the bad road and scanning the horizon for signs of trouble. Leah couldn't think of much to say, either, so the three of them traveled for the most part in silence. *If you don't count the screaming in my head,* Leah thought.

Everyone was on edge by the time they broke for lunch, because they could sense they were drawing closer to their quarry. The trail had looped northward, then cut toward the west, and they had just intersected with the main road when they pulled off to take their meal. They were in fairly desolate countryside now as the road paralleled a long, low line of rocky hills that seemed to consist of red granite and scrubby green bushes in equal proportions. The land that stretched out south of the road supported little but wild grass and creeping ivy, and Barlow said there wasn't a town or homestead for twenty miles.

"Every trader prays his wagon doesn't break down anywhere along this route," he told Leah and Yori as they leaned against the elaymotive and ate their unappetizing meals. "You're stuck until someone comes along and offers to help you. No water till the next town, either. Nothing."

Leah barely listened to him. Her eyes were on Chandran, thirty yards away, deep in a quiet conversation with Jaker. She thought she saw Jaker nod, ask a few questions, then nod again before leading Chandran to the elaymotive he was sharing with one of Darien's soldiers. She didn't know if she should be unutterably relieved or unspeakably terrified. Probably both.

"How far is it from here to the ocean?" Yori asked.

"Five days in good weather." Barlow swept a doubtful glance across the seventy or so vehicles pulled off the road onto the rocky ground. "Well, maybe six or seven when there are so many traveling together."

"Do you—" Yori started to say, and then paused, tilting her head as if listening to some distant sound.

"What is it?" Barlow asked.

"I think I hear motors."

Leah had thought she was already as tense as anyone could be, but at those words, she felt her whole body tighten with anticipatory dread. She bent forward, straining to hear. Was that a low rumble from an approaching elaymotive or just the blood roaring in her ears?

Whatever it was, others in their group had heard it as well. At a shout from the captain, the soldiers mobilized. About a dozen hopped into their own elaymotives and drove them across the pavement, creating a roadblock three and four cars deep. Roughly half of the remaining soldiers took up a military formation behind the imperfect cover of the smoker cars, facing east and readying their weapons. The rest ranged along the side of the road, prepared to charge in any direction.

"Where's Chandran? I need to find Chandran," Leah said.

Yori stopped her with a hand on her arm. "He'll find his way to Darien," Yori said, her voice kind but unyielding. "You don't need to be in the middle of those negotiations. You need to be focused on Mally, when she's returned to us."

Leah stared at her, hearing the echo of Darien's voice in Yori's words and knowing that he had issued this directive. *Yori—Leah is emotional and unstable. I need you to stay with her and keep her steady. Don't let her interrupt my conference with the prince.*

He might be right. She couldn't be sure. She couldn't think straight. "Will I get a chance to say goodbye to him?" she whispered.

"I don't know. None of us knows how this will go."

"But I—"

"Trust Darien," Yori said.

She didn't, of course. She didn't trust Darien, she didn't trust anyone, but she was, in this particular circumstance, powerless. There would be nothing she could do except fling herself at Chandran, beg him not to throw his life away—and that would net her nothing except the loss of Mally. It was an impossible choice. She was paralyzed.

"Did he send you here to watch me?" she finally managed to ask.

Yori only nodded.

"Then let's find somewhere that we can sit and see how this unfolds."

Barlow came with them as they hiked about fifty yards up the hillside and found seats on an outcropping of sun-warmed red stone. Their vantage point not only would allow them to watch everything happening on the road below, but it also would let everyone in the approaching caravan know that Leah was here.

"Mally might see you," Yori said in an encouraging voice. "It will give her hope, knowing you're nearby."

"I'm not sure she'll be able to make out my features from so far away."

"She'll see you. She'll know it's you."

They were barely settled in place when the building hum of the approaching motors grew suddenly louder, and the whole convoy burst into view. There might have been fifteen elaymotives, traveling fast and sticking close together, and they weren't prepared to encounter obstacles in the road. There was a great tumult as brakes squealed and passengers shouted and the three lead vehicles slammed into the Welchin elaymotives blocking their way. More shouts, more crashes, and the heartstopping sound of dozens of weapons locking into place as the Welchin soldiers took aim over the barricade. Karkan guards instantly deployed in a semicircle around the caravan, and they aimed right back.

For a long, tense moment, the tableau held. No one advanced, no one retreated. Then a single shape detached itself from the line of Welchin soldiers and marched slowly toward the Karkan convoy.

"There's a brave man," Barlow said admiringly.

Yori nodded, her eyes fixed on the distant scene. "Volunteer," she said. "Darien doesn't order anyone to take a risk like that."

"What's he doing? Why is he going over there?" Leah demanded.

"To ask for a parley. Invite the prince—or more likely, one of his people—to come into our camp and talk terms."

"We have more soldiers than they do," Leah said. "Or we will when the rest of our troops catch up. Won't the Karkans have to surrender? We could just kill them all, right?" She'd never been the bloodthirsty type. It was appalling to think she could look at almost a hundred living, breathing people and wish them all dead, as violently as necessary.

"We could," Yori agreed. "But they have something we want, so they know we won't."

"But if they just give Mally back to us—"

"Then they have no leverage," Yori said. "And even if they agree to return her, they might insist on keeping her until they're at the port. I would if I were the prince."

"*Five more days?*" Leah said, appalled.

"Maybe. Let's see."

The Welchin emissary made it safely to the Karkan perimeter and conferred briefly with someone whose head poked through the bristling line of weapons. Leah couldn't tell if the Karkan negotiator was a man or a woman. *I wonder if Seka Mardis will speak for the prince,* she thought. It was probably a great honor to be the prince's emissary; all his attendants would fight for the opportunity.

It definitely wasn't a woman who separated from the Karkan contingent a few minutes later and followed Darien's guard through the double line of soldiers. Leah had been focused so hard on the Karkans that she hadn't noticed the activity under way in the Welchin camp, so she was surprised to see that a sizable tent had been pitched some distance from the road. This was no doubt Darien's makeshift conference room, Leah thought. He might even have brought comfortable chairs, writing paper, elegant amenities like wine or fruited water. He would be prepared to negotiate through the night.

The Welchin guard stopped at the entrance to the tent, but the Karkan ducked his head and went in.

"Now what?" Leah asked.

"Now we wait."

"I don't see Chandran. Is he in the tent with Darien?"

Barlow spoke up. "No. He's over there with Jaker. See?" He pointed.

"Darien wouldn't want to tip his hand," Yori said. "He'll say he wants to make a trade, but he might not be specific at first."

"Maybe he won't even need to trade," Leah said hopefully. "Maybe he'll just sign the treaty. That's what they want anyway, isn't it? Then they give Mally back and they don't even have to know about Chandran."

Yori's face showed dissent, but all she said was, "Let it all play out. No one is better at these games than Darien."

It's not a game! Leah wanted to wail. *It's life and death! It's Mally and Chandran! It's everything I love, and I'm going to lose someone I cannot afford to lose, and I will die of it. I will.*

But she wouldn't. She couldn't. Not if she got Mally back. *I have to get her back.* She folded her hands together so tightly the knuckles turned white, and she stared down at Darien's tent as if her gaze might somehow burn through the rough canvas and allow her to view the colloquy inside.

It might have been twenty minutes later that the Karkan emissary emerged and was escorted back toward the convoy.

"That didn't take too long," Barlow observed.

Yori shook her head. "Just an opening gambit. Not the real offer. Everyone knows it."

How? How do they know? Leah wanted to ask. But she said nothing. She no longer trusted herself to speak.

The emissary slipped past the lines of soldiers and into the Karkan stronghold. Leah took a moment to study the way the Karkans had responded to the roadblock. Like Darien, the prince seemed to think they would be here for a while, and he had set up his own tent amid the chaos of crashed smoker cars and milling attendants. His was made from brightly striped blue and green fabric and featured a small, impudent banner waving from the center pole.

I wonder where Mally is? she thought and stared hard at the collection of elaymotives in the Karkan caravan. Several were quite large, maybe thirty feet long and eight or ten feet wide; they were practically small houses on wheels. A young girl could easily be held captive in one of those, along with a watcher or two, and travel in relative comfort. Because surely they were treating her well—feeding her—giving her a safe place to sleep—promising her that no matter what happened, she wouldn't be hurt, no, not the slightest bit—

"What was that?" Barlow asked as a single sharp report echoed off the rocky hillside. Every soldier in the opposing camps snapped to attention, but none of them made an aggressive move. A moment later, there was a flurry of motion at the entrance to the blue and green tent. Two men emerged, carrying something heavy between them. They pushed through the ranks of soldiers, hauled their burden to the side of the road, and dumped it. Yori caught her breath.

"What is that? I can't see," Leah demanded.

"The Karkan emissary," Yori said. "It's the prince's way of saying he won't accept the offered deal."

"Killed his own man?" Barlow asked in a disbelieving voice. "Just to say no?"

"He wants to let Darien know he's serious."

Leah heard a sob break from her own mouth, and she turned away, pressing a hand to her lips. If the prince would murder his own messenger, he would kill anyone else who displeased him. Who encumbered him. Who enraged him. Mally. Chandran. Anyone.

"He's crazy," Barlow said with conviction.

Yori shrugged. "Or merely cruel and powerful."

"So what happens next?"

"He sends another emissary."

"Who'd agree to go?" Barlow demanded.

"I'm not sure any of his people have a choice," Yori answered.

Or they don't mind the risk, Leah thought, still turned away from the scene below. She remembered how eagerly Seka Mardis had talked about trying to find favor with the prince, how she hated the other sycophants at court who were always clawing for a better position. *Seka Mardis would take the challenge. She would undergo any danger for her prince. She's nothing without him. She'd die for him.*

Leah closed her eyes and concentrated on her breathing.

"Hey—look at that," Barlow said, which made Leah open her eyes again. Down the road, past the Karkan encampment, a cloud of dust and motion was roiling in from the east. "Are those the rest of Darien's troops?"

Yori nodded. "Looks like it. We've got them boxed in."

"That'll make the prince more eager to deal, won't it?" Barlow asked.

Yori just shrugged.

It didn't take long for the big transports to arrive and disgorge their occupants in a quick and orderly fashion. Now the Karkans had Welchin soldiers blocking them on three sides and the rocky hill offering a barrier on the fourth. They were effectively surrounded. *Is that good? Is that bad? I can't tell,* Leah thought.

The Welchin soldiers had barely finished taking up their positions when a lone Karkan made his way from the prince's tent to the front line. The prince's new emissary. "I bet *he's* nervous," Barlow observed.

Leah abruptly rose. "I can't sit here any longer," she said. "I can't watch. I have to go back to camp."

Yori was instantly on her feet. "I'll come down with you."

"You don't have to."

The guard offered a slight smile. "I'm supposed to be watching you, remember?"

Barlow pushed himself to a standing position and they all made their way down the hill, weaving between the stands of scrubby brush and piles of tumbled boulders. Once they reached relatively flat ground, Barlow peeled off to find Jaker.

"Maybe you should rest awhile," Yori suggested to Leah. "I could put up your tent in ten minutes and you could sleep. Nothing's going to be decided here for another few hours."

"I won't be able to sleep." *I'll never sleep again.*

"Maybe not, but you could close your eyes. Rest a little. Build up your strength."

I have to be strong for Mally. "All right," Leah said. "If it's not too much trouble. Thank you."

Yori gave her a ghost of the old insouciant grin. "Have to keep myself busy somehow," she said. "This waiting is hard on all of us."

Fifteen minutes later, Leah was lying on her mat, alone in the tent she had shared last night with Chandran. *And might share with Mally tonight. Or tomorrow. Or maybe the day after that,* she told herself. The day was chilly and brisk, and she felt cold even wrapped up in all of her blankets, all of Chandran's. The coarse weave of wool still held the scent of his body, and she pressed it to her face, inhaling that fragrance over and over, holding each breath as long as she could. She couldn't remember the last thing that had ever seemed so precious.

TWENTY-SIX

Heaviness. Disorientation. An insistent, wayward thread of music tickling at her brain. Cramped muscles, hard mattress, and a sense of foreboding dread. And that music, thin, plaintive, pleading. *Come find me. Come find me.* Over and over.

Where am I? Leah thought, struggling to turn over on her uncomfortable bed. She was tangled in blankets, lying in some cold, unfamiliar place—

Then memory slammed her awake and she shoved herself to a sitting position, looking around wildly. She must have fallen asleep—here, today, of all times and places, while Darien negotiated for the lives of the two people she held most dear. She could tell by the quality of light seeping through the tent walls that she had been sleeping for at least a couple of hours. Anything could have happened, *anyone* could be dead by now, and she wouldn't know—

She fumbled free of the covers and stumbled out of the tent, brushing at her ear to make the faint music go away. Yori was sitting just outside, but jumped to her feet when Leah emerged.

"What's happening?" Leah demanded.

"Nothing we can tell from out here," Yori said. "The second Karkan emissary is still meeting with Darien. Chandran has gone into the tent—I guess to prove he's really here—but he's come out again. We're still just waiting."

Maybe that was good news, maybe that was terrible news; once again, Leah couldn't tell. Her stomach tightened from the effort of not screaming. "Where's that music coming from?" she asked next.

Yori looked mystified. "What music?"

"That—that— It sounds like a flute, except not exactly."

"I can't hear anything."

"Really? You could hear the Karkan convoy from two miles away."

Yori grinned. "Maybe I'm more attuned to dangerous sounds than artistic ones."

Just then the music swelled for three long, supplicating notes that made Leah's heart squeeze with desolation. "You didn't hear *that*?"

"Hear what?"

Leah stared at her. "If you— I wonder—" She frowned.

"You wonder what?"

Leah turned and did a slow scan of the landscape around them, her eyes running over the rough slope of the rocky hills, the bunched military forces of the two camps, the open, endless, barren prairie spreading from the edge of the road to fill the whole southern horizon. Not many places to hide. Her gaze went back to the hillside. Not so high that it would be hard to climb all the way to the top and over to the other side. Someone could be crouching there, just out of sight, sending up a private signal. *Come to me, come to me.*

"Seka Mardis," Leah said abruptly. "She's out there. Probably across the hill. She wants me to meet with her."

Yori's eyes narrowed. "How do you know that?"

Leah brushed at her ear again. "This music. There's a thing called a Darnish pipe—it plays at a frequency only a few people can hear. Seka has one and she knows I can hear it."

Yori didn't bother expressing astonishment or skepticism. She just turned to study the hillside, the way Leah had. "There's a small pass just beyond that big mass of boulders—see it? Probably easy to slip through there."

"Then let's go."

Yori moved to cut her off. "You realize she could be setting a trap for you. Probably is."

"I know. She can't be trusted. But she wants something, and maybe she'll help us make a deal."

"I should alert the regent."

Leah shrugged. "I'm going. Now. Come with me or not."

Yori eyed her speculatively for a moment, and Leah realized that the guard was trying to decide if she should disable Leah and report this development to Darien. She could do it, too; no question about that. Leah said, "She might know something about Mally."

Yori nodded and let her pass, then fell in step behind her as Leah headed for the hill. They made a wide detour around the Welchin soldiers before hitting the incline and beginning the climb. It was later than Leah had realized; the first faint patches of peach and saffron were beginning to streak the western skyline. It would be dark within an hour, and then this long, difficult day would finally come to a close. They'd better be off the hillside by then. With all the loose stones, footing was tricky even in daylight. Descending after nightfall would be an invitation to disaster.

The higher they climbed, the louder the music sounded, till Leah could practically picture it swirling around inside her skull. That was good, though—at least she knew they had guessed correctly about where Seka Mardis was most likely to be.

It took them nearly twenty minutes to make it from Leah's tent to the top of the hillside and the narrow pass cut between two heavy walls of granite. Yori insisted on going first, though Leah whispered, "Seka doesn't trust you." Yori whispered right back, "Well, I don't trust her, either." Yori had to turn her small body sideways to slip through the shallow opening, and Leah could see that she kept her attention split between the loose rocks at her feet and the potential hazards waiting on the other side.

Once she was through, Yori stood still for a moment and silently reconnoitered. Leah watched her gaze sweep the whole vista laid out on the northern half of the hill, which appeared to be a mirror image of the landcape on the southern side. Almost immediately, Yori's attention narrowed to one spot. After a few seconds of study, she waved Leah forward. Leah thought she might get stuck in the narrow pass, but she managed to shove herself through. Then she skidded on the loose gravel, dropping to her knees and sliding another few feet. She could feel the abrasions on her skin through the thick fabric of her trousers.

But she hadn't whimpered or cried out, and now she picked herself up and brushed the dirt from her clothes. She looked at Yori and then in the direction of Yori's pointing finger.

There was Seka Mardis, perched on one of those rough red boulders, her eyes closed, the mother-of-pearl pipe lifted to her lips. She looked different, odd, and for a moment Leah thought it was just the heart-breaking rapture of the plaintive melody. But then she realized. There were no jewels braided into Seka's blond hair, no cosmetics on her face; her clothes were severe and plain. This was Seka at her rawest and most unadorned, and she looked like a woman in mourning.

Leah glanced at Yori, who nodded silently. Leah stepped forward, her feet making small noises as she dislodged stones and crunched over dry sticks. But Seka just kept playing, her eyes closed and her face lifted, as if she still didn't realize anyone had come in response to her song. Leah stepped closer, close enough to touch, then stood still.

"Seka. I'm here."

Seka's eyes flew open and she dropped the pipe. "Leah!" she exclaimed, jumping to her feet and flinging out her arms. For a moment, an expression that looked like genuine joy gave her face its customary beauty. "Oh, I was sure you would hear me! My soulmate."

Because it was so clear Seka wanted it, Leah stepped into the other woman's embrace, which almost crushed her bones. Before releasing her, Seka drew back just enough to plant a kiss on Leah's mouth, then she smiled and dropped her arms. "I knew you were here," Seka said. "I saw you this afternoon, sitting on the hillside, and that's when I knew what I had to do."

"Seka, what's going on? Why did you want to talk to me? Do you know what's happened to Mally?"

Seka's gaze went over Leah's shoulder and her happiness dimmed. "Yori. Of course you brought her. Well, I can't blame you for being cautious." She brightened again. "But at least you *did* come."

Leah placed her hands on Seka's shoulders and stared at her, trying to focus the other woman's attention. She wondered if Seka had taken a stimulant of some kind, or if she was merely unsteady from tension and lack of sleep. She seemed wilder than usual, less in control—and Seka had always been a woman who seemed capable of throwing off every restraint.

"Seka," she said firmly. "What's going on? Why did you want to see me?"

Seka lifted one hand and ran it delicately down Leah's cheek, smiling as if she was stroking a panel of gold. "So beautiful," she said softly. "It took me half a day, but I realized. She looks just like you."

Leah caught her breath. "Mally?"

Seka nodded, then abruptly changed the subject. "I've done everything for him, you know. *Everything*. Nothing disgusted me. Nothing horrified me. Of course I was jealous when he would find others and try to replace me, but he always came back to me, because no one was as good as I was. No one was as loyal."

"You mean the prince?"

Seka nodded again. "And then—this little girl. Why shouldn't we take her? Why should she be any more precious than anyone else? Little girls suffer all the time. They get stolen away from their families, they get sold into slavery, they die. Why should I care what happens to this one?"

"She's my daughter," Leah whispered.

"She's your daughter. My soulmate's daughter. When I realized that, everything was suddenly clear. I knew what I had to do."

What? What do you have to do? Leah thought wildly. She felt her hands tighten so much she had to be bruising the bone, but Seka didn't protest. "Can you help me get her back? Please? I'll do anything."

"Kill me," Seka said.

Leah's grip slackened in astonishment. "What?"

Seka cupped both hands around Leah's face. "Kill me," she repeated, her voice almost a croon. "He'll know I betrayed him. If he takes me alive— Oh, you don't want to know the things he'll do to me. You might hate me, but you wouldn't wish such terrible sufferings on anyone."

"I don't hate you," Leah said, amazed that the words were true. "But I can't kill you."

"Yes, you can," Seka said, and leaned in to kiss her again. Then she dropped her hands and pulled free and turned businesslike. "Quickly. Over here. I'm surprised no one has noticed yet that we're gone."

"'*We're* gone'? Who's with you?"

Seka didn't answer, just spun away and strode as quickly as she could over the uneven ground. Leah followed, sliding on patches of slick stone, trembling so much she couldn't have kept her balance if they were on absolutely level ground. There—another mound of boulders, shaded by one of those low bushes and the dramatic shadows thrown by the setting sun. Inside that patchwork darkness, a length of blue fabric wrapped around a small and sturdy shape—

"*Mally,*" Leah breathed, and then ran to her, falling only once on that mad dash, then falling again as she reached the girl's side. Mally was sitting on the ground against the rock, her eyes blindfolded, her hands tied before her, but her expression alert, her head tilted to catch any sounds.

"Leah?" she asked tentatively.

"Oh, Mally Mally *Mally,*" Leah chanted, drawing that frail shape into her arms for a single convulsive hug. Then she pulled back and ripped off the blindfold and began picking frantically at the ropes. "Are you all right? Don't be afraid. Oh my darling girl, you're with me now—"

Two figures materialized nearby. Yori dropped to her knees beside Mally and produced a knife, which she used to cut through the ropes with a few efficient strokes. Seka kept to her feet, leaning over them nervously.

"Quickly now," Seka said. "It took you longer to get here than I thought it would, and I'm sure someone is searching for us by now."

Leah pulled Mally back in her arms and looked up at Seka. "Thank you," she said, her voice so rough she almost didn't recognize it. "I don't know why you did it, but thank you."

"To atone," Seka said simply. "For everything. Everything I've done."

Yori was on her feet and tugging at Leah's elbow. "She's right. We have to go."

Leah stood up, holding one of Mally's hands tightly in hers. "I can't carry you," she said to the little girl. "The ground is too dangerous—I keep falling. Can you run? Can you walk?"

"Yes," Mally said. "I'm fine."

Yori turned away. "Then let's go."

Seka caught Leah's arm. "No, not yet," she said, her voice rising. "You have to kill me. You have to."

Leah stared at her. "Seka—"

Seka's grip tightened. "Soulmates," she insisted. "We would do any-thing for each other. Anything."

"I can't kill you," Leah said.

For a moment, Seka stared at her, her face a study in grief and shock. Then her features contorted and she loosed a howl of primal agony. She shoved Leah so hard that Leah lost her footing and toppled over, drop-ping Mally's hand as she somersaulted twice down the rocky slope. Before she could come to her feet, Seka was upon her, punching her, slashing at her, trying to wrap her hands around Leah's throat. All this time she continued to howl out wordless wails of betrayal and despera-tion. Leah kicked and rolled and pushed herself to her knees, digging for her concealed knife—but suddenly Seka jerked backward, gurgled a choked cry, and then fell forward in a lifeless sprawl. Leah, breathing heavily, saw Yori standing behind her, wiping a knife against her tunic.

"Guess we had to give her what she wanted," Yori said in a cool voice. "Come on. Let's go."

"Mally," Leah breathed, but Mally was right there, crouched on the balls of her feet, watching everything with her eyes big and her face impassive. Leah crawled over, gave her a brief hug and said, "I'm so sorry you saw that. We can talk about it later."

"She wanted to die," Mally said. "She said so. She told me."

Leah hauled herself to her feet, ignoring the flashes of pain from the blows Seka had inflicted and the scrapes she'd accumulated in her fall. She would be a mass of cuts and bruises if she ever got to safety, but she wouldn't care. If she really *made* it to safety with her daughter in her arms. "She did," Leah said, "but we don't. Come on. Let's run back to camp."

Of course, there was no *running* over the treacherous terrain, but they went as fast as they could, bent forward to keep their balance, hands now and then touching the ground to steady themselves. Yori was in the lead, scrambling up the hillside with the grace of a wild creature, but even she had to slow down now and then to find better footing. Mally was between them, never more than an arm's length away from Leah, silent and focused. What was she thinking? What terrors had she endured in the past three days? Leah wanted nothing so much as to scoop her up in a tight embrace and promise her the world was safe, but it wasn't and she didn't have the leisure to lie right at that moment.

Yori made it to the top of the hill, paused at the pass to glance back at the other two, then angled her body through the slash in the rock face. Leah took Mally's hand to steady her as the little girl followed the guard, then Leah forced her own body through the narrow passage, picking up a few new cuts and scrapes as she did so. The instant she was on the other side, she grabbed Mally's hand again.

Yori was standing at stiff attention, staring down and to the left, in the direction of the Karkan camp. She spoke a single flat expletive and kept staring. Leah followed her gaze.

Maybe twenty Karkan soldiers were swarming up the hillside, angled in their direction. The sun was so low on the horizon that it was difficult to see if they carried weapons in their hands, but they hardly needed to. There were too many of them, they were too close, and no one in the Welchin camp seemed to have realized what prize they were after. *We can't outfight them and we can't outrun them,* Leah thought, her body flooding with adrenaline and terror. *They will kill us or kidnap us, and no one can save us.*

She snatched Mally into her arms and cradled the little girl against her chest, because at least if Mally was going to die, she would die in the arms of love. "Should we go back? To the other side?" she panted at Yori.

"First, let's see if we can create some commotion, and maybe some of the Welchin soldiers will notice us and come help," Yori said. "When the Karkans get close enough, we'll slip through."

"Makes sense," Leah said. Though it didn't. Nothing made sense today.

Yori had already begun to shout and wave her arms. *"Here! Up here! Deke! Carver! Anybody!"*

Squirming against Leah's tight hold, Mally twisted her head to see what the trouble was. "Soldiers," she said against Leah's chest.

Leah kissed her hair. "I know, baby," she said. "I don't think we can fight them. I'm so, so sorry."

"They'll fall down," Mally whispered.

Leah bent her head closer. "What? What did you say?"

Mally didn't answer, just continued staring at the approaching troops. The closest three were only ten yards away. Yori had struck a defensive pose, knives in each hand. "Back to the pass," she hissed, edging that way.

Then the hillside began to rumble.

Leah felt a shudder at her feet as if the ground below her had re-arranged itself. A few loose stones began skipping down the slope, small ones, then slightly bigger ones. There was that sound again—as if the earth itself had growled in annoyance—and another temblor, this one stronger. Leah couldn't keep her balance; she sat down abruptly on the patchy soil, Mally still in her arms.

"What was that?" Yori demanded. She was still on her feet, but she'd dropped into a squat, low to the ground.

"I don't know—I think—"

Suddenly the whole hillside started shaking, tossing them back and forth till they all clutched at handfuls of grass and shrub to keep them-selves from pitching down the incline. More rocks fell, bigger ones, boulders the size of a man's head, of a woman's torso, rolling down the hillside in a crescendoing rush and clatter. The Karkan soldiers shouted and screamed and tried to move out of the way, but more stones poured down the hillside, knocking them to the ground or smashing into their bodies, crushing them under the accumulating weight. Leah saw two men swept up in an onslaught of stone, cartwheeling down the moun-tain in an indiscriminate rain of gravel and boulders. Three more men tumbled down the slope in a hail of red rock.

The immediate landscape was swept clean of soldiers, but the rocks kept falling, landing with noisy force on the tents and elaymotives of the Karkan delegation. Leah saw soldiers streaming away in all directions, trying to outrun the avalanche, heard shouts of pain and terror as hands and heads and hip bones were crushed by the heavy boulders. But none of the rocks rolled past the demarcation line of the westbound road; not one stone spilled over into the tidy confines of the Welchin camp.

Leah clutched her daughter more tightly to her chest and whispered, "Mally, make it stop."

The hillside ceased its trembling. A few loose stones bounced down freshly exposed scars of red earth, then settled. The silence was so loud that Leah felt a buzzing in her head.

She had practically breathed her words, but somehow Yori had heard them. The guard stared at Mally, then lifted her gaze to Leah's face, her expression incredulous. Leah merely nodded.

Yori pushed herself to a more upright position and surveyed the scene below. "No more Karkan soldiers headed our way, so that's good," she said, with only the slightest strain in her voice. "I see a few survivors in the Karkan camp—some of our people on the way over to make sure everything's secure. Oh, and there's the prince. Looks like he made it out alive, more's the pity."

Leah could tell her voice was shaking, though she tried to match Yori's cool tone. "We don't want him to die on our soil, so it's just as well."

Cautiously, as if not sure that the ground would hold her, Yori came to her feet. "Is it safe to climb down?" she asked.

I don't know, Leah was going to answer, but it turned out Yori wasn't addressing her. "Yes," Mally said. "But it might be slippery."

Yori held out her hand to pull Leah up. Leah set Mally down first, and soon they were all standing cautiously, working to keep their balance. Yori said, "Then let's get going."

They were halfway down when people from their own camp began to collect at the bottom of the hillside, waving and calling out to them. Most didn't seem too keen on the idea of charging up the hill to meet them halfway—understandably, Leah thought—but Rhan plunged forward with his arms outstretched and no regard for his own safety. He swooped down and swept Mally off her feet, then leaned over to kiss Leah on the mouth.

"When we realized where you were—what had happened—and then when we saw the soldiers were going after you . . ." Keeping Mally in his arms, he pivoted and continued the descent with them.

"And then when you saw the hillside coming down on top of everyone," Yori added in a conversational voice.

Rhan nodded. "Darien wants to see you," he said.

Leah strangled a laugh. "I imagine he does."

"So what's the situation down here?" Yori asked.

"Darien was making terms with the prince's latest emissary when everything started shaking," Rhan said. "I didn't do a head count, but it looked like the damage was pretty severe in the Karkan camp. But no fatalities in ours. A miracle."

Leah risked glancing up from her feet to give him a straight look. "Not quite."

He met her eyes and nodded. "Did you know?" he asked quietly.

"I suspected. You?"

"No. But I find I'm not surprised. With her heritage—" He shrugged.

"Stop talking about me," Mally said.

Rhan laughed and hugged her tighter. "But you're so very interesting," he murmured into her ear. She hid a smile against his chest.

Darien was waiting for them outside his tent, and he waved them all inside. It was outfitted with two tables and several padded chairs, and Leah sank into one with boneless gratitude. Rhan and Mally sat in another, but Yori remained standing, as did Darien.

"Report, please," Darien said to the soldier, and she reeled off a crisp accounting of their trek up the hillside, Mally's rescue, and Seka's death.

"How did you know she had Mally?" Darien demanded.

Leah stirred on the seat cushions. "We didn't. She was playing a flute that only I could hear—don't ask me to explain, I don't understand it—so I realized she was sending a message to me. I knew I had to meet with her. I hoped she would have information, but I didn't think—" Her voice was too choked to allow her to continue.

"Why did she decide to betray the prince?" Darien asked.

"I can't be sure. She said she made her decision when she realized Mally was my daughter." *We're soulmates,* Leah thought. And then, in instant dissent, *We're not.* "But I got the impression that there had been some kind of rupture with the prince. He had turned to other people for support instead of her. She was hurt and angry, and this was how she chose to get her revenge."

"Now that we have Mally back, he's got nothing to bargain with, right?" Rhan said. "This is over. Right?"

"We'll get to that in a minute," Darien said. He nodded at Yori and she left the tent. Darien took one of the remaining seats and regarded Leah thoughtfully. "Am I right in believing that the avalanche was not a natural event?"

"You are."

"Does this mean that you have been revealed as Taro's heir?"

It was almost worth having this entire adventure for the opportunity to see Darien's face. "Not me," she said. "Mally."

His expression was all she'd hoped for. Though, being Darien, he quickly regained his composure. "Impressive control for one so young," he said.

"I'm not a baby," Mally said.

"Clearly not," Darien said, eyeing her. "I can see I have to get to know you much better."

"Although I agree with Darien," Rhan said, smoothing Mally's hair. "Pretty impressive."

Darien's face grew darkly serious. "But my question now is, is it common for the heir to have this degree of power? While the prime still lives? Or—" He didn't complete the sentence.

Leah put her hand to her mouth. "Taro," she whispered. "Oh no— surely not—with Zoe and Nelson and everybody there with him . . ."

Darien looked at Rhan. "Your father is a prime and your brother his heir. Can you shed any light on this question?"

Rhan was frowning. "Kurtis has always been able to do small tricks with fire, ever since we were boys. But small, as I say. Nothing on this scale."

"Mally has had some abilities ever since I've been in Chialto," Leah said in a constricted voice. "When there was a thief in the store one day, she brought a box of stones down on his head. I thought I knocked them over when I fell against the shelves, but I think it was Mally."

Mally yawned and leaned her head against Rhan. "And the man who was hurt. I helped him," she said.

They all looked at her. "What man? Who was hurt?" Rhan asked.

"He was all cut up. I kept his feet warm," Mally said.

Leah felt a shiver skitter down her back. She'd forgotten that incident. Or rather, it hadn't occurred to her that Mally's touch had contributed to any of the healing that took place that night.

"So you've had some abilities for a while," Darien said to Mally.

"Yes."

"Was today any different? Did you have more—power?"

"It was different because I was afraid."

Rhan closed his arms around her and kissed her head again, shooting Darien a look that said, *Stop asking her questions.* "Well, you don't have to be afraid now," Rhan said.

Darien might have stifled a sigh. "I suppose we can't know about Taro until we've returned to Chialto," he said. "I've sent a messenger ahead, and he's prepared to travel through the night. But I believe we should make haste back to the city."

Rhan waved at the tent wall, vaguely indicating the Karkan camp. "What about all of them?"

"I will have a detail of soldiers accompany them to the ocean and see them on their way."

Leah swallowed a yawn. She was suddenly exhausted. It was just past sunset but she felt as if this day had been a hundred hours long. "No treaty?" she asked.

"No treaty," Darien said coldly. "I informed the prince that I have been in negotiations with both Cozique and Malinqua for the past few ninedays."

"Of course you have," Leah murmured. "Just as you've been in private negotiations with Soeche-Tas."

"You *have*?" Rhan exclaimed. "I wondered why none of their people had accompanied the Karkans on this wild venture. You've driven a wedge between them?"

"I doubt that," Darien said. "Merely, I found a way to divorce their interests in Welce from the interests of the Karkades."

"So what other deals have you been making in secret?" Leah asked.

He looked faintly annoyed at her tone, but he answered anyway. "Everyone knows that Cozique recently invaded Malinqua, so everyone has assumed that the empress of Malinqua would be quick to join with anyone arrayed against Cozique. But the two nations have settled their differences by arranging for a betrothal between the empress's nephew and the queen's daughter. That is not generally known yet, but Corene told me all about it, which put me in a much better bargaining position. And, as it turns out, neither the queen nor the empress has any love for the Karkans, and they are willing to make friends with the Karkans' enemies."

"So what did you tell the prince?" Leah asked.

"I told him I would rather ally myself with those nations than with his. And now that he can no longer blackmail me with Mally, I will tell him I want him off my land as quickly as possible."

Leah felt a rush of relief so intense that it left her giddy. "Mally is safe and you didn't have to trade Chandran to get her back," she said. "The prince goes home empty-handed and we go home happy."

The look on Darien's face was indecipherable, but for some reason uneasiness made all her joy drain away. "As to that," he said, "there's a problem."

"What?" she said so sharply that Rhan looked over at her in astonishment and Mally lifted her head. "You didn't give Chandran to him, did you? He's here in the camp, isn't he? *Our* camp?"

"He's here—but we had made significant progress in our talks to effect the exchange," Darien said soberly. "It seemed likely that he would be joining the Karkans before the night was over."

"No," Leah moaned, surging to her feet. "Oh no. Oh no. *No!*"

"What is it? What's happened?" Rhan asked urgently, jumping up with Mally still in his arms.

"Chandran," she choked out. "He's been poisoned."

TWENTY-SEVEN

Leah ran out of the tent, knocking past soldiers and transports and cook fires and the accumulated detritus of camp, racing for her tent. But Chandran wasn't there. Why would he be? He had been nowhere near when Yori set it up and urged Leah to nap. *She had slept away her final hours with Chandran!* She paused at the tent flap, panting, terrified, trying to think.

Jaker. Chandran had obtained his drugs from Jaker; he would have returned to check for an antidote. She spun around, peering wildly through the growing shadows of the camp. There it was, the small, tidy elaymotive that Barlow had been driving ever since they set out on this rescue mission. A few people were reclining in its seats and clustered around its frame—surely one of them was Chandran. She gulped for air and ran in that direction.

Yes—that was Chandran, settled on the narrow front seat as if resting his bones after a long and trying day. Jaker and Barlow hovered nearby, as well as a few other people she didn't know and didn't care about. She pushed past them all and clambered into the seat next to Chandran, practically kneeling on top of him, and begged, "Tell me you didn't take the corvier."

He smiled at her, his teeth very white through the heavy cover of his beard, his dark eyes warm. "Leah," he said, lifting his hands to cup her face, much as Seka Mardis had. "Barlow tells me you brought Mally safely down the hillside. Is that true?"

"Yes, yes—we got her back—Seka Mardis betrayed her prince as her great act of atonement," she rattled off. "But you—what did you—"

"Ah," he said, still smiling. "I forgive her all of it, then. Every crime, every horror. Because she saved Mally. And she is dead now?"

"Yori killed her at Seka's insistence," Leah said baldly. She clutched the front of his tunic and almost shook him. "*Chandran*. Did you swallow the corvier?"

"I did," he said. "About two hours ago."

"Then take the antidote. The antitoxin. Whatever you have to take."

He smoothed back a loose strand of her hair, then cupped her cheeks again. "No such drug exists," he said.

"Did you ask Jaker?" A stupid question. Of course he had asked Jaker. Why else was he here, conferring with the trader and his friends?

"I did. But I knew before I took the dose that there was no turning back."

He was so tranquil that she was infuriated. Now she did actually shake him. "Then you have to make yourself sick! Vomit up the poison! Come on—now. Take something vile or stick your fingers down your throat—"

"Leah. It is too late. It has already been absorbed into my body."

"You don't know that," she said desperately. "It will take a few days to kill you, right?"

"Three. That is what Jaker said."

"So it hasn't done any damage yet. If you get rid of it—"

A shadow fell over her and she looked up to see that Jaker had moved close enough to hear them. His face was wracked with guilt and compassion. "Leah. I thought it was best. I gave him the dose, and I explained—but I didn't realize—I'm so sorry."

She glared at him. "But if he throws up," she said. "If he finds some way to expel it from his body—"

"I've never known anyone to recover from this high a dose once the drug has been in his system longer than an hour," Jaker said gently.

For a moment, she stared at him, not entirely comprehending his words. *It won't work. He's been well and truly poisoned and there's nothing you can do about it. Chandran will die.* Then she shook her head fiercely. "No. I don't accept that. Give him something—something that will clear out his stomach and his bowels. We have to try. We have to do *something*."

Chandran dropped his hands to Leah's shoulders, gripping tightly. "Leah. No. I do not want to spend my last hours with you doubled over in pain and nausea. I want to spend that time laughing with you, loving you, telling you all the things I have stored up to say."

"How can you?" she whispered, feeling the tears gather and fall. "How can you stop fighting to live? How can you so calmly leave me behind?"

He leaned in and kissed her on the mouth, a benediction. "Because I have given my life for you and no other gift could have made me so happy."

"But you *didn't* give it for me! *Or* for Mally!" she exclaimed, crying harder. "It's a wasted sacrifice!"

"I do not believe that," he responded. "I think my sacrifice was a counterweight in the great balance of justice. Because I was willing to give so much, Seka was willing to give so much. My actions in some sense inspired hers, even though neither of us knew what the other was planning. She probably slipped from camp with Mally in her arms the minute I swallowed the fatal dose. The universe loves such symmetry."

"But, Chandran—"

He kissed her again. "The minute Mally was taken, this was the only outcome," he said gently. "Accept it and be at peace."

She couldn't. She collapsed against his chest, sobbing uncontrollably. Around her she heard the murmur of voices as Jaker and Barlow and other bystanders debated what to do. None of them were rash enough to offer comfort. There was no comfort anywhere in the world.

It was Chandran who eventually tugged on her sleeve and put his hand under her chin and tilted her head up. "It looks like everyone is making camp for the night," he said. "Let us go to our tent and rest and talk of happier things."

She pushed herself off of him and shakily climbed out of the wagon. Her body was sore all over, cramped from clinging to Chandran, bruised from her sojourn up and down the hillside. She couldn't even imagine how dreadful her face looked, red and puffy, or her disordered hair. As she waited for Chandran to disembark, her eyes sought Jaker in the small group of onlookers.

"What will happen?" she demanded. "What will his symptoms be?"

Jaker still looked as wretched as any accidental murderer could be. "He'll grow tired and lethargic. He'll still be lucid and very much himself tonight, but by morning he will be hard to rouse and he may have bouts of amnesia. Tomorrow he will drift in and out of consciousness, becoming a bit more forgetful all the while. He will develop difficulty breathing. The day after tomorrow he will mostly sleep. And then—" He hunched his shoulders.

"Will he be in pain?"

"No. Corvier offers a kind exit from this world. The old and weary, or those who are very sick and in unrelenting pain, will often take it to ease them on their way."

"So I have tonight, then," she said.

"And bits of tomorrow."

She wiped her sleeve across her face and nodded. "All right." She took hold of Chandran's arm. "Let's go to the tent."

He leaned on her, or she leaned on him, as they wove their way through the orderly camp. Yori had made a small fire just outside their tent, and she crouched in front of it, settling two small clay containers in the coals.

"You're probably not hungry," Yori said, "but I brought you something to eat anyway."

"Thank you," Leah said.

"How thoughtful of you," Chandran said. "I do have an appetite, as it happens."

Leah glanced around. "Where's Mally?"

"With Rhan. He thought— He wasn't sure you were up for watching her tonight."

Chandran settled himself in front of the fire, sitting cross-legged on the rocky ground. "I would like to visit with her, at least for a while," he said to Leah. "Unless that would be too hard on you."

She stared down at him hopelessly. "Seeing the two people I love the most together for one last hour?" she said. "I think I want that more than anything in the world."

Yori slipped to her feet. "I'll go find her."

Leah knelt beside Chandran. "How are you feeling?"

"Good. A little tired," he said. "My thought is to stay awake as long as I can tonight, since apparently I will spend most of tomorrow sleeping."

Leah nodded. "I expect the troops will move out early in the morning, since Darien is impatient to get back, but we can leave later if we feel like it."

"Whatever is easiest on you," Chandran said.

None of this is easy on me. "Maybe Darien would let us use one of the bigger transports. So you can lie down in comfort while we travel."

"I don't expect it matters much," he replied.

A brief silence fell between them. Leah felt panic and sadness and resentment spike through her body. *My last few hours to tell Chandran everything I need to let him know and I can't think of anything to say.* It took all her willpower not to start crying again.

She was almost relieved to see Yori returning with Mally in tow, even though Rhan accompanied them. *I should have told her to leave him behind,* she thought. But she didn't have enough energy to be truly irritated.

He seemed to sense he wasn't wanted, though, because he halted a few paces from the campfire and stood there uncertainly. Yori said something to him and disappeared into the gathering dark, but Mally came forward without hesitation.

Leah took her hand and pulled her down so they were sitting next to Chandran on the patchy grass. The fire snapped with bright enthusiasm, but did little to dispel the chill of the evening. Or maybe the chill had just come to permanently reside in Leah's bones. "Do you remember my friend Chandran?" she asked, trying for a cheerful tone. "You met him at the shop a while ago."

Mally nodded. "We sat in the window and built things out of rocks."

Chandran smiled at her. "Just so. You made towers almost as tall as you are."

"Did you find out yet?"

"Find out what?"

"Your affiliation."

"I did not. I have not had a chance to ask your friend Taro what he thinks I might be."

"Maybe I could tell you," Mally said.

Chandran glanced at Leah, a question in his eyes. She said, "It turns out—none of us knew, but—Mally is the heir to the torz prime. She has started to exhibit some of his particular powers."

"Ah," Chandran said. "Thus your facility with stones."

"And landslides," Leah said dryly.

"That is a very exciting development," Chandran said to Mally.

She wrinkled her nose. "Maybe," she said. "I don't feel any different. I just feel like me."

"And that is a good thing," he said firmly. "It is always good to know who you are, what matters to you, and what you are capable of."

Leah glanced down at Mally. "Do you really think you can tell what his affiliation is?"

"Maybe," Mally repeated. "If I touch him."

Chandran held out his hand. "I would be curious to see."

Mally laced her fingers with his and concentrated for a moment. When she looked up at his face, she was frowning. "There's something wrong with you," she said.

"Because I do not have an elemental affiliation that you can detect?"

"No, something else. Something *bad*."

"Ah," he said again. "Yes. I am dying."

"But you're not sick."

"No," he said. "There is poison in my body, and it will kill me in a day or two."

"Do you want to die?" Mally asked solemnly. "Seka Mardis did."

"I did want to," Chandran said softly. "Now I do not."

"Then make the poison stop," Mally said.

"I would," Chandran said. "But I cannot. No one can."

"I can."

There was a moment of utter silence. A log shifted within the campfire, falling into the embers with a crash that seemed as loud as a mountain coming down.

"Darling," Leah said finally, "what do you think you can do?"

Mally was still holding Chandran's hand in one of hers, but she pointed at him with her other one. "I can make the poison go away."

Leah felt dizzy. "No you can't," she whispered.

Rhan had hung back all this time, but clearly he had been near enough to eavesdrop. Now he came closer and dropped to his knees on the other side of the fire. "Maybe she can," he said, his voice low and excited. "I've seen my father put his hand on a madman's head and bring him straight to sanity. I've seen Mirti Serlast press her fingers against a woman's shattered rib cage and heal every last bone."

"She's a *child*," Leah said. "She has no *training*. She doesn't even know what she's talking about! And what if she tries something—and it goes wrong—and *she* is the one who ends up poisoned?" She couldn't bear to hope that Mally could save Chandran—and she certainly couldn't allow Mally to exercise her newfound powers in a way that might bring harm to herself. No matter how much she wanted Chandran to live.

But Mally was shaking her head. "That's not how it works," she said.

"You don't even *know* how it works!" Leah exclaimed.

"Yes I do," Mally said. She extended her other hand to Chandran, and after a moment's hesitation, he slipped his fingers between hers.

"What should I do?" he asked.

"Just sit there," she said.

They all just sat there, hardly moving, barely breathing, glancing at each other and then looking away. *I shouldn't let her do this, I should make Rhan carry her away, I am putting her at risk, and all because I love him!* Leah thought. But Mally seemed so calm, so sure of herself, as she held his big hands in her tiny ones and appeared to concentrate on the shape of his knuckles beneath the skin. *She's been kidnapped—taken away—held by strangers,* Leah thought, hysteria rising despite her attempts to keep it in check. *She's seen a woman killed in front of her. She's caused a* mountain *to come down! And now she's trying to heal a stranger using power she doesn't even understand. I cannot let her do this. I have to protect her—*

"Darling," she said, wrapping her arms around the small body and tugging it toward her. "It is so very generous of you to try to help him, but—"

Mally wriggled free of Leah's hold and closer to Chandran. "I'm almost done," she said.

"Let her finish," Rhan murmured.

"But she—"

"She wants to," he said simply. "And he deserves it."

Leah shook her head but had no other answer. Just in case it could help, just in case Mally needed her support, she put her hands on the small hunched shoulders and tried to feed her own heat and energy into Mally's little body. She could feel the slight tension in Mally's neck and back, then the coil and release of her muscles as Mally dropped Chandran's hands and sat back.

"I fixed you," she said.

Chandran rolled his shoulders and moved his head experimentally from side to side. "How odd," he said. "I feel—quite good. As if I have just woken from a very long sleep. Or eaten two keitzee balls. Or plunged into a cold mountain stream and climbed out on the other side."

"The torz prime has an affinity for the body and the earth," Rhan said, his voice subdued but threaded with excitement. "If Mally really did go in and heal you—"

"At this moment, I feel as if she did," Chandran said.

"I did," Mally said. "But I'm so hungry. Can we eat something now?"

Leah was in shock, staring between her daughter and her lover and trying to make herself believe that both of them were out of danger. *He tried to save her and she ended up saving him,* she thought, almost too dazed to put the thoughts together. *If she did. If she really did.*

Chandran pushed to his knees and began poking at the clay pots Yori had left in the fire. "I believe this food was meant for us," he said. "Could you hand me that long spoon? Good. Let us take the lids off and see what we have."

Rhan climbed hastily to his feet and motioned to Leah, so she stood up and followed him into the darkness just outside the circle of firelight. "I think she did it," he said in a low voice. "I think she cured him."

"Maybe," she said. "I hope so. But did it take too much out of her? I need Zoe or your father or someone to explain this to me—"

"We'll talk to them as soon as we get back to Chialto," he promised. "But, Leah. I think what this means is—I've never seen Kurtis do anything like this. Nothing like playing tricks with a man's brain. I wonder if—I hope not, but I'm afraid—"

Leah nodded and whispered, "Taro's dead."

. . .

They accomplished the trip back to Chialto with almost as much speed as the outbound journey, despite the fact that the circumstances weren't quite as dire. But Darien Serlast, as Jaker observed, didn't like to waste anything, and that included time. In fact, Darien and a contingent of soldiers departed the minute the sky was light enough to make out the terrain. The rest of them followed as quickly as they could break camp.

Jaker served as the driver for Leah and Mally, while Barlow and Chandran occupied the elaymotive just behind them, and Rhan rode with Yori. Jaker could not have been more delighted with Chandran's recovery if he himself had stumbled on the antidote. "And he was wide awake this morning? Lucid?" he asked three times during the first hour of their journey.

Leah didn't mind repeating the details as often as he wanted to hear them. "Wide awake, full of energy. Said he hadn't felt this well in years." Leah squeezed Mally, who sat on her lap and watched with interest as the barren countryside rolled by. Leah supposed that, to the torz prime, even the most monotonous landscape was full of hidden beauty. "I think Mally must have rummaged around inside his body and healed old scars and repaired damaged tissues. Or something."

She could feel Mally's shoulders rise and fall in a slight shrug. "I just fixed everything," she said. "It wasn't very hard."

"That's amazing," Jaker said.

Leah leaned over and whispered in Mally's ear. "Did you hear that? You're amazing. Everybody thinks so."

About a dozen times an hour, she turned around to make sure Chandran was still sitting upright next to Barlow, still exhibiting signs of his miraculous recovery. Whenever she looked, he smiled and waved; once he clasped his hands together and raised them over his head in a gesture of triumph. Every time they stopped for food or water, she hurried to his side and demanded, "How are you feeling?" Every time, he replied, "Healthy and whole."

Every time, she touched him, just to be sure.

By sunset, they were only a few hours from the city, but road conditions were poor enough that the sergeant in charge decided they should stop for the night. There was no sign of Darien, and Rhan speculated that the regent had pushed on despite the hazards. There wasn't even enough moonlight to show the rutted road before them.

"But the newest elaymotives come with lighting systems," Rhan told Leah. "I have to assume Darien's in one of those."

"I wonder if he's heard anything about Taro," she said. "He sent a messenger to Chialto the minute we rescued Mally. If the messenger has had time to make it back to Darien—"

"Well, everyone will know the news soon enough," Rhan said with a sigh.

Dinner was hasty but unexpectedly flavorful, as Barlow did the cooking and threw in a few specialty spices. Halfway through the meal, Leah caught herself looking at the faces of the people who had gathered at her fire. It was an odd collection, to be sure: Mally, Chandran, Rhan, Yori, Jaker, and Barlow. Two that she loved, one that she *had* loved, three that she considered friends so close she would trust them with her life. With her daughter's life. *How did this become my circle?* she asked herself. And then, an even more surprising question: *How did I manage before I found them?*

TWENTY-EIGHT

By noon the next day, the whole caravan was crossing the canal into the city. Yori waved goodbye and headed off with the soldiers, turning her elaymotive onto the Cinque in the direction of the palace. Rhan crammed himself into the vehicle with Jaker and Mally and Leah as they made their way toward the wealthy residential district where Darien had his house.

They found the whole street blockaded with horse-drawn carriages and smoker cars; guards clustered at the front door. Rhan and Leah exchanged sober looks. The guards meant Darien was inside. The presence of so many visitors meant something momentous had occurred on the property. Most likely, the death of a prime.

"People are going to be curious about Mally," Rhan said to Leah in a low voice as they climbed out of the elaymotive and gathered in the street. Chandran and Barlow came over to huddle with them. "Staring at her. Trying to get close to her. We need to shield her. Give her time to adjust to all this before—"

Leah nodded. "I'll take her straight upstairs. You can handle any questions."

Rhan jerked his head in Chandran's direction. "They'll be curious about *him*, too."

"I will also go upstairs and hide," Chandran said. "Mally and I will amuse ourselves. I am sure she has boxes of stones somewhere in her room."

"Yes," Mally said.

"What you should both be doing is *sleeping*," Leah retorted. "You've had a very challenging set of days."

"I'm not tired," Mally said.

"I feel quite energetic," Chandran said.

Jaker touched Leah's sleeve. "I don't see that you have much need for us anymore," he said. "So we'll retrieve our own car and be off."

"I'm sure Darien will want to express his thanks in some impressive way, so you could wait around for that," she suggested.

"We didn't do anything special," Barlow said.

"And we have lives of our own to return to," Jaker said. "But we'll be back in Chialto in a few ninedays. We'll be in touch."

She threw her arms around Jaker, then turned and hugged Barlow. The men all exchanged respectful nods, and then Jaker leaned down to pat Mally on the head. "I have a soft spot for Zoe," he said, "but I think you're going to be my favorite prime."

A few more farewells, another round of hugs, and they were gone. Chandran and Leah took hold of Mally's hands, and Leah shared another quick glance with Rhan before he straightened his shoulders and strode up the walkway. The three of them followed behind him, nodded at the soldiers, and pushed through the door and into the kierten of Darien's house.

They stepped into a party.

The kierten was cluttered with discarded plates and glasses; the air was filled with the appetizing scents of bread and cheese and sweets and wine. A burst of laughter greeted them from an interior room, and when they moved into the big chamber just through the kierten, they found knots of people standing around, talking, smiling, sipping from their glasses.

"It does not appear funereal," Chandran observed.

Leah's hand tightened on Mally's. "Then—maybe—"

At that moment, a group of people surged in through a far door, moving in one untidy mass. Taro was at the center.

"*Mally!*" he roared, flinging his arms wide.

Mally broke free of Leah's hold and dashed across the room. Taro swung her up over his head, laughing at her, shaking her so her arms and legs jittered and danced. "What have you been up to?" he demanded. "Throwing boulders at the enemies of Welce and saving men from death by poison? Who taught you how to do such tricks?"

"I just figured it out," Mally said, beaming down at him. "It wasn't very hard."

Leah missed the rest of their exchange as people converged around the prime and his heir, calling out questions and expressing congratulations. *We didn't do a very good job of shielding her from the public,* Leah thought. *But I don't suppose she's quite as vulnerable as we thought, since Taro's still alive.*

She took a moment to savor that. *Taro's alive. Taro's alive!*

Chandran looked down at her. "That is the torz prime? The one you feared dead?"

"Yes."

"Then you have been blessed with a series of miracles."

Rhan was close enough to hear. "Prime magic," he said. "I can't imagine any other country in the southern seas has anything to equal it."

"I have traveled some," Chandran said, "and I am inclined to agree."

"I'm going to find my father," Rhan said, "and learn how things unfolded here."

He disappeared into the crowd. Leah glanced at Chandran with a question in her eyes. "Do you want to make the rounds and meet people, or would you rather disappear quietly? This might be a little overwhelming."

"What do they know about me?"

"Probably everything," she said. "That you were prepared to sacrifice yourself for Mally and that Mally was able to save you. That you're from Cozique, that you were married to a Karkan princess—all of it."

"I have been away from royal courts too long," he said with a faint smile. "I had forgotten how quickly news spreads when it is connected to the palace."

"So had I," she confessed. "But now that everyone knows Mally is the heir, I'm back in that world for good. It will take some getting used to. And you don't have to try to get used to it today."

He smiled and took her hand. "But it is a day for celebrating miracles," he said. "We have been braced for grief and sorrow. Let us go forth instead and drench ourselves in joy."

The next few hours were a bewildering blur of introductions, explanations, exclamations, and embraces as Leah and Chandran moved through the crowd and made their presence known. She had been right; everyone had learned Chandran's name and history, and they eyed him with varying degrees of admiration and speculation. She was almost as much of a curiosity as he was, since she had not been well-known in society when she lived there five years ago. And now everyone knew *her* history as well—that she had been Rhan's lover, that Mally was her daughter, that from now on she would be raising the decoy princess who had most dramatically been revealed to be heir to the torz prime.

Everyone wanted to hear her story. She barely finished telling it to one person before another one came up and demanded the same details. It wasn't long before she and Chandran were separated, first by a few feet, then by half the width of the room. Leah gave up trying to make her way back to him and simply plunged into the next conversation with the next group of inquisitive strangers. It was a relief to occasionally come across the people she knew. Josetta and Rafe. Nelson and Beccan. Virrie. Zoe. She fell into their arms as if into brief, welcome moments of sanity, and laughed, and tried not to cry.

"I have a message from Annova," Zoe said, once they'd progressed beyond tears and hugs and laughter. "She says she has been at the shop every day, at least for a few hours, to make sure nothing is amiss. And to feed your fish."

"The reifarjin!" Leah exclaimed. "I haven't even had a moment to worry about it. Thank her for me five thousand times."

"She says he misses you."

"How can she possibly tell?"

"She says she dangled her fingers in the water and he didn't make any attempt to bite her. In fact, he just swam away. So she could tell he was pining."

Leah laughed and spread her hands. "I never expected that fish to care if I was alive or dead."

"Well, that's the lesson, I suppose," Zoe said. "We can never predict who will love us or where we'll feel love in return."

Leah was still mulling that over a few minutes later when she came across Taro—who was, for one astonishing moment, alone. He crushed her into the most ferocious hug of the afternoon and said, "You and I have a great deal to talk about once we get rid of all these people."

"You *love* being at the center of all these people," she scoffed. "If it was up to you, you'd never send them home."

He laughed and released her. "I *am* enjoying myself," he admitted.

"But you're well now? Whole? You looked so fragile the last time I saw you."

"Hearty and strong," he assured her. "I'll live another twenty years. We'll have lots of time to train your little girl in everything she needs to know."

"You knew," she said. "About Mally."

"I was fairly certain," he said. "But not until the past few ninedays. I'm glad it didn't occur to me back when she was playing decoy for Odelia! I don't know how we would have balanced a prime with a princess."

She laughed. "Now I almost wish you'd been forced to try."

Someone came up behind Taro and drew him into conversation, so Leah did a slow pivot, looking for Chandran. She had just spotted him in conversation with Nelson and Kurtis when a footman approached and told her Darien wanted to meet with her in his study. She threaded through the press of people, pausing to lift a glass of fruited water from the buffet, and made her way to the room at the back of the house. Darien was seated behind the enormous desk, going over some papers, but he looked up when she stepped inside and dropped noisily into a chair.

"Finally!" she exclaimed. "Some blessed quiet!"

Darien smiled. "We can sit here in silence for a minute if you would like to collect yourself."

She sipped from her water glass. "I keep telling myself to get used to it. This is what my life holds from now on."

"I'm glad you realize that," he said. "Though such events will not take place all day, every day. You will be able to manage an ordinary enough existence for much of the time."

"Well, that's a relief."

Darien folded his hands before him and studied her across the desk. "But your life *has* changed," he said seriously. "And we must at some point discuss its new boundaries."

She eyed him. "I realize there is some irony here," she said. "I came back to Welce so I could reclaim my daughter from Taro—but it turns out I have to share her with him after all so he can teach her what she needs to know. But that's no hardship. We will split our days between the city and his estate."

"Mally will need to spend time at the palace, too, because when she becomes prime, she will be part of court life. Fortunately, that environment is already familiar to her from all the time she was there pretending to be Odelia."

"So far, I'm not seeing that many new boundaries," Leah said.

Darien smiled. "You must ask yourself how you wish to fit your life around Mally's," he said. "Do you still want to be a shop owner? Would you like to find some other occupation? Would you prefer to be a woman of leisure? Where would you like to live? There are always apartments available at the palace for the primes and their families." He gestured at the walls around them. "Or you could stay in this house as long as you choose—and as long as you do not mind the continuous influx of other guests who are connected to me in some fashion."

She settled back in the chair and regarded him a moment. Darien always had motives behind motives; she couldn't guess what he was really trying to maneuver her into doing. "Do you *want* me to continue running the shop?" she asked bluntly. "I might be more cooperative if you would just come out and tell me your preferences."

"I was trying to be neutral and refrain from influencing your decision," he said.

"Ha."

He smiled again. "I like the shop. I like having someone I trust in a position to meet so many citizens and visitors. If you would be willing to continue to operate it, I would be happy to continue to back it."

"Then that's another parameter we don't have to change," she said. "So I guess the big one is where I'm going to set up my household."

"And who you're going to set it up with."

Now she grew very still. She stared at him with narrowed eyes and said, "I hope you aren't thinking of asking me to give up Chandran."

"Of course I'm not."

"Because I'm not going to. I'm keeping them both. Mally and Chandran. I could have lost both of them in the past nineday, and I didn't lose either of them. And I don't care what you threaten me with, I'm not living without either one of them."

Darien looked mildly affronted. "People are always accusing me of being much more sinister than I really am."

"I think that would be difficult," she replied with some heat.

He waited a beat, then went on with his usual calm. "I like him. I spent some time with him in recent days, and I admire his intelligence as well as his honor. But he's a foreign national of some standing, and if he is living openly in Welce, there are certain requirements of diplomacy regarding his safety and the quality of his housing."

She was wholly bewildered. "What?"

"We have to treat him well," Darien elucidated. "His father is a cousin to the queen of Cozique."

Leah flopped back in her chair. "*What?*" she said more faintly.

"Ah. I thought Chandran had shared that part of his history with you."

"No—he said—his father was a merchant. Who had trading treaties with merchant families in the Karkades. That's why his father arranged his marriage—"

"Technically true," Darien said. "His father was the Minister of Commerce for thirty years. And, of course, you already know Chandran's wife was part of the royal family of the Karkades."

Leah rubbed her forehead. "All right. *This* might be a different parameter."

"I wouldn't try to restrict his movements," Darien said. "But I would want to take steps to make sure he's safe."

"You want to assign guards to him."

"They would be discreet."

"If I say no—if *he* says no—will there still be guards?"

Darien made a graceful gesture with both hands. "They would be even more discreet."

She nodded. "All right. After the last few ninedays, I'm not sure I would mind knowing there was protection nearby. But I'll talk to him and get back to you."

Darien cocked his head. "So I am correct in assuming you plan to set up a household with him?"

She couldn't help a smile. "Well, we haven't had much chance to make plans, since it seemed unlikely we'd live to see them to fruition, but yes, that's my assumption as well. Maybe you should give me a little time to put my personal affairs in order before you start trying to organize my life."

He smiled in return. "But, Leah," he said. "You're the mother of the next torz prime and romantically involved with a high-ranking envoy from a powerful foreign nation. Your personal affairs impact the public good. You give up your privacy or you give up the ones you love. Those are your choices."

She came to her feet, feeling contrary impulses to throw a tantrum or to break into laughter. She figured she'd be battling those twin desires for pretty much the rest of her life. "I'm not even bothering to answer that," she said. "We'll talk more later."

"Yes," he said as she stepped through the door, "I'm sure we will."

She found Mally in the river room with Natalie, Celia, and a tumble of Ardelay cousins. "You. Bedtime. Now," she said, once she pulled Mally from the crowd. "You've had a very long few days."

Mally nodded, but instantly began negotiating. "I have to say good night to Taro first."

"You'll see him tomorrow morning."

"And Chandran."

"Him, too."

"And Rhan."

"He'll be around a lot."

"But not in the *morning*."

Leah certainly hoped not. Then again, she was starting to enjoy having Rhan nearby. On this latest adventure, he had proved himself both loyal and loving when it came to his daughter. It wasn't going to be as hard to share Mally as she'd feared. "All right. Five minutes. Then I'm taking you up to your room."

Mally scampered off. Leah went in search of Chandran and found him conversing with Rafe and Josetta, apparently enjoying himself a good deal. "I need to talk to him alone for just a moment," she said, and pulled him to a quiet corner just outside the kierten.

"I thought we wouldn't have any more secrets between us," she said. For the life of her, she couldn't muster anger or even indignation; curiosity was about as intense as she could get. She was too happy that he was alive. "I thought you said you had told me everything."

He looked surprised. "Have I not? What information do you think I am withholding?"

"The fact that you're closely related to the queen of Cozique."

Now he was astonished. "And how did you discover that?"

"Darien knew. I have to guess Princess Corene found out. I know she and Darien have been corresponding about all the excitement here. Including you. So why didn't you tell me?"

He shook his head. "I have not been in touch with anyone from my family since I left the Karkades. I did not want them to have to decide whether or not to tolerate a murderer in their midst. I have assumed they think me—or wish me—dead."

"Well, not anymore," Leah said. "Darien plans to treat you like a foreign diplomat, so I imagine it won't be long before your family knows you're still alive. Maybe they'll revile you, maybe they'll embrace you, but one way or another, you'll have to factor them into your life going forward."

He took a deep breath, let it out, and nodded. "Then I shall," he said. "It seems a less onerous challenge than many of the ones that we have faced this nineday."

Leah laughed. "Indeed it does! And I want to sit down with you and talk about all of them sometime in the very near future, but right now I have to put Mally to bed."

He smiled and kissed her lightly on the mouth. "At least there *is* a future," he said. "The last time we stood in this house, there was not."

"I know," she said, kissing him back before turning away. "I can't wait to find out what will happen next."

Five minutes later, she took Mally upstairs, cleaned her up, and tucked her into bed. Once the little girl was settled, Leah stretched out next to her, facing her, both of their heads on a single pillow.

"Do you think you'll be able to fall asleep?" Leah asked. "Or do you want me to stay here awhile?"

"I want you to stay," Mally said. There was a burst of laughter from below, faint but audible, and Mally smiled. "I like having all the people in the house," she said.

Leah kissed her forehead. "That's because you're torz. Torz folks *love* to be surrounded by as many people as possible."

"Do you?"

Leah considered. "For a long time I didn't. People were what made me unhappy, so I wanted to get as far away from them as I could. I wanted to be separate and alone. But now—everything's changed. I feel connected to certain people with such intensity that I want to be around them all the time. And I don't think that's ever going to go away."

"What people?" Mally asked.

"You, of course. Chandran. Taro and Virrie and Zoe and Celia and Josetta and Rafe and Annova and Yori and—lots of people."

"Rhan?"

"I'm connected to him," Leah acknowledged, "but not as much as you are."

"He's my father."

"Did he tell you that?"

"I just knew."

"I think he'll be a pretty good father."

"He said he would buy me a bracelet," Mally said. "With all my blessings on it. Just like Zoe's."

"That'll be pretty."

"You could get a bracelet, too."

"Maybe I will."

"Because then you never forget," Mally said earnestly. "You look at your bracelet, and you always know what your blessings are."

Leah gathered the little body closer for one final hug. "Oh, Mally," she whispered. "I will never, ever forget. My blessing is *you.*"